Jean Ingelow

Don John

Jean Ingelow

Don John

ISBN/EAN: 9783337398804

Printed in Europe, USA, Canada, Australia, Japan

Cover: Foto ©Andreas Hilbeck / pixelio.de

More available books at **www.hansebooks.com**

NO NAME SERIES.

"Is the Gentleman Anonymous? Is he a great Unknown?"
DANIEL DERONDA.

———◆———

DON JOHN.

BOSTON:
ROBERTS BROTHERS.
1881.

THE MOTHER OF MARIA JANE AIRD, WHO WAS THE
MOTHER OF ——

"I suppose, whatever you may have thought all your—all your life,
you—you—you never thought your mother was a fool?"—PAGE 29.

DON JOHN.

CHAPTER I.

WHILE I listened, like young birds,
Hints were fluttering; almost words, —
Leaned and leaned, and nearer came ; —
Everything had changed its name.

Sorrow was a ship, I found,
Wrecked with them that in her are,
On an island richer far
Than the port where they were bound.

JEAN INGELOW.

IT may be doubted whether in all London there is,
considering its width and the size of its houses, a
more gloomy street than Upper Harley Street.

The houses in this fine street are too deep to be
lighted well within; and so high as to give it on a dull
day very much the effect of an exceedingly long railway cutting between two high hills.

Some years ago, a very young woman in a widow's
cap was furtively peeping out from an upper window
in the front of one of these houses, and as she gazed
down towards Cavendish Square and up towards Harley Place she made the above comparison in her mind.

It was rather a dull day in the beginning of April,
but she did not find the gloom of a London spring at
all depressing, for she was sometimes allowed to take
the baby, now lying in a frilled bassinet behind her,
into Oxford Street, where she could feast her eyes on
the splendid contents of the shop windows, or she
might stroll into the Soho bazaar, or she would be

taken for a drive in the park with her charge by the baby's mother, for she was wet-nurse to the said baby, and thus found herself for the first time in her life a personage of great importance, whose tastes were to be consulted, whose dinner was by no means to be delayed, and whose comfort and even pleasure were considered to be of consequence.

To do her justice, she gave herself fewer airs than most of her class, and did her best for the baby, who was the child of a lawyer in excellent practice.

His name, the very same as that of his son, was Donald Johnstone; he was of Scotch extraction, but his family had been for two generations settled in the South.

Maria Jane Aird, such was the name of the nurse, had been highly recommended to her present place; and, in order to take it, had left her own young infant under the charge of her mother. But that she fretted after him now and then, she would have been thoroughly content; she had not much loved the young husband whom, to please her mother, she had married. She was consoled now, for he had been already dead six months; the main regret she still felt was that during his long illness (he was a carpenter) all his savings had been spent, so that she had nothing whereon to begin life again, and had even become familiar before the birth of her child with both want and cold.

She was a sweet-tempered young creature, had never done any particular good in the world; but then what opportunity had she found? for the same reason possibly she had never done any particular harm.

She had one habit which Mrs. Johnstone, the baby's mother, did not like; she was constantly reading books from a circulating library. Some of these were dirty, and smelt of tobacco; Mrs. Johnstone had remarked more than once that she did not approve of books of that kind in the same room with the baby.

He was her only son, and a very precious infant; everything that love and money could do was to be lavished on him. His three little sisters were in the country under the charge of an old servant, and just as Mrs. Aird withdrew her head and cautiously shut down the window, a boy with a telegram in his hand came up the street, containing a very important message concerning them. They were expected home that very afternoon, and their father was gone to fetch them.

Mrs. Aird, as she turned, looked about the wide chamber, with that kind of exaltation which comes of a fresh and advantageous change.

It was before the date when the browns we use on our wall-papers began to be reverently studied from Thames mud, and the greens and yellows from mouldy cheese. No one as yet toned down tender dirty drab within to match the formless smoky drab without; no one adored rhubarb tints, or admired the color resulting from mixtures of cocoa and milk.

The walls here were all one flush of comely cabbage roses making the most of themselves in quantities enough if they could have been gathered to fill several clothes' baskets. They sprawled quite innocent of artistic propriety over a paper satin-soft, and glossy, and in hue of a delicate dove-color. There was gilding about certain picture-frames, and pink flutings and embroidered muslin draped the dressing-table. The baby, as a little god of love, was half smothered in lace frillings, his little quilt was edged with swan's-down, and all his surroundings were enriched with fine needlework. All was gay and fresh and clean.

Mrs. Aird, hearing a step on the stairs, thrust away her novel, took up a piece of needlework, and at the same moment Mrs. Johnstone came in, looking very much flushed and agitated.

The nurse set a chair for her, but she was too restless to sit down. She had a telegram in her hand.

" This has just come from Mr. Johnstone," she said ; " it is about the little girls, nurse."

" Indeed, ma'am."

" Mr. Johnstone telegraphed from Reading Station."

" Indeed, ma'am," repeated the nurse ; " I hope there 's nothing wrong ? "

"I don't know, I hope not; but he says my eldest little girl has a slight rash on her neck."

"Dear, ma'am!" exclaimed the nurse, "don't flurry yourself so; consider how ill you have been. I dare say it's nothing; might I see the message?"

With a trembling hand Mrs. Johnstone held out the telegram. It ran thus:—

"Have only just observed that Irene has a slight rash on her neck; seems unwell, and is cross. Send baby into lodgings before we arrive. I hope nothing of consequence. If doctor says so, can have him back to-morrow."

Upwards of twenty words; how these gentle-folks throw away their money! This was the nurse's first thought; after it crowded in others that nearly took her breath away.

"I understand, I am told, Mrs. Aird, that your mother lives at Dartford, and has the care of your baby."

"Yes, ma'am; it is a very nice clean place."

"Oh, I have of course no thought of sending you there for only one night."

Mrs. Aird showed no disappointment in her face; she only said,—

"This handsome street and these squares about here never have any card up to show they let lodgings."

"Oh, no, no; and there is so little time; what can I do?"

"There's Kew; is that far off, ma'am?"

"Kew, yes, of course it is; but why?"

"I have a friend there, close to Kew Green, a very respectable woman that comes from the same place in Oxfordshire that my poor husband did, and she told me this very morning that an artist gentleman had just left her, and she wished she could hear of another *let*."

"I hope it would be only for a night," mused the mother.

"She is the cleanest woman that ever was," urged the nurse, "and I am sure she would not charge much."

"It would be sure to be for two nights," thought Mrs. Aird. "I can telegraph as well as other people, and I might get a sight of my blessed baby."

"Ma'am, I would not deceive you for the world," she cried, the clear color at a thought of this possibility flushing up all over her face and throat.

"You mean that this person is really clean and respectable?"

"Yes, ma'am."

"And no other lodgers taken?"

"Oh no, ma'am, the house is too small for that."

"It is a healthy place?"

"Oh yes, close to the gardens."

"And in half an hour they will be here; ring the bell, Mrs. Aird."

"The baby is ready dressed to go out," proceeded the nurse as she rose.

"And the carriage," sighed the mother, "is already at the door."

It had been ordered in fact to take Mrs. Johnstone out.

"If I trust you for this one night," she pleaded, "you will not leave my dear baby for a moment?"

"No, ma'am, it cuts me to the heart to see you so trembling. I would not, I assure you, as I am a Christian. But I'll be bound there's very little the matter with little miss; perhaps it's scarlatina she's got coming on, and all children must have that; the baby could not have it at a better time."

The sight of Mrs. Johnstone's nervous anxiety and changing color wrung these words from the nurse almost in spite of herself, and though she longed to go; but the bell was soon answered by a housemaid who was told to help Mrs. Aird at once in packing the baby's clothes.

Mrs. Aird observed with excitement and joy that though the baby was to come back to-morrow, enough clothes were put up to last him at least a week. She herself was told to take a box of clothes with her, and in a very few minutes all was ready.

"I shall hope to drive over for you to-morrow," said
Mrs. Johnstone, and in the meanwhile she gave her
twelve postage cards and three pounds, in case she
should not be able to come, charged her not to return
without further orders, and took leave of her baby, with
floods of passionate tears.

In the comfortable closed carriage the nurse was
driven through the streets· in a state of exultation
scarcely to be described; here at least was absolute
freedom for twenty-four hours, and if it proved that
there really was any danger of infection, she might be
left there some days, and manage to send her mother
money to Dartford to buy a third-class ticket with, so
that she might be willing to bring over the baby.

This would be a costly pleasure certainly, but her
circumstances as she understood them were so comfortable that she could afford it well.

That very afternoon, having taken a friendly leave of
the coachman and footman, and established herself in
all state in the clean tidy lodgings which were everything she had described, Mrs. Aird wrote to her mother
to relate these circumstances, dwelt on her longing to
see her child, and expressed a *naïve*, and perhaps not
unnatural, hope that the *rash* might turn out to be
scarlatina, in which case she was likely, as she thought,
to have her time to herself for at least a week, and she
should take it hard if her mother did not spare a day to
bring the baby.

The next day passed and no notice was taken of Mrs.
Aird; Mrs. Johnstone did not appear, and a card was
posted to her according to her directions.

The following day Mrs. Aird's spirits were put into a
flutter by the arrival of a telegram, in which she was
informed that the little Miss Johnstone really had got
scarlatina, that Mrs. Johnstone's doctor would pay her
a visit that day at four o'clock, and that he would give
her any directions which she might need.

Mrs. Aird was ready to receive the doctor, she was
so fresh, clean, cosy, and cheerful, that she looked a
very ideal nurse, and the baby only six weeks old (her

own being one fortnight older), looked already the better for her ministrations.

The little lodgings were so neat, the house so detached in its pretty little garden, the air so pleasant,
that altogether the doctor was very well satisfied.
" You may be here a week yet," he observed, knowing
that if she was found to be doing her duty she would
be there much longer. " Of course it is perfectly understood that you are never to go into London."

" Oh, yes, sir, and I have no such wish, I am sure.
I have not a single friend there."

" Nor are you to go into any houses here."

" Sir, I have not a single acquaintance anywhere
near."

" Of course you are to have no communication with
Mr. Johnstone's servants, not even by letter."

" You have not been there, then, sir? "

It was taking a great liberty in the nurse to say that.
" Certainly I have," he answered a little sternly ;
" that is another thing, doctors understand these matters, doctors never convey infection."

" No, sir," answered Mrs. Aird, as an echo of his
words, but not as conveying any opinion of her own ;
" I hope the little girl is not very ill? " she continued.

" Oh, no, quite an ordinary case."

The doctor then stepped out into the road.

" You are in a position of great trust, Mrs. Aird.
Prove yourself worthy of it for your own sake. Mr.
and Mrs. Johnstone are both rich and kind. By-the-
bye, I may be expected to drop in any day."

" Yes, sir, at what time? "

" At any time."

" Then I had better never take the baby out of sight
of the house."

" I don't say that, I will always send a telegram an
hour or so before I come, and if you take care never
to be away more than an hour I shall be sure to find
you."

He thus effectually prevented her from doing more
than take the baby for a walk, but she by her absolutely

contented face when he spoke, prevented his thinking it needful to come! She evidently did not mind the restraint at all, and he left her without having the remotest intention of going near her any more. The baby was thriving, the nurse was well, the lodgings were all that he could wish, the young woman had no friend, and believed herself liable to frequent supervision.

But why was the nurse so well contented to stay at home? Because she had got an answer to her letter from her mother, and it set forth, to her great joy and surprise, that this frugal and respectable woman, having made up her mind to leave her lodgings at Dartford, where she got as "Maria well knew such a poor living out of the washing," was coming up with the baby to her old quarters at the back of Kensington Square, and to-morrow might be expected to drop in to an early dinner, and, if it was not an ill conveniency, could enjoy a pork chop or two and a green gooseberry pudding.

Mrs. Aird could hardly believe her good fortune. She saw at once a reason, though not the reason, for this sudden resolution. She was herself to have every comfort; if more pork chops were eaten than could have been expected, no questions would be asked provided the baby was well and flourishing. Her mother intended, of course, to come and share in some of the good things. The friend in the lodgings would never tell that she might now and then have cooked for two instead of for one. Moreover the mother had hinted already that she might as well constitute herself the baby's washerwoman as allow any other woman to have that post. Mrs. Aird was rather late the next morning, and was about to dress the baby, who, having only just been washed, was sprawling on her knee, a little red, limp, crying creature, when, to her delight, her mother with her own baby came in.

"Oh, mother, mother, take this one," she cried, "and give me mine!"

The exchange was instantly effected, and Mrs. Aird

began to devour her own baby with kisses. Her mother
laid the little Johnstone down on the bed, and let him
comfort himself as well as he could with his own tiny
fist, while she carefully took off and folded her own best
shawl, and put on an apron.

" A nice little fellow," she then said, looking at him
critically. " A fine boy I call him, for he's as big as
yours already, and a fortnight younger. A nice fresh
skin," she continued, taking him up and turning him
over on her competent motherly arm, " not a spot nor
— nor — nor, a mark about him. Yes, he's as near as
may be the same weight as yours."

The young mother, absorbed in her child, took no
notice of these remarks, but tenderly cuddling her own
baby against her neck, said sighing, —

" And to think he's weaned! Oh, how much more
interesting he does look than that other woman's child."

" La!" cried her mother, " how can you say so,
Maria! I call that real, real foolish. Interesting indeed, one's just as interesting as — as the other, same
size, same blue eyes, and what little down there is on
their heads, just the same color."

" Well, mother, you were all for my having a nurse-
child, so you're bound to make out it's for the best."

" And I hope it'll prove for the best, my — my girl,"
said the mother, with a slow, quiet impressiveness.
" Well, if this child ain't gone off to sleep! I'll just
wrap him in — in the nursing apron and put him in his
cot. I've brought you a bundle, Maria," she continued, cautiously lifting the child. " A bundle with your
two old print gowns in it, no need for you to go tramping up and — and down these dull roads in your good
new clothes. Did you manage to — to get those library
books returned? I should be loath for you to get into
trouble, through their being sent for to the house, such
a lot as you had too by what you wrote."

" Yes, mother, I got them back ; I had to send them
from here by the carrier, and send the ninepence too in
stamps for the reading of them."

" See how you waste your money," answered her

mother, cautiously laying the baby in his cot, "read, read, for ever read; that's what came of—of my settling at Kensington, and your going to S'Mary Abbots' schools. What a man the old vicar is, to be sure! If all the S'Mary Abbots' scholars can't read the—the smallest print and—and write the longest word as soon as look at them, it's not for want of his worritting after them. Little he cares, I'll be bound, what your mother had to pay in that very High Street for novels for you to read by candle-light in bed (all along of his being so keen after the learning). It's a wonder you did not burn the house down!"

"Mother," said Mrs. Aird, "I don't want Mrs. Johnstone to know I was brought up at Kensington; she's not aware but what we've lived at Dartford all our lives, instead of only while poor Lancey was with us."

"Of course not," answered her mother, with gentle deliberation, which derived emphasis from a very slight impediment in her speech. "And she never need, Ma—Maria."

She showed this imperfection of speech very little unless she was excited or agitated, and this is the exact contrary of what happens in most cases.

"She hates the notion of my so much as looking at poor people, as if the very air of them could foul her child," said the daughter.

"Most of 'em do."

"And as to your coming all the way from Dartford through me wanting to set my eyes on my own just for an hour, she'd never believe it."

"Just like 'em again, *but most of us is even with 'em,* *Ma—Maria.* And it does see—seem a good deal to act out for—for an hour or two, it does in—deed, Maria."

"Well, mother, it does; but you see I sent the money."

"Ay," continued the mother, Mrs. Pearson by name, with her gentle, slow hesitation, "and don't you go hiring your rubbishing no—novels here. It might be found out. And—and—and I've—I've lit on two or

three first — first-rate ones, that I brought with me,
shilling ones, I got half — half price — Ma — Maria."
"Why should mother be so put out about the novels?" thought Mrs. Aird; "I've not heard her talk so
badly I don't know when."

"What are you doing, mother?"

"Well, I'm not fond of washing frocks constant!
you're crumpling the child's robe, and he — he — poor
little fellow·! has — has but one. I'll lay it by till we
— we — go home. And how's Mrs. Leach, Ma —
Maria?" (Mrs. Leach was the landlady.)

"She's well, and full of joy; got work for nine days
to come, morning till night, charing. I'm to have my
dinner cooked at the bake-house, and I shall oblige her
by making my bed, and that."

Master Lancelot Aird, having been divested of his
best frock, was now laid in his mother's bed, with his
bottle, over which he also fell asleep. Mrs. Aird let
her mother know that now she could do as she liked,
she dined at twelve, and then she could enjoy her tea at
four o'clock, and eat a good supper by half-past eight.

"I wonder how you'll do when you've weaned this
child?" observed the mother, her capricious impediment
quite gone; "you'll find a difference then, my girl."

"Don't talk of that, mother; I hope that won't be
for six months at least."

"It'll be no trouble," replied the mother, "be it
sooner or later — sooner or later, Ma — Maria. For by
what you told me, he has been used to have the bottle
once a day from his birth. I had no trouble with —
with yours my — my — my girl. And — and if their
being as like as — as two peas is any — any rule, you'll
have none with — with him."

"There she goes again," thought Mrs. Aird, quite
impressed by the uncommon degree of discomfort that
her mother was suffering.

Then it all went off again, the dinner was carried into the tiny parlor, the two babes slept in peace, and the
two women, leaving the door open, sat down to enjoy
themselves, a pot of porter, and some new bread, and
other luxuries being set on the table.

"Mrs. Leach does n't so much as know I brought your child," said Mrs. Pearson, the young widow's mother.

"Why should she, mother?" answered Mrs. Aird sharply, "she might take it into her head to tell Mrs. Johnstone."

The mother nodded with an air of wisdom and triumph. "The children have all got the scarlatina now, my girl, and one of them is very ill."

"How do you know, mother."

"I went and inquired. Said I to the cook, she was cleaning the steps, ' *Mrs. Thompson's* love, and has heard the little Johnstones are ill, and I was to inquire.' She told me all I wanted to know. Mrs. Johnstone's very unwell herself, and the servants say she 'll certainly fret herself sick, so ill as she has just been, and she won't leave the children a minute. ' Well,' said I, ' you won't forget to give Mrs. Thompson's love to your lady ; ' and I left. You 've some days to yourself, my girl, yet."

"So I think, mother."

" *Then — then — then do — your best.*"

"Yes, mother, why not ?" answered Mrs. Aird carelessly, when at last her mother had managed to utter these words. Mrs. Aird now went into the little kitchen and fetched in the pudding, she was by no means too proud to wait on herself when her friend and landlady was busy.

And now that this comfortable meal was over, Mrs. Pearson, to her daughter's great surprise, expressed a strong wish to see Kew Gardens. "But as you 've never dressed the baby, Maria," she continued, "along of his being asleep, you have no call to come too, you can see them any day: There he is awake, I hear him stirring, and yours 'll wake too directly." She stepped out into the road, and before her daughter had recovered from the surprise of feeling that there was something unusual about her mother, she was gone. "I 'll — I 'll — I 'll be in by tea-time, my — my girl," she said ; "undo the bundle and put in any — anything you have for the wash, and I 'll take it with me."

CHAPTER II.

MRS. PEARSON had no sooner departed than the Johnstone baby began to cry lustily. His nurse took him up, and while she sat on the side of the bed, satisfying his little wants, she gazed at her own child with tender love.

Two or three tears rolled down her comely cheeks, while the alien baby made himself at home at her breast, and half choked his greedy little self, over the nourishment she had sold away from her own.

As she held her nursling with one hand, she drew towards her the bundle her mother had brought, with the other, untied the knots, shook out her two gowns, and three shabby little volumes fell away from them on to the bed. She lifted one, and a sudden touch of self-consciousness made her feel how odd it was that her mother should have accidentally lighted on such a story; but she put it aside without another thought, for she had read it before, and it was not interesting. Then she took up the next, and when she saw that it was on the same subject — a very common and favorite subject with writers of fiction — she no longer thought there was any accident in the matter. Her mother, she perceived, had brought these books to her on purpose to suggest what she did not dare to say. She took up the third book — one very dirty volume from an old-fashioned story called "The Changeling."

She turned very pale ; her first thought was one of almost unreasonable anger against her mother. If she had been minded to do this thing, as she now perceived,

2

she could not have done it without an accomplice, without doubling therefore the slender chance of escape from detection. She felt that a longing that such a thing could have been done had already existed deep down in her heart. She accused her mother as alone having given it form and possibility. The little nursling, now fed to the full, was awake and quiet in her arms; but temptation was too new to be acted on. She put on his fine and ample clothes all but his robe, and laying him down beside the other babe, began to recall the things her mother had said. They had the same colored eyes, the same colored down on their heads, they were about the same size; but as to bringing the remote romances of a by-gone age into families that lived in Harley Street and sent a baby with his nurse to Kew — now, at this very present time — it was a thing too arduous for thought, too wicked for every-day life. An Irish castle — tumble-down, haunted by ghosts, and full of retainers — had been the scene of one of these stories. A fugitive family hundreds of years ago had stolen away the heir of the house, in another; and had left their child in its stead.

In the third, children were also changed at nurse — but there was a gipsy in the case, and there were awful midnight incantations, and the nurse was conjured into the crypt of a ruined chapel, far among the Scotch mountains; and there the baby was charmed away from her, and an elf-child left in her arms.

She mocked at her mother, and was sore against her in her heart. She was holding up the broidered robe of her nursling; did it look like anything that her child could wear upon his pretty low-born limbs without detection? Yes! There was nothing to choose. He was the finer child of the two; at least, if there was anything to choose between them.

It was time he had his bottle. She would warm its contents for him. She did so, and her tears fell fast, as she leaned over the little kitchen fire.

When he had finished this meal — each child being full dressed, excepting that it had its frock off — she

thought she should like to see how her child would look
in the beautiful robe. She put it on ; and to her fond
eyes he seemed to become it far better than the other
did. To change them ! Oh, that such a thing could
be ! But she was not unreasonable ; she knew as well
as possible that it could not; but, for the moment —
only for the moment — her child should look like the
gentleman's son. Nature was not unfair at the first ;
the carpenter's baby as he had come from her hand was
as fair, as refined, as innocent in aspect as he could be.
It would only be when art stepped in and educated him,
that he would be, however he might dress, all the cock-
ney and all the carpenter.

His mother (over the Johnstone baby's robe) put on
the delicate blue cashmere cloak, enriched with swan's-
down, and the pretty satin hood, with its lace cockade.
And sat hanging over him with a yearning sense of envy
against the other baby and a rapture of pride in him.

She did not care whether her mother came in or not.
She would by no means do this thing. In fact, it could
not be done with the least chance of success — but not
the less, her mother should know she perceived she had
been tempted — not the less — A sudden qualm at the
nurse's heart. A noise of wheels ! A dust rising up !
A carriage ! — oh misfortune, a carriage, — and both
the children in the house ; she herself, sitting in the
little bedroom, which was on the ground floor and led
out of the sitting-room, must have been plainly seen by
its one occupant — a lady ; and this lady was now de-
scending. It was Mr. Johnstone's mother. Something
must be done, and done instantly. But nothing could
ever make things come right if it were discovered that
two babies were in the house and one of them her own.
She had but one instant to decide ! the lady was coming
up the tiny garden. The little Johnstone was lying con-
tentedly on the bed — no time to dress him, no time to
undress the other. She kept her own baby on her arm,
and in sheer desperation opened the bedroom door, and
shutting it behind her, came to meet her guest with a
curtsey and a welcome. Something sadly like a prayer

was on her trembling lips — her situation was terrible
— and for the first few moments while the supposed
grandmother — a fine capable woman little more than
fifty, who had just come up from Scotland — lifted the
baby's lace veil, kissed him, chirped to him, and asked
how he was, she trembled so as to attract attention —
he was lying flat on his mother's arms staring at
the nodding feathers in the visitor's bonnet.

" You look very pale, nurse !" exclaimed the grandmother.

" Oh, ma'am," answered Mrs. Aird, the ready lie
rising to her lips. " I was afraid you might be come
to say the children were worse."

" The children are worse, I am sorry to say," was the
answer. " I have not seen them, of course, that would
not be prudent — but Mr. Johnstone writes me word
that Miss Irene causes them a good deal of anxiety."

" You may put your bonnet on, nurse. The darling
is dressed — you shall take him out with me for a little
airing in the carriage."

What! and leave the other baby all alone on the
bed? Mrs. Aird felt as if her heart stood still.

" Oh, ma'am !" she exclaimed, lying again, " I am
so sorry. but the person of the house is gone out for an
hour or so, just to do a little shopping, and I promised
to see to the house while she was away — and she has
locked the back-door and given me the key."

" Oh, well, another time, then," said the lady slowly,
and as if Mrs. Aird's manner surprised her.

" You are quite well?" she inquired.

" Oh, yes, as well as can be, ma'am," and all her soul
was in her ears. What if the Johnstone baby should
cry !

" Pretty little man," said the grandmother, again
caressing the baby, but not taking him from the nurse ;
" I hope he is thriving." She had not seen her grandson before.

" Oh, ma'am, he is as good-tempered and as contented
as he can be." The nurse had now recovered her color,
every moment that the other baby remained quiet was

a great gain, she was beginning to pluck up courage, and was trying to look cheerful.

" Well, well," said the lady, smiling kindly, " I confess I do not see much virtue in a baby's contentment, when he has as good cause for it as I hear you give this one."

" Thank you, ma'am ; I am sure I try to give satisfaction."

" I am very well satisfied," answered the grandmother graciously ; " I shall write to my daughter that I am."

A few more commonplaces, a few more adverse chances to be overlived, a few more flutterings of the heart on the part of the nurse, and then her visitor got up and took her leave and went back to the carriage, followed by the nurse with her own child in her arms. It seemed to her that she had never listened and never looked before.

That baby on the bed, how her ears were open to him ! That velvet mantle she was following, how she noted every fold and every " frog " upon it !

But now her curtsey was made and the carriage was gone.

She ran back into the house, laid her child on the bed, and burst into tears ; for the first time in her life she knew what bitterness there is in the fear of detection. " The wages of sin are hard." Her ruin as regarded this situation and the character she hoped to have from it would have been irretrievable if anything had been found out.

Even if she had·meant really to do the thing, and keep to it, such an interview would have been more than she could have borne. What if Mrs. Leach had walked in, and it had come out that she had not left the house at all ! What if the other baby had begun to cry ! And yet how sweet that one of her own had looked when the strange visitor had nodded and chirped to him, and he had twisted his tiny mouth into the promise of a smile !

It was not worth while to go through so much.

No, that was not exactly it. She loved herself as
well as her baby. She had not expected to be so
frightened. The least questioning would have betrayed
all. She never could so much as *act* such a thing again,
and she pulled down the broidered robe, even tearing it
in her hurry, and threw it aside from her own child.
Then she took up her nursling, dressed him in all his
bravery, and waited her mother's arrival with an easier
heart. She had not known herself before. She was
aware now what shame and dread had come of the mere
prophecy of a crime in her heart.   .

What, then, would experience be! Well, it might
be a pity, perhaps it was ; but she was not one of those
who could stand such a thing. It was not her conscience that was awake, but her reason ; even if she
could do such a thing successfully, she should suffer
constant fear of detection ; she would not do it.

Master Johnstone had enjoyed his supper, and was
in his cot, and Master Aird had enjoyed his bottle before Mrs. Pearson came in.

She entered slowly, and as if she would not startle
her daughter. Mrs. Aird had one of the babies on her
knee. Mrs. Pearson never cast her eyes on him.

" La, Maria, my girl," were her first words ; " such
queer things as I have seen ! "

" No, have you, mother?" answered Mrs. Aird, with
a keen consciousness that her mother cared about the
said things nothing in the world.

" If some of those cactus things was n't just like an
— an old man's head all over white hairs, my name's
not Fanny Pearson," said the mother, without any signs
of hesitation. " There was a — a glass-house full of
such. The last time I saw them was the first bank
holiday Parliament made. The shops all shut up, and
yet the Punches going, and barrows of fruit *cried* all
about the streets, it was just like — like a wicked Sunday, that had got sorted wrong and come in the middle
of the — the week."

Her daughter, with a baby on her knee, remained
silent.

" And so tea's ready, Maria, my girl, and very acceptable, I say." She glanced at her daughter, and noticed the signs of tears upon her face. " I'm always glad of — of my tea," she continued ; " how quiet the dear children are ! " she added, as she drew her chair to the table.

" One of them has been crying pretty hard," replied the daughter, without specifying which.

She had a little white pinafore in her hand, and seemed to be giving her attention to the sleeve which she was folding back with a button.

Her mother glanced keenly at her, but did not dare to look at the face of the child she had on her knee.

Tea was now poured out. Mrs. Pearson had begun to feel the silence rather awkward, when at last her daughter said, " Those three novels you brought me, mother, I wonder you should have thought I had n't read them, they're old things every one of them."

" Well," answered the mother, with obliging suavity, " if you don't mean to read them again, I 'll take them back, Ma — Maria."

" No, I don't," said Mrs. Aird. She knew she was making her mother uncomfortable, but a certain slight perversity of temper afflicted her just then. " I saw you 'd looked them over before you chose them," she continued.

Her mother reddened, she was not at all sure that the thing suggested had not been done. " Maria's so deep," she reflected, " that she's quite capable of playing at innocence with me. Still ' Least said is soonest mended,' and I wish she would hold her tongue."

" I 'll take them back," she managed to say, with many breaks and repetitions through the return of her impediment, and she rose and tied them up in a blue handkerchief, and returned almost meekly to the tea table, she was quite at her daughter's mercy now ; she could not articulate tolerably. The least little smile hovered about Mrs. Aird's lips, such a subtle small smile as justified at once her mother's assertion that she was " deep."

"I should burn them, mother, if I was you," she observed calmly, "not that they signify."

Her mother answered nothing.

"I've read dozens such — dozens," continued the daughter. "I've not forgót one of them. They're enough to dishearten the willingest sinner that ever breathed."

"I don't know what you mean, Maria," the mother burst out, anger overcoming her hesitation. She hardly knew whether she was most angry with her daughter for "giving words" to the matter at all when perfect silence would have been most prudent, or for thus leaving her in some doubt what she had done or meant to do, or for (as it really seemed) not being perfectly certain whether she dared trust her own mother.

"Don't know what I mean, mother?" rejoined the daughter, that small smile hovering over her upper lip; "well, I call them disheartening because after *they've* (whoever they may be), after they've done it so beautiful, you know, they're always found out." The mother looked very red and irate. "No," she continued, appearing to cogitate, "I don't remember one but what's found out, nor one but what's brought to shame for it."

And what was the effect of this speech on the mother? She caught the subtle smile as it went and came, it never rose higher than the lip or warmed the eye, and she was in doubt. Something had put Maria out she thought; perhaps though she meant to do the thing that had been hinted at, the peril of it mixed as wormwood with the sweetness of her hope.

"They're always found out," repeated the daughter.

The mother recovered speech. "*No, they're not,*" she replied angrily, "*I know better than that.*"

The significance of her manner was inexpressible. Mrs. Aird gave a great start, and with frightened eyes gazed at the woman who had claimed for herself such awful experience. But having said so much, the mother either could not or would not say more. She poured out some tea, cut her daughter more bread and butter,

and still not looking at the baby, scarcely looking in
his direction, left her words to work their due effect.

What she had to do was finished. She had made
a certain suggestion, and her daughter surely was
aware that she might count on her help to carry it
out.

There was silence; then Mrs. Leach, the landlady,
came in. She had a promise of several days' charing,
wanted for many days to be away till eight o'clock at
night, was very anxious to propitiate. Did Mrs. Aird
think she should mind answering the door herself if anybody came to see the baby? Mrs. Aird was sure she
should not, and also was quite willing to have a baked
dinner for the next few days.

Mrs. Leach had not seen the second baby who had
made his appearance on the scene, neither the mother
nor the daughter cared to mention him. He was lying
on his mother's bed with his bottle. The little Johnstone, taking it into his head to be very fractious, Mrs.
Aird carried him into the bedroom, and there, shutting
herself in, comforted him and contemplated her heir.
The mother and Mrs. Leach meanwhile (tea being
over) proceeded into the back of the house together, to
inspect a new copper, and were a long while away, so
that Mrs. Aird had plenty of time for thought.

It was nearly three quarters of an hour before Mrs.
Pearson returned and saw her daughter sitting by the
window with a baby on her lap. He was dressed in the
robe that had been folded up so carefully in the morning, had on the neat little gray cloak and hood familiar
to Mrs. Pearson's eyes, he had also a fine handkerchief
trimmed with imitation lace lightly laid over his face. A
bundle of clothes to be washed was lying beside her.
The nurse explained that the omnibus her mother had
wished to go back by was very nearly due, and that she
had dressed the baby ready. The grandmother did not
look either at her or at the child with anything but a
hasty glance.

She took the child upon her arm and advanced to the
open door, but the omnibus was not yet visible. She

could not stand waiting, she felt too much excited, and
she proposed, as well as her impediment permitted, to
go on and let it overtake her. She was just stepping
out when, as if by an irresistible impulse, the daughter
exclaimed, " Oh, I must have another kiss of him."
She flung back the handkerchief, and, behold, it was the
same baby that had been brought, it was the carpenter's
child ! the grandmother could not doubt it, and anger
reddened her face and filled her soul.

Then Maria had not done it after all — after the trouble she had taken to come and live at Kensington — after
the day's work she had given up in order to bring the
child to Kew. She was so wrath that she would have
liked to box Maria's ears. So irate in fact when Maria burst into a little chuckling laugh that she trembled
all over till she was fain to step inside again and sit
down, setting her bundle beside her on the floor. Mrs.
Aird, after that small laugh, darted into the bedroom
and appeared with the other baby in her arms and an
air of simple innocence. The omnibus went by and
neither of them noticed it till too late. The mother was
trying hard to calm herself, and the irate hue of her face
was fading ; the daughter had the subtle smile about her
lips when their eyes met, but it gave way to a gleam
of surprise when her mother spoke as pleasantly as
if nothing had happened.

" I wish you could have managed to take him off
my hands for two days while I look about me, Ma —
Maria, he is a great handful."

" Why, mother, it would be found out, you know it
would."

" Mrs. Leach don't know he's here ; you couldn't
help your own crying now and then in the night, but
there's no ne — eed they should ever bo — oth cry together, for the other you can always stop. They'd
only — only seem to be one."

" So I could, mother ; how I should love to have him
till you bring the clothes back ! "

" The doctor is to send a telegram if ever he comes.
There's a girl in the cottage round by the green that

would take him out at what's calling time for ladies, Ma — Ma — ria."

"To be sure," answered the daughter; "they never lunch till nearly two, they cannot possibly get here till three at earliest; I might send the blessed babe out at that time of day. The girl need never see my nurse-child. Well, mother —"

"Well, you'll take him off — off — my hands then, till the clothes are — are — are ready."

Mrs. Aird took him, that is, she got her mother to lay him in the cot, for her own arms were full, and she agreed with her mother to send on the girl who had been mentioned to speak to her. The temptation, as she herself looked upon it, was over, she had not yielded. She now thought she could enjoy the sweet for that little time without the bitter. She could have her own baby to sleep in her arms for those two nights, and send him away during the afternoon, so that she could no more suffer as she had done during the grandmother's visit. She was glad at heart. It was only safety she wanted. Not to do the right, but to be safe in doing wrong. So the baby was left, and Mrs. Pearson departed with a light step and considerable confidence in her mind as to what would be the end of it. There never was such a chance, as she told herself as she went home — babies altered from week to week, who could challenge them? The mother who could at this moment tell her child out of a hundred was sure not to come near him for fear of infection; and though she might in her jealous love and care send a friend almost every day to look that he was happy, clean, and cared for, the visit would be of no use as regarded the child's real danger, the only danger that threatened him.

Mrs. Johnstone did indeed send almost every day, and was consoled by letters from various friends who came at her desire. They always found a charming, fresh, healthy young nurse, a clean room and a fat baby. They never found any one with the nurse. She seemed glad to see them, and always expressed much sympathy with Mrs. Johnstone.

CHAPTER III.

It's more asking than answering in this world, asking back and asking on. — ADELINE D. T. WHITNEY.

AT about ten o'clock on the morning of the appointed day, Mrs. Pearson entered the cottage at Kew with the baby Johnstone's clean clothes.

Mrs. Aird looked tired and flushed. "Such a night as I have had, mother, you wouldn't believe!" she exclaimed; "as fast as one was quiet the other set off crying, and it's been nothing but cry, cry, one or the other, all the time I've been washing and dressing them. They're both just fed, and I hope they'll take a spell of sleep now, for I'm about tired out."

The clothes from the wash were then spread on the table, and Maria proceeded to pay her mother for doing them.

"And now, mother, sit down," she proceeded. "You are the washerwoman, you see, sit down, but in case anybody should come in, leave the money and the clothes on the table to look natural."

"Nobody will come to-day," answered the mother, rather seriously.

"Why not?"

"That — that little girl that was first taken ill — she's dead, Maria."

"Mother!"

"Yes, I inquired, and — and the cook told me;" she gave a little gasp here, as if making a supreme effort to overtake and run down her words, then went on quite easily. She said, "They've just sent the death to the *Times*, and — and you'll see it to-morrow, ' Irene, beloved child of Donald Johnstone, aged three years and three months.'"

" Yes, she was their eldest child. Poor Mrs. Johnstone! I wonder how the others are, mother?"

" Very ill by what I hear; the cook said Mrs. Johnstone was very ill too, and the master was so knocked down by that, and his trouble at the child's death, that it was a pity to see him."

" He is very fond of her; I wonder whether she is going to have the fever."

" Nobody will know that yet, with grown-up people it seldom shows before the fourteenth day. But — but — but, dear me, my girl, you do look tired out."

" I am tired. I 'm sorry at my heart for the Johnstones. Mother, I 've done a deal of thinking since we parted."

" Thinking about what, Ma — Maria?"

" Well, partly about you, mother, and what you let out the other day."

" I suppose, whatever you may have thought all your — all your life, you — you — you never thought your mother was a fool?"

" No, I never did; but I have thought there might be things —"

" Things as you 'd have a right to hear when you was older. Well, there might be, or again there might — might — might not be, Ma — Maria."

" But if you go on like this, mother, I shall know as clear as can be that you 're not easy in your mind about trusting me, and don't seem to like it; if so, I 'd as lief not hear anything."

" I 've no call to be uneasy, Ma — Maria, what I had a hand in is done constant — constant, Maria."

" Mother!"

" And if I tell it you now, it 's — it 's for your good."

" Yes, mother, what else should it be for?" but the daughter blushed, and the mother looked anywhere rather than at her face.

" Before I married your father, when I was in service — nursemaid to Mrs. Plumstead — we were in Italy, and the baby died."

"Yes, I've heard you say so."

"But she kept me, Ma — Maria, for there was another expected very soon, and the master was going so fast in con — consumption, that she was glad enough of me to help to nurse him."

She lifted the edge of a Paisley shawl she had on. "She was very free-spoken. This very shawl, such a good one it was, she gave it me the first par — particular talk we had. She said she knew *he* (she — she always called him *he*, and whispered as if she was cautious about being overheard) — she knew *he* could n't live long, and she did so wish for a boy. Once when — when we talked she said, 'If — if I have a girl, I shall be a nobody; but if it's a boy, he will inherit the estate, and I shall have a handsome allowance for — for bringing of him up.' She said, 'Fanny Slade, my husband is very dark, as — as dark as most Italians. It's likely his son should be dark. Don't you think,' she said, very soft and gentle, 'Don't you think I can manage to have a boy?' I knew a — a good many of her thoughts by that time, I said, 'You would n't be so cruel, ma'am. What! and — and leave your own child, if it's a girl, with these nuns and people.'

"She laughed me to scorn at that. 'Leave my own, if it's a girl,' she said; 'for shame of you, to think of such a thing, but why — why — why shouldn't I have twins, Fanny Slade?'

"She had a curious smile, Ma — Maria. Many an hour I sat and thought on it after I left her. A little smile like — like yours. She was so deep that I could never make out more of her than — than she liked to explain. Yet she seemed so free-spoken. I often wondered over her. She would sit and look up in the bare sky, not a bit afraid of it."

"Why should she have been afraid of it?"

"Why — why, wait till — till you see it, everything wiped clean away betwixt you and heaven; seems as — as if *they* must see down so awful clear — everything you're doing, and that for — for weeks and weeks together. When — when I came to have things on my

mind I hated that sky, and there seemed to be nothing
worth breathing, it was so clear. All the time before
you were born, I — I often sat and thought how she
would paint her flowers, and smile when he was n't looking at her. He — he was very fond of her. She had
a dove-colored quilted satin gown, and she would be
dressed in it for him to admire her, and then when he
fell asleep she would smile.

"She said, 'Why should n't I have twins, Fanny
Slade?' and she looked at — at — at me so quiet. She
would be often painting, and — and she would send me
out under the olive-trees to — to gather flowers for her.
I did n't like it. You — you may think your mother
soft, Ma — Maria, but I often cried over that work, I —
I assure you."

"Why, mother?"

"They were so mortal beautiful; they stood so thick
together, white, and crimson, and blue, in the shadow
among the green wheat, all scent and glory. I was
afraid of them, for — for — for I knew the Lord would
never have made them like that, and not often be coming down to look at them."

All this time the daughter listened wide-eyed, and the
mother whispered, "We had been all the winter in that
little island I told you of, they call it Capri; and now
we was journeying — we — we was journeying slowly
home, Ma — Maria. The orange-trees were full of
blossom, and what with their scent and the sun I — I —
I used to feel quite giddy.

"We stopped once at a little — little village inn, for
the master was very faint; he went indoors, and he laid
himself down on the bed to rest a couple of hours. We
sat down on a bench under a vine. As we sat we saw
a young girl with a very young baby on — on her arm.
Down there they fix them out straight. Mrs. Plumstead
called her, and began to whisper to her, and she sat —
sat down almost at her feet. She could speak Italian
quite well, but the master could not, at — at all, no, nor
understand it.

"Such a pretty young girl she was, and by — by

what Mrs. Plumstead told me, she had no father for her babe.

" Well, I went in to see how the master was, and — and we dined there ; after that they sent for me, and when I came she said, ' Fanny Slade, Mr. Plumstead has — has just noticed that my diamond ring is not on my finger, and he is sure I had it this — this morning.' ' Sure,' said he. She looked at me so — so calm and gentle. Said he, ' I seem to recall the sound of some small thing that I heard roll on the floor before dinner,' and he thought it had rolled under the skirting. Well, I searched, and when it was not found, if he did n't have all the flooring up! she encouraging him. But my thought was that she had given it to the girl. Well, we — we slept there, and — and — and the next day he was better. We went on and then stopped (because she said she was tired), in the market-place of a little small town, and there to — to — to my wonder, I saw that same girl forty miles from her home, looking out for us. I — I looked at missis. She said, so gentle and sweet, ' Love, I wish you were not so short-sighted,' she said, ' there is such a pretty cos — costume down there,' that was said to him, but it was meant for me, he — he could not see the girl. We had a vast deal of talk that afternoon, she and I. Then we went on and — and again, in a little village by an inn door was the girl, she had gone on before us, Mrs. — Mrs. Plumstead saying what — what inn she should drive to. We did not move any more. That — that night Mrs. Plumstead was taken ill, and about dawn her baby was born, and — and, Ma — ria, it was a girl.

" As soon as the doctor was gone I knocked at — at Mr. Plumstead's door. Well, it — it was shocking to hear him thank God for my lie. I told him he had twin children born, a son and a daughter."

She gave a little gasp here in this the crisis of her story, and as if her words could not be commanded, went back to an easier part of it.

" Mrs. Plumstead had said to me, ' I mean to have that girl for a wet-nurse, and I have told her also to —

to wash her baby and bring him to me to — to look at.'
I could see in the dawn light how — how wan Mr. Plumstead looked ; but he gave thanks as — as well as he could
like a Christian ; and — and said he, ' It's a sin — singular thing, Fanny Slade, that Mrs. Plumstead has more
than once expressed to me a sort of pre — sentiment,
that she should have twins.'

"I was obliged to leave him, ill as — as he seemed.
When I went to him again he seemed to rally a bit,
but little as I knew then about sickness and death, I
knew that death was nigh.

"And — and he would send me out for flowers.
There never were such people for flowers. They were
easy enough to get, the olive-yards were choked up
with them, spread-out anemones, and tulips, and Jacob's
ladder. I pulled an armful, but I was frightened, for
— for there was a sign in the sky."

" Mother ! what sign?"

" I had — had seen too many pictures of angels not
to know what sign. It was a vast way off. It was an
angel, you could not make out the form of its — its body,
but his two long pointed wings just like a gauze cloud
were tilted towards the world as — as if he was flying
down. I saw the — the faint shadow of them, it fell
just where I stood."

" You saw only the white wings?"

" Yes, I tell you only the wings. The sky being so
clear there, you can see things, Maria, that — that here
are invisible. It was the Angel of Death passing —
passing down and going to stop.

" I ran in. He was propped up with pillows, writing
to his father, to express the birth of the twins. He —
he directed the letter and sent me to his wife with his
dear love, and how did she feel herself? When I got
back, dying he was with the letter in his hand. I
could see his face change as I gave him the — the message. He expressed he was pleased, but he soon began
to ramble in his talk, and just at noon that day he died
in my arms, as softly as could be.

" We kept the — the girl about us, and when Mrs.

3

Plumstead was able to travel, we took her and the —
the boy-baby too, for it was made out that the poor lady
was — was too delicate by half to nurse her child.

"When we got well away, Mrs. Plumstead had to
give the — the girl a very heavy bribe, to leave her
child. She was a thief and a good-for-nothing little
— little hussy; but she loved her baby, and at last
Mrs. Plumstead got out her jewel-case and sat smiling
at her, and showed her — her two diamond earrings;
and she sat staring as — as if she would eat them.
Then Mrs. Plumstead put them in her ears, and gave
her a little hand-glass to look at herself; but she kept
sulking and pouting. Then Mrs. Plumstead gave her
a pink coral brooch, and she began to talk and smile
and show her pretty white teeth; and — and at last
Mrs. Plumstead shook out a long gold chain, and looked
at her and smiled, and put it round her neck, and —
and the girl started up and gave a great cry, and ran
out of the room, never looking back, and took herself
off, and — and we saw her no more.

"That's all about it, Maria, it was very easy done.
We soon hired a wet-nurse for the boy, and came out of
Italy to a place they — they call Mentone.

"But nothing seemed to go right, for here the little
girl-baby died, and Mrs. Plumstead took on most —
most fearful, and made out that I'd encouraged her to
do the thing, and the death of the baby was sent to punish
her. She fretted and used to put herself quite in a rage
over the letters she got from her relations. She must be
— be thankful, they all said, she'd got her dear boy left.

"She was all brown, her cheeks were soft and brown,
and her eyes like — like brown velvet. The baby was
not as brown as she. Well, Maria, in a few months we
came to England, and there I did a — a foolish thing —"

The daughter, all eyes, sat listening; tears were on
the mother's cheeks.

"A foolish thing, and lost my hold over her. I
married your father. He came to see me, and vowed
he would not wait any longer. And I married him."

"Well, mother, many's the time you said he made
you a good husband, and he never drank."

" No, my girl; but *she* had promised me two hundred pounds, and she — she said she could not get at it before I married, for — for she must not part with any more of her jewels. Afterwards she was engaged to be married again, and I — I heard it. I was bent on having that money. I thought if she put me off any more, I would threaten her that I would speak;. and as soon as I got well, after you were born, I took you on my arm and went to her house. Oh, Ma — Maria! it cuts me to the heart to think on it. I 'd done my level best to serve her, and nothing was to come of it.

" ' You cannot speak with Mrs. Plumstead to-day,' said the butler, ' she 's distracted with — with grief; we 've lost Master Geoffry.' I did see her, though; she was hiding herself in her dressing-room. She did not wish it to be seen that she had no tears to shed. But oh! she was vexed. He had died of croup. I saw it was a bad chance for me ; she — she put me off with promises and promises."

" Then why did n't you say you would speak of it?" asked the daughter eagerly.

" Where would have been the use, my girl? And — and she promised me so fair. Who could I tell it to either — nobody cared? He was out of the way of the next heir, and — and — and the girl could never come and seek her own ; she did not so much as know our names. But, Maria, it — it seemed hard."

" Mother, did n't I say that those stories never end well? They are alike for that."

· " I got but ten pounds of her, Maria, and when I was put out she smiled — yes, she did ; she — she looked at me and smiled ! "

" It was a shame."

" Ay, and she soon went to Scotland with her new husband, and had five fine boys, one after the other; but — but she never gave me aught but their old clothes for mine, and paid the carriage of the parcels — I will say that : she — she paid the carriage."

" You 've no writing for the two hundred?" asked the daughter.

"No — and there's nothing to be done. I — I — I can't punish her without ac — accusing myself."

"If you think so, mother —"

"I know it, my girl, and it seems to hold me back; and me only five and forty and a widow, to think of my missing such a payment after — after, as you may say, it was fairly won!"

"I'm sorry I vexed you the other day, mother," said the daughter with absurd compunction.

"Ay, Ma — Maria, my girl, it was not dutiful of you." The daughter kissed her, and the mother wiped away some tears. Then there was a long silence.

"You'll stop and dine, mother? We could both dine in the kitchen; and, if anybody called, I could leave you and baby there," said Mrs. Aird at last.

"No, I'd best not; but if you could keep him another day or so —"

"To be sure, mother. Why, I find nobody ever comes except between three and six. As to Mrs. Leach, she'll not have a day at home for the next fortnight, so she'll never see him. Leave him, mother, and, when I want you to come for him, I'll drop you a post-card."

So Mrs. Pearson departed, not having stayed more than an hour or seen either of the children.

Mr. Johnstone's mother drove over again that afternoon, and wept as she told the story of the little Irene's death, and the father's distress. Her daughter-in-law, she said, was causing great anxiety to them all by the way that she appeared to be sinking under this trial. Maria Aird won golden opinions for herself by the tears she also shed when she heard this.

One baby was gone out for a walk, in charge of the girl; the other was lying on her knee: which was it? If it was not the same that Mrs. Johnstone's mother had seen two or three days before, she certainly did not notice any such fact.

Maria Aird, after that, expected at least one visitor every day, and never failed to have one. The day following the grandmother's visit came a telegram from the doctor. She was in every way ready for him ; the house very clean, the baby fast asleep (she said she had just nursed him), the other baby away.

" I shall not be able to come again," he said as he departed. " Mrs. Johnstone's mother will now see that you have what you want. At the same time, if anything should ail the child, you will of course telegraph to me ; for in such a case, you understand, I certainly should come."

So he took his leave, having done mischief which, when it disclosed itself, he was truly sorry for. But what are doctors to do ? He had changed his coat after his morning visit to Harley Street, and, as we all know, doctors never convey infection.

Mrs. Pearson had agreed with her daughter that a card should be posted to her when the baby was to be fetched, but she was very much surprised when a fortnight within one day had elapsed, and the expected card had not arrived. " But Maria is very deep," she reflected, " and, *if she is going to do her duty* by her own child, she'll yet be wishful that I should not know it — know it, for certain. Very like I may go on to the end of my days and never hear the real truth from her own mouth ; but I shall feel sure about what it is for all that ; and she thinks the child may alter a good bit in a fortnight. Besides, she'll have weaned the other."

The same evening a letter arrived : —

" DEAREST MOTHER,

" I feel myself very ill. Come as soon as ever you can to-morrow morning and fetch away Lancey. They are both so very fractious, I don't know where to turn. [" *Both so fractious, are they? I expected it of one of them,*" *mused the grandmother.*] I shall get up as early as I can, and have mine ready. I do so want you to take him ; I cannot do with them both [" *That looks well !*"], for my head aches so, night and day, and his fretting makes me feel worse. Mother, don't fail to come. Your dutiful daughter,

" MARIA JANE AIRD."

At nine o'clock the next morning, Mrs. Pearson walked in. Her daughter Maria, who seemed to be sitting up with difficulty, was dressing one baby; the other — presumably her own — was already in cloak and hood.

The mother's keen glance made her at once aware of something more the matter than she had anticipated. The daughter acknowledged no discomforts but headache and sore throat, and was presently so giddy that her mother made her go into the chamber and lie down on her bed.

And now, as is often the case, the daughter found herself more than commonly under the dominion of her natural qualities of mind, just, as it seemed, because it was more than commonly needful to success that she should escape from them.

She preserved an open innocence of manner, and said nothing at all to her mother, who knew, or thought, at once that no confidence would be reposed in her, and that all depended on her own keenness of observation. So she left her on her bed, and, taking her time to examine the children, to cogitate, and to make her arrangements, sent, in about an hour, by a passing child, to fetch the girl always trusted to carry out one of the children, put him into her arms in the little gray cloak and veil, and, having already despatched a telegram for the doctor, sat nursing the other child till his carriage appeared, and out he bustled. Mrs. Pearson met him.

"My daughter wrote me word, sir, last night, that she felt herself ill, and I have just come over to see her."

"What is the matter?"

"I hope, sir, considering that — that she has done her best," the mother began, following him into the little chamber.

"Take the baby out of the room," were almost his first words.

"I feel so confused, sir, and my throat so sore," said the poor young creature.

Mrs. Aird felt more confused as the day wore on, but she knew her mother was sometimes present, and that both the babies were gone.

She was quite able also to take pleasure in the knowledge that she was to be nursed at the charges of the Johnstones, and she did not forget that, when her mother said to the doctor that she knew very well how her daughter had caught the infection which had deprived her of her situation, he looked concerned, said not a word, but put his hand in his pocket and gave her a sovereign.

She was skilfully and carefully nursed, and was never seriously ill — scarcely in bed more than a fortnight.

Then began her education.

She sat up, thin, white-handed, and with eyes full of brooding thought and doubtful cogitation. She was to remain in the little lodgings at Kew for a full month, and then to have change, that the Johnstones might not have it on their consciences that anything was left undone for her good, or to prevent the further spread of infection.

Mr. Johnstone's mother had fetched away the baby, and happily he did not have the fever. The other child took it, and, of course, was nursed in the little lodgings at the back of Kensington Square.

Always in doubt, turning things over in her mind, Maria Aird would sit out in Kew Gardens, pondering over what she had done. "Was it worth while to have done this thing? No, but it was now not worth while to go through the far worse misery of undoing it. But was it done, after all? That depended entirely on what had been her mother's opinion of matters when she had been left alone with the children. But, oh, to be well again!" thought the young woman, "and see the baby again. I shall know whether it's my own or not. If it is, after all I've gone through, I think I shall be glad, though it may seem hard, when I'd got it done, to have it undone. Yet if it is not — oh! I do think I must confess it, come what will!"

But all sense of the possibility of such a thing as

confession and restitution was soon over, and every day she got more used to the dull brooding pain that had worn itself a home in her breast. She knew and felt that she had done a criminal action, but she did not, strange to say, by any means think of herself as a criminal.

A criminal seemed to be some one whose crime was a part of himself, some one with whom crime was ingrain, and she felt, in spite of all Bible teaching and school teaching, as if her fault was external to herself — something into which she had been tricked by circumstances.

And yet she knew it was wrong to dislike, as she did, the notion of having to work for, and bring up, and act mother to, the Johnstone baby. Very soon, almost all her sense of wrong-doing attached itself to this dislike.

She longed to go to service again, though she should have to pay her mother half the money she got to take care of this child and bring him up. And how soon could she make interest for his being got into some orphan school? Then she could go abroad and see him no more. Better by half never to set her eyes upon her own son again than have that other woman's son always beside her!

CHAPTER IV.

And shut the gates of silence on her thought.
JEAN INGELOW.

IT was nearly the end of July when Maria Jane Aird, getting out of an omnibus, passed through Kensington Square to her mother's lodgings.

She was expected. Her sister, a girl of fourteen, ran and snatched up the baby, and, thrusting him almost into her face, expatiated on his good temper, and demanded her eulogies in the same breath. "Ain't he grown?" she exclaimed, giving him a sounding kiss.

The mother, having greeted her daughter, turned again at once to the ironing-board and looked away, while Mrs. Aird, without taking the child, gazed at him with earnest, anxious attention.

"What ails you?" asked her sister.

"He's so changed," she murmured.

The thing sat boldly up, and stared at her — she stared at him.

Though it was a hot night, she began to shiver; she remembered so well the two babes she had parted from, and all the small but unmistakable particulars of feature and countenance in which they differed; but this differed from both.

This little fellow had a certain small amount of speculation in his bead-like blue eyes; he was more than five months old. He clutched the little sister's hair, and tried to suck it; when she tossed him up, he uttered an ecstatic squeal to express approval; he turned his head when he heard the click of the iron as it was set down; when she took him in her arms he cried, for his dawning intelligence seemed to assure him that she was a stranger.

She had thought incessantly on the two children ever since they had been taken from her. This child was not the least like her faithful recollection of either.

"By my not knowing him," she reflected, "I am sure he is not mine; mine I shall certainly know, and I shall never rest till I've seen him."

"He kicks ever so when he wants me to put him down," observed the zealous little sister; "he likes to lie on the floor on the woolly mat."

Mrs. Pearson then came forward to show off some of his accomplishments; he took a great deal of notice, it appeared.

"Toss him up and make him laugh, 'Lizabeth." No sooner said than done. The baby crowed and cooed, and showed his toothless gums, and, at the sight of this reality, her remembrance faded away.

She took him and pressed him to her bosom with a sort of yearning, for he might be hers; but she soon put him down again, for — oh, strange uncertainty, he might not!

The baby, the two sisters, and their mother, all slept in one room that night; there was but one other — the living-room, which also served for a kitchen. There was scant opportunity for such conversation as the young widow might have been supposed to long for with her mother; but it was characteristic of both the women that, so far from wishing to talk, they dreaded to be alone together. The mother, having for so many years kept her own secret, felt a kind of resentment against her favorite child for having been so tardy, so unwilling to take a hint as to have at last forced it from her; the daughter feared to ask a direct question, lest her mother should prevaricate in her answer, and so make her feel doubtful evermore in spite of any protestations that might come after. No, she should certainly find her own child less altered; she should know him easily enough. She would wait, and in the meantime try to be good to this one.

Some weeks after this the Johnstones came back to London for a short time preparatory to an autumnal sojourn at the seaside, and Mrs. Johnstone received a letter, which she thought a very nice one. She was quite well herself, and her little girls were well, so was the baby — indeed, he had never been otherwise.

" Madam," ran the letter, " I have long been perfectly recovered, and hope never to forget how good you have been to me. I came home some time ago and found my baby very well under mother's charge.

" Madam, I feel such a great wish to see your dear babe ; might I take the liberty to come some morning to set my eyes upon him? I hope he was none the worse for my being ill so suddenly. Hoping to hear from you, madam, I am,

" Your humble servant,
" MARIA JANE AIRD."

" Kindly creature ! " said Mrs. Johnstone, handing over the letter to her husband. " Many women feel a great love for their foster-children. I shall be pleased to show baby to her."

So one morning, about the end of September, Mrs. Aird was shown up into the nursery at Upper Harley Street. She was to dine there and spend the day. Mrs. Johnstone brought her up herself. The boy was asleep in his cradle ; he was a great, fat, heavy child, almost half as big again as the active, lean little fellow she had left at home. She had all but made up her mind — the want of maternal yearning towards the baby at home having persuaded her most of all — yet she longed to recognize this child, and so be sure for ever. She fully looked for certainty, but this child also was so much changed, that, as she stood looking at him, she could not help shedding tears. He awoke, rosy and cross, and would not come to her, and she knew she must now tell all to her mother, and get the real truth from her, or else for ever be uncertain which was which. She looked round at the pretty little sisters ; there was no special likeness between him and them ; just so she had recalled all her own and her husband's relatives as

far as she had known them in childhood, and she found
no decisive likeness to either child there. The children
were both fair, both blue eyed; this was a fine fat baby,
but then he had never been ill. The other had had an
attack of scarlatina, had been pulled down by it, and
was not fat; that was all. ·

Maria Aird did not get out of the omnibus which
brought her to Kensington High Street till about seven
o'clock in the evening; the day had been hot and the
street was more shady than dusk, though the weather
was remarkably overcast.

As she walked on, she saw a stretcher preceding her.
It was borne on the shoulders of four policemen, who
were pacing carefully along. At first she knew not what
was upon it — it was something brown. Then suddenly
it revealed itself plainly to her — a woman's gown. Yes,
poor creature, it was a woman.

Bandages were swathed round and round her and the
stretcher, but she did not move or show any sign of life.
Mrs. Aird could make out her figure, and, as she went
on, still the stretcher preceded her up a street, through
the square, then down another street, then to the little
court where she lived, and there — oh, terror! it stopped
at her mother's door.

A cry from within echoed her agonized voice without,
" Oh, mother, mother!"

The dull misery of the day was as nothing, now this
more acute agony absorbed all her thoughts.

The poor patient was carried to her bed, and her
daughters were told of her having been run over in one
of the narrow streets near, and from the first, having
been insensible, showing in her face no expression of
pain.

A kindly neighbor proposed to take charge of the baby
for the night. The young widow let him go, scarcely
looking at him; she remembered every few minutes,
with a flash of fear, that she might now perhaps never
be able to ask the question on which so much depended.
She loved her mother, and between this love and this
fear it seemed as if nothing could exhaust her. That

night and the next day, and through the next night, her
untiring eyes kept watch; her unwearied hands were
busy about the silent patient.

Sometimes a little better, there would seem to be intelligence in her mother's eyes, then again there would
be a wandering and aimless gaze.

The daughters were told to hope, and hope assisted
in sustaining them; but as yet no communication was
possible. At last Maria Jane Aird felt that she could
do no more, and left her place by the bedside to her
sister.

Another weary day and night passed, still they were
told to hope; then, just at dawn, the tired sister crept
to Maria's bed and woke her with, " Mother has spok-
en quite sensibly several times;" and she got up, and
came to take her turn at the nursing. The red flush and
solemn light of sunrise was on the ceiling, and seemed
to be cast down on her mother's pallid and wasted features. She saw at once an improvement of a certain
kind, but the face was no longer calm; she laid her
hand gently on her mother's, saying, in a soothing tone,
" You must be quite still, mother dear, and not fuss
yourself about anything — there's no occasion."

Such a commonplace reply, — " Me not fuss, and
your silk gown gone to the pawnbroker's?"

" Don't trouble about that, dear mother."

" And your watch — I heard you both express that
you'd do it when you did not think I noticed."

" Well, mother dear, I can get them out when you're
better," said the daughter soothingly.

" I — I never loved to see the dawn, I told *him* —
told *him* that lie, just at the dawn."

" It did no harm in the ending of it, mother dear,"
she answered, understanding her instantly.

" Then it — it don't signify, Maria, my girl?"

" No, nothing signifies but your getting well."

" And where's the child?"

" I paid fourpence to have him taken care of for to-
night. — Mother?"

. " Ay, my girl."

"The child — we were talking of the child. *Is he mine?*"

She leaned down with a face full of earnest entreaty and anguish; the mother gasped, and seemed to make an effort to speak.

"Is he mine?" murmured the daughter. "Did you change him, mother? Say yes, or say no."

And yet neither could be said. There seemed to be some effort first to speak, then some effort to bear in mind the matter that should be spoken of, and after that the little glimpse of sense and reason was gone. The daughter thought she whispered, "*Some other time;*" then her eyes closed, and the fallacious hope of recovery was over.

It was about a month after this that Mrs. Johnstone got another letter from Mrs. Aird, and was touched by the simple filial love and grief that breathed through it. Her dear mother, the best of parents, had been knocked down by a cab in the street on the very day that the writer had spent in Upper Harley Street, and had met with injuries to her head. The last sentence Mrs. Johnstone read without any thought of the anguish which had wrung it from the writer, or of how much it concerned herself.

"She died, and, O madam! there were words I longed above all things to hear from her poor lips, and she could not say them."

"Poor thing!" said Mrs. Johnstone, quietly laying the letter aside, "I like that young woman; there 's something so open and sincere about her."

"But I rather think this is meant for a begging letter, my dear," observed Mr. Johnstone; "this is rather a telling sentence as to her not being able to maintain herself in service again on account of the *burden* of her young child."

He had a newspaper in his hand, and, as he spoke, he looked down and aside from it at the little Donald, who was now seven months old, and was crowing and kicking on the rug — a puppy nestling close to him, and receiving meekly various soft infantile thumps from his fat little fist. A red setter, the mother of the puppy, looked on with a somewhat dejected air, as if she knew her offspring was honored by the notice of this child of the favored race, but yet could have wished those dimpled hands would respect her treasure's eyes. Mr. Johnstone, from looking at his heir, got to whistling to him. " You 're a burden — a very sore burden," he said, smiling, to him ; " did you know that? "

The baby stared at him, understanding the good-will in his pleasant face, but nothing more. He was old enough already to answer the paternal expression, and presently he smiled all over his little face.

As long as only the puppy had been procurable as a playmate, he had been contented with it ; but now, conceiving hope of a more desirable slave, he made vigorous efforts to turn himself over, and, clutching his father's foot, soon got himself taken up, and began forthwith to amuse himself and make himself agreeable according to his lights, dashing his hand into his father's breakfast-cup, and, when this had been withdrawn and dried, seizing various envelopes, dropping them on the floor, and beginning to crow and screech with the peculiar ecstasy of a baby in full action, while he worked his arms and legs about, reckless of the trouble it was to prevent him from wriggling off. Meanwhile Mrs. Johnstone smiled with some quiet enjoyment, and carefully removed all the knives and all the crockery out of his reach.

" Well, love," she said at last, " have you had enough of it? " Thereupon Mr. Johnstone called to the dog, " Die, ring the bell ; " and the setter walked forth from under the table, and, grasping the bell-handle in both paws, pulled it down, while his master, still struggling with the baby, exclaimed, " This boy has more life in him than all the girls put together. I defy any fellow to hold him, and take care of him without giving his whole mind to it and to nothing else."

" There goes the milk ! " said the mother ; " I did not think he could have reached it. Look, my baby, dear ! does baby know what he has done? "

" He looks as if he did ; the sapient air he gives himself is something wonderful. It is evident that a man-
child from the first is different from girl-babies. What
shall I do with you, my son, when you are older ? "

" Don't afflict thyself, love," said his wife, caressing
his hand ; " he is just like the others ; but you know
you were never in the habit of having them downstairs
at breakfast time, nor of otherwise troubling yourself
with the charge of them."

The nurse now appeared, and had no sooner carried
off Master Donald Johnstone, and shut the door behind
her, than Die the setter started up with several little
yaps of satisfaction, and, seizing her puppy by the
neck, deposited it in Mrs. Johnstone's lap. The setter
knew very well that her puppy was a thing of no account when the baby was present, and she sometimes
testified her dissatisfaction, and expressed her sensation of dulness in his society, and the neglect brought
her, by uttering a loud and somewhat impertinent
yawn. Now she was happy, and probably thought
things were as they should be ; her puppy had curled
himself up in the upstart baby's place, and she was
watching him, with her chin upon her master's foot.

Mr. Johnstone was a man about thirty-four years of
age ; he was about the middle height ; in complexion he
inclined to fairness ; he was neither handsome nor plain ;
he walked much more like a soldier than a civilian, and
he had one remarkably agreeable feature — his eyes,
which were of a bright light hazel, had a charming
power of expressing affection and frankness. He was
a man whom everybody liked, and most of all those
who had the most to do with him. People who made
his acquaintance often found themselves attached to
him before they had discovered why.

Mrs. Johnstone, on the other hand, was much above
the middle height ; she had not one good feature, and
yet she was exceedingly admired by the other sex, and
had been won, with great difficulty, by her husband
from several other suitors who sighed for her. She had
that hair which, of all the varieties called red, is alone

beautiful. It was so light and bright that it crowned her like a glory, and she had blue eyes and thick light eyelashes.

An easy, cordial manner, and that observant tact which always characterize a much-admired woman, were in her case mingled with real sweetness of nature and wish to do kindness. These good qualities, however, by no means accounted for the love which had been lavished on her. That must be indeed an unamiable woman whose lovers can find no good quality to quote in excuse, or perhaps as a reason (!), for the extravagance of their love. Mr. Johnstone had never raved about her virtues; that was, perhaps, because he had taken them all for granted; and when, after some months of marriage, he discovered that her charm was an abiding one, and that she was just as sensible, just as devoted, and no more extravagant than other men's wives, he could hardly believe in his own good fortune. He also showed himself a sensible man. Of course she was lovely — most men thought so — but he never had her photographed. Photographs deal with facts, and when the photograph showed him rather a long upper lip, eyes by no means lustrous, and a nose neither Roman nor Grecian, he destroyed it, all but one copy, which he intended to keep carefully hidden for himself, and begged her never to be photographed again.

Then she laughed, but not without a certain tenderness, and said, " Oh, Donald, what a goose you are ! "

" Do you think so, my dear?" he answered, still looking at the portrait rather ruefully, and then at her as she sat by him on a sofa.

" Of course," she answered, looking him straight in the face, as if lost in contemplation.

" Well?" he asked.

" And yet I always did — and I suppose I always shall — think you the only man worth mentioning."

But that little scene had been long over at the time when Die the setter put her puppy into Mrs. Donald Johnstone's lap. A discussion took place which con-

cerned Mrs. Aird, and which ended in a handsome
present of money being sent her by post-office order,
with a letter from Mrs. Johnstone, who told her that, if
ever she did go to service again, she might depend on a
good character from her as an honest, sober, cleanly,
and thoroughly trustworthy person.

Having written this kind letter, and shown herself
just as able as most of us to judge of character — that is,
just as unable to divide manner from conduct, to make
allowance for overwhelming circumstance, and bridge
over the wide gap, in her thoughts, which rends apart
the interests of the rich from those of the poor — Mrs.
Johnstone almost forgot Maria Aird. She had a letter
of thanks from her, but she was never asked for the
"character;" the very dangerous illness which had
caused her to want this young woman's services, and
the loss of her little girl, began alike to recede into the
background of her thoughts. She could think of her
precious little Irene without tears. Her two little girls
were healthy and happy, her boy was growing fast, and
she was shortly hoping to add another boy to her little
tribe. Of course it was to be a boy; her husband's
great desire for sons always made her feel as if her girls
were failures. He was fond of them, and imagined that
he made no difference between one and another of his
children; but his little daughters, though by no means
able to express a contrary opinion, not only held it, but
would certainly have justified it, if they had known how ;
they shared their father's views, and considered that
their " boy-baby " enhanced their own dignity.

It was about the longest day ; Mr. Johnstone, coming home to dinner, was advancing along Upper Harley
Street on foot, when a young man, who seemed to be
loitering along, looking out for some one, met him and
suddenly stopped short without addressing him.

Mr. Johnstone for the moment stopped short also.

" Sir," said the man, turning as he went on, and
walking beside him, " I am aware that I am speaking
to Mr. Johnstone."

" Certainly you are : what do you want with me ? "

He paused, for he had reached his own steps. He had spoken with the brusque manner that an officer uses in addressing a soldier. He now looked the young man straight in the face, and saw, to his surprise, the signs of great and varying emotion, and a strange flush of anger or shame. "Not drunk," thought Mr. Johnstone. The man looked at him, and at that instant the footman answered his master's knock.

"Well?" said Mr. Johnstone.

"I can't say it," exclaimed the young fellow; and, turning round, he almost ran away.

"Queer!" thought the lawyer, and he entered his own house, pondering on the matter; but he soon forgot it, for Mrs. Johnstone was not at all well.

In the course of a few hours there was another infantile failure in Upper Harley Street.

The father, intensely grateful for this endeared wife's safety, went to bed in broad daylight; but, first putting his head out of the open window to inhale the early air, he saw, looking up — but it flitted away almost at once — a female figure that seemed familiar to him. Surely that was the nurse — the young widow, Mrs. Aird? Odd of her to be gazing up at his window at three o'clock in the morning — and with her was (or he was very much mistaken) the identical young man who had accosted him in the street, and then so suddenly taken himself off!

Mr. Johnstone closed the window, and very soon fell asleep, looked down upon by hundreds of cabbage roses — for this was the same room where Mrs. Aird had been sitting with his boy-baby when the telegram came in that sent them out of the house.

A few days had passed, Mrs. Johnstone was said to be "as well as could be expected," when one evening, just as he had dined, her husband was told that a young man wanted to speak with him.

The young man had been shown into a library at the back of the house, the light was already going, but Mr. Johnstone recognized him instantly.

" You accosted me in the street the other day? "

" Yes, sir."

The clear hazel eyes looked straight at him ; his next speech seemed to be in answer to them, — "I am not come here to deceive you, sir."

CHAPTER V.

" Man is born to trouble as the sparks to fly upward."

MR. JOHNSTONE rang the bell, and a shaded lamp was brought in. The young man did not speak till the servant had shut the door; then, looking at Mr. Johnstone as he stood on the rug, "I should wish to prevent mistakes," he began.

" You had better sit down," was the answer.

The young man sat down. " I am not come to ask your professional aid, sir," he continued; " I know this ain't the place to do it in, and I know you've nothing to do with criminal cases either. But, sir, it is a crime that I'm come to speak of. Well — no, I don't know what it is, and nobody else does."

Here Mr. Johnstone naturally felt some astonishment, and his clear, keen eyes held the young man so completely under their control that he seemed to find nothing to say, but to repeat his former assurance.

" I am not come here to deceive you, sir — why should I? I might have kept away and never said a word. But, oh, it's hard upon me that I should have it to do!"

" It seems to me that you have to accuse some one else, then?" said his host, intending to help him.

" Yes."

" By the way you express yourself, I gather that the crime, whatever it may be, is not committed yet? It might be a burglary, for instance, projected but not accomplished?"

" Oh, no, sir, no — they were both as honest as the day, poor things!"

" Women, then ? "

" Yes, sir."

" Well, man, speak out ! "

" Speak out ! " repeated the young man passionately ;
" speak out ! when it 's my own wife, that I have n't
been married to three weeks, and when I don't know
what you 'll do to her? Speak out ! If you 'd ever
loved a woman as I love her, you 'd — you 'd be more
merciful, sir."

Excited as the young man was, he perceived at once
that this exclamation was, in the ears of his listener,
absolutely absurd. Donald Johnstone had, as if involuntarily, lifted his eyes ; they rested on the wall,
behind where the young husband had been ordered to
sit. He saw for a moment, in their clear depth, not
the assertion, but the evidence, of a passionate love
which, even in the first freshness of his own, brought
his thoughts to a pause. Then there was something
deliberate in their withdrawal which checked the young
man's desire to glance behind him. Something like a
flash of displeasure met his gaze. He perceived that
he was supposed to have taken a liberty. There was
no answer to his speech ; he must begin again as well
as he could.

" It 's my wife and her mother," he said in a low
voice, " that I 've come to speak of — what one of
them did, as we are afraid (for, mark you, sir, we are
not sure) — what one of them did, and the other let to
be done — what one of them did, and then died, and
we think wanted to speak of first, but could not find
the words."

" Your wife and her mother?" repeated Mr. Johnstone with a weighty calm ; " and you feel that you
must lay it before some one? You want advice — is
that it?"

" No, sir, not advice ; my wife wants forgiveness, if
you could forgive her."

Mr. Johnstone looked surprised, but not at all
alarmed.

The young man wiped his forehead. " I fell in love

with her when she had her widow's cap on a full year ago," he said; "but, when I offered to her, she would not have me. I was so fond of her; I said, 'I ain't capable of taking a denial without a reason.' Then she says, 'Have the reason: *I've something on my mind.*' Her name was Maria Jane Aird."

Mr. Johnstone was not surprised; he remembered how he had seen this young woman when he looked out of the window in the night. Pity for the husband arose in his mind.

"She was in a situation of trust," he said, "and I am afraid you mean that she abused it?"

"Yes, sir — alas! she did. But at that time she would not tell me what her fault was. 'You, may be, would not hold to your wish to take me,' was all she said, 'if you knew what I have on my mind;' but I did hold to it — I could not help it — and she never did speak, though, in the end, she married me."

His distress was such that Mr. Johnstone tried to help him again.

"And then she probably told you that she had unfortunately taken something of value out of this house — some jewel, perhaps? If so, you are come to return it? Well, I pity you, and I forgive her."

"Bless you, sir!" exclaimed the young man, quite impatient at his calm; "I told you they were honest. Sir, don't make it harder for me and yourself too. You will have it that this thing is nothing to you. It is; I think, if you would sit down, I could speak better; won't you, sir? There, that's it! I'm talking of my wife, Maria; she was wet-nurse here."

"Yes."

"And you sent her away from the house with your baby?"

"Yes."

Now, at last, something like fear began to show itself in Donald Johnstone's face, but it was a vague fear.

"You never ought to have done it, sir."

"He was quite well," answered the father, amazed and pale, "quite well all the time; he cannot have met with any injury? She must have done her. duty by him."

"You should not have done it," repeated the young man. "As I make out, you were so afraid of an illness you had in the house that you never came near him or set your eyes on him for two or three months; and how were you to judge, when you had a child back, whether it was the same? Sir, sit down; don't look like that! There! it's quite possible the children were not changed."

"Changed!" exclaimed the father, shuddering.

"I'm sure I don't know how to tell it you, but my poor wife, all on a sudden, was taken very ill, and sent for her mother, who came with the baby — Maria's baby. Maria did not see either of the children again, being so ill. I don't know how to tell it you, but I'm afraid that woman, wishing her own grandchild in a better position — I am afraid those children were changed."

No need now to tell the father to take this thing seriously; he trembled from head to foot, and could not speak.

"But we shall never know," proceeded the young man. "'Is the other child living?' I seem to think you would ask. Yes, sir, and as well as can be."

"It's impossible your wife should be in any doubt," exclaimed the other, recovering his voice and starting up, white to the lips. "Impossible she should not know! She must know, she does know, whether this wicked, base, cruel crime was perpetrated or not. And what makes her even suspect such a thing?" he added, sinking back faint between his passion and his despair.

"Her mother many times tempted her to do it, sir, and was angry with her because she would not," said the young man in a deprecating tone. "They had words, and Maria was angry with her mother too."

"No, that story won't do. Angry with her, and then send for her, and leave her alone with all opportunity to do her worst?"

" It seems bad, sir," continued the young man with studied gentleness and patience. " And it's only a fancy of Maria's that she might have done it. We have n't the least proof, Mr. Johnstone."

" If she connived at it, she is a wretch, as lost to all justice and mercy as her mother."

" And that's what lies so heavy on her mind," said the husband, still in a low, deprecatory voice.

" How did she tell it you? Let me know the worst — for heaven's sake let me hear it all!"

" We had but been married three days, and it was Sunday. Maria was putting the little chap's coat on. I says, ' He's a credit to you, Maria.' ' He'll be my punishment before he's done,' she makes answer; ' for, David, *this child is what I have on my mind.*' She was kneeling on the ground; she put on her things, but you may think we did not go to church that morning. I carried the child into Richmond Park (I live and have my trade at Richmond). There we sat down, and I said, ' Maria, my dear, it's now time to speak. I've often seen you fret — and so it's concerning your child?' ' Yes,' she makes answer again, ' for I give you my plain word for it — and what I say I mean, David — I don't know whether he's mine or not.'"

It will be observed that this version of the story was not the true one, for Maria Aird did change the children. All her doubt was as to what her mother had done, otherwise she would have known well enough that the child her second husband was so willing to be good to was not hers. The young man, however, did his best to make the thing plain; he gave the version he had received. His wife's sorrow and repentance were genuine — this he had perceived at once; and that she was capable of fretting over her fault, and yet misrepresenting it, never entered his head. She screened herself at the expense of the dead. He never supposed that her misery, in the sense of this uncertainty, was half owing to her doubt as to whether or not she had secured a better lot in life for her child in return for her own distress of mind. If she had been

sure this was the case, she would have felt herself repaid; but to have lost her own child utterly, and yet to
have no reward — to be unable to love the one she had
in her arms, and yet not be sure that she did not owe
him a mother's love — was more than her half-awak-
ened conscience could bear. She had turned herself
out of the paradise of innocence; she had gathered the
apple and not tasted its sweetness: how was she to
know what a common experience this is? How could
she suppose that the promised good in evil was all a
cheat, and that she should find nothing but bitterness
in it from the very first?

The everlasting lie had been uttered to her also.

There was silence now, and the young man did not
dare to break it. His heart was beating more freely,
for the dreaded words had been said. He felt a strange
consciousness of the picture that he knew was hanging
behind him; but, though Donald Johnstone's head was
bowed into his hands, it seemed impossible to turn and
look at it. But this poor gentleman was thinking of
her whom it represented. "Oh, my wife!" the young
man heard him murmur. The words gave him a lump
in his throat; he longed to be dismissed; he thought of
rising, and proposing to take his leave, but did not see
his way to this. How long would Mr. Johnstone sit
with his face in his hands?

Mr. Johnstone lifted it up at last, and the young
man had never been so astonished in his life as he was
at the tone and manner, at the most unexpected words,
and the most keen expression of countenance with
which he accosted him.

"What is your name, Mr. David ——?"

"My name is David Collingwood, sir."

"And what is your calling, Mr. David Collingwood?"

"I'm a carpenter, sir, the same as Maria's first husband was."

"Oh! Have you any thought of going abroad — of
emigrating?"

"Yes, sir!" exclaimed the young man, very much

astonished; " that's what I think of doing as soon as
ever I can. I 'm saving money for it."

" I thought so ! ".

" Sir?"

" A child would be a great burden to you on a voyage."

" So Maria has always said, sir."

" She has, has she? Mr. David Collingwood?"

" Yes, sir?"

" You know nothing of me?"

" No, I don't."

" For instance, as to whether I am a man of my
word or no?"

Mr. David Collingwood here began to look a little
alarmed; involuntarily he glanced towards the window.

His host was looking straight at him.

" Don't be frightened," he said again, coming close
to Mr. David Collingwood's thought. " I have no intention of throwing you out of that ! "

David Collingwood rose quietly, — " Sir, I 've said
what I had to say."

" Yes, but you have not heard what I have to say ! "

" No, sir, but I can't make out what you should have
to say as I need be afraid of ! "

" Why are you afraid, then?"

" I 'm not ! " said the carpenter, but he trembled.

" Do I look like a man who may be expected to keep
to what I say?"

" Yes, you do."

" Well, I say, then, if you will confess to me that all
you have said to-night is a lie — "

" A lie ! " shouted the man.

" Yes, a lie, and that you — not unnaturally — feeling what a burden this child will be to you, and hoping
to get rid of him, have persuaded your wife — "

" A lie ! " shouted the man again, almost in a rage.

" Have persuaded your wife to bear you out in this
story, I will give you, David Collingwood, two hundred
pounds, and no man out of this room shall ever hear a
word of the matter."

" Why, what good would that do? " cried the carpenter, so much astonished that it almost overcame his anger.

Mr. Johnstone was silent. There was a long pause.

" It wouldn't help me to get rid of the child," reasoned David Collingwood at last, almost remonstrating with him, " because, anyhow, one of them must be my wife's, and thereby one of them must be on my hands to bring up."

" You don't think so? "

" Don't I, sir? " said the carpenter, almost helplessly, and with an air of puzzlement indescribable.

" No, you are just as well aware as I am that, rather than let you two take over to Australia — (you a stepfather as you are, and she a worse than step-mother, as she must be, whether her tale is true or false, and whether the boy is hers or not) — rather than let you two carry away for ever a child who may be my child, I shall take him off your hands — do you hear me? — take him off your hands and bring him up myself. Do you mean to tell me you have not thought of this and counted on it? "

David Collingwood trembled visibly.

" I may have gone so far as to think — " he began.

" To think what? "

" That maybe I should do so if I was you, sir, and one of the children was mine."

" And what did your wife say when she and you talked it over together? "

" We never did talk it over together."

" You never said to her, then, that if you two stuck to this tale, the child was secure of a good bringing up? "

" No, I didn't."

" She never wept over the boy, and said it would be a sore distress to her to part with him? "

" No, she didn't; she has not a mother's feelings for him, because of her doubt."

" Well, David Collingwood, I offer you two hundred pounds to confess that this is all a lie, and a plot between you and your wife to get rid of her child."

David Collingwood was silent.

" I should only add one condition — that is, that you would stay here, in this room, till after I have seen your wife, and seen her alone. I should tell her of your confession, and then you have my word for silence ever after."

" My wife would be frightened out of her senses ! "

" Why ? "

" She thinks, and I was afeard, you would have the law of her — take her up and prosecute her for what she's done."

" But she did not do it."

David Collingwood was sitting down with arms folded ; he had looked very much puzzled, and sat long silent. At last he lifted his face, and when Mr. Johnstone saw its expression, he involuntarily sighed.

" I've had mean thoughts in my mind, like other men," he began. " Sir, you may go to my wife, if you have a mind, for I think you have a right so to do. In short, come what may, I don't see, now I've once spoken, what I've got it in my power to do for her. Yes, you may go, of course, to her ; it ain't in my power to prevent it. I seem to observe now what you mean, sir. If I would own to a lie, it would what you lawyer gentlemen call discredit me as a witness, and then you could get alone with my wife, and perhaps make her tell you a different tale, and so you'd buy your own son, and be sure you'd got him. But I say — "

" Yes, David Collingwood."

" I say, be hanged to your two hundred pounds ! If my poor wife has done you the base wrong she says she has — (well, I mean the wrong she owns to have let her mother do, wishing and hoping it was done) — that money ain't of any use. It is only of use in case she has told you and me a lie. I may have had a mean thought as well as another man, but I'm not a villain. You want, by means of that money, to bring out the falseness of the tale. It cuts me very sharp to say it to you — the tale's not false ; worse luck ! it's true."

No answer to this. Donald Johnstone, looking

straight before him, very pale, but not convinced, was searching over his recollections. David Collingwood went on, —

"She never told me this that was on her mind through any thought that I should up and tell it to you. It slipped out along of her feeling how fond I was of her, and to relieve her own mind. She cannot keep a secret. And when I broke to her that it must be told to you, she fell into a great faint, and said you would take her up and she should be imprisoned. Through that I went to a lawyer."

"Oh! you did?"

"Well, I did, sir, and told him all except the names and the places. If he had said you could and would prosecute, you would never have heard a word from me. He said, ' The weak place is ' — but you know what it is, sir."

"Go on."

" ' What is the woman afraid of ? ' he said ; ' there is no witness — not one! The person is dead that is accused of having probably done this thing.' ' I was afraid she might be prosecuted for a conspiracy,' said I. ' No,' said he, ' there was no conspiracy.' ' It's her opinion,' said I, ' that it's more than likely the thing was done.' ' But,' said he, ' she cannot be prosecuted for an opinion, and one that, if she is frightened, she is not obliged to stick to. If there had been any evidence whatever, but what is to come out of her own mouth — if she had ever breathed a word of this, or if the other woman had — ' "

Here he paused.

" Then the supposed father might have brought an action in hope of obtaining more evidence — more witnesses — was that it? How do you know that I shall not do so even now?"

" Well, I satisfied him fully, and had to pay for it. I satisfied him that the thing — the whole of it — was in my wife's mind and nowhere else."

" And then you went home and told her you believed it? What was the lawyer's name?"

" Oh, sir, you 'll excuse me."

" You paid for his information — I am willing to pay for mine."

" I could n't tell you, sir."

" If he was a respectable man, he told you, first, that he would have nothing to do with the case ; and, secondly, that he believed it was a got-up story intended to extort money from an unfortunate father. He advised you to drop it, and said you were playing with edge-tools."

David Collingwood's look of astonishment and intense dismay seemed to show that something very like this had actually been said to him ; he sat silent and became angry. Donald Johnstone never took his eyes off him, but, with a pang not to be described, he saw the astonishment subside, the anger fade away, and the young man said, meeting his gaze with tolerable firmness, —

" And what do you think yourself, sir? Do you think it is a got-up story ? "

" I don't know what to think."

" No, sir ; and as to your wanting to turn it against me, you 've met with such a cruel wrong that I should be a brute if I could n't take it patiently — only — I 've met with a wrong too, sir."

" This concerns my own son — my only son. By what you say, I am never to know — never can know — whether the child I am bringing up is my child or not."

" And you 've tried one way and another to find out whether I 've lied, and you have a right — I know it cuts — but it does n't cut you only."

" No, I am truly sorry for you, David Collingwood. *If this is true —* "

" For she 's not what I thought she was, and I 've only been married to her three weeks."

He broke down here, and shed tears, but the other had no tears ; he was extremely pale, and he trembled as he sat looking at the portrait on the wall with unspeakable love and almost despair.

David Collingwood sat some time trying in vain to

recover himself. Not a word was spoken, his host
knew neither what to say nor what to do. How should
he tell this beloved wife, who had almost died to give
him birth, that he knew not whether their one son was
theirs or not? how should he bear it himself? Suddenly
a bright hope came into his mind. The other child
might prove to have no likeness whatever to himself or
to his other children; he might prove to be specially
unlike them. At least there would be comfort in this if
he did.

David Collingwood spoke while he was deep in this
flattering hope. He rose and said sullenly, "What do
you want me to do, sir? It's late — my wife — "

"Your wife will be uneasy?"

"Yes, sir."

"I am afraid that on this one occasion you cannot
consider her feelings."

"What am I to do, then?"

"I am going to Richmond. It is essential that I
should see her before you do."

"I never said she was at Richmond; she is in the
street, waiting for me."

"And the child with her?"

"No, sir, she's alone."

"Then you stay in this room and I will call her in."

"You may turn the lock on me, sir, if you please."

Donald Johnstone put on his hat, left the young husband, and, opening the front door, looked keenly right
and left. There was not far to look: a woman in black,
near at hand, was dejectedly pacing on. As she came
absolutely to the foot of his door-steps, he descended
and looked straight into her eyes. She stood and gazed
as if fascinated, the color fading out of her face, and
her hands clenching themselves.

"You — you won't prosecute me?" she entreated
helplessly, and stammering as her mother had done.

"No, you base woman," he answered, "because it
would be useless. Come here!"

"Must I — oh, sir! — must I come in?"

She entered. He was even then mindful of his invalid upstairs, and shut the door most deliberately and gently behind him; then he entered the dining-room, locked the door, put up the gas, and turned. She had followed him but a little way into the room, and was already on her knees; her terror was far from simulated, and his quickness of observation showed him in an instant that no probable fault of her dead mother's could ever have brought that ashen pallor and deadly fright into her face.

"Maria Collingwood," he began, almost in a whisper, as he stood leaning slightly towards her and looking straight down into her eyes, "you have told lies to your husband — do you hear me? — lies!"

Her white lips murmured something, but it hardly seemed to be a denial. She was kneeling upright, and with folded hands.

"But you may look for all mercy that is possible from me, if you will now speak the truth."

This was far from the way in which he had intended to begin. Her own face had brought his accusation upon her. She stammered out, "He — he would hate me; he — he would cast me off, if — if I did. Oh, have mercy!" Then she *had* deceived her husband; there was no plot, the man was her dupe.

"I will have mercy if you tell me all the truth."

"And he shall not know?" she moaned.

"I'll give you no time for meditation, and for the inventing of fresh lies; unless you speak, and instantly, he shall know what you have already said; but if you speak, and I feel that you speak the truth, he shall not."

And then, at a sign from him, she rose, took the chair he pointed to, and told all her miserable story in few words.

Donald Johnstone ground his teeth together in the agonizing desire to keep himself silent, lest he should frighten back the truth, and never have a chance of hearing it more. He allowed all to be told — her temptation, her yielding, her illness, her intention of sending away the wrong child, and then her doubt as to what her mother had done. All, he perceived, depended on what had been the mother's opinion. She had no conscience.

" And you incline to think this second villainy was accomplished — why ? "

" Mother could n't look at me, sir, when I got home."

" And, on the other hand? "

" On the other hand, when I saw the baby here, I seemed to think he was the most like what I remembered of mine."

CHAPTER VI.

Let me be only sure ; for sooth to tell
The sorest dole — is doubt.
JEAN INGELOW.

THAT was a miserable night for Donald Johnstone. It was twelve o'clock before the guilty woman and her husband were sent away — David Collingwood almost with kindness, and his wife without one word. The possible father had got what he wanted — two distinct tales, differing from one another, but, as he listened to the details of the second, he shared in the unsolvable doubt.

He ordered David Collingwood to bring the child the next morning, and, having dismissed the pair, he sat till daylight filtered in between the leaves of the shutters, and could not decide what to do further.

It was the doubt that mastered him and confused his mind. And what father in real life, or in any true history, had gone through such an experience as would be a guide to him? He was the victim of an unknown crime — as truly unknown in life as well known in the penny theatres. His distracted thoughts dragged him through all the phases of feeling, even to scornful laughter that left a lump in his throat. "Have you a mole on your left arm?" asks the supposed father in *Punch.* "No!" "Then come to my arms, my long-lost son!"

He laughed bitterly, and could not help it; then he moaned over his wife. How would she bear it, and how and when could he tell it to her?

There was tragedy indeed here, and yet what a hateful, enraging smack of the ridiculous too! He perceived that he could not possibly let such a story come out; all London would ring with it. When the children were taken out with their nurses, people would collect at his door on purpose to look at them! No, not a soul must hear of it. How, then, could he do his duty, and satisfy his love towards his son?

He was in his room only three hours or so. When he came down to breakfast, he said to the footman, " I have told Mrs. Aird to bring Master Donald's foster-brother here. When they come, show them in." He had a headache, and sighed bitterly as he sat down ; the hand trembled that poured out the coffee. The moment after, there was a modest knock at the door, and the little child who *perhaps* had so vast a claim on him was *perhaps* come to his rightful home.

He looked up ; David Collingwood and Maria Collingwood were standing stock still within the door. Maria did not lift up her eyes, she was mute and pale, and she held a lovely little boy in her arms.

" Put that child down," was all Mr. Johnstone could say ; and he did not rise from his place at the table. But, lo ! the small visitor, not troubled with any doubts or fears as to his welcome, no sooner found himself on the floor than he began to trot towards the rug, on which was lying the old setter, with a puppy as usual. This one was about two months old. She seized him as the baby advanced, and slunk under the table. Then the pretty little . fellow laughed, and showed a mouthful of pearls, pointing with his finger under the table.

" Boy did see doggy," he said, fearlessly addressing the strange gentleman ; then, coming straight up to him, he laid his dimpled hand on Mr. Johnstone's knee, and stooped the better to see the dog.

" Up, up ! " he next said in an entreating tone. Mr. Johnstone took him up on his knee with perfect gravity and gentleness, and looked at the man and woman who were standing motionless within the door. The man was trembling ; the woman, white and frightened, held herself absolutely still. " You may go," he said.

" One — for — Laney," lisped the child, pointing to some strawberries on a plate.

"You may go," repeated Mr. Johnstone; he could not trust himself to say more.

" Yes, sir; when is she to come back for him?"

" Never!"

" One — for — Lancy," repeated the child with sweet entreaty.

The possible father put one into his little hand.

" I mean, sir, what are we to do — when is she to take him back?"

" I know what you mean : I answer, *never!*"

The young man whispered to his wife, and she, without once looking at the child, turned to the door. " I wish you good morning, sir," he said, and in another moment they were gone.

David Collingwood had caused his wife to spend money of his in dressing the little Lancy. The child was healthy and rosy, clean, well arrayed, and without the least shyness. He was a more beautiful little fellow than the treasure upstairs, but not quite so big. He talked rather better; his hair was a shade browner than that of the two little girls in the nursery. Little Donald's, on the contrary, was a shade lighter; and there seemed to be no special likeness, in either child, to himself or to his wife.

Left alone with the little Lancy, all the pathos of the situation seemed to show itself to him. He could endure it well enough, he thought, for himself; but, like many another sympathetic and affectionate man, he had already begun to suffer for his wife ; her supposed future feeling was worse to him than his own present distress. If he could be sure that she could bear it, he thought he could bear it very well.

Of course the child's face did not help him. At such an early age, children rarely show strong family likeness, unless the appearance of the parents is peculiar indeed.

When we see family likeness, which we constantly do, we think how natural it is ; but when we see family unlikeness, which we also constantly do, it never costs us a moment's surprise, a moment's thought. In life, no-

body is ever surprised if, or because, a brother and
sister are diverse in feature, complexion, or character,
and yet we all have a theory concerning family likeness,
and generally it is an exaggerated one.

A fresh series of observations, if theory could be set
aside, would perhaps show that strong likeness is almost
always founded on peculiarity.

A man of average height, with no exaggerated feature, with somewhat light hair, gray or hazel eyes, and a
certain freshness of complexion (neither pale nor ruddy),
together with a figure rather firmly built, though not
stout, — this description would suit many thousands of
Englishmen ; add a shade of auburn to the beard, and
it would suit many thousands of Scotchmen ; add a
shade of blue to the eyes, and it would suit many thousands of Irishmen. These are the men who transmit
national likeness.

But here and there you may meet a man with a nose
like an eagle's beak, stalking about his fields with his
young brood after him. In all probability, a like nose
is in course of erection on their youthful faces. Or you
fall in with a man who has a preposterously deep bass
voice — too deep for ordinary life — much deeper, in
fact, than he is himself — his children, more likely than
not, echo that voice, sons and daughters both. Or you
see a man, lanky, and so tall that, when he has done
getting up, you think how conveniently he might be
folded together like a yard measure, his children rise
and step after him like storks. Ten to one his very
baby is taller than it ought to be. Such men as these
transmit family likeness.

The little Lancy soon slipped off Mr. Johnstone's
knee, and began to talk and scold at the puppy, because
he would not come and be friendly — in other words, to
be tormented.

The old mother knew better than to leave him to the
tender mercies of a baby-boy. She rose, and, taking
him in her mouth, walked slowly away round and round
the table, the child following, and just not overtaking her.
This game was going on when Mr. Johnstone caught

sight of a parcel lying on a chair close to the door. He had told David Collingwood to ask his wife whether she had any photograph in her possession of her first husband — if so, to bring it.

He now cut open the little package, but there were no photographs in it, only two letters — one from a lady, giving an excellent character to *Maria Jane Pearson* as a housemaid, setting forth that she was honest, sober, and steady. It seemed to have been preserved as a gratifying testimony of approval, but did not bear on the present case. The other letter was from David Collingwood, and was as follows : —

" SIR, — As it ain't in my power to say what I meant to say when I see you, along of my feeling so badly about this matter, I write this to inform you that my wife has no portraits of her first husband, for he was very badly marked with small-pox, and never would be taken, and she says he had no brothers nor sisters, and his parents are not living. Herewith you will find her marriage lines. She has always kept herself respectable, and do assure me she never did wrong in her life but in the one thing you know of. And she humbly begs your pardon.   I am, your obedient humble servant,
                    " DAVID COLLINGWOOD."

A baby hand was on his knee again. He looked down ; tears were on the little flushed cheeks ; the long slow chase had been useless.

" Boy did want doggy," he sobbed. Mr. Johnstone felt a sudden yearning, and a catch in his throat that almost overcame him. He took up the child, and pressed him to his breast. For a moment or two the child and the man wept together. He soon recovered himself ; it was a waste of emotion to suffer it to get the mastery now ; there would come a day when he and his wife would weep together — that was the time to dread. He must save his courage, all his powers of consoling. flattering, encouraging, for that ; the present was only his own distress — it was nothing.

There was rejoicing in the nursery upstairs that morning ; the baby Aird, as he was called, had come to spend the day. He made himself perfectly at home ; the little Johnstones produced all their toys for him. "What a credit he is to his mother!" said the nurse. "His clothes quite new, and almost as handsome as *our* children's."

David Collingwood, as he led his wife to the omnibus which was to take them home, could hardly believe his own good fortune. The child, "the encumbrance" that he had perforce taken with her, and had meant to do his duty by, had, contrary to all sober hope, been received into another man's house, and there he had been told to leave him. His wife, though confused and frightened, did not seem to feel any distress at parting with him.

"Is this all?" he repeated many times to himself as they went on. "Is this over?" "Is she truly going to get off scot-free?"

If so, the sooner he took her away the better. At the other side of the world he felt that he should have more chance of forgetting that, which while he remembered it made his love for his young wife more bitter than sweet to him.

"Is it over?" No, it was not quite over. They got out of the omnibus at their own cottage door. A hansom cab stood there, and Mr. Johnstone was paying the cabman. He followed them in. Maria Collingwood sank into a chair. Mr. Johnstone, not unnaturally, declined one ; he stood with a note-book in his hand. "If you 've — you 've altered your mind," Maria began, "I 'm willing, as is my duty, to take back the child."

David Collingwood darted an indignant look at her, but Mr. Johnstone took no notice of the speech. Various questions were asked her, and answered ; the husband weighed the effect of her answers as each was given : "He can make nothing of that;" "He can make little of that;" "He sees she speaks the truth there;" "He'll not give the boy back for that!"

He was mean, as he had said, but not base.

The little sister — Mr. Johnstone wanted her address. She was in a place : the address was given.

" Where was she when your mother came home with the child ? "

" She was in a place then, and till a month after."

" Can you prove that? "

The matter was gone into. Donald Johnstone hoped then for a few moments, and David Collingwood feared ; but their respective feelings were soon reversed, for Maria did prove it. The sister was in a place as kitchen-girl at a school, and did not come home till it broke up for the holidays ; consequently, she never saw the child till after her mother had brought him home to Kensington.

" Where did Mrs. Leach live? " Her address was given. It was asserted that she had never known there was more than one child under her roof ; consequently, that she could not have harbored any sort of suspicion bearing on the case. " Where was the girl who had carried one of the children out? " David Collingwood had ascertained that she was dead. Mr. Johnstone stood long pondering on this matter ; finally he took David Collingwood with him to the cottage of Mrs. Leach, and asked a few questions, which abundantly proved the truth of what Mrs. Aird had declared. He therefore said nothing to excite her astonishment ; but gave her a present of money and withdrew.

Donald Johnstone came back to London in the course of the morning, and found the nurse who had lived in his family when the little Donald was born. She was very comfortably married, and he agreed with her to take Master Donald's foster-brother under her charge for a little while. Mrs. Aird, he informed her, had married again, and he intended to be good to the child. Less could hardly be said ; and what his own servants might think of this story, he considered it best to leave to themselves.

In the course of time, Mrs. Johnstone perfectly recovered, the London season was just over, and the quietest time of year was coming on.

The worst, though he did not known it, had already been endured. His anxiety as to its effect on her had so wrought on him that she had discovered it, and a heavy portion of it was already weighing on her own heart. It was necessary that she should now be told, and she was so fully conscious that a certain something — she knew not what — was the matter, that when he said she had something to hear which would disturb her, she was quite relieved to find that he now thought her strong enough to know the worst.

She soon brought him to the point. It was not his health; it was nothing in his profession; it was no pecuniary loss: but when she saw his distress, she was sure that more than half of it was for her, and she did her very best to bear it well for his sake. And yet, when the blow fell, it was almost too much for her. She had all a woman's horror of doubt. Let her have anything to endure but doubt; yet doubt had come into her house, and, perhaps, for ever was to reign over her. She, however, took the misfortune very sweetly and bravely. In general, the woman bears the small misfortunes and continued disappointments of life best, and the man bears best the great ones. Here the case was reversed: the woman bore it best, but that was mainly because of the supreme comfort of her husband's love and sympathy.

If we consider women whose lot it is to inspire deep affection, we shall sometimes find them, not those who can most generously bestow, but those who can most graciously receive. All is offered; they accept all without haggling about its possible endurance; their trust in affection helps to make it lasting, and their own comfort in it is so evident as to call it forth and make it show itself at its best.

Donald Johnstone's wife had a disposition that longed to repose itself on another. Her peculiar and almost unconscious tact made her seem generally in harmony with her surroundings.

All she said and did, and wore, appeared to be a part of herself; there was a sweet directness, a placid oneness about her, which inspired belief and caused contentment.

"Why am I so calm, so satisfied, so well with myself in this woman's presence?" men might have asked themselves; but they seldom did, perhaps because her loving, placid nature was seasoned in a very small degree with the love of admiration. She had a gracious insight into the feelings of others, and used it not to show off her own beauties, but to console them for defects in themselves.

Many people show us our deficiencies by the light of their own advantages, but Donald Johnstone's wife showed rather how insignificant those deficiencies must be since she who was so complete had never noticed them.

A sincere and admired woman, her firm and open preference for her own made her own for ever satisfied; yet she always gave others a notion that she felt she had reason to trust them, sense to acknowledge their fine qualities, and leisure to delight in them.

Reverend in mind, and, on the whole, submissive, she yet was in the somewhat unusual position of a wife who knows that her husband's religious life is more developed and more satisfying than her own.

Master Donald's foster-brother was now sent for to dine in the nursery again, and delighted the nurse and her subordinate by the way in which he made himself at home, tyrannizing over the little Donald, picking the grapes out of his fat little hand, and trotting off with them while he sat on the floor and helplessly gazed at his nurse.

"Run after the little boy, then, Master Donny," cried the nursery maid; "why, he ain't near so big as you are!" But the little Donald placidly smiled; either he had not pluck yet, or he had not sense for contention; and, in the meantime, the little Lancy took from him and collected for himself most of the toys, specially the animals from a Noah's ark, which he carried off in his frock, retiring into a corner to examine them at his leisure.

Mr. Johnstone came upstairs soon after the nursery dinner, and said the little Lancy might come with him and see Mrs. Johnstone; so the child's pinafore was taken off, and, with characteristic fearlessness, he put his hand in " gentleman's " hand and was taken down.

Mrs. Johnstone was in the dressing-room; her husband, having considered the matter, had decided to spare her all waiting for the child, all expectation. He opened the door quietly; she did not know this little guest was in the house; she should guess his name, or he should tell it her.

She had just sent the nurse down to her dinner, and was lying on a couch asleep — the baby in her bassinet beside her.

Fast asleep as it seemed; yet, the moment her husband came in with the child in his arms, she started as if the thought in his mind had power over her, and, opening her eyes, she looked at them with quiet, untroubled gaze. The time she had been waiting for was manifestly come. She rose, and slowly, as if drawn on, came to meet her husband, with her eyes on the little child, who was occupied with the toys which he still held in his hand. Neither the husband nor the wife spoke; she came close, laid her hand on the child's little bright head, and her cheek against his.

" Lady did kiss Lancy," said the child; then, looking attentively at her, and perhaps approvingly, he pursed up his rosy mouth and proffered a kiss in his turn.

" Lady must not cry," he next said, almost with indifference; then, as if to account for her tears, he continued, " Lady dot a mummy gone in ship — gone all away."

" Does Lancy cry for his mummy?" she asked the child, who was still embraced between them.

He shook his head.

" Why not? — I feel easier, love, now I have seen him," she murmured; " our children are not like him. — Why not, sweet baby-boy?" she repeated.

" 'Cause boy dot a horse and two doggy." He

opened his hand and displayed this property. Nothing more likely than that this infantile account of himself was true. The animals from the ark had driven all the mother he knew of clean out of his baby-heart.

" He talks remarkably well for two years and a quarter," she said, and that was almost an assertion of her opinion, for the little Donald had only reached the age of two years, two months, and a fortnight. Mr. Johnstone heard it almost with dismay; his own opinion was drifting in the other direction.

She dried her eyes and held out her arms. " Will Lancy come to lady?" Of course he would; she took him, and sat down with him in her lap on the couch.

" I know how this will end," she exclaimed, holding him to her bosom with yearning unutterable. Then she burst into a passion of tears, kissing the little hands and face, and bemoaning herself and him with uncontrollable grief. " O Donald! how shall I bear it?"

She was bearing it much better than he could have expected. He was almost overcome himself, thinking how cruelly she had been treated, but he had nothing to say. He could only be near, standing at the end of the couch, leaning over her, to feel with her, and for her.

Then the child spoke, putting his arms round her neck — " Lancy loves lady." He seemed to have some intention of comforting her in his little mind.

" Estelle!" remonstrated her husband.

" But I shall know," she exclaimed, " I shall know in the end. You are making all possible inquiry?"

" My bright, particular star!" was all he answered; the tone was full of pity.

" And is nothing found out, Donald, nothing?"

" It is early days yet. If anything more can be done, I am on the look-out to do it."

" And you find nothing to do at present?"

" No."

" I know how this will end," she repeated. " I never will love *my own* less; he is so dear to every fibre of my heart."

" He is most dear to us both."

" But this one has come so near to me already, and the nearness is such a bitter pain — such pain. (Oh, you poor little one !) I know it will end in my so loving him, from anxiety and doubt, that I shall not be able to bear him long out of my sight."

" All shall be as you wish, my Stella," said the husband ; but he thought, " You are far happier than I, for it will end — I know it will — in your loving both the boys as if they were your own ; whilst I feel already that, if the shadow of a doubt remains, I shall not deeply love either."

CHAPTER VII.

THE time was a little past the middle of the century; the "Great Exhibition" had not long been over; the Metropolitan Railway had not yet begun to burrow under London, encouraging the builders to plant swarms of suburban villas far out into the fields; Londoners paid turnpikes then before they could drive out for fresh air, and they commonly contented themselves with a sojourn in the autumn at the sea-side, or in Scotland, instead of, as a rule, rushing over and dispersing themselves about the continent.

But Donald Johnstone decided to take his wife there that autumn, baby, nurse and all. First he would establish the children at Dover; then he would propose to their mother that the little Lancy — "boy," as he more frequently called himself — should be sent to them, and have also the benefit of the change; then he would take her away and reproduce for her their wedding tour.

This had been to Normandy and Brittany, where they had seen quaint, sweet fashions, even then on the wane; beautiful clothes, which those who have not already seen never will see; and peaked and pointed habitations, so strange and so picturesque, that nothing but a sojourn in them can make one believe them to be as convenient as those of ugly make.

Estelle should see again the apple-gathering, the great melons, and the purple grapes drawn into market with homely pomp; the brown-faced girls gossiping beside their beautiful roofed wells, dressed in garments such as no lady in the finest drawing-room puts on at present; creatures like countrified queens, stepping after their solitary cows, each one with the spindle in

her hand.   He would take her to Contances, and then
on to Avranches, and there he would unfold to her a
certain plan.

She fretted much over the doubt, which at present no
investigation availed to solve., Time had not befriended
her: the more she thought, the more uncertain she became.

Yet he hoped that time might bring them enlighten-
ment in the end.   He would take her to Avranches,
where lived his only sister, the widow of a general officer, who, from motives of economy, had settled there,
and did not often come to England.

In his opinion she was one of the most sensible
women to be met with anywhere — just the kind of
creature to be trusted with a secret — a little too full
of theories, perhaps, almost oppressively intelligent,
active in mind and body, but a very fast friend, and
fond of his wife.

He felt that, if the two boys could be parted from
Estelle for three or four years, and be under the charge
of his sister, it would be more easy, at the end of that
time, to decide which of them had really the best claim
to be brought up with his name and with all the prospects of a son.   It was quite probable that, in the
course of three or four years, such a likeness might
appear in one of the boys to some member of his family
as would all but set the matter at rest.

Nothing could be done if they remained in London,
brought up among his own friends, and known by name
and person to every servant about him.   But if he left
them at Avranches with his sister, among French servants, who knew nothing about them — each known by
his pet name, and not addressed by any surname — and
if they themselves knew nothing about their parentage,
there could be no injustice to either in the choice the
parents might eventually make, even though they should
decide not to take the child first sent home to them.

He was desirous, for his own sake as well as for
theirs, that they should hear of no doubt; that would
be cruelty to the one not chosen, causing him almost

inevitable discontent and envy, while the one chosen might himself become the victim of doubt, and never be able to enjoy the love of his parents, or any other of his advantages in peace.

"We must be their earthly providence," he said to his wife, when he had unfolded this plan to her; "we must absolutely and irrevocably decide for them. We must try fully to make up our minds, and then, whichever we eventually take, we must treat altogether as a son."

"And the other, Donald?"

"The other? I think one's best chance of peace in any doubtful matter is not to do the least we can, but the most; we must give them both the same advantages in all respects, and so care for, and advance, and provide for, and love the other — so completely adopt him, that if we should ever have the misfortune to find that, after all, we have made a mistake, we may still feel that there was but one thing more we could have given him, and that was our name."

"Then, even in that case, the choice having once been made, you would keep to it?"

"What do you think, my star?"

"It would be a cruel thing on the one we had taken for our own to dispossess him."

"Yes; but if we allowed things to stand, the loss and pain would all be our own; they would be nothing to the other. Some wrongs are done in spite of a great longing after the right, and such I hold to be irrevocable."

"I see no promise of rest in any plan. Perhaps my best chance will be to leave it altogether to you; you often talk of casting our cares upon God. I have tried, but it does not seem to relieve me of the burden. I can — I often do cast them upon you, only I hope —"

"What, Estelle?"

"I hope your sister will not say, as your mother did when our little Irene died, that it was one of those troubles which was ordained to work for my good."

"She was only quoting Scripture."

G

" When she used to come and pray with me, and read with me, I felt at last able to submit; and I found, as she had said, that submission could take the worst sting of that anguish out of my heart. But no one must talk so to me now. I have not fallen into the hands of God, but into those of a wicked woman. This is different."

" Is it, my wife?"

" Your sister may say it is a rebuke to me for having loved this present life, and my husband, and my children too much, or she may say it is a warning to me that these blessings can — oh, how easily! — be withdrawn. I will try to bear it as a discipline, as a punishment; let her teach me, if she can, to submit; but I cannot bear to hear about blessings in disguise. My own little son; he was the pride of my heart; and now, when I hold him in my arms, and see the other playing at my feet, I wonder which has the best right to me. I know that nothing can make up to me for the doubt. I shall never be so happy any more!"

So she thought; but she was utterly devoid of morbid feelings, and quite willing to let time do all for her that it could. She had a sincere desire to be well and happy. A woman, with any insight into man's nature, generally knows better than to believe that, in the long run, delicacy can be interesting, and low spirits and sorrow attractive.

She did not aggravate herself with anger against the nurse. She knew she was to part with both the boys for years, while a doubtful experiment was tried. Yet she let herself be refreshed by the sweet weather, the rural signs of peace and homely abundance; and when she drove up to the quaint abode her sister-in-law had made a home of, she could be amused with its oddness; the tiled floors, numerous clocks, clumsy furniture, thick crockery; the charming kitchen, full of bright pots and pans, so much lighter and more roomy than the drawing-room; the laundry in the roof; its orchard that stood it instead of a flower-garden, almost every tree hoary with lichen, and feathery with mistletoe; its little fish-pond and fountain, with a pipe like a quill, and its wooden arbors, with all their great creaking weather-cocks.

And there was one little child, a girl, in the house — a small, dimpled thing, about six months younger than the two boys.

That first evening passed off, and both husband and wife shrank from entering on the subject of their thoughts. Mrs. O'Grady, Charlotte by Christian name, was full of talk and interest about all manner of things. She had the disadvantage of being very short-sighted, and so missed the flashing messages and expressive communications that passed between other eyes.

This defect makes many people more intellectual than they otherwise would be, and less intelligent, throwing them more on thought and less on observation. But in her case it was only a question of wearing or not wearing her spectacles. When she had them on, "all the world was print to her;" when they were off, her remarks were frequently more sensible in themselves than suitable to the occasion.

Politics, church parties, family affairs, the newest books, the last scientific theories — nothing came amiss to her, every scrap of information was welcome.

Mrs. Johnstone looked on rather listlessly, and soon it was evident that her husband could not make an opening for the matter that was in their thoughts. He was letting himself be amused and interested while waiting for a more convenient season.

When they had retired, she said, —

"I shall be so much more easy, Donald, when you have managed to tell her our story."

"But what was I to do?" he answered. "I could not suddenly dash into her sentence with a 'by-the-bye,' as she does herself. 'By-the-bye, Charlotte, we don't know whether one of our children is, in fact, ours or not!'"

"That would at least astonish her into silence for a time."

The next morning just the same difficulty! They were in the midst of a discussion before they knew that it had begun.

The baby was taken out after breakfast, by her nurse, into the apple orchard.

"You have no servants who speak English, have you, Charlotte?" asked Mr. Johnstone, thinking to open the matter.

"No," she answered; "and I prefer the French as servants, on the whole, to the English. But I like that young Irish woman, Estelle, that you have brought with your baby. There is something sweet about her that one does not meet with here. Do you know, I have long noticed that, of all modern people, the Irish suffer least, and the French most, from the misery of envy?"

"Do you think so?" said her brother, only half listening.

"Yes, and hence the Irish chivalry towards the women of 'the quality,' and the total absence of any such feeling in a Frenchman. He, frugal and accumulative, thinks, 'I am down because you are up.' The poor Frenchman would rather all were down than that any should have what he has not; but it is the material advantages of those well off that he envies them; but the poor Irishman, wasteful and not covetous, could not do without something to admire. One of these two takes in anguish through his eyes, whenever he casts them on beauty or riches not his; the other takes in consolation through his eyes. He is not wholly bereaved of grandeur or loveliness if he may look on them, and he troubles himself little that they are not his own."

"When demagogues leave him alone!" her brother put in.

"It is singular, though," she continued, gliding on with scarcely any pause, "that though the Irish can do best without education and culture, they repay it least, they are least changed by it. Now the English, of all people, can least do without culture and education, and repay them most. What a brute and what a dolt a low Englishman frequently is! but a low Irishman is often a wit, and full of fine feelings."

"Marry an Irishman," said the brother with a smile, "and speak well of the Irish ever after."

"Of course! I always used to say, ' Give me an Irish lover and a Scotch cousin.' "

" Why an Irish lover? "

" Because he is sure to marry me as soon as he can, just as a Scotch cousin, if he gets in anywhere, is sure to do his best to get me in too."

" You want nothing English, then?"

" Yes, certainly, give me an English housemaid. Let a French woman nurse me when I am ill, let an English woman clean me my house, and an Englishman write me my poetry! For it is a curious thing," she went on, " that sentiment and poetic power never go together. The French are rich in sentiment and very poor in poets. How rich in sentiment the Irish are, and how poor the English! We call the Irish talk poetical, yet Ireland has never produced a poet even as high as the second order. How far more than the lion's share England has of all the poetry written in the English tongue — or, if you speak of current poetry, you might add, ' and in all other tongues.' " Here she chanced to put on her spectacles, and immediately came to a full-stop.

" Well?" said her brother; but she was no more to be lured on, when she could see, than stopped when she could not. His chance had come.

" If you will put on your bonnet, Charlotte," he said, " we will go out about the place. I have something important — to us — to say to you."

She rose instantly with the strange sense of defect and discomfiture that she often felt when her spectacles showed her other people's eyes, and thus that she had been at fault because her own were not better.

It was a difficult story to tell, and at first she could not be made to believe that all had been done which could be done.

An unsolvable doubt seemed just as unbearable to her as it had done to the mother. She sat down on a bench in the apple orchard with nothing to say and nothing to propose.

" I do not believe this thing ever was done," she said hesitatingly at last. " I think the nurse's baseness be-

gan and ended when she planted this horrid doubt in
your hearts. She foresaw that it would rid her of her
own child. What could you do but take him?"

" But you have told me this," she presently said,
" because you think I can help you?"

" Yes, you can help us —what we want is to gain time."

He then unfolded his plan. Each of the little fellows
called himself by a pet name. One went in the nursery
by the name of "Middy," so called after a favorite
sailor-doll they had ; the other generally called himself
" Boy."

If they could be taken charge of till they were five or
six years old, and the parents denied themselves all in-
tercourse with them during those years, it was not in
nature that the one truly theirs should not show some
strong likeness either to one of his parents or to some
of his brothers and sisters — for there might well be
both by that time — or a likeness as to voice or even
disposition might show itself ; and, failing that, there
was the other child. He might begin to betray his parentage ; the Johnstones had no likeness of Aird, but
could never forget his wife.

An irrevocable choice must be made at the end of that
time ; and when the father and mother came over to
make it, neither child would have heard anything about
his story. The one selected would soon return their
love and subside into his place with the unquestioning
composure of childhood, and the other would be equally
contented with his position, having long forgotten all
about his native country and his earliest friends.

Little more than a week after this, Mr. Johnstone
was sitting on the sands of a small French bathing-
place, his sister with him. He had brought over the
two tiny boys, and they were playing at their feet, while
Mrs. O'Grady scanned them eagerly.

" Yours — I mean the one you call ' Middy '— is the
most like our family, and like you in particular," she
observed.

" Yes, we think so."

" And he is the one whom you brought up till the

nurse herself put it into your heads that he might not be yours?"

" Even so."

" The other has slightly darker eyelashes and browner hair than either yours or Estelle's."

" Of course we have noticed that."

" And yet you doubt?"

" We fancy that ' Boy ' is a little like our dear child Irene."

" Estelle says she wants me to dress them precisely alike, and treat them absolutely alike."

" Yes, we have decided on that. We shall leave photographs behind us. When they see these in your book, they can be told to call them father and mother. And we shall never take these names from either, but only teach one of them to understand that he is an adopted child."

The parting with the boys was very bitter to Mrs. Johnstone. She held each to her heart with yearnings unutterable, though, as was but natural, only one fretted after her at all, and that for a very little while.

And when they were brought into the quaint house near Avranches, it was doubtful whether either had the intelligence to be surprised. One was perfectly fearless, and found out directly that the " 'tupid mans and womans could not talk to ' Boy ;' " the other listened to the babble about him with infantile scorn, and sometimes, baby as he was, showed himself a true-born Briton by laughing at it.

But that stage of their life was soon over; their French nurse made them understand her very shortly; and before they had discovered that little Charlotte's English was worse than their French, she was taken away — gone to Ireland to her grandmother, as they were told. They thought this was a pity ; her mother, with a touch of bitterness, thought so too ; but the grandmother had long urged it, promising to provide for the little Charlotte, and but that the Johnstones had known of her intended absence, they would not have proposed their plan.

The poor must do — not what they would, but — what they can.

Even if her little Charlotte was left unprovided for at the grandmother's death, the mother felt that here was a chance of saving several hundred pounds for her. Donald Johnstone's payment was to be liberal in proportion to the importance of the interest at stake. And, in the meantime, the little Charlotte cost her mother nothing, and the two boys were just as happy together when she was gone.

They had not been a year in France before they spoke French as well as French children, which is not saying much. In less than another year they spoke their English with a French accent, loved their nurse more than any living creature, excepting one another, and had altogether lost the air of English children, for their clothes were worn out, and they wore instead the frilled aprons and baggy trousers of the country; their hair was cropped perfectly short, as is there the mode, and every article they had about them was equally tasteless and unbecoming.

But their toys were charming.

Their aunt, as they both called her, was careful to waken in their infant minds a certain enthusiasm for England; they had many pictures of English scenes in their nursery. The nurse also did her part; she frequently talked to them about the dear papa and mamma, caused them to kiss the portraits of Mr. and Mrs. Johnstone every night before they went to bed, and instilled into them something of the peculiar French tenderness and sentiment towards a mother.

They both loved this pretty mother, and they grew on in health and peace till they were nearly five years old, about which time it became evident that the Johnstones could not make up their minds to be absent much longer.

Mrs. O'Grady had not, for some time past, found it possible to doubt which was her brother's child, but she loyally forebore to make the least difference in her treatment of them, or to convey any hint to her brother.

And now the children were told that dear father and mother were coming, and this important news was a good deal connected in their minds with the growth of their own hair. It was much too long now, their nurse said, but English boys wore it so. They thought it would have been impossible for father and mother to come and see them while it had been cropped so short. Their aunt also had sent to London for complete suits of children's dress for them. Their nurse was very gracious as regarded these. Melanie, the cook, came up to see them dressed *à l'Anglais;* she agreed with her that there was much to be said in favor of the English style. Certainly, but for these clothes, the dear father and mother would never have taken the trouble to come; it was to be hoped they would like them.

How slight was the feeling of the children as to this expected interview! how intense were the feelings of the parents!

A door opened, and a pretty little boy, who knew nothing of their arrival, came dancing into a room where were seated a lady and a gentleman close together.

In an instant he knew them, and stood blushing. Then that lady said, —

" Come on, sweet boy ! " and he advanced and kissed her hand, and that gentleman looked at him — oh, so earnestly !

This was the dear mother; she had tears in her eyes, and she took him on her knee, and kissed his little face and head, and stroked his hair. So did the dear father.

" Did he know them ? "

" Oh, yes, and he and Middy had wanted them to come for a long while. The dear mother was quite as pretty as he had expected," he continued looking up at her. He spoke in French, and paid her a little French compliment as naturally as possible. Then he blushed again with pleasure as she caressed him, and was glad he had all his best things on.

After a time, his aunt came in, and quietly took him out of the room.

" I should not have known him, he is so much grown and altered," sighed Mrs. Johnstone; "but he has made it evident that it is Middy whom we have not seen."

" This is a most lovable, pretty little fellow," said the husband.

" And not at all unlike our little Irene," she answered.

But, in a minute or two, another child, equally unconscious of what awaited him, opened the same door, and marched boldly in. A sudden thrill shook the hearts of both. The child paused, drew back, and trembled; then he put up his arm before his face, and burst into tears.

What it was that he felt or feared, it would have been quite past his power to express; but the dear mamma was there; she had tears in her eyes; was she going to kiss him? He did not know what to say; what should he do?

He could not look, he was crying so; and somebody carried him to her, and put his arms round her neck, and called him his dear little son.

" Mamma, I never meant to cry," he presently said, with all naïveté — and mother was crying too, and so was father — well! it was very extraordinary, when he thought he should have been so glad. And presently he *was* very glad because they were so kind.

They said they had wanted him so much for such a long time, and he should go to England — go home and see his dear little sisters. They said he was just like the others, and there was a baby brother at home; he must teach him to play. So Middy was very happy indeed, as in a child's paradise he nestled close to the long-lost mother, and admired his father, and thought how nice it would be to go to England with them.

It would have been hard to doubt any more; the little flaxen-haired fellow was so like the children at home; they were so vastly more drawn to him than to the other, and yet he too was greatly altered. He was not such a fine child for his years as when they had left him. But if they could have doubted, his own love and agitation would have settled all. The shy and yet delighted gaze, his contentment in their arms, the manner in which he seemed to have thought of them, — all helped them to a thankful certainty. The mother had not been without her sorrows. Since the parting she had lost two more little girls in infancy, and had longed inexpressibly to have her boy back again.

Charlotte came in at last; she still had him in her arms. There was no mistaking the father's look of contentment. Charlotte had her spectacles on, and saw the state of the case at once.

" Of course," she exclaimed ; " how could it be otherwise? I am afraid, Middy, father and mother will be rather shocked when I tell them that you have forgotten your other name."

" I thought I was Middy," answered the child.

Of course he did ! Great pains had been taken to prevent his thinking anything else.

" But that is a baby-name, my sweet boy ! Don't you know what your father's name is ? "

" Yes, Donald."

" Well, then, you are Donald too."

CHAPTER VIII.

"I NEVER had any doubt which of the children was yours," observed Mrs. O'Grady the next day.

" It was the more good of you to say nothing, then," replied the mother.

" But now I hope you really feel at peace?"

" Yes, at peace; but, in order to do so, I must adopt your theory, and believe that Maria Aird or her second husband invented the story of the changing of the children, — that supposes baseness enough — but how far easier to do than to effect a real change!"

" And you, Donald?" asked his sister.

" My dear, I suppose myself to be quite satisfied which is my child; but I am not satisfied to leave the other out of my care and influence for an hour."

" It is certainly time Donald was taken home," observed his sister; " he is a complete little Frenchman. And you would not like to leave Lancy, then, in my charge a little longer?"

" If I had no other reason I should still think it his right to be brought up as an Englishman also."

" Then he must not breathe this air and eat this diet much longer. Race has not half so much to do with national character as people think! Why, some of the English families brought up here by English parents talk like the French, and cannot produce the peculiarly soft sound of the English 'r,' they either ring it or slur it over."

" Companionship, my dear, nothing more."

" But Charlotte would not deny herself the society of her one child, unless she felt what she has been saying very strongly," said Mrs. Johnstone.

Donald Johnstone looked at his wife. Tall, placid, fair, she was at work on a piece of knitting, and took her time about it. All her movements spoke of tranquillity, and she observed what was going on about her. Then he looked at his sister, who was netting. Even the movements of her small ivory shuttle had an energetic jerk which seemed to suit the somewhat eager flash and sparkle of her clear hazel eyes; her thoughts were swift, her words were urgent for release, she longed to spread her theories, and scarcely noticed how they were received if she could but produce them.

" No, Estelle, companionship is not all ; your boys have hardly any companions, English or French, but they do not play half so boisterously, and they are not half so full of mischief as they would be if they had been brought up in equal seclusion on English soil. The French child is more tame in early childhood than the English. It is France that does this, not his race."

" You really think so ? "

" Of course I do ; the world is full of facts that bear on this point. In many parts of Germany, the men have a most unfair advantage over the women. They are better made, taller in proportion ; they are far more intellectual, and you must admit, Donald, that they are handsomer. All this mainly results from the superior diet of the men, specially in the towns. Many of them regularly dine out excellently well, leaving their women-folk at home to cabbage-soup and cheap sausages."

" Mean hounds ! " exclaimed Donald Johnstone, laughing.

" Yes, but unless the climate of Germany had already caused an inferiority in the women, they would not allow themselves to be so ' put upon.' It is the intense cold of their winter, together with poor diet, which dwarfs and deteriorates the women ; the same cold, with good food, braces the men. There is no nation in Europe where the height, strength, and wits of the sexes are so equal as in France. In fact. I think the French woman has the best of it ! It is partly the excellent climate — not hot enough to enervate, not damp to induce them to

drink — and partly it is the excellent food. Soil influences air — air influences food : these together influence
manners, and are more, on the whole, than descent."

" I shall always feel, Charlotte, that you have a right
to preach to us, and to put forth as many theories as
you please," said Donald Johnstone, when at last she
came to a pause.

" Because you feel that there is a great deal in what
I say?" she inquired.

Then she put on her spectacles, and caught a smile,
half amused, half tender, flitting over her sister-in-law's
face. Her brother was openly laughing at her.

" Not at all," he replied, " but because you are, as
you always have been, the best of sisters and the most
staunch of friends. You can understand people ; you
are willing, and able too, to help them in their own
way." Then, observing that she was a little touchy
and not at all pleased, he quietly stepped out over the
low window, and left her to his wife, for he knew that
it would be difficult for him to set matters straight
again.

The two little fellows were very docile children, and
less independent than English boys of their age.

" Donald," as Mrs. O'Grady was now careful to call
him, " Donald has fewest faults, but he is the least interesting. Lancy is a very endearing child."

" Has he any special fault?" asked Mrs. Johnstone.

" Well," she answered, " I hardly know what to say
about that."

Mrs. Johnstone looked up a little surprised ; her
sister-in-law appeared to speak with a certain caution.
" He is a very endearing little fellow," she repeated.

" But if he has any special childish fault, I ought to
know it, Charlotte."

" Yes, my dear. Well, I must be very careful not
to make a mountain of a mole-hill, and you must
try, if I tell you what has occurred, not to think too
much of it. He was but a baby, Estelle, when he first
did it."

" Did what, Charlotte?"

" But I have taken great pains not to make light of it, and also, I could not let you know, because it is a fault so rare in our rank of life, that it would have appeared to be a telling piece of evidence against him in your mind. It would have diminished his chance."

Estelle colored with anxiety.

" The fact is, he has several times taken little articles that were not his own, and appropriated them. They were things of no great value. Can this be hereditary? Were the father and mother honest?"

" I cannot tell. But what a fault, Charlotte! Does little Donald know?"

" Yes, but you need not be afraid for him. Lancy was scarcely more than three years old when, walking home from the town one day with his *bonne*, a minute toy was found in his hand that he could give no account of. They had been into several shops, but I never supposed that he had taken it. I thought some child must have dropped it, and that he had picked it up on the road. But, a few weeks after, I was in the market, bargaining for some oranges. I saw Lancy, who was with me, looking red and roguish, and was very much vexed when I found that he had snatched up an orange, and evidently meant to carry it off. The woman, with nods and winks, pointed this out to me ; she evidently regarded it as a joke. I told her how wrong she was to laugh at him, made him give it back, and for several days, in order to impress his fault on his little mind, I deprived him of his usual dessert, though the oranges were always on the table."

" This was two years ago?"

" Yes."

" Then I am afraid it is not all."

" It was nearly all that I know of till last Christmas, when Donald sent over a box with some English school books, and a number of little presents for the boys ; among these were two silver medals. Middy lost his almost at once, and there were great searchings for it. Lancy helped to look, but it could not be found ; then, one night after they were both asleep, *la bonne* was turning out the pockets of their little coats for the wash, and the two medals rolled out of Lancy's coat. One had been tucked into the lining. Poor little fellow! when I took him alone into my room the next morning, and showed them to him without saying a word, he wept piteously. And, Estelle, I believe he is cured. It was very touching to see the distress of both the little fellows when I made Lancy give back the medal and confess to Donald that he had taken it. Donald is much the most affectionate of the two, and when Lancy saw how much he was shocked and how sorry he was for him, he seemed to think all the more of his fault himself. I did all I could to deepen the impression, to show them the sin of stealing, and the punishment too. For several days they were both very *triste.* Then Lancy said to me, ' *When Middy says his* prayers to-night, he's going to ask God to forgive me.' I could do no less than say I was sure God would forgive him. But I have not let the matter drop; and you must be on the watch, Estelle, to help the poor little fellow against himself." And so, with all tenderness, the childish fault was told, everything that watchful love could do being extended to Lancy afterwards, and to all appearance he was cured, and as a rule, was a better boy than his foster-brother.

The two little Frenchmen were brought back to their native isle. At first, they took it amiss that there was no soup at the nursery breakfast, but then the nurse never expected to have hold of their hands when they walked out. And the dogs did not understand them; they thought this must be on purpose; but, on the other hand, they were allowed — indeed, they were encouraged — to climb the trees, and the *cher père* had given them some spades and a wheelbarrow. There were no drums, swords, and shrill French pipe to parade the garden with, but these spades were better than nothing. The *cher père* said they might dig as deep as they liked with them.

"But the clay would stain their new coats."

"Oh, that could not be helped!"

" Might they dig down to the middle of the world, then ? "

" Certainly, if they could."

They began to think England was a nice place to live in, and after a short sojourn in it contrived to make as much noise and do as much mischief as any other two little urchins breathing, for they were in the country now. The *cher père* had a rambling, homely old house in the country, and there they gradually mastered English, learning it from the little sisters, though they continued, to the great scandal of the servants, to jabber French, and *tutoyer* one another when they were together.

Childhood is long to the child, and his growth is slow, though to his parents he appears to " shoot up."

Donald and Lancy shot up, and, neither of them showing the slightest taste for any branch of learning whatever, they gave their governess a great deal of trouble.

The nurse said there never were two such young Turks. That was partly because, being of the same age and size, whatever piece of mischief attracted one, the other was always ready to help him in. Then the little girls were always trying to imitate them. It made them so rude " as never was." As to the nursery children, specially Master Freddy, who would have been as good as gold but for them, they took delight in leading him astray, and had taught him to speak French too, on purpose that she might not understand what they said to him.

Master Freddy kept his seventh birthday without having had any broken bones to rue, which was wonderful considering the diligence with which he had studied the manners and actions of his two brothers, as they were always called. But, about this time, they were sent off rather suddenly to school, it being at last allowed by governess, nurse, and even mother, that they were past feminine management.

Mrs. Johnstone was excessively fond of them both. None of the anguish of doubt remained. Her boy

was her own, and he was intensely fond of her; yet
towards Lancy she felt a never-satisfied yearning. She
was rather more indulgent to him than to Donald, as if
she could never forget her period of uncertainty; and if
there was a soft place in Lancy's heart — which is doubtful, for little boys are often hard-hearted mortals — it
was probably reserved for her. It was certainly to her
that he always complained when he had any grievance
against the nurse, and in her arms that he cried when
the governess punished him for any grave delinquency
by making him stop in doors on a half holiday.

Lancy remembered long after he went to school
(that is to say for nearly six weeks) how dear mother
had talked to him when he was in his little bed the night
before he went. She kissed him a great many times,
and she cried, and he promised he would be so good,
and never make her unhappy by doing naughty things.
And then she talked to Donald. And Donald declared
that he was never going to get into any mischief any
more; he would promise her that he never would, and
he would always say his prayers; and he would never
fight with the other boys — at least he wouldn't if he
could help it; and certainly he would never tell a lie
whether he could help it or not.

The house in Upper Harley Street was a far more
comfortable abode when they were gone, and they saw
very little of it for several years to come, their holidays
always taking place when the family was in the country.

As to their entrance on school life it was much like
that of other little boys. It was rather a large preparatory school to which Mr. Johnstone took his son and
his adopted son, both the little fellows chubby, brave,
according to their years, truthful and idle. They had a
box of cakes and other *prog* with them. He knew better than they did what would become of it. They had
also plenty of money. He did not, of course, expect
that they could have much to do with the spending of it,
but he found out two of the bigger boys, whose fathers
he was acquainted with, gave each a handsome tip,

turned his fledglings over to them, and left them, feeling the parting, on the whole, more than they did.

Under the auspices of these their new friends, the two little boys, when their own prog had been consumed, were privileged to put their money into a common purse, which happened just then to be nearly empty ; a great deal more prog, some of it very unwholesome, was then bought and consumed, after which the school sat in judgment on the new boys, kicked some of their caps round the playground, and ordered them never to wear them any more ; tore up some of their books as being only fit for the nursery, and then decided that such a name as *Donald Johnstone* was not to be borne. There had been another boy whose name was so spelt, but he called it Johnson, why could n't this fellow do the same. Yes, it was a troublesome name to pronounce — not really long, of course — but it sounded long. It was an uppish name ; they were sure he was proud of it. Half of it was quite enough for any fellow ; from henceforth he should be called Don John.

Don John accepted the verdict, and took it in good part. His father had impressed on both the boys that they must never be " cheeky," or it would be the worse for them. He thought when they next decreed that Lancy should be called Sir Lancelot, that they were rather inconsistent, but he did not take the liberty to say so, and the two little fellows made their way pretty well on the whole, seldom getting into trouble, excepting by a too ardent championship of one another. To learn how to disguise this, their only deep affection, was their first lesson in duplicity.

Always to take one another's part, right or wrong, when they dared, was their natural instinct ; their fealty and devotion was far stronger than that felt by most true brothers, they were never known to quarrel. They were always side by side in their class because Lancy would not learn as fast as he might have done, lest he should outstrip Don John, and get into a higher form, and they were always together in their play because

Don John did not care to outdo Lancy, and have to be with stronger boys instead of with him.

But the longing for companionship, a certain *camaraderie* as they would have called it, was not Don John's only reason for keeping close to Lancy. For a long while the childish fault had been almost forgotten ; if ever alluded to, it was by Lancy himself; but when the boys were twelve years old, and had just returned to school after the Easter holidays, Don John showed symptoms of illness, and was seized upon and sent home again forthwith.

He had the measles, and was away for nearly six weeks. There never was much the matter with him, and he returned ; but in a day or two a very slight something, he hardly knew what it was, seemed to let him know that Lancy was watched, and that he knew it.

Lancy did not meet his eye ; and that alone was strange.

An opinion seemed to be floating in the air that it was better not to leave things about. It was hardly expressed, but it was acted on, and the first hint he saw of such action drove the blood to Don John's heart ; he remembered the medal.

The next day the two boys were alone together in a class-room for one minute. Don John looked at Lancy, and putting his head down on the high desk, whispered with a long sigh that was almost a sob, —

" They don't *know* anything against you, do they, Lancy ? "

" No," answered the other little fellow in a frightened whisper, and feigning to be busy with his dictionary. " Don't seem to be talking to me. They only suspect."

Lancy's guilt was thus taken for granted, and confessed at once.

A boy, dashing into the class-room, called them out to cricket.

" Where are *the things* then ? " sobbed Don John again. " Can't they be found ? "

"I've buried them," replied Lancy, and they darted out together, pretending to be eager for the game.

As the two passing one another were for an instant apart from the rest, Don John cried out,—

"Where?"

"You can't get them out," replied Lancy, as after an interval they passed each other again. "I buried them in the garden, and you know the door is almost always locked."

"Say whereabouts it was," answered Don John. But the two did not meet any more till the game was over.

"What do you want to get them out for?" asked Lancy, as crestfallen and sad they left the cricket-field together.

"Because I know one of them is Marsden's watch. You always said last half that it was a far better watch than either of ours. He never will rest till he gets it, or till they find you out."

He spoke in French, using the familiar "tu." He was not angry with him, and the other was less ashamed than afraid.

"He only suspects," repeated Lancy, sick at heart, and already feeling the truth of those words, "The wages of sin are hard."

"And I took some money too—Oh, Don, how could I do it?"

"You might have known I should have plenty when I came back. Why couldn't you wait?"

"I don't know. I took two sovereigns, one was an Australian sovereign. He left them on his locker, and when he was telling the boys that it was gone, he said he knew that it was not a safe place to have put it on, and he looked at me."

"Then we must get back that very sovereign," said Don John; "one of mine will not do."

Lancy said no, they only suspected him, and now he knew the misery that came of taking things he should never do it any more. He then explained exactly where he had buried the watch and the two sovereigns. On the head-master's birthday they always had a holiday, and were allowed to range all over the place. While he was walking about in the garden on that day, miserable on account of what Marsden had just said, he found that the other boys had fallen back from him, and then dispersed themselves; he was quite alone. He hastily pushed a hole in some loose earth, close to a melon-frame, by which he was standing, dropped in the watch and the money, and with his foot covered them, just as some boys drew near. It was five days since this had occurred, and the first shower would probably uncover this property again. In the evening of that very day Don John had come back with lots of prog, lots of money. "And then," said Lancy, "I wished I had n't done it."

Don John burst out with, —

"If you were found out you would be —" he stopped awe-struck.

"I know," said Lancy, "and father would be sent for — oh what shall I do — and mother would know too."

"It was wicked," answered Don John, "I won't go to sleep all night thinking what we can do. It was wicked; *it was worse than being a cad.*"

Yes, Lancy felt that it was worse than being a cad. Human language could go no further; they had both, as it were, made their confession, and their minds for the moment were a little relieved.

CHAPTER IX.

THE morning after this conversation two remarkable things occurred.

There were four other boys in the dormitory where Don John slept; these were Lancy, Marsden, and two younger fellows.

When they began to get up Don John complained that his left arm hurt him horribly. It was very much swollen, and he could not dress himself.

The weather was hot, the boys had been out rather late the previous evening in the playing-field. Don John was a great climber, he confessed to having had a fall; he must have sprained it then, Marsden said. He seemed to have no opinion to give on the matter.

His room-mates gave him a good deal of awkward help, which hurt him very much; but when they found that his jacket could not be put on, they went and fetched their Dame, and she took him away.

Don John asked if Lancy might come too.

"Oh, not by no means; he was better by-half by himself."

So she bore him off to a little study set apart for such contingencies as hurts and accidents which were distinct from illness, and there she much consoled him for his pain by giving him a little pot of hot tea all to himself, two eggs, and a plate of buttered toast. He felt much better after this, but he wanted Lancy.

Presently the head-master came in, and with him a surgeon.

"How had he managed to hurt himself so much?"

"He had been climbing a tree, and he could not get down, so he sprang from the end of a bough, and fell on his arm."

" Then it did not hurt him much at first?"

" No, it felt quite numb."

Neither asked when this had taken place ; that it had been just before going to bed the night before was taken for granted.

Yet the surgeon did testify a little surprise.

" It's extraordinary what boys will sleep through," he remarked.

" You should have mentioned it last night, my boy," said the master kindly. " Why did n't you?"

Don John said nothing, but he turned pale.

" It gives you a good deal of pain, does n't it?" he proceeded.

" It did n't, sir, until I began to talk about it," answered the boy.

In fact he could not bear the pain and the fear of detection together ; he began to tremble visibly.

But he had much worse pain to bear before the surgeon had done with him, for it was found that his wrist was badly sprained, and that the small bone of the upper arm was broken.

Soon after this the other remarkable thing occurred.

At twelve o'clock, when the boys came out of school, their Dame asked to see Marsden.

" Master Marsden, you 're mighty careless of your things," she exclaimed, when he and some of the other boys came running up. " I was just a having your dormitory cleaned out, and when we moved the box atop of your locker, look here — if there was n't your watch and the two sovereigns behind it that you 've been making a work about."

Marsden took these things and blushed as he had never blushed in his life before ; what to do he did not know ; but Lancy just then passing by and looking as usual crestfallen and miserable, he obeyed a good impulse, —

" I say, Sir Lancelot," he exclaimed, " look here, I must be an uncommon stupid ass !"

Lancy looked with all his might, there was the Australian sovereign, and there was the watch and the other sovereign.

"They were found at the back of my box!" proceeded Marsden. "I could have declared I had looked there, but it seems I did n't."

A friendly boy at that instant stepped up, and stared him full in the face.

"Hold your tongue," he whispered; "we were mistaken; don't *let out* that we suspected him."

"They were found at the back of my box," repeated Marsden.

"Oh, were they?" said Lancy; "well, I'm glad you've got them again," — moderate and quiet words, but his gratitude was deep; he was reprieved.

"Of course it's nothing to you," said the blundering Marsden, "but I thought you'd like to know."

Several other boys in an equally blundering spirit betrayed their former suspicions by making like speeches, and showing a sudden desire to play with Lancy.

Nobody but Don John, he was sure, could have done this — but how?

This was how; but Lancy did not know it till some time afterwards.

The boys went to bed as usual, and the others — even poor Lancy — soon fell asleep. Don John then began to carry out the hardest part of his projected task; this was to keep himself awake till the dead time of the night, for he well knew that if he once went to sleep he should not wake till he was called in the morning.

He sat upright in his little bed and cogitated. There were three ways of getting into the garden; and once in there were several ways out, but they were all difficult.

It was well-known that to get in otherwise than by the door, you must go through the kitchen, which involved a long tramp down dark passages, and a great risk of making a noise. Or if you did not go that way you must descend the principal staircase (which had a nasty trick of creaking), and go past the head-master's own bedroom door; or, finally, you might creep along the corridor and descend by the washhouse roof. This,

in hot weather, when the corridor window was wide
open, was by far the shortest and easiest way, but then,
unless the garden-door, which was always locked inside,
had the key in it, how should he get out and get back
again? He could not come through the kitchen, the
bar would be up ; and that he could only remove on the
other side. He could jump down from the washhouse
roof, but he could not get up to it again without a short
ladder, which would betray him. Even if he could sur-
mount that difficulty it was doubtful whether he should
not make more clatter in creeping up the tiles than in
creeping down.

Therefore, if the garden-door was locked, he would
have to climb to the top of the high garden wall, by the
branches of the trained fruit-trees upon it, and creep
along the top of the wall till he reached a certain tree
whose branches hung out over it; from one of these he
must spring, or drop himself down as well as he could.
He would then be in the playground. To break a pane
of glass, and so undo the fastening of a window, push
up the sash, get in, shut it down again, and softly come
upstairs to his little chamber ; all these things had to be
done successfully, if Lancy was to be saved.

And if he himself was found out, what would happen?

" Why, if he had the watch and the two sovereigns
upon him, it would appear that he was the thief, and,
moreover, that he had committed the high misdemeanor
of getting out at night, perhaps to perpetrate more
thefts. Certainly for no possible good purpose. Perhaps it would end in his being expelled ; and mother — "
Here Don John choked a little.

" But then, if he did not do it, Lancy in the end was
sure to be found out, then *he* would be expelled. And
father — " Here he choked again. " Well it 's no use
funking or *arguing*," said Don John to himself, " because you know it 's going to be done, and you 're going
to do it."

It was almost like a nightmare when he thought of
it afterwards, but he certainly enjoyed the deed while it
was adoing.

To slip out of bed, listen all breathless, and watch his room-mates, while the clock in the corridor, the wheezing old clock, swung its clumsy pendulum, this was the only difficult thing he really had to do. It was the beginning; his own assurance to himself that the daring thing was to be attempted.

But a stealthy exultation in the strangeness of the adventure was damped by that obtrusive tick. The old clock was disagreeably wide awake; it seemed quite vicious enough to run down just at the decisive moment, and wake the second master, who might — who naturally would think a boy must be at that moment climbing down by the washhouse roof into the garden.

It seemed equally natural that he should look out, and catch the boy.

No, that clock must be stopped at all risks. He stole out of the open door and along the bare corridor, full of dim moonlight and confused sounds of snoring.

A childish figure in a long white night gown; he stopped before the clock, and gently opening its door, seized the great pendulum in his hand, and with one long gasping click the clock stopped. Then was his real danger; the cessation of a noise so often wakes people, yet nobody did wake, not even the master.

What a wicked boy he was! he felt as if he had choked off the incorruptible witness. He held the pendulum squeezed hard in his hand for two or three minutes, then stole back to his room and put on his clothes.

Often in his dreams it all came back to him afterwards; how he had tied his slippers together, and slung them round his neck, and how, as he got out, there was a white cat on the washhouse roof. In the dim light, her eyes gleamed on him strangely. He all but slipped — yet no — he reached the eave, and jumped down safely into the soft mould underneath. Then he stooped and put on his slippers, and effaced the marks of his feet in the mould.

The cat had jumped down after him, and was looking on. Here he was in the garden at one o' clock in the morning, and the moon was fast going down.

How beautiful those tall white lilies were. They enjoyed themselves in secret all through the night, gave out their scent, drank in the dew, and never let men and women find out that the night time was their life and their day. The great evening primroses, too, white and yellow, were in their glory, and it seemed as if they also were keeping it secret, and still. The cat was very jealous of his being out to see it all. It would be very unlucky for cats if people in a body should discover how much more jolly it was to be out in the warm golden mist of moonlight, when all was so fresh and sweet, than tucked up in their heated bedrooms under the low ceiling that shut out the stars.

Don John shared in the still stealthy delight of the flowers; he knew all was easy till he had to get into the house again, and he put off thinking about that till the last moment. But the moon was fast southing; it behoved him to be quick, unless he meant to stay out till day dawned. So with a beating heart he went softly across the dewy lawn among the wet flowers, the cat following him every step of the way, and looking on, while he secured the plunder, while he effaced the traces of his search, while he climbed the wall by means of the spread-out branches of a fig-tree, and while he softly crept along the top.

Oh, to be a cat for two minutes then; for cats never slip, and cats can see even under the branches in the dimness of a summer night!

Don John sprang into the tree successfully, but whether he mistook a branch for a shadow, or whether the white cat, springing after, startled him, he never knew, but the next instant he was on the grass at the foot of this tree, and his arm was under him.

He was on the right side of the wall, in the playground, that was his first thought.

He felt as if he had no arm, it was so perfectly numb. He was very cold, but presently thinking of himself, far more as a sneak than a hero, he got up and crept slowly towards the house.

"I'm glad I'm not obliged to be a burglar, too," he

said to himself, as he drew near, for a window was partly open, and he could get in without breaking a pane.

He had got the watch and the two sovereigns, but now the deed was done there seemed to be no glory in it, that was perhaps because he had hurt himself. He stole up to his little bed, thinking what a bad boy he had been to have thought the first part of the adventure such rare fun. But now neither he nor Lancy would be expelled, that was something. It was as much as they could expect, and they must make the best of it.

It always seemed to him afterwards as if the cat understood the whole matter better than Lancy did. . Have cats a natural sympathy with wickedness? probably they have, for the cat was the fast friend of Don John from that day forward; and when his "dame" came in would march in after her, gravely inspect his sling, and smell at his nice savory dinner.

And Lancy? Why, Lancy at first was very much relieved, and also very sorry that Don John was hurt, but both the boys felt, — one as much as the other, that to have a broken arm was as nothing compared with being expelled, and it did not signify to either, which had the broken arm so much as it should have done. Father and mother now would never know. What real gratitude Lancy felt was mainly on that account. Don John loved them far more keenly than Lancy did, and this was but natural, but Lancy loved no one better. They were his all, and Don John's brothers and sisters and home were his too. The boys never set themselves one above the other, everything about them appeared to point plainly to their being equals, and little as Lancy had been told about his parentage, it satisfied him, and he asked no questions.

He had always known that he was a dear adopted son, that his father's name was the same as his own, that he had died before his child's birth, and that his mother had married again and gone to Australia.

It was Don John who asked awkward questions,

Lancy did not care; what did it signify who gave him
all he wanted so long as it was given? No such thought
had shaped itself distinctly in his young mind, thought
was lying dormant as yet, and the love that cherished
him and the well-being in which he lived kept it from
expansion.

Once Don John asked his mother why Lancy's
mother never wrote to him, and she answered that
mothers did not all love their children as much as she
did. The boy looked up at her with clear blue eyes
full of surprise. It had seemed as natural that a mother
should love as that a flame should burn.

His arm was just well when she said this unexpected
thing. She had a very long string of amber beads
round her neck; he loved to rub the larger ones against
the sleeve of his jacket, and make little bits of paper
stick to them. He always remembered afterwards how
she looked down upon him as he sat by her, when he
asked what was the use to any fellow of having a mother
if she did not love him, and she moved his thick flaxen
hair from his forehead while he made another little bit
of paper leap to the beads, and then he put his arm
round her waist and leaned his head against her shoulder to cogitate. She was never in a hurry, this sweet
comfortable mother. She always had time to listen to
every grievance about hard lessons, and childish scrapes.
She even sympathized when tops would not spin. She
generally knew when her children wanted to say something to her, and would wait till it came. She was
expecting something about Lancy now, and hoped the
question might be easy to answer, but though Don John
was thinking about Lancy, it concerned what he himself had lately done for him, and when he spoke at last
she was a good deal surprised.

"Oh, mother," he said, "you don't know how wicked
I often feel."

She looked down on him, but said nothing, and he
went on.

"And I think Mr. Viser is a very odd man — particularly for a clergyman."

"What have those two things to do with one another, my dear boy," she answered.

"Oh, a great deal," answered Don John. "But you know, mother, you are the soul of honor."

"Yes," she repeated, without smiling, "I am the soul of honor."

She meant that when things were confided to her by her children she always kept them strictly to herself. Sometimes the confidence related to quarrels, and then she generally managed to persuade the penitent to make them up, or they concerned misdoings, were in the nature of confessions, and she was to tell their father, and persuade him to forgive. They all had a very wholesome fear of their father.

"And you never think of telling."

"Of course not!"

"I listened to his sermon yesterday — I never used to listen, but I did, and — well, if it's of no use punishing one's self, what *is* of use? you know fathers, and mothers, and masters are always punishing boys."

"Yes, they are."

"To make them better?"

"Yes."

"But if I had done something horrid — told a good many lies, for instance — and invented a story, which could not be confessed to father so that he could punish me, I think it extremely mean of Mr. Viser to make out that it's of no use my punishing myself instead."

The mother did not startle her penitent by asking, "Have you told a great many lies?" She only said, "And have you punished yourself, my boy?"

"Yes, mother," he answered, "and here is the punishment. I did it up more than a week ago, when first we came home for the holidays. It almost choked me when father and you were so pleased with my papers. And you know you talked about trusting me when I was out of your sight, and feeling sure I should be a good honorable boy. Oh, you know what you said." He produced a small brown paper parcel. "I meant — meant at first to dig a very deep hole and bury it —

but I am afraid I might afterwards not be able to help
digging it up again, for that mouse really is such a — ”

He paused, and still she did not smile or hurry the
penitent, whose hand trembled a little, and who looked
rather red and irate, and he presently went on, —

“ So whatever Mr. Viser says, you are to take the
parcel, mother, and lock it up — and mind, I am never
to have it any more.”

“ Very well, my boy,” she answered, not at all as if
she was surprised, and asked calmly, “ What is there
in it?”

“ There ’s all my money that grandmother sent, and my
mechanical mouse that runs round and round when it is
wound up, and several other things that I like.   Now I
have punished myself!”

“ Yes.   Can you repeat Mr. Viser’s text to me?”

“ No, not all of it.”

“ Get me a Bible.”

Don John fetched a Bible, his wrong against the
vicar did not seem less present to him when he had read
the verses in question, the beautiful and well-known
verses beginning “ Wherewith shall I come before the
Lord,” and ending, “Hear ye the Rod, and who hath
appointed it.”

“ You see it is all in the Bible,” she observed; “ and
what did he say it meant, but that we must not think
we can please or propitiate God by depriving ourselves
of our goods, or even of any earthly thing, though we
love it best.   Not to punish yourself, but to confess your
sin and forsake it, is the way to obtain forgiveness.”

“ Yes, but I did say that I could not confess this;
that would be worse than doing it.   I cannot tell the
real thing, the thing of consequence, but I can tell you
a little more, and you will be sorry.”

“ Yes, I shall — tell me as much as you can.”

“ What I said to father when he questioned me about
how I broke my arm, and when I did it, was all a lie —
all my own invention.   I made it up — I am in such
a rage sometimes after I go to bed and think about it,
that I can hardly help crying.   I wish father could pun-

ish me for it, and then forgive me, and I should be all right then." •

" But that cannot be unless you c mfess your fault to him."

" Oh, mother, I did tell you I could not confess it. So if punishing myself won't do, I suppose it's my duty to be miserable about it, when I don't forget it," he added with boyish naïveté.

" I dare say Lancy knows," she next said, and when he made no answer, " Don't you think he would be glad if you confessed?" she asked.

" Why, of course not, mother," the boy exclaimed, and then she never doubted that she should hear the whole; but no, Don John was very loving, very penitent, yet he stuck to it, that he must not tell her anything more, though when she asked him afterwards whether he had at least confessed his fault to God, he answered, —

" Oh, yes," with a fearlessness that surprised her. She was surprised both that he should have done so, and that he should think nothing of telling her that he had. Like most other boys he was in general extremely shy of all such subjects.

She urged him again to confess his fault to her, and he paused, as if considering the matter. " As God knows everything," he began, and then broke off.

" Yes, my dear boy?"

" And Mr. Viser does n't, I shall not take back my mouse." Here being hard put to it not to smile, she held her peace.

" When boys are at school," he went on with a certain quaint simplicity that was natural to him, — " when boys are at school, it's not at all easy to think about God. But HE knows what I mean. Boys are not so good, mother, as you suppose. If you knew everything just as God does, without my telling you, I should be very glad."

This was all his confidence — childhood was nearly over, not precisely even in that fashion could he ever talk to her again.

It was only Lancy who seemed never to have anything to hide.   Seemed — he was such a sweet little fellow, so ready to confess a fault, so apparently open ;
Donald Johnstone and his wife always felt themselves
repaid for the kindness and the love they had shown
him, and the family circle appeared to be incomplete
unless he was in it.   But of course Mrs. Johnstone
never asked him anything about Don John, how he
broke his arm, and why he was *obliged* to tell lies to his
father about it.   She would not have been " the soul of
honor " if she had done such a thing as that.

CHAPTER X.

THE family circle, as has been explained, never seemed perfect unless Lancy was in it, and this was more true than ever when, after another year, the two boys came home healthy, cheerful, and well-grown.

Lancy had not got himself into a scrape since the memorable stealing of the watch, and consequently both the boys were happier.

A somewhat singular circle it was. The house in Upper Harley Street had been let. The long rambling homestead in the country suited the mistress and the children far better. Her easy household ways often surprised Mr. Viser, her children inherited her placid temper and her unruffled ease.

They were all " characters " already; observed with amusement by the neighbors, both rich and poor; at home everywhere, and perfectly independent.

Mr. Viser and his wife, Lady Louisa, had a large, young family, but none of their children, though taken great care of, showed half the strength and spirit of the Johnstones.

Sometimes Lady Louisa came to call on Mrs. Johnstone, and made quiet observations on the manners and fashions of that gentlewoman, but it did not occur to her that these had anything to do with the sparkling eyes and high health of the children.

Once she had known Mrs. Johnstone to take up a parasol, when a very great noise of shouting and laughter almost deafened them, as they sat in the drawing-room. She went out into the garden, Lady Louisa

accompanied her; the boys and girls were easily found
by the said noise.

Were they told to make less? not at all; they were
merely admonished to go a little further off.

The little Visers never shouted; they never went out
of doors without a nurse or a governess; they wore
gloves, and generally had parasols.

A buttoned glove! handcuffs.are hardly more powerful to restrain. Such an article was never put on to the
little Johnstone girls, unless when they went out in the
close carriage to pay calls with their mother, then they
had also the regulation quantity of ribbon and feathers,
and behaved accordingly.

The groom in that establishment acted as an under-
gardener; he also went out on errands occasionally,
but when Mrs. Johnstone ordered the pony-carriage, she
never troubled herself to inquire whether he was ' at
home or not. Why? The boys of course could bring
the pony up from the meadow, run out the little carriage,
and harness the docile beast as well as he could. And,
to be plain with the reader (at the same time hoping not
to shock or displease), the girls could too.

When Mrs. Johnstone heard the wheels of the pony-
carriage, as it was brought round to the front door,
she would step forth equipped for the occasion, and
serene as usual. In holiday time she always found one
of the two boys ready to drive her; he would have
brushed himself up a little and put on a tolerably good
hat.

The carriage had a moderately comfortable seat in
front, the back of it was somewhat like an open square
box. There was a movable bench-like seat in it,
under which old Die was generally lying, for she liked
the air. The white cat was not unfrequently there also
(she had followed Don John from school).

"So long as you keep yourself to yourself," Don John
would say, "there's no objection to your seeing the
country." A third passenger would be Peterkin — old
Die's grandson. She knew why he was brought. He
was not to be trusted at home by himself. It was all

very well to bark at tramps, "but Peterkin was such a cad, that he would bark at the honest poor."

The mother and son would then set forth in homely state; but if their errand was to the town they would be sure to overtake Lancy and the elder girls, perhaps Mary and Freddy also, about a mile down the hill. These young people, as a rule, would be arrayed in flapping sun-bonnets and " over-all" garden pinafores, but you perceive " that there would not have been time to ' dress up,' and mother did not mind."

They also had errands to the town, which was about four miles off. A couple would get in behind, when mother told Don John to drive slowly, at the same time nests, and ferns, and flowers would be put in. Some did not attain to the town, but lingered in the lane picking up property till the return journey, then they would perhaps all get on board the somewhat clumsy craft pulling out the dogs to follow on foot. Sometimes on a sudden they would all get down, excepting the boy who was driving, and scurry into the little wood on either side, turning in like rabbits.

This was when a farmer's smart phaeton, with the farmer's lady in it, appeared at the top of the hill, or when Mr. Viser and Lady Louisa drove into the lane in their landau.

Such a feeling as shyness was quite alien to their natures, but they felt that their garden pinafores rather disgraced mother, filled as they would be with cowslips, blackberries, or nuts, as the case might be. It was as well, therefore, to make themselves scarce.

Mrs. Johnstone never took any notice of these proceedings. Occasionally Mr. Viser could see flitting figures and bright eyes peeping through the hedge, while the placid and admired mother exchanged civilities with her neighbors ; but, of course, he took no notice, and never looked back ; while the children stole out again, and quietly got into the carriage without stopping it, as the pony labored slowly up the hill.

Their purchases were as strange as themselves.

Once he saw a gawky girl, the eldest of the brood,

dart into the wood with a good-sized tin kettle in her hand. That kettle, which had cost two and eightpence had, together with a cuckoo clock, exhausted the whole resources of the family, the clock had cost eleven shillings, two shillings of which had been borrowed of mother as an advance upon next week's allowance.

Mother was not fond of advancing money, but this was for a great occasion. These were birthday presents for a particular friend.

Here it is really needful to give some account of the friend, together with certain other friends, their place, and their surroundings.

Within thirty miles of London there is a good deal of rural scenery. If any doubt this let them go and look about them — not south of the metropolis, of course, and not west. There are some little towns also with a general air of being old-fashioned and altogether behindhand with the world.

One of these was the little town beyond that long hill that the pony hated and the children liked; because his natural pace as he climbed it enabled them to fling their wildings into the back of the carriage without asking to have it stopped. They generally got out when they came to the steep part, and often, in a chivalrous spirit, gave the lumbering machine an unanimous push behind, while mother took the reins.

Mr. Johnstone had a "clarence," but this carriage was mainly used for taking him five days in the week to and from the station, which was more than four miles off. His expenses were large, and he had three sons to educate and to provide for, when there should have been but two. But his wife had persuaded him to let their town house for a term of years, so that it became a source of revenue instead of an expense to him; and when he found that she enjoyed her quiet life in the country, where there was next to no "neighborhood," that she looked more charming and fresh in her country attire than she had done when they mainly lived in London, where her milliner's bill was six times as high, and that all her children were healthy and happy, he fell back on his old thought that he was the luckiest husband going, and let himself take the same cheerful view of things that she did.

His abode was called "the house," and about two fields off, with no means of reaching them but a foot-path, which led, without any compromise, through his stable-yard, were six cottages called "the houses." Each of these had a nice plot of vegetable garden at the back, but in front it had scarcely six feet of flower-border, divided from the field by a simple wooden rail-ing, and having no outlet to any road or lane, and yet this field, a charming field in its way, might al-most itself have been thought of as a lane, for it was very long and very narrow, and was divided from its neighbor field by a running brook, edged with haw-thorn and maple, and a wasteful tangle of brambles and whitethorn. Very bad farming prevailed in those parts.

In the first of the tenements, dignified by this name "the houses," lived the very particular friends for one of whom the tin kettle and the cuckoo clock had been purchased. Her cottage consisted of a very neat and rather roomy front kitchen, a little washhouse behind, and upstairs two tolerably comfortable bedrooms. By calling, she was a humble dressmaker; she and her sister worked for Lady Louisa's children and servants, made the little Johnstones' common clothes, worked for the farmer's ladies, and did odd jobs generally.

In the next cottage (they were all detached) lived the cobbler. His name was Salisbury. The particular friend's name was Clarboy — Mrs. Clarboy, and she was aunt to the nurse up at the house. The houses were supposed to be Mrs. Johnstone's district; if the people there were ill it was her special business to look after them; she also lent them books and tracts, and persuaded them to join the parish coal club and go to church.

So far as the young Johnstones were concerned, these cottages constituted "the neighborhood," very frequently went on their own invitation to drink tea with Mrs. Clarboy, who was a widow, and her sister Jenny. They generally trundled the loaf, the cake, the butter, and the tea, they proposed to consume, through the fields in a child's wheelbarrow, frequently they added radishes out of their own little gardens or some fruit.

If the sisters confessed that their coal was low, the wheelbarrow, after having been duly emptied, was trundled on to the last cottage, which was called the shop, where there was often as much as a whole sack of potatoes on sale, a matter of three or four "hundred" of coal, gilt images made of gingerbread in the window, bull's-eyes and yellow butter, together with a jar of treacle, with other like dainties, and a moderate allowance of bacon, all of inferior quality and somewhat the worse for keeping. A quarter of a hundred of coals would be purchased, and if the young Johnstones had not the requisite cash to pay at the time, they brought it the next day, but if it was at the beginning of the week, and they had plenty of money, they bought half a hundred and wheeled it to its destination at twice. They then made up a good fire. The sisters had a capital pair of bellows, presented to Miss Jenny by the same young friends on a previous birthday.

They used them liberally. Mrs. Clarboy and Miss Jenny, proud and pleased, looked on, at the same time continuing to stitch; they never thought of interfering with the preparations.

A great deal of toast was made, sally-lun cakes were buttered, tea set on the hob to "brew," then radishes were washed and the cloth was laid.

Some of the company sat on Windsor chairs, others on tall stools or boxes set on end, which they had imported from their home.

The hostesses enjoyed their meal to the full as much as their guests. Nothing ever interfered, the sisters never had any other engagements. If they were very busy, the girls helped to hem frills, or were trusted to run seams afterwards, or at least they threaded needles, while the boys made themselves popguns, or dis-

ported themselves in or beside the brook, catching
caddis-worms, or sailing boats.

Mrs. Johnstone knew all about this?

Certainly.

What a singular woman Mrs. Johnstone must have
been!

There was a sweet gentleness about all these children, and an untroubled air of quaint independence.

Where, indeed, was their governess?

Why, she was at her lodgings in the nearest farm-
house, where she spent her evenings, and where she
slept.

It was as much to her enfranchisement as theirs;
but very few mothers would have deliberately ban-
ished her, and undertaken herself all the supervision re-
quired between five o'clock one day and nine o'clock the
next.

It made the governess — a very good woman — extremely happy; it gave an early sense of responsibility
to the children, for if they got into any scrape, or perpetrated any mischief, they were expected to go and
tell, which they did.

Lady Louisa called one evening when they were present. She only stayed a minute.

"We've come to tea," the company told her.

Mrs. Clarboy, rising, colored and curtseyed.

Lady Louisa did not look or express the least surprise. She had several small books nicely bound in
her basket, and she said, —

"Mrs. Clarboy, the Rector has had his course of
Easter sermons published, and he wishes me to present
you with a copy."

Miss Jenny was a Methodist, so to her Lady Louisa
merely bowed.

She then took her leave and went on to the next cottage.

Mrs. Clarboy, a shrewd, industrious woman, more
than sixty years of age, was rather silent after Lady
Louisa's visit. She was in the habit of going out to
work as well as of taking work in. She hoped her enter-

tainment of the party would not stand in her light as
regarded work at the rectory.

Could Lady Louisa disapprove? Well, though it
might be a liberty to think it, what business was it of
hers?

Mrs. Clarboy took up her needle again with great
vigor the moment tea was over, the Methodist sister
having first said a long grace, expressive of fervent
thanks for the meal. She said just the same grace
when the two sisters had only partaken of stale bread
and the weakest of tea with no milk in it, but she imparted to the words on these occasions an unconscious
fervor.

" You had need not overdo yourself to-night," she
remarked, " for you're going to the Hall Farm to work
to-morrow."

" Yes, I had need," answered Mrs. Clarboy; " for
they look to it there that they get their money's worth
out of me."

" Is n't it very amusing, Mrs. Clarboy, dear, going to
so many different houses?" asked Lancy.

Lancy was waxing Mrs. Clarboy's thread.

" Well, Master Lancy, yes, I may say it is. Not
but what two shillings a day is harder earned working
out than working in; but you must count in the exper'ence you get of life. You see the world. As I
often say to Jenny, ' Jenny,' I say, ' what should I be
now if I had never seen the world, and what would you
be either ; not that you go out, my pore girl! you hav'n't
the nerve for it.' "

Miss Jenny assented by rather a foolish simper.

" Nobody can never be dull," she remarked, " with
such an one as sister to talk to, as we sit and sew.
She's better by half than any printed book that *I* ever
had the reading of."

Don John, sitting cross-legged on the floor, was labori-
ously threading needles. It took him nearly as much
time to perform this operation as it did the two sisters
to work up the thread. The little girls were elaborately
hemming the frills for the sleeve of a kitchen-maid's

new gown, which was to be finished and taken home that night.

"But I look for no thanks — let the fit be as good as it may — from that sort of customer," observed Mrs. Clarboy. "It's your ma that's the lady to say she's pleased or she's satisfied. To be sure that best — bed furniture I put up for her after it had been calendered was the intricatest thing I ever got the better of."

"But then you had your reward," said Miss Jenny, simpering; "the head house-maid showed you the drawing-room while the family was at dinner."

"She did, Jenny; and I've wished times and again you could see it, so frequently as you complain that you can't make a picture to yourself of what heaven's like. But you hav'n't the nerve to go up to the house. You'll have to wait. It might be an advantage to you, though, if you could see it."

"Do you think it so very pretty, then, Mrs. Clarboy, dear?"

"Pretty ain't the word, Miss Marjorie. It fairly made the tears start, so full of great looking-glasses, and gilding, and silk hangings. I felt quite solemn. I said at the time, 'It makes me think of heaven;' so clean, too, and so cheerful."

"I know heaven's not a bit like that," observed Don John, with conviction, at the same time handing up another needle, the thread of which, from much handling, was not quite so clean as it should have been.

"Well, and you may be right, sir," answered Mrs. Clarboy, with due gravity; "and the Scripture says, as we all know, 'eye hath not seen.' And yet it stands to reason that very beautiful things and places must be more like than such as are not beautiful at all."

The company were not able to give an opinion here; but they were not much surprised at what they had heard, being already accustomed to look at things through other eyes, and different points of view from that of their own class.

"There's not much to see at the Hall Farm," said Miss Jenny.

"But to them that can take notice," observed Mrs. Clarboy, "it's all interesting; it shows one people's ways. I know what it is to have two candles as good as whole ones all to myself, and I know what it is to have to share the end of a dip with two others working by me."

"You like as well as anything working at the Red Farm," observed Miss Jenny, "where you sit in the kitchen with the mistress. There's plenty to hear there, if there is n't much to see."

"Ay, I've worked for three generations of the Hollyoakes."

"He was one to argue, was the old Mr. Hollyoake," proceeded Miss Jenny; "you always said so. Why, he would argue with a ghost!"

"Ay, but you've no call to talk of ghosts now," said Mrs. Clarboy. "You've not an ounce of discretion in your whole body, Jenny."

"You mean because of us," said Marjorie; "but we often play at ghosts at home, Mrs. Clarboy, and father and mother don't mind."

"Are you sure, miss?"

"Oh, yes! and we often go to the Polytechnic and see the ghosts — real ones, you know."

"Oh, well, miss, I was not aware. Well, as Jenny was saying, old Jem Hollyoake was so given up to arguing, that he would argue even with a ghost. He had brought up his brother's son. The lad died, and his ghost rose, got into the kitchen, and pointed his long finger at his uncle.

"'Uncle Jem,' said the ghost, 'as you brought me up —'

"'Bring you up, did I?' interrupted old Hollyoake, beginning at once. 'Bring you up, did I? Little enough of that you needed; it was impossible to keep you down!'

"'I mean,' said the ghost, obliged to explain himself, 'as you've brought me up to speak with you out of the silent tomb.'

"'I did nothing of the sort,' says Mr. Hollyoake, very much frightened.

" ' You did,' said the ghost.

" The family was gone to bed, but I dare say old Jem had drunk enough to keep his courage up, and argue he would.

" ' How dare you tell such a falsehood,' said he. ' I wish nothing more heartily than that you would keep in your proper place. Is n't your headstone to your mind?'

" ' Yes,' said the ghost, ' it 's a real handsome one. But, Uncle Jem, you 've brought me up by for ever thinking and thinking about those seven silver spoons you 've lost. *I took them !*'

" Mr. Hollyoake said he was sorry, and the ghost went on, —

" ' They 're at the bottom of the least of the two old hair trunks in the garret, hid under my velveteen coat.' Then he vanished."

" Are you sure the ghost said all that?"

" Yes, Master Lancy. But you 'll think it strange that when, the next morning, old Hollyoake related all this, and got some of the neighbors to go with him into the garret, they found the trunk and the old coat in it; but the spoons were not there."

" Not there?"

" No."

" Then I don't believe the story!"

" Why not, sir? Oh, you may depend it 's true. It was a story against himself, and how disrespectful he 'd been arguing with the ghost."

" You said he was alone when the ghost rose?"

" Yes, sir, smoking his pipe in his own kitchen."

" He must have been dreaming!"

" Oh no, sir, not he, the kitchen is tiled. Why, he has shown me many a time the very tile the ghost stood upon. It was a yellow one — all the others are red. The tile is there to this day!"

" Well, ghosts are mere bubbles," observed Don John, repeating something that he had heard at the Polytechnic.

" No, sir, the man was most like a bubble here,"

said Mrs. Clarboy, "for he broke, and never paid but two and eleven-pence in the pound, whereby we got no more than that for making the mourning his wife stood upright in when she cried at the ghost's funeral."

Here the story ended. The young Johnstones pondered over it with deep interest and attention, as something that would do capitally to act. They were fond of play-room theatricals, but thanks to the Polytechnic they were, so far as ghosts went, perfectly fear-proof.

"Oh, mother," said Lancy, when they got home, "Mrs. Clarboy told us such a jolly ghost story. Will you come into the playroom to tea to-morrow and see us act it?"

"You should not have asked mother in that unconventional way," said Naomi, "when you know we planned to send a proper note on pink paper, and paint a monogram for it."

"Oh well, I think it had better be considered then that I know nothing about the tea at present," said the mother.

Naomi was mollified.

"And, mother," said Don John, "may we have two more chairs for the playroom? I told you last week that we had got a Fetch."

"And I did not know what you meant, Don John."

"Why, mother, you must have noticed that when droll or ridiculous anecdotes are invented for the papers, or told in books, they are often palmed off on people who had nothing to do with them. Well we have invented two characters. We act them. And we palm off our funny things that we say upon them. They are Fetches of our own imagination, mother."

"What do they want with chairs, then?"

"Now, mother, it's not fair to laugh. Why, we have a *séance* twice a week; we keep minutes of it. Our Fetch is frequently called to the chair, so we want one, to pretend that he is in it."

"Ah, I see."

"Robert Fetch Fetch, Esq.; that's his name. We

have pretended a large house for him in the rectory glebe. It seems quite odd to go there and find nothing in it. And Fanny Fetch is his old cousin, who lives with him."

"And you want a chair for her, too?"

"Oh, yes, that we may know where she is sitting. Of course their chairs will not appear to us to be empty. When we act them and do their voices, you cannot think how real they seem."

"You'll come and hear the *séance* sometimes, won't you, mother?" asked Naomi.

"Certainly."

"You'll like them much better than our charades; for sometimes, you know, you think those are rather long."

"I have thought so once or twice when they lasted more than an hour."

"Well, it takes a long time to dress up; but may n't we have the two chairs? It's very awkward for our Fetches to have to sit upon stools."

"You may take two chairs out of the blue bedroom."

"Oh, thank you, mother; and you shall see every bit of the ghost acted before tea," cried Lancy, with effusive gratitude.

He wagged his longest finger.

"It's a jolly one. '*Uncle Jem, as you've brought me up*'—mind I'm to do the ghost, Naomi. '*Uncle Jem, as you've brought me up.*'"

Here Lancy, delighted at the prospect, turned head over heels, and the young people shortly departed together.

CHAPTER XI.

SHORTLY before the boys were sent off again to school, Mr. and Mrs. Johnstone went over to Normandy to be present on an interesting occasion. Mrs. O'Grady married again. She married a somewhat impecunious military man, and forthwith proceeded with him to India.

Her one little girl, Charlotte by name, had been brought up near Dublin, but had lately come home to her mother; her paternal grandmother, who had taken charge of her, having died. She was pretty, very clever, very awkward, and extremely shy. Quite different from most girls of her age, and keenly conscious of it.

She had never been accustomed to the society of boys and girls of her own age, and when she heard that she was to go back with her uncle and aunt, and be educated with her cousins, she wept with shyness and a sense of disadvantage.

Her behavior when first she appeared in the playroom was so stiff, her discomfort was so evident, that she made the young Johnstones feel almost as ill at ease as herself.

As for Don John, at first he almost hated her. Boys are extremely intolerant of awkwardness and causeless fear. But in a short time what kindness he had in his heart was touched for Charlotte, and while he scolded he roughly encouraged her.

"Now then, Charlotte, hold up your head. What are you so shy about?"

"I can't help it, indeed; it won't go off, Don John."

"Won't it? Well we can't stand this much longer.

Do you think it would go off if I gave you a good shaking?"

"No-o."

" Suppose I try?"

He advanced ; they were in the garden. Charlotte, taking all for sober earnest, turned, and, fleet of foot as a fawn, darted along the grass walk and across the first field, he after her whooping, and with all the Johnstones at his heels.

She reached the brook, he was gaining on her, he was close behind. She checked herself for an instant on the edge, gave a shriek, made a spring, and instead of clearing it, splashed into its very midst.

Astonishment, and the water bubbling about her, brought her instantly to a dead pause. Then she heard shouts of laughter behind her. She turned cautiously round, and when she saw Don John gaping at her in dismay on the bank, and all the others laughing, she could not help laughing too.

" Keep as still as ever you can!" shouted Lancy, as he came up breathless. " Well, I don't know whether this was most *funky* or most *plucky!*"

Charlotte by no means wanted courage, and shyness could not stand against such an adventure as this. The water was almost up to her shoulders, and it was not without some difficulty, and the help of the cobbler's — Mr. Salisbury's — bench that she was extricated, for she was standing on a little shoal, and the water was deep on either side of her.

Breathless was the interest of the folk from " the houses," while Charlotte, dripping and blushing, was taken to Mrs. Clarboy's house. Marjorie having rushed home for the nurse, that functionary soon appeared with dry clothing, and Charlotte was arrayed in it.

When she appeared outside, Don John met her looking very sheepish, but instead of apologizing, he said bluntly,—

" You 're not to do that again ; it 's more horrid of you even than being shy. I was only in fun."

" I shall not do that again, unless *you* do that
9

again," said Charlotte, not without a certain audacity ; for she was still excited and her shyness for the moment was gone.

She shook back her thick black hair. She was a pretty little girl ; but Don John cared not for her good looks, for the lustre of her dark blue eyes, and the soft carnation flush which had spread itself over her small oval face.

" Well, let's be friends," said Don John bluntly ; " you know it was hateful of you to be so shy."

" Yes," said Charlotte, " I know it was."

" If you'll be nice to us," he continued, with a sudden burst of generosity, " I'll let you write the minutes of our society, and tell you all about our Fetches."

Hints of the Fetches had reached Charlotte. She was devoured with curiosity about them.

" Come ! I don't like writing, and you can write so fast."

He held out his hand as a token of forgiveness. She was the culprit, of course. Charlotte looked at matters in the same light.

The minutes of our society. These were fine words ; they meant the meagre and badly-spelt notes, written in ruled copy-books, of these children's fantastic doings.

Charlotte held out her hand, and amity was proclaimed then and there.

The little girl was now at her ease with this especial company, and did not know that the desired state of things had not come about by any resolution of her own, but only through accidental circumstances.

Poor little Charlotte ! She was more utterly at home and at ease than most people with those whom she did fully know and love ; but she had a fresh access of shyness with every stranger, every visitor, and even every new housemaid that appeared on the narrow scene of her life. If she went to drink tea with the young Visers, she made herself ridiculous by her stammering and her blushes ; if a farmer's lady made a polite remark on meeting her in a lane, she left the Johnstones to answer it and retreated behind them, flushing furiously.

Sometimes, as time went on, and she was more shy than ever, she would, say it was hard when her cousins laughed at her.

" Then you should n't write verses, Charlotte. Only think of a girl of your age writing verses," observed Marjorie on one such occasion.

" It can't be that," answered the poor little victim, drying her eyes.

" Oh yes, it is," said Don John, with youthful certainty and inconsequence. " Father says it's the poetical temperament that makes you so shy."

" But I've tried to leave off writing my poetry, and it makes no difference," said Charlotte, choking a sob ; " I have n't written any for a fortnight."

" And those verses she did for poor Peterkin's epitaph were perfectly stunning," observed Lancy.

Charlotte was consoled.

" And mother says she thinks it's extremely interesting to have the poetical temperament," remarked Naomi, the second girl.

" So now, Charlotte, don't be mooney ; set off ! — proceed ! — go it ! — and finish the minutes. Don't you know that Fetch is coming to tea — and mother," exclaimed Don John.

Don John and Lancy were now fourteen years old, Marjorie was nearly sixteen, and Naomi fifteen. But the two boys were quite at the head of the family — bigger, stronger, cleverer, and bolder than the sisters, they reigned over all, especially over Charlotte, though she alone had the touch of genius, which guided their fancies and suggested their most amusing play.

The boys were just come home for the midsummer holidays, and had been to pay a short call at the houses. There was poor Mrs. Appleby, who was a cripple, and lived with her daughter ; to these patient women they took some tea, and a little shawl, bought with their own money. Then they paid their respects to Mr. Salisbury and his wife, and were astonished to find the cobbler at work in his little back kitchen, and the front room with a new square of carpet spread over its brick floor, a sofa with a soft puffy seat, some new chairs, smartly covered with rep, and a good-size looking-glass; while, standing on a small wicker-table, was a lady's work-basket lined with quilted satin, and filled with odds and ends of colored threads.

Mrs. Salisbury answered the door when they knocked. She had on a clean gown and a white apron.

" Glad to see you, young ladies, and you, Master Lancy, and you, Master Don John. Salisbury and me we have promoted ourselves into the wash'us."

Mrs. Salisbury looked a little confused.

" We've got a lodger," she continued, " that is out at the present time."

" But who might be coming back," said Marjorie instantly, feeling that to come in might be to intrude. So the boys, having been assured by Mrs. Salisbury that they " were so growed as never was," proceeded with their sisters and Charlotte to Mrs. Clarboy's cottage.

" Fine doings, young ladies, and gentlemen, at Salisbury's," exclaimed Mrs. Clarboy, when the usual greetings had been exchanged. " You've heard of the lady, no doubt."

" What lady, Mrs. Clarboy?"

" It's a very 'sterious thing," began Miss Jenny, quite solemnly.

" Ah! you may say that, my pore girl! Jenny has had a shaking of the nerves lately, pore thing; but a truer word she never said, Mr. Don John, than that as has just passed her lips. There's a lady come to lodge here! She have our front bedroom all to herself (and put in the best of new furniture); and eight shillings and sixpence a week paid regular she has promised us for it. And she has Salisbury's front room for her parlor. And it's a 'sterious thing."

" She came in yesterday was a week," observed Jenny.

"And," said Mrs. Clarboy, "I told her truly when first she walked up to the door, and asked if we had lodgings to let, ' No, ma'am,' said I, ' not for a lady

like you.' ' It 's not what I 've been used to, I 'll allow,'
she said, rather high, ' but I feel as if I should take to
this quiet place ; and I 've seen the world, so I can make
allowance.' She was all in silks and satins, and had
a long gold chain, and a gold watch! ' Why, ma'am,'
said I, ' just look round. There 's not so much as a
high road to look out of the window at, and see the
carts, and carriages, and what not pass, when you 're
dull. A narrow field and a few bramble bushes are all
very well for poor folks, such as we, to have for a prospect. But you, that I make no doubt might lodge in
the best street of the town! Besides,' said I, ' we 've
no accommodation.' She did n't seem convinced, but
she went on to Salisbury's, and there they said the same
thing."

" But I think I would rather be in these houses than
in the town," said Marjorie.

" There now ! " cried Miss Jenny, and shook her head
as much as to say " they none of them have any sense,
these gentlefolk."

A great deal of folding and measuring of flounces
followed ; the girls lent their aid ; but when all was set
in order, and the sisters could take up their needles
again, Mrs. Clarboy resumed the subject so much in
her thoughts.

" Jenny, pore girl, has seen little of life, to be sure,
and her nerves are not strong, so she is not to be
judged (she pronounced this word jedged) like other
folks that have had exper'ence. I went out to work
next day. When I came home she said — you did,
did n't you, Jenny? — she said, ' Often do I pray against
the fear of the world, but I 'm afraid the love of the
world and the handsome things in it has got the better
of me this day. Elizabeth,' she said, ' the lady has been
here again, and I was that dazzled with her beautiful
gown, made of the best corded silk, and her things in
general (and the picture of a gentleman hung round her
neck) ; but though you had said our place was too
humble for such as she, I took her upstairs when she
told me, and showed her our front bedroom.' "

" Yes, that was what I said," Miss Jenny answered. " Only I did n't lay it all out so straight on end as you can, sister, and I went on to her, as was my duty; I said, ' It 's a poor place, ma'am, for such as you.' ' I think, Miss Jenny,' she says, ' if you and your sister was to sleep in the back room, and put some new furniture in here, it would do for me very well.' "

" And here she is," said Mrs. Clarboy, cutting the story short, for she observed that it did not much interest her young visitors.

" But I hope it 's not wronging her to take the eight shillings and sixpence a week," continued Miss Jenny, who for the moment was irrepressible, " being as it is so much more than our whole rent. And it 's strange and worldly to come down of a weekday morning as she does in a silk and cashmere costume almost as good as new."

" That 's nothing to us," said Mrs. Clarboy, austerely, and the young people took their leave. They could not stay to tea, they said, their mother was going to drink tea with them in the playroom, and they must go back at once to receive her.

But Don John had spent the morning at the town, and had not come home in time for the early dinner, his noontide refection had been limited to two buns, he was therefore about to have a " meat tea," with the addition of gooseberry pie and beer.

" You here ?" exclaimed Lancy, when he and Don John entered the playroom, and he saw Mary and Freddy seated in a corner with all humility.

" No, you can't stay, you must slope !" proceeded the other young despot. " Did n't we tell you you might make the raspberry wine in the nursery ? "

" But we don't see any fun in that."

" Oh, you don't ! Well, now, I wish you would do something really useful for me."

" Yes, we will, Don John."

" Take two or three matches out into the garden, and strike a light, that you may see whether the sunshine 's of the right sort. If it is, bring me word."

" We wanted to hear you do Sam Weller."

" Don't sniff," proceeded Lancy.

" And the cake smells so good," continued Mary, in a piteous tone, and twinkling away a tear.

" Oh, the cake!" exclaimed Don John. " Yes, my young friends, that's fair. Now then, 'share and share alike,' as the tiger said to the washerwoman ; 'you shall mangle the skirts and I the bodies.' "

" That's meant for Sam Weller," Lancy exclaimed. " Now you 've heard him ! "

" Pass a knife," proceeded Don John.

The little sister handed him a handsome ivory paper-knife. Don John was wroth.

" What! my prize — my carved knife that father gave me? Well," he continued, falling into thought, " ' I don't see that it can be put to a better use,' as the Queen said in the kitchen at Balmoral, when she stirred up the porridge with her sceptre."

" And there 's no other knife," said Freddy humbly.

" And," Mary put in, " we 've often seen you cut with this one yourself."

Don John was feeling the edge of the knife.

" That 's nothing," he answered uttering a great truth without perceiving its importance, " things are perfectly different, and are always reckoned so according to the person who does them."

He dug the knife into the cake, and carved out a handsome quarter. But just as the operation seemed about to terminate successfully, a hard piece of citron got in the way. A portentous crack was heard, and the heft broke off short in his hand.

The little brother and sister seized their share and immediately took themselves off. Under the circumstances, how could they hope to be tolerated in the playroom any longer. The company set chairs, Lancy nicked out more portions of cake with his pocket-knife, and then they bethought themselves of ringing for what they wanted.

When Mrs. Johnstone made her appearance, the

paper-knife had been put away and forgotten. Don John was pouring out a glass of beer, and saying, — " ' I like my drink frothed, and plenty of it,' as the porpoise said in the storm."

Then, when the foam disappearing with mortifying rapidity, he went on in more natural fashion, — " Oh, mother, don't you think father might let us have the beer a little less *powerfully* weak? It really reminds me of the old story he told me himself, that the proper way to make small beer was to tie an ear of barley to a duck's tail, whip it round the pond with a bunch of hops, and serve out the liquor. No, mother, you are to sit at the head of the table opposite to me. That chair is Fetch's seat."

" Is he here?" asked Mrs. Johnstone.

" Not yet, mother; he was here yesterday," said Lancy, " and Fanny drove over in the pony chaise to convey him home. ' Oh, Rob,' she said — his Christian name is Robert — (here Lancy fell into a soft foolish tone), ' I left your boots at Salisbury's to be patched. He certainly is an ugly fellow ; I little expected ever to see him, though I have heard of Salisbury plain all my life. And I have yet to learn, my dear, why they calls him Salisbury plain, instead of plain Salisbury.' "

" And then," said Charlotte, " Fetch told us this anec-dote, and said we were to enter it on the minutes. Three men, after a hot day's work in the hay fields, got very drunk ; their names were Miller, Wright, and Watt. When their wives came to fetch them home they had tumbled down in a heap, and were fast asleep on the hay. Wright's wife said, ' Wright 's wrong.' Miller's wife said, ' My man 's so jumbled up with the others, that I don't know which is which,' and Watt's wife said, ' I don't mind which is which, all I care for is what 's Watt.' "

" After that," observed Marjorie, " we had great fun, Lancy did Fetch, and Don John was Sam Weller! He 's generally Sam Weller now."

" Rather ambitious," remarked Mrs. Johnstone.

" Yes — we read Charlotte's epitaph on poor Peterkin,

and Sam Weller said, ' Very affecting, " I incline to blubber," as the whale said when he was half seas over.' There you see, mother laughed at that quite naturally, and without trying!" exclaimed Naomi. " I told .you I was sure it was funny. And then Fanny Fetch interrupted — the stupid thing continually says what has nothing to do with the subject. ' My pretty Rob,' Naomi simpered, ' if you were to steal a joke, would that be burglary or petty larceny?' There! mother laughed again."

" But I wish Fetch to come," said Mrs. Johnstone; " I like him to be present."

" We can't always make him be here," Lancy explained; " sometimes we have nothing for him to say. But he told some more anecdotes yesterday. He said a man met one Mr. Tooth, and a lady supposed to be his mother. The man said, ' Is that your own tooth, or a false one?' She answered, ' He 's both.' "

" If it 's not a breach of confidence, I should like to know who made Fetch say that? "

" Well, mother, it would be a breach of confidence to tell you her name; but perhaps I may whisper to you that her initials are C. O'G. Don John was so much pleased with the minutes and her anecdotes, that while she was writing this morning he invented a Sam Weller for her. ' You can't speak to me now, I 'm composing,' as the little boy said when he was making the dirt pie, and sticking it round with barberries."

" Oh, here 's Fetch! " exclaimed Don John, rising up and shaking hands violently with nothing. " How d' ye do? — how d' ye do? You find us in the midst of our simple meal — consommé de bread and cheese, seed cake au naturel, and small beer à la maitre d'hôtel."

Fetch was then bowed into his seat and introduced to Mrs. Johnstone.

" Having had nothing to eat for some hours, my friend," said Lancy, as Fetch, " I think I could enjoy a slice of that cake."

" Good," said Don John, " that 's quite fair."

Lancy accordingly began his meal over again; but

Mrs. Johnstone proposing that the cake should be served all round, stopped the conversation for a few minutes.

"And now, my friends, *the minutes.* Charlotte, get out the book," said Don John, as Fetch. "I wish to have placed on record an anecdote of my own family that I thought of last night."

Fetch spoke in a high raised voice, and Don John and Lancy produced it equally well.

"But I wish you were not so proud," said Charlotte, "always boasting — about something — I'm tired of writing down — about *my* property — *my* family."

She spoke quite sharply.

"*My* old clothesman — *my* undertaker," interrupted Don John. "Yes, it's too true, Charlotte, I am proud!"

"The minutes don't seem natural with so many anecdotes," persisted Charlotte.

"Well," said Lancy, as Fetch, "but what am I to say if I can think of nothing else? Don't be so peppery! Some people are never satisfied. Come! I'll tell an anecdote about that. I invented it some time ago, but I never got an opportunity to bring it in. There was once a Titan who had the largest hand ever seen. Jupiter proposed to give him a ring. 'I know it won't be big enough,' grumbled the Titan. Jupiter was determined it should. He ordered it to be made as large round as the earth's orbit. And yet when it was sent home, the Titan declared he couldn't wear it. He pretended it was too big."

"Mr. Fetch, I consider your anecdote very good," said Mrs. Johnstone. "But is it true that you have ever boasted of your undertaker?"

Lancy not being ready, Marjorie answered, —

"It's true, mother, that Fetch signed a paper securing his funeral to a particular undertaker, and he received a small sum down for doing it."

"That shows Fetch's frugal mind," said Don John.

"My cousin Fanny is very saving — very frugal too," said Lancy, as Fetch. "In fact, I often tell her she is even mean. I said to her only yesterday, 'Fanny Fetch, you are so selfish, that if the whole sea was yours, you'd still charge twopence a bucket for salt water.' Mother," continued Lancy in his own character, "the most disagreeable thing about this game is that when we have invented anything funny, we can't find an opportunity to bring it in. Now, Don John said yesterday, when Freddy was tootletooing in the garden with his fife and pretending to drill Mary, ' " I always adored the military," as the young lady-elephant said when she heard her lover trumpeting in the rice swamp.' But you know if we were to wait for a year, nothing would happen to enable us to bring that in naturally."

" I am afraid, my boy, this sorrow of yours is common to all wits; yet you see you have managed to bring it in ! "

CHAPTER XII.

ABOUT that lodger.
We often think we are of great importance to certain people ; that they must be thinking of us and our affairs, that they watch our actions and shape their course accordingly. In general it is not so ; we are quite mistaken.

The young Johnstones and Lancy never had any such ideas as regarded the lodger ; never supposed that she walked up and down the little path through the fields between the wood that skirted their garden and " the houses " on purpose to catch a glimpse of them ; never thought that when she was not taking this monotonous exercise, she was often peeping out between the small damask curtains of her so-called parlor, which had been the cobbler's front kitchen, in case they should pass by ; never thought anything of the kind ; and they too were mistaken. She thought of hardly anything else but of them and their doings, specially of one of them. But through the bushy tangle of the wood they could always see whether she was in the field, and so surely as she was they kept out of the way.

What a bother that lodger is, Don John would say, when he would notice her trailing her fine flounces among the buttercups. She was far too gay too look otherwise than vulgar in such a country solitude, and if there was anything pathetic in her longing to see them, and in their always thwarting her, they did not know it.

Sometimes, if it was hot and she was tired, she would bring out a folding camp-stool and sit upon it in the shade of the wood, knitting. She was come from

London for the sake of country air, so she said. Nobody at the house thought of inquiring her name, or cared at all about her excepting that the young Johnstones wished her out of their way.

At the houses, when they begged to ask what they should call her, meaning " What is your name, ma'am ? " she answered, —

" You can call me ' the lady.' "

But they did not.

They called her " the lodger."

They all knew in spite of her shining gold watch and chains, and satins and rings, her handsome silks and her fastidious ways, that she was not what they were pleased to consider a lady, by which they meant, if they had known how to use the English language correctly, a gentlewoman.

Those women who have an undoubted right to the title of lady, and yet are without that culture, that style, that consideration which would enable them to pass muster as gentlewomen, are always very unpopular among the rustic poor. The lodger, of course, had no right to the title of lady ; and because she wanted to pass for a gentlewoman, which she was not either, they gave her even less than was her due.

She was rich ; free with her money ; not difficult to please ; moderately civil to her hosts ; but they rewarded all this by disparaging comments.

" She was not a lady born, not she ! She's not like Mrs. Johnstone ; but she's well enough, and she pays her way."

But an important day was approaching ; a friend's birthday.

The young Johnstones collected a quantity of excellent prog, and bought several presents, among others a box-iron and a Brighton reading lamp.

The two boys were allowed to have the pony-carriage and go into the town in the morning to fetch home these things. " We girls," said Marjorie, half enviously, " are never trusted to drive by ourselves."

" I should think not, indeed ! " said Lancy ; " girls

must always be properly attended," and he ran off into
the wood, where the good things were being collected
preparatory to being carried off to Mrs. Clarboy's cottage.

"How good they smell," said little Mary. "Choco-
late — and O! toffee — and tarts, and muffins; what
lots of money you and Lancy have. Oh, Don John, I
wish I was a boy!"

Don John as purveyor-general was looking on.

"It's lucky," remarked Lancy, in reply, "that being
a girl is not infectious. If I thought I should catch it
of you, Mary, I would never come near you or any other
girl, any more."

"Of course you would n't," said Mary, with conviction.

"But you two little wretches are always thinking
about eating," said Lancy, rather contemptuously. "It
makes me feel that if we did our duty by you, we
should not think of letting you go to these tea-parties."

"Oh, Lancy!"

"Yes, it does; most likely you'll never be allowed
to go to any one but this. Now be off, Button-nose,
and you too, Freddy, and fetch the other parcels."

"You are always hard on the kids," said Don John.
"I rather like to hear them talk their talk, and play
their little rigs in holiday-time."

"But they bother one," said Lancy. "And you
really did encourage them yesterday, till there was no
bearing their *cheek*."

Then Don John burst forth in these noticeable
words. —

"'It's always a graceful thing to unbend,' as the
goldstick-in-waiting said when he balanced a pepper-
mint-drop on his nose, as he stood behind the queen's
chair."

"Charlotte," shouted Lancy, "here! Don John has
broken out in a fresh place; come and write this down,
and stick it in the minutes."

"That's a good one," said Charlotte, "but I don't
think the goldstick does stand there."

" It does n't signify," said Don John, "everyone of you now, who reads the minutes, will be obliged to think of him as if he did!"

" Tell us a Sam Weller, too," said Button-nose, otherwise Mary, coming back with the parcels.

" We like Sam Weller better than Fetch," observed Freddy.

" You 're not to interrupt your betters. Charlotte has n't done writing yet. Yes, I 'll tell you one presently about — "

" Yes, Don John, *about?* "

"About something to eat. I am happy to see, Button-nose, that you can blush. When I was in the town this morning, and saw all the shops, the butchers', the bakers', the pastry-cooks', and the rest, I sighed deeply."

" Oh ! "

" And said what should we be without these. Man is made of what he eats. ' This is the stuff our heroes are made of,' as the Prince of Wales said when he peeped into the Eton boys' ' sock ' shop." Fetch, who was listening, burst into tears and said, "Alas ! "

" Why, Don John? "

" Because he thought it was so good of the Prince of Wales to take notice that we are made of what we eat, and because he remembered that asses are too."

" Is that all the story? "

" It is ; now let the procession be formed."

Don John marched first, a somewhat thickset boy, broad-shouldered, fair-haired, with light eyebrows and lashes, a martial walk, and a sweet-tempered expression ; Lancy came next. They cut across the lodger's path, so that she paused and waited a moment. She looked at Lancy with all her eyes. He was not so big as Don John, he had fine brown hair, pleasant blue eyes, a general air of roguery, and an elastic walk. Lancy was brandishing the box-iron, and singing at the top of his voice. Then came the four girls, all small for their years. Charlotte very pretty, the others not pretty, but sweet and rather graceful ; Freddy brought up the rear.

Lancy was rather a handsome boy, the lodger saw
his face well for the first time, and a perfectly unreasonable pang shot through her heart as she observed the
utter indifference of his manner towards her. How
should it be otherwise. She dragged herself on to
Salisbury's cottage, trembling ; while Mrs. Clarboy shed
tears of pleasure, as peeping through the blinds she
saw her guests coming.

She only wiped them away just in time to receive
their congratulations.

" Well, and I 'm sure I 'm obliged to you, young
ladies and gentlemen, more than I can say ; and to
think of you always knowing the very things I should
like to buy myself, if I could afford them. You 'll stay
to tea with Jenny and me, now won't you? It 's but a
loaf of bread we 've got in the house, and a bit of butter."

Mrs. Clarboy always offered hospitality in these words,
and always feigned not to see the parcels of eatables till
they were actually presented to her.

"Well, I never did ! such a noble lot of cakes, and all
so good and acceptable," she exclaimed, "on the present occasion. And there now ! I priced that very box-
iron yesterday was a week, when Jenny and I walked
into the town. You bought it of poor Robinson's widow,
now did n't you, sir? "

" Yes," said Lancy ; " she was selling off."

" ' Ah,' says I to her by way of being neighborly, for
I knew she was going to *settle*, ' I hear Cupid's been at
his old tricks again.' ' Yes,' says she, ' I 'm going to
marry the butcher.' "

With talk like this the time sped till the cloth was
laid, and all the good things were set out, and then
just as the tea was poured out there was a light tap at
the door.

Mrs. Clarboy knew it well, but vexation kept her
silent, and Lancy jumping up went and opened the
door.

The lodger !

" I would n't intrude on any account," said the lodger,
a little hurriedly. " I was only just going to pass up-

stairs to my room," and she moved a few steps forward, and then came to a sudden pause, and turned excessively pale.

" Ma'am," exclaimed Mrs. Clarboy, " don't you feel yourself well?"

" You 're all of a tremble, ma'am," said Miss Jenny.

" Oh," sighed the lodger, " let me sit down just for a minute."

A chair was set for her. She was a fat young woman, extremely fair, and now as pale as a lily.

" If you would n't mind letting me sit a few minutes and taking no notice of me," she began.

Marjorie in the meantime brought her a cup of tea, and Lancy handed her a biscuit. Even Lancy noticed her face when she looked up at him, it was full of entreaty, full of love. What does she want? thought the boy. What a bother that she should have come to spoil our fun.

She began to sip her tea, and such a rapture of tenderness made all her nerves thrill and her pulses tingle, that she quite forgot to consider her position as an unbidden guest. Don John sat full in view, with his side towards her. She could look at him at her ease, she felt almost repelled by him, a sense of conscious dislike towards him, as having been the cause — innocent enough, certainly — of a great deal of misery to her made her shrink from his talk, tremble at the sound of his laugh, and feel offended and hurt when Lancy spoke to him.

How familiar Lancy was with them all, commanding and admonishing the two little ones, making fun of the girls, arguing with Don John. " And what a real young gentleman he is," she felt with tender love and pride. " I could never have brought him up wherever I had put him to school, to talk and to look like that. Oh, that I should long to kiss him, and may n't; it 's hard."

Just as the tea-drinking was all but over, one of the girls said to Mrs. Clarboy that if she had done reading a certain book, which she had lent to her, her mother rather wanted it, and she would take it home.

10

Then the lodger with somewhat affected flurry was shocked to think that she had got it. She had quite done with it. She would fetch it.

"Don't trouble yourself," said Lancy. "I can go."

"It's on the table, sir, I think, in my parlor," said the lodger.

Lancy and Don John said they were going down first to the brook to look after a hedgehog, and after that the book should be fetched.

They departed, and went whooping to the brookside, their two dogs after them; and the lodger, quietly rising, went out the back way into the little kitchen garden and so over the little low fence, not two feet high, which divided this from Salisbury's garden.

She hardly knew what she wanted to do — surely not to say anything to Lancy — no, she thought not. No, it could only be to look at him while he was finding the book. Stop! the Salisburys were both out, but the least little noise in her parlor warned her that Lancy had already come in. There was a minute window, consisting but of two small panes let into the wall, between the front and back room. A thin muslin curtain was hanging before it. The lodger, trembling with a pleased agitation, stepped up to it, and through a narrow opening in the muslin looked and saw — what?

At first astonishment made her incredulous. What was he doing?

He was standing almost with his back to her, and gazing, as if fascinated, at a small desk which stood on a table under the window; her keys were dangling from its lock, and it seemed as if he meant to open it.

No, he turned away, took the book, and with a boyish whoop sped to the door, then all in a moment he turned on his heels and — what a sight for her! she saw him go back to the desk, and turn the key, — and lift it, — and look in.

He dropped the book on the floor, and with his now disengaged hand lifted a little drawer, while he held the desk open with the other. There was a small canvas bag in it. She saw him shut the desk, saw him slip certain gold coins into his palm, then in one instant return them to the bag which he put in his pocket, and let the desk fall to. Then he darted out of the house, taking the book with him, and leaving the door of her parlor wide open.

She stood trembling, but not now with tenderness so much as with distress.

Through the open door she saw him run down again to the brook; and shocked and amazed, she stepped back again through the garden and into Mrs. Clarboy's house.

She crept in pale as a lily, all her joy and excitement over, she sat down in her former place, and scarcely heard a word that passed about her.

Presently the two boys came in again, Don John had a dog under each arm, Lancy had the book. She looked earnestly at him, as it seemed to Lancy, appealingly. For a moment his guilty mind appeared to assure him that she must know, and he felt ready to sink into the floor with fright and shame. Oh, to have the last ten minutes over again, and put that money back.

But in another moment his better sense, as he falsely thought, came back to him; it was quite impossible that she could know. He certainly had not been one minute in her room; and he had left her door wide open, so that the inhabitants of six houses had easy access to it.

He was a bad boy, guilty, and utterly unprincipled; but he had not done this out of mere wantonness in theft and greed of gold. No, Lancy knew what it was now to be in bondage to a boy who had found him out, and who was always threatening him with betrayal. He had taken ten sovereigns. To this boy two of them had to go, as the price of his silence. "And if I am suspected," thought poor Lancy, "but it's not likely, I'll run away."

As the young Johnstones and Lancy retired, the lodger went upstairs to her bedroom, threw herself on her bed, and wept. She knew the door of Salisbury's cottage was wide open, that he and his wife were gone to the town, and were not likely to be back till dusk, and she knew why he, whom she called "her dear boy, her only dear, her precious Lancy," had left it so. He had not only taken the money, but he was more than willing that some innocent person should be accused of the theft.

"Do they keep him so short of money, that he cannot forbear to take mine?" was her foolish unreasonable thought. "Oh, I must, I will speak to him now. Tell him I forgive him! Tell him it shall all be his, and I have plenty for us both. Oh, my Lancy, you are breaking my heart!"

The next morning, Mrs. Johnstone sent Lancy over to the town on an errand. What could be more opportune? He got a post-office order, and sent his young tyrant the two sovereigns. She had given him a shilling and told him to get his lunch there, for he and Don John were to meet Mr. Johnstone at the station, and walk over from it with him. Lancy had three or four hours therefore to spare, and he wandered about in the little town and amused himself as well as he could.

It was market-day; Lancy, as any other boy might have done, sauntered about in the market, bought a few early jennetings, looked at the gingerbread stall, kept his dog in order, inspected some young dormice, and declined to purchase, saying that he had not enough money. Nobody looking at him would have supposed that he was a boy who had anything on his mind, or that he dreaded the moment when he was to go home and walk with his adopted father through Salisbury's field.

But that time came at last; Lancy, with Don John, went at the appointed time to the railway station; Mr. Johnstone, at the expected moment, stepped out of a carriage, and they all proceeded home through the field.

And there just as he turned towards his own house, skirting the wood, the lodger saw them.

He was walking with somewhat of a martial uprightness, coming on steadily and straightforward; Don John walked at his right side, with precisely the same carriage. The two were talking together; Lancy now a step or two in front, now behind, meandered about them with a boyish gait.

" Who is that person?" said Donald Johnstone, when he caught sight of the trailing skirts.

" Oh, that's ' the lodger,'" said Lancy.

" Humph!" said Donald Johnstone.

" Father," exclaimed Don John, " Salisbury's house was robbed last night, did you know —"

" Robbed!" said Mr. Johnstone, " why, I should not have thought the worthy soul possessed anything worth stealing."

" No; but it was their lodger's things that were taken. It seems she left their door open last night, and I think it was open all night, by what I hear."

Lancy's terror was intense; and Don John spoke so coolly that it was evident he had no suspicions.

" It is to be hoped she did not accuse the poor honest people," said Mr. Johnstone.

" Oh, no. She had left the keys dangling in her desk; she felt sure, she said, that nobody in the houses was dishonest."

" That's a queer story," said Donald Johnstone, " Who ever passes there in the night?" and he went marching on; while she, afraid to turn too sharply out of his path, lest she should attract more observation, came on, hoping he would not look at her.

He would not have done, but just as they met, both the boys lifted their hats. He had not been aware that they had the slightest acquaintance with this person. He looked up with momentary keenness of attention, the boys, one on each side of him, went on a step or two; he came to a dead stand, and she saw in a moment that he knew her.

Twelve years' foreign travel, plenty of money, fashionable clothes, had not so much changed Maria Jane Collingwood that she could pass the scrutiny of those keen eyes unknown. He gave her no greeting of any sort, but after his involuntary pause went on again, and the boys lingering slightly he was soon between them.

CHAPTER XIII.

DONALD JOHNSTONE walked on to his house and said not another word.

Maria Jane Collingwood in his field — *the lodger* whom he had heard his children talk of. He had recognized her instantly; to what end could she possibly have come there that did not bode disquiet, if not disaster to him and his.

He walked straight to his wife's room, and there remembered that he was to entertain a party at dinner that night.

Mrs. Johnstone was just dressed, her maid had stepped back to survey her. The two elder girls, who loved to assist at their mother's toilet, were tying up some flowers.

Tall, upright as a wand, slender, and placid she stood. He looked fixedly at her, and sighed.

"Father," said Naomi, "mother has got our favorite gown on. Does n't she look sweet?"

He continued to look at her, but said nothing.

"It's so thick and soft," said Marjorie, feeling the folds of the satin; "and just the color of cream — and, mother, these roses are exactly the same color — and look at their little soft brown leaves."

The mother took her bouquet and smiled at their enthusiasm.

"You look well, my star," said her husband. He felt that there was no time now to say anything to her, and he hastened off to his dressing-room.

There, while he dressed, he saw the fat little woman, who had been the plague of his life, waddling along the path through his field, and he hated the sight of her.

He trembled with irritation and impatience, for nothing could be done. He must entertain his guests, and he absolutely must leave his boys and girls to wander all about the fields that evening, though she might have come there on purpose to say to them what he most wished them not to hear.

His wife's unconsciousness calmed him a little, however. They were alone together for half a minute in the drawing-room before the first guests entered.

" Estelle," he began, " I met that woman this evening whom the children call *the lodger*. I wish they had not seen anything of her."

A tentative remark. She answered with perfect serenity.

" Oh, yes, my dear — I wish it too — but there is no harm done ; and I have told them not to go into the field at all, but to keep in our woods and garden this evening."

" No harm done ? " he repeated in a tone of inquiry.

" I meant that there is no reason they should not associate a little with the honest poor ; but this person, a vulgar, second-rate woman, as I gather, is just the sort of creature we should like to guard them from."

" Ah ! exactly so," he answered ; and added mentally, while the first guests were announced, " if we can."

" Well, I hope there is no harm done," he reflected ; " and yet if that woman had wished to say anything to either of the boys, surely she might have found opportunity to say it by this time. It must be a month, or nearly so, since I first heard them mention her."

He made rather an inattentive host that evening ; he was nervous, and sometimes absent, but not half as much so as he would have been if he could have known what was coming to pass.

Lancy's punishment had begun.

The young people, while their elders dined, were having their supper in the playroom. It suited Lancy to appear to be in excellent spirits. All the girls began to talk of the supposed robbery, and then, frightened as he was, he had to feign interest and curiosity.

" Does the lodger mean to have a policeman come ? " asked Don John.

Lancy turned cold and sick.

" I don't know," answered Charlotte, who had been sent to Mrs. Clarboy's house with a message about some needlework ; " Mrs. Clarboy and Jenny were both crying when I got there. They said they were wretched for fear they should be suspected — and so were the Salisburys ; and yet — "

" Well ? " said Lancy.

" They said they wished they had never seen her, and yet, when Salisbury came in the morning to break it to her, that the door had been open all night, and her keys were dangling in her desk, where, of course, she never could have been so careless as to leave them, she said, ' I know I have been robbed ; I know all about it.' "

" Extraordinary ! " exclaimed Don John.

" She too had been crying bitterly they say."

Lancy was so giddy with fright that if the least suspicion concerning him had crossed Don John's mind, and he had looked at him, he must have discovered all. As it was, dismissing the contemned lodger from his mind, he said, —

" Well now, Charlotte — *the minutes* — call in Fetch and let 's have some fun."

How Lancy got through the next hour or two he never could remember afterwards. He knew he was frightened, miserable, guilty ; he knew that in order to satisfy his tyrant he had risked and lost the happiness of all his future life.

He gave Button-nose a kiss when she was going to bed. It seemed to him almost for the first time in his life that he loved these so-called brothers and sisters very much — that no fun would be so well worth having if Don John was not there to share it with him ; that if father and mother found out what he had done, he never would be so happy any more.

Why had he done it? At least he need not have taken so much. If he had contented himself with the sum that he so sorely needed, the lodger might have thought herself mistaken, when counting over her money she found less than she expected. And, oh, why had he taken the bag. And now one and another went off to bed. Lancy was left to the last; he wrote a letter and cried over it, and at length he too stole into his little room, and, holding the letter in his hand, sat down at the foot of his bed. The letter was full of lies — lying came just as naturally to poor Lancy as thieving, and he could already do both with a practised hand.

Sometimes when people think intensely of us it makes us think of them. Was that the reason why, in the middle of the night, Mrs. Johnstone had a singular dream?

She dreamed that she saw Lancy sitting on the foot of her bed in his long white night-gown; the moonlight was streaming in, so that every lock of his brown hair, every line of his features was distinctly visible as he sat with his side-face towards her, and he had some coins in his hand which he was counting and laying out upon the quilt.

She thought she spoke gently to him, thinking that he had been walking in his sleep. " Lancy, Lancy," she said, and then he turned, and looked earnestly at her and at his adopted father. She thought he whispered in a mournful tone, " Oh, mother and father, oh, mother and father ! " still sitting on the bed ; and then she thought he went into the moonbeam and that he walked in it through the open window, and so on and on in the air till he was lost in a cloud.

With a start she awoke, the moon had gone down, all was perfectly dark and perfectly still. Whenever anything aroused in her a solicitude about one of the children, the feeling soon spread till it had embraced them all. She prayed for Lancy as she laid awake thinking of this dream, and then she prayed for all the others. At last sleep came to her again, and she did not awake till it was nigh day. Lancy was gone.

He sat on his little bed a long time, reflecting, and fearing, and repenting, but he saw no opening for confession.

To confess such a deed as he had done, even to Don John, was past his courage, because, to have any effect, it must bring other confessions in its train.

Could he possibly put back the eight sovereigns which remained, and having done so could he stay in his happy home, and brave all the talk he should hear on this subject without betraying himself.

He hoped, he thought he could. A flattering fancy showed him a picture of himself stealing up between the hollyhocks, softly undoing the casement-hasp, and slipping in the money. They would not hear.

Something like genuine repentance made him sigh and sob as he stole downstairs, got away into the garden, and crept round the bushes into the wood. The stars, which moonlight left visible, looked so bright and so near, that they seemed to be prying at him.

Lancy walked down the wood-path till he came opposite to Salisbury's cottage. He was full of tremor and fear — night-beetles bumped against his face; a great white woolly moth sailed up smelling of musk, little mice ran across the path, and all of these startled him. He passed between the bushes. There was no light burning within; the moonlight struck the little casement-panes without, and made them glitter. He pushed his finger into his waistcoat pocket, and felt the eight sovereigns in the bag. The great experiment was soon to be made. He stole nearer, constantly thinking of how Don John had done that very thing before; surely as he wished to do well — good would come of it; surely he should be helped to do what was right.

The lodger did not really know " all about it," as she had said. She could only have meant that she strongly suspected some person, the wrong person; and if he could only put so much of the money back nobody would believe her story. He must, he would risk everything, for he was lost and ruined, if once investigations were made.

His heart beat high, his breath came in little pants, he was quivering with agitation, in which was far more hope than fear. He crept on behind the bushes at the further side of the brook. It was nearly midnight when he stole across the narrow field and risked several times being seen, so sore was his longing to get close to the casement window.

He reached it at last, and his hope was quenched. He laid his cheek against the glass, and put his fingers on the fastening. The curtains hung a few inches apart, and to his alarm he heard soft whispering voices within. Salisbury and his wife — perhaps a policeman, who could tell — were sitting up ; evidently on the watch.

He edged himself back among the hollyhocks, and quite calmly went away by the back of the house. His last chance had failed, his home was forfeit ; go he must.

He hardened his heart — had he not tried his very best to repair his fault ! — he must now keep the eight sovereigns, that was manifest. He supposed all that money would last a long time, and then when he had nothing left, why, he could go to sea.

In the meantime he had always heard that the best place to hide oneself in was London.

Lancy was young for his years, he was strangely undecided, he had often longed to see the world, and wished he could go to sea. But he loved comfort more than adventure, and to a certain extent he loved the parents who had adopted him, and the brothers and sisters with whom he had been brought up.

He thought he would wait another hour before he started ; he went and took leave of his rabbits, and of old Die, it was a sore wrench to leave them behind. He would stay for this one hour in the church porch, surely something would turn up — surely he was not going away forever ?

The shadows were long now the moon was southing. He could steal along by the hedge and not be seen, and he came and leaned against the old wall of the church tower and shed some miserable, contrite tears. But there were strange creakings and groanings up aloft. He could hardly believe that the old clock in the tower was responsible for them all, and then there seemed to be running up and down and jumping in the body of the church. He turned very cold, something appeared to fall; a squeak almost human followed; in the day-time he might have thought of rats, but now his mind was on more awful things. The clock "gave warning," it was an awful sound — a new sound — and when midnight began to strike, his guilty conscience drove him forth as if the brazen echoes were proclaiming his guilt to all. He ran away in good earnest, glad and almost thankful to go.

About seven o'clock on a sultry evening a decent-looking woman was laying the cloth on a small round table in a moderately clean and very scantily-furnished parlor in London.

Now and then she glanced curiously at a fine boy, who looked very tired, and was sleepily watching her operations.

"He can hardly keep his eyes open," was her thought; "what ever shall I do?"

Lancy — for Lancy it was — had walked during the previous night to within four miles of London; and then a fit of indecision had come upon him, and he had lingered about, losing his way, and lamenting his fate till it was high noon, then finding himself close to the railway by which Mr. Johnstone came up to London every day, he walked across the country from it till an omnibus overtook him, and getting in he coiled himself up in a corner. It did not matter in the least where he was going, for he himself was not bound to any place in particular. He dozed, and ate gingerbread, and in course of time the omnibus stopped at the King's Cross Station, the terminus by which he was accustomed to enter London.

"Father" never came up at that time of day; but yet Lancy did not much relish finding himself at the foot of Pentonville Hill, a locality so familiar to him.

He dived into a side street, and observed almost at once that nearly every house had a card in some window, or over the door, setting forth that lodgings were to let in it.

He remembered that he must sleep somewhere, and

if he went to a hotel he should be far more liable to discovery than in a quiet street such as this.

So Lancy took some cheap lodgings for a week, a tiny room called a drawing-room, with a tiny bedroom behind it. He was tired and hungry, but he was not equal to the task of ordering dinner, because his landlady seemed to be examining him and cogitating over him.

He went out and subsisted on refections of buns, tarts, and fruit. At last he came back to his rooms, and his landlady helped him by asking when he would have his supper, and what he would like. He did not know what to have. She told him, and requested money to pay for the various items, looking curiously at him while he took out his well-filled purse and gave her what she wanted.

He had felt very forlorn during the afternoon. There was a little bird shop not a hundred yards from the station, to which he and Don John always paid a visit when they came to London. The station was not visible from it, and Lancy had felt irresistibly drawn to it. There were squirrels as well as birds, dormice, young tortoises, and goldfish. There you might buy a cock redbreast for sixpence; a chaffinch for twopence, and various other English birds at moderate prices.

Lancy had laid out a small sum in the purchase of two green linnets in cruelly small cages, a bag of seed, and a little tortoise, in a lidless wooden box, lined with a damp sod.

His landlady, having laid the cloth, brought him up some mutton chops, potatoes, tea, and bread and butter, and left him. Lancy had never in his life been so glad of a comfortable meal. She told him to ring when he wanted her to clear away.

She was a little bustling, clean woman, motherly and observant. Her eyebrows had a peculiar faculty for raising themselves. Lancy knew as well as possible that she was making observations on him, and that frequent sensations of surprise made these eyebrows go up into her forehead as two black arches, which left her large eyelids full of little veins, to droop over her inquisitive brown eyes, which for all their penetration made him feel a certain confidence in her. He thought she was a kind, good woman.

When she came in to clear away, he had set the two cages on the table, and was shaping two small wooden perches for his miserable little thralls. He evidently did not wish to look at her, and having nothing else to do was whiling away his time by feeding and attending to these new pets.

As he did not speak to her, she made an opening for herself by saying, " You'll have to pay for the use of the castors, sir."

Lancy looked up.

" For the mustard, and pepper, and vinegar inside 'em, I mean," she explained.

" How much? " asked Lancy, a little uneasily.

" Ninepence a week."

On hearing of such a small sum, the interest and uneasiness of her young lodger immediately subsided; he pushed the perch into one of the cages, and when the linnet had ended its distressful fluttering she said in a clear, decided tone, —

" Not much used to taking lodgings, I reckon? "

Lancy said nothing.

" And your luggage, sir, when might that be coming? "

" I have no luggage," answered Lancy, blushing.

" Left it at home, I reckon? " and before Lancy had time to reflect his answer had slipped out, " Yes."

She folded up her cloth. " They're in a fine taking about you *there* by this time, I'll go bail," she observed.

" I don't know what you mean," said Lancy, flushing up.

" Just as if I didn't know as well as if you'd told me that you'd run away from home ; but now here you are as safe as can be, and you've got at least a whole week to think it over."

" I don't know what you mean," repeated Lancy.

" Why, I mean that you've paid for these lodgings for a week — and you can turn things over in your mind. They're fond of you, I'll be bound — you can turn *that* over." She lifted up her tray. "I have a son that ran away to sea three years ago come Michaelmas; I'll assure you he has bitterly enough repented it ever since, poor fellow."

If Lancy had not supposed himself to be utterly beyond fear of detection he would not have answered at all; as it was, wishing to shirk further discussion, and so confirming her in her thoughts, he said he was sleepy and should now go to bed, which he did, and in spite of uncertainty as to his future, sorrow for his fault, and for the parting from all he held dear, he slept as soundly and as sweetly as the most innocent boy in London.

It was ten o'clock before he had finished his breakfast the next morning, and he ordered his dinner, which was to be at five o'clock, with the air of one who so fully intended to eat it, that his landlady was sure she should see him again, and hoped he might be in a better humor for answering questions than he was at present.

And yet, as he was about to go out, she did hazard a question.

"And where might you be going now, sir?"

"To the Polytechnic," he answered carelessly, and off he set.

"To the Polytechnic, why, you poor innocent, misguided child — for child you are, and loves childish pleasure still — what ever am I to do for you! Who would think it?" While the landlady said this she looked after Lancy as he walked down the street, and her eyebrows went up almost to the roots of her hair.

Yes, Lancy was actually going to the Polytechnic; he had nothing on earth to do. "Pepper's ghosts" just then were all in their glory; he had money enough, as he supposed, to last nearly three weeks. Of course, he should not go to sea till the last minute. He and Don John had been trying to produce Pepper's ghosts by means of a magic lantern and two looking-glasses. He should stop there the whole day, and to-morrow (unless he altered his mind and went to see the beasts feed at the Zoölogical Gardens) to-morrow he would go to the docks,

To say that Lancy was happy at the Polytechnic
would be to make a mistake ; but he certainly had intervals of enjoyment, when he forgot the past and the
future, and puzzled himself over " Pepper's ghosts," and
afterwards listened to a lecture, which was enlivened by
various chemical experiments, that made noise enough
to delight (and deafen) any boy of average tastes.

He came home, ate his dinner, and played with his
bird and tortoise. He was more cunning than he had
been the previous night. His landlady got nothing at
all out of him. He went to bed, but did not sleep so
well. He must not spend all his money, he now thought,
before he had even decided whether he would go to sea
or not. There might be an outfit to buy, and if it cost
anything like as much as his clothes did at school, he
had not half enough money for it even now, unless he
sold his watch.

Yes, he must go to the docks. He ordered his dinner as before and set out. Where should he get a cheap
map of London, for he had not a notion how to get to
the docks? He sauntered on till he reached the Gower
Street Station of the Metropolitan Railway ; for a few
pence, as he knew he could go a long way to the east-
ward, he took a ticket and descended. Then, since a
merciful Providence had ordained that, in spite of his
crime, he should yet have a chance of well-doing, he
found that he had ten minutes to wait, and that on a
dark, dingy book-stall there were maps and the daily
papers ; he asked for a map of London, and while the
selling-boy dived under the back of the stall he glanced
at the rows of *Times* newspapers, *Standards*, *Telegraphs*,
&c., &c., and his eye carelessly ran over the first advertisement on the top of the second column of the
Times.

" To L. A. — L., it is all discovered ; but yet there
is time. L., only one person in this world knows. Will
you trust that one, and all shall be forgiven and made
right again? Do not throw away your home and your
prospects. Trust me, and come to the Euston Hotel.
Write your own name on a card, and send it up to No.
16."

Lancy read the whole of this before it occurred to him that the initials were his own. With a start his eye then passed on to the *Standard*, and there was the same advertisement to L. A. He was instantly sure that the message was to him. How could he doubt that, any more than Don John had put it in.

But where had the money come from? A trembling seized Lancy. He began to be sure that this going to sea was a horrid and unbearable thing; that to give up his home and his family would bring misery and ruin. He had more than five pounds in his pocket: if Don John had contrived to borrow the money here was something towards it, and he would sell his watch besides. Oh, to be at home again; oh, how sweet the promise that all should be set right. "I don't want the map," cried Lancy, as the boy came forth; but he snatched the paper, threw down a shilling, and ran out into the road and on towards Euston Square, never daring to stop lest fear should get the better of him and he should change his mind.

———◆———

CHAPTER XIV.

THE Euston Hotel.
Lancy reached it, got in front of the railway terminus, and looked right and left with a longing hope that he might see Don John glancing out at some window. His heart beat wildly, as if all the life he had was thumping at his left side. His hands trembled, his lips were white. What if after all there was some mistake!

But what mistake could there be?

Don John had written obscurely, but that was because he was afraid of being found out. Lancy had written a letter to his adopted parents, setting forth that he longed to see the world, and so — he had run away. But Don John would have had time now to put that and the stealing of the ten sovereigns together. He

11

had no doubt jumped to the right conclusion, and would save him ; but Lancy did not relish having to face him. Whenever he had committed any peculations, it was Don John who was sick with shame and rage, not only with fear of detection, which was what Lancy felt, but with horror at the deed itself.

He had written his own name on a card, and though he was full of hope, yet the dread of what Don John would say, and of what he might have risked in order to bring about this interview made Lancy tremble.

" Is there a young gentleman waiting here for me? " he asked of the porter.

" What is the young gentleman's name? " was the not unnatural answer.

Lancy hesitated, sank into the one chair which graced the vestibule, and gave it, " Master Donald Johnstone."

A young woman, who was seated in a kind of glass case, began to examine some books.

" No, sir," she shortly answered, " we have no such name here."

Perhaps Don John had not dared to give his own name. Lancy now felt that he must follow the directions given.

" I was asked to give this card, and inquire for No. 16."

" No. 16! Ah, yes, sir, that's it," exclaimed a waiter, starting forward almost with alacrity, and taking the card. " Yes, sir ; follow me, if you please."

Lancy rose to follow, but slowly. It seemed to him that the young person who had searched the books looked at him with amusement, and that the porter at the door was observant too. He was taken upstairs and along some almost interminable passages ; then a door was opened ; he was announced, — " Mr. Lancelot Aird," and turning from a table in the window, and coming slowly on as if not to startle him, he saw, not Don John — but, *the lodger.*

" There's some mistake! " exclaimed Lancy aghast, and starting back.

"No, there's no mistake," she answered, looking at him with that never-to-be-forgotten expression in her eyes. "No; 't was I that advertised, — Lancy!"

Something indescribable in her face and in her manner astonished him almost to the point of making him forget why he had come.

She had passed between him and the door. She leaned against it, and held the handle, while he sank into a chair.

"Lancy," she began again, and said no more: The silence that followed was so full of wonderment to Lancy that no words, he felt, could add to it whatever those words might be. And yet they did give him a kind of shock, she said them with such difficulty and such distress.

"I saw you take it," she whispered, after that pause. "Lancy, I saw you open my desk and steal the ten sovereigns; and I — I am as miserable as you are."

Lancy looked at her as she still stood supporting herself against the door. He was subdued by her paleness, by the distress and misery in her voice, and the yearning in her face. He burst into tears.

O, it appeared so long before she spoke again!

"I want to save you. Do you know why?"

"Do I know why?" he repeated, almost in a whisper. "No."

He looked at her, and his heart seemed to whisper to him what this meant. He put out both his hands as if to entreat her not to come nearer to him yet.

"I took those lodgings in Salisbury's house that I might see you — only you," she continued.

"Why should you care about me?" he burst out. "I don't know you. What are you to me?"

"Your mother."

Yes! He was almost sure now that this was what he had foreseen — this was what he had known she would say.

He trembled from head to foot; the ten sovereigns were far away now, lost in a wild whirl of disaster, and grief, and change.

"I can't love any other mother than that one at home," he said bitterly.

She answered, in a piercing tone of distress and remonstrance, "But you have run away from her, my Lancy. And could she forgive you if she knew all?"

"I cannot say."

"But I do know — and I do forgive — and I will forget. Only repent, my son, my only dear; or you'll break my heart."

"I have repented. Oh, forgive me, and let me go! I have left them all, and lost them. But —"

"But you cannot take me instead. I know it. You cannot love me all on a sudden."

Lancy was too much astonished and agitated to arrange the many thoughts which were soon to press for utterance. Only one came to the front, and he uttered it.

"It is late in my life for you to ask me to love you for the first time."

"Yes," she sighed.

She stood pale and mournful of aspect and leaned against the door. He knew that her distress for his fault was overpowering the joy of recovering him. He revolved in his mind the circumstance, and vaguely gazed about him at the commonplace room, the commonplace woman only distinguished from many others by the over-richness of her dress, and the fineness of her gold ornaments. Nothing helped him.

And she said she was his mother! Which was best? to run away to the docks and see what ships were like, and make trial of the hardships of the sea; or to bind her to secrecy, and let her save him as she had said?

It was easy, this last plan. It was a respite; but he felt instinctively, for he was not calm enough for any decided thoughts — he felt that to run away bore with it the blessed possibility of coming home again and being forgiven. But to stay as her son was to give up the home, he could not have both. Then he looked at her, and for the moment was even more sorry for her than for himself. And he rose and came towards her, for this Lancy was not always to act basely and with un-kindness. He dried away his tears.

" But I know very well that you love me now," he said, with her last word still ringing in his ears. " You would like to kiss me, would n't you? " and he bent his fresh young cheek to her lips.

She kissed him, and with what joy and gratitude no words can tell. Holding him for a moment round the neck, — " Promise you won't run away from me," she entreated.

" No, I will not." Then astonishment getting the better of his emotion, he went on, " You — no, I need not fear that you will betray me. But if you are my mother, how comes it that my own — I mean my other father and mother — do not know you? "

" Mr. Johnstone does know," she answered, sobbing. " When I met him in the fields I saw that he recognized me. So then you know nothing at all about me, Lancy? "

She trembled. She was seated on a chair next to him now, had taken his hand, and was pressing it to her heart. He scarcely cared about this, or noticed it. He perceived that he was saved, but then he was lost ! This mother who had found him would want to keep him, and she could never be admitted as an equal in the adopted mother's home.

" I know nothing but that your name is Collingwood," he answered, with a sigh.

" Oh yes ! my name is Collingwood. You know nothing more, my son? Think."

She looked intently at him, and he added, —

" They said that my father's name was Aird, and after his death that you married again." It's quicker than lightning. I have no time to think, was his re-flection, and he held up his hands to his head.

" Yes, but nothing more? " she asked.

" Nothing, but that you never wrote to me, which we thought was strange."

" We ? "

" Don John and I." Then there was a pause, and they both wept.

" Can't you say *Mother* to me, Lancy?"

" No," said Lancy, dejectedly. "I love the other one. I don't mean — I don't wish to love any but her."

" But surely — " she sighed as if deeply wounded — " surely you are thankful to be saved?"

A lump seemed to rise in Lancy's throat then, and he trembled even more than she did.

" I am not saved," he answered hoarsely; " I don't wish to say anything wicked to you. Let me alone, or I shall."

" I 'll only say one thing, then," she persisted. " That ten pounds : you are welcome to it. Consider that I gave it to you. It is yours."

Lancy's chest heaved ; there certainly was some relief in that sigh.

Presently she spoke again.

" I heard what you wrote in your letter to Mrs. Johnstone — all the servants and children know — that you had run away to sea. Nothing could be like the astonishment of them all. I think it was as good a thing as you could have said ; and so, when I got here, I said the same thing, that my son had run off to sea ; but I said I hoped you would come and take leave of me, and I bribed the waiters to look out for you."

Oh ! what a world of difference there was between this speech and anything that had ever been said to him in his lost and forfeited home.

But it suited poor Lancy, and he gradually became calmer. He was to be aided with this lie that concealed a theft. She hoped by means of it to conciliate and make him lovingly dependent on her ; and he, by the same means, hoped to pass for nothing worse than an extremely ungrateful, bad, and foolish schoolboy, to obtain forgiveness and get away from her. Each was subtle enough to conceal such thoughts. Lancy at once determined that he would try to be more pleasant to her, and she began to throw out hints of projected visits to Paris and to Switzerland, which, without distinctly asking him to go with her, seemed to show that his company at home, or abroad, would always be a pleas-

ure to her. A clock on the mantelpiece struck one.
Now was the decisive moment.

"You'll stay and have your lunch with me, of
course?" she said.

"I suppose so," he answered dejectedly; and then,
on reflection, added, "If you please."

The color came back to her face. She knew her
game was won. She rang the bell, quietly ordered
lunch for two, and added, but rather slowly, "And this
young gentleman — my son — will sleep here to-night.
I shall want a room for him near to mine."

The waiter tried, but not very successfully, to conceal his interest and amusement. Lancy, with a disconsolate air, was looking out of the window. Mrs.
Collingwood put a small piece of paper in the waiter's
hand, on which was some writing.

"You'll see that this goes at once?"

"Yes, ma'am."

It was a telegram addressed to Mr. Johnstone, at
his house in the country, and was thus expressed: —

"Sir, Master Lancelot Aird is with me at the Euston
Hotel; I await your wishes. M. J. C."

As the lunch drew to its conclusion, Lancy became
hopelessly restless. Mrs. Collingwood noticed this,
and asked what he would like to do.

He had nothing to do. He had thought of going to
see the beasts fed; but it was too early. Lancy brought
out this plan in his most boyish and inconsequent
fashion.

"But he had two green linnets and a little tortoise
in his lodgings. He should like to have them with him
at the hotel, for he had nothing to do."

Mrs. Collingwood said she would go with him and
fetch them.

"And as I've got some money left," continued
Lancy, sighing between almost every word; "money
that you have given me now, I should like some more
creatures. I saw a puppy at the shop yesterday — a
stunning one, a skye — and, perhaps, if I had it" —
here a great many more sighs — "I shouldn't be so
miserable."

So an open fly was hired, and Lancy appeared at his
late lodgings to claim his property. His landlady was
a good woman. She was pleased to see him with a
fine lady, who thanked her for having been kind to her
son.

" Does he owe you anything?" she asked.

" No, ma'am, nothing."

" Excepting for the castors," said Lancy.

" Well, now," exclaimed the landlady, " to think of
your remembering that, sir; and to think of my forgetting !"

Mrs. Collingwood paid a shilling for the use of the
castors, and generously forbore to take back the three-
pence change.

Lancy felt rather less forlorn when he reached the
hotel again with his tortoise, his two linnets, a skye
puppy, and some wood and wire with which he meant
to enlarge a cage for a starling, that he had added to
his menagerie. He was very clever with his hands,
and being much occupied, took no notice when a telegram was brought in for Mrs. Collingwood. It ran
thus, — " I will be with you to-morrow morning, about
ten o'clock."

So after breakfast the next morning — a meal during
which Lancy was still disconsolate — Mrs. Collingwood
asked him if he did not wish to see Mr. Johnstone, and
ask his pardon for having run away.

Lancy said " Yes," but not with any hope that this
wish would so soon be realized. In two minutes the
waiter announced Mr. and Mrs. Johnstone. A tall lady
entered, and with a jealous pang, Maria Collingwood
saw her boy rush up to her.

" Oh, mother — mother !" he cried. His face was
on her bosom, and her hand rested on his forehead.
" Ask father to forgive me," he cried.

His arm was round her neck, and she kissed him.
How beautiful she was, how motherly, how tall. The
other woman looked and envied her from the bottom
of her soul; her face was colored with agitation, and
her eyes flashed. She had but vaguely noticed, she

was scarcely aware of Mrs. Collingwood's presence ; but Mr. Johnstone was, he walked up to her, as she sat slightly turning away from the unbearable sight of her Lancy's love for another mother.

"How much does that boy know?" he inquired, looking steadily at her, and speaking low.

"Nothing, sir — "

"Nothing?"

"I have told him that I am his mother, sir," she whispered, "but nothing else ; nothing at all."

Donald Johnstone turned ; Lancy had made a step or two towards him, but before he took any other notice of him, he said, —

"Set your mother a chair."

"Yes, father," said Lancy.

And as Mrs. Johnstone sat down she made a slight movement of recognition to Mrs. Collingwood, who was keenly aware that her Lancy was standing humble and crestfallen for what seemed a long time before the adopted father, whose steady, penetrative eyes appeared to look him through and through.

It seemed a long time, but it could not have been many seconds. When he did speak his face changed, and his voice, which was low, trembled with impassioned emotion.

"Have I ever denied you any one thing that was good for you all your life long?"

"No, father."

"Have I made any difference between you and the dearest of my dear sons?"

"No, father."

"Look at me."

Lancy lifted up his daunted face, and looked entreatingly at his judge.

"Your mother, as we drove along this morning, •begged me to forgive you, Lancy, — *for running away.*"

Lancy's eyes fell.

The steady, clear emphasis imparted to those last words shook him, and frightened Mrs. Collingwood no less. There was more meaning in them than .met the

ear. How could he have discovered what she only had
seen? And if he had not, what did he suspect?

He sighed deeply.

"For running away," he repeated; "and I said—
I would."

Another pause.

"Have I anything else to forgive you for?"

Lancy's head was bent, as he stood, but he murmured
something in his fright and confusion. It seemed to be
"No."

Then the other mother spoke. She said, "Oh, yes,
my Lancy; yes. Your father has to forgive you for
long distrust of his anxious goodness, and care for you.
If you were unhappy at home, why did n't you say so?
If you longed so much for a sea life, why did you never
tell it even to me? Why have you done this to us? We
deserved better things of you, Lancy. You have been
ungrateful and unkind."

He does know, thought Mrs. Collingwood, and *she*
does not.

Lancy was completely overcome. He staggered as
he stood, and in another instant the adopted father was
holding him by the shoulder; he made him sit down,
and unfastened his necktie. As he bent over him to do
this, Mrs. Collingwood saw Lancy lean his forehead for
a moment against Mr. Johnstone's breast.

"You won't tell mother?" he faltered. And Mrs.
Collingwood heard the words with a passion of jealous
pain. Of course he did not care that *she* knew.

She heard the whispered "No." Then she saw him
put his hand on her boy's head. He said, —

"May God forgive you, my poor child, and grant you
time to retrieve the past."

A silence followed. The adopted mother and the
true mother both wept. Lancy, now the terrible ordeal
was over, felt almost as if he was in his former place,
and was going to his home as if nothing was changed,
but yet the many strange things that had come to pass
flashing back on his memory, enabled him quickly to
overcome his emotion.

"Mother," he burst out, addressing Mrs. Johnstone, "this — this lady says that she came home from Australia on purpose to see *me*. She says she is —"

"*She says she is your mother*," said Mrs. Johnstone. "Well, my son, you always knew that I was not; we always told you that you were a dear adopted son."

"You won't let her take me from you?"

"Lancy," cried Mrs. Collingwood, "I have been very good to you, and this I cannot stand. But for me, you would have been on shipboard by this time."

"Father," repeated Lancy, "you won't let her take me from you?"

"No," he answered, just as decidedly as if the whole matter was in his own hands.

"Sir, you may find that I have something to say as to that," sobbed poor Mrs. Collingwood.

"I have no doubt of it," he replied, "and now is the time to say it. If Mrs. Johnstone will let Lancy take her to his sleeping-room, you can speak as you could not in the presence of the boy, and I can tell you my intentions."

Still taking in all respects the upper hand, he was soon left alone with Mrs. Collingwood, and while she dried her eyes, he said, —

"Mrs. Collingwood, I am sorry to begin with a disparaging question. You went away declaring that you did not know, and had no means of knowing, which of those two children was yours — how is it that you come back, to the full as sure as we are, if not more so?"

No answer.

"This certainty of yours almost ties me down to the thought that you did know always; but that in an unworthy hour you yielded to your husband's desire to get rid of your child, and made up a story which you knew would provide him with a kind father, and a better mother than you had been."

"No, sir," she replied, moving her hand as if to put all this aside, "don't."

"How is it, then?"

"I came to see which you had chosen, and the moment I set my eyes on Lancy, I felt—I was sure—I could have sworn that he was my son. I loved him so. I knew that you were right. I saw your son, sir, several times first, and felt that I did n't like him, that he was nothing to me. But Lancy—oh, sir! you *know* he 's mine as well as I do."

" I *believe* he is, so does Mrs. Johnstone."

" I have plenty, sir. My husband's—Collingwood's—relations in Australia left him four hundred a year; they had been so prosperous. It all came by David's will to me."

" That I have nothing to do with."

" Sir? "

" You can leave it to Lancy, if you please; but that is nothing to me."

" I am ever deeply thankful for all you have done for my Lancy. You have made a gentleman of him; but I meant, sir, that of course I should wish to take him off your hands now, and finish educating of him, and provide for him myself."

" Quite impossible."

" How so, sir."

" You cannot prove that the boy is yours."

" Prove it?—no, of course not."

" Nothing on earth but proof will do for me. That it is to the last and uttermost *improbable* he can be mine, I fully admit; but I will not give him up unless you can prove that it is *impossible*."

" Why, you have five, Mr. Johnstone—five beside him—and I have none."

" The thing is entirely your own doing."

" But my poor husband, Collingwood, had no doubt in the world; when, after some years—we had plenty of money and no children, and he so fond of me—I told him at last everything. How I concealed from poor mother and denied that I had changed the children, and so—"

" And so she did it herself; yes, probably."

" Oh, you 'll let me have my boy, then? "

" No, never."

"I'm a miserable woman; but there's law. I take the law of you, sir." ·

"You are talking nonsense; there is no law for such a case; and if you make it public, you will cover yourself with disgrace, and make your son detest you; we have never told him anything at all against you. To the utmost of my ability, I am bringing him up as I would if it was proved to me that he was mine; and whether he is to be my honor or my disgrace, so help me God, I will never forsake him."

CHAPTER XV.

DONALD JOHNSTONE'S words, no less than his manner, which seemed to announce no doubt whatever that he both could and would keep her boy, were too much for poor Maria Collingwood. She wept passionately, but she was highly irritated also. "You're extremely unforgiving and hard upon me," she sobbed;. "and, as for Mrs. Johnstone, if I had been the dirt under her feet, she could hardly at first have taken less account of me."

"She did not see you. She was thinking of the boy; and she never said one word of reproach to you when she did see you."

"She was very high — very, and it hurt my feelings — before Lancy and all. She's not so very much above me *now*."

"Listen to reason, Mrs. Collingwood, and acknowledge what you very well know, that my wife is immeasurably above you. She has been as noble as you were base. She has never said one word against you to the child through whom you wrought her for some years such unutterable pain."

"They can't both be yours," sobbed the poor woman; — she still remonstrated.

" 'They are both mine in one sense, and in the same sense neither can ever be yours; for if you gave me any serious trouble about this matter (which I am sure you will not do), I should tell Lancy — the one whom you want — the whole story. He would probably believe himself to be yours. I leave you to judge what he would think of you compared with the woman who has brought him up. But it is possible that he might do worse ; he might, spite of all that *we* think, entertain a lurking fancy that, after all, he had the best of rights to every single thing we have done for him. And what chance would you have of anything but hatred and repulsion from him in such a case as that ? "

" It is but right — *you 'll own it 's right* — that I should see him sometimes," she sobbed, when she had pondered this last speech.

" Yes, I own it; and if you will do my bidding, I will make this thing as little bitter to you as I can."

" I had not left him in your parlor in Harley Street a day — not one day — before my heart began to cry for him ; not but what I truly was in doubt then, sir. But David — he was so jealous of the child, and I was that desirous to please him, and that he should not have the expense of his bringing up ! It was years after, when he got fonder and fonder of me, that I relieved my mind with telling him all — and he did so reproach me ! ' If you 'd had a mother's heart,' said he, ' you would have known there was no reasonable doubt ; and now,' said he, ' I want that child of yours ' (that was when he was ill), ' since I 've none,' said he, ' of my own ! '

" But I give way, sir; I did wrong; and if you won't tell him anything against me, I 'll do my best to be patient. You 'll let me see him sometimes ? "

" I will ; and now I am afraid I have to ask you a question which will give you pain. His father, Lancelot Aird — "

" Yes, sir."

" Well, the thing must be said. Did he ever get himself into trouble, as they call it ? — was he ever taken up for any — larceny ? "

The color rushed over her face and neck, and she drew herself up, and darted a reproachful look at him.

" I think you will do well to answer," he said.

" He was in trouble once — only once," she whispered. " Oh, sir, I know — my poor boy !"

" It seems as if it must be hereditary," he murmured. " What do you know, Mrs. Collingwood?"

She was silent, and shook her head.

" It is said that you were robbed three days ago."

Still she was silent.

" When my own dear boy found that Lancy had run away, he was naturally very much distressed, and told me Lancy had no real desire to go to sea. He also confessed to me something which had happened some years ago at school, which instantly excited a terrible suspicion in my mind. I could not but perceive what my boy thought, as I now perceive that you understand me."

" I promised him I would not betray him," said the poor, shamed, and sorrowful woman.

" Then, Mrs. Collingwood, I must myself make him confess all."

But there proved to be no need for this. Mrs. Collingwood, with all her faults, was not a foolish woman ; she soon was made to feel that the boy's best chance of being cured of his propensity and duly looked after lay in his being under Mr. Johnstone's supervision. She gave way. She would part with him then and there, only she begged that she might not have to see Mrs. Johnstone again.

Lancy was therefore sent for to return to the room he had left, a little note from Mr. Johnstone asking his wife to remain where she was. Accordingly, Lancy appeared, but it was with an altogether new expression on his face. He looked dejected and ashamed, but the craven air was gone. He walked straight up to Mr. Johnstone. " Father," he said, " I have confessed it all. I have told mother everything."

When Maria Collingwood heard this, she felt as if Lancy was saved, but yet that he was all the more lost to her. She had now no hold; the other woman was supreme, and she was nothing.

"And she has forgiven me," proceeded Lancy, in a whisper.

"May God forgive you, my boy," answered Donald Johnstone, solemnly, "and bring you to a better mind. Understand me."

"No, father," Lancy burst out; "I am not daring to ask *you* to forgive me yet; but I will — I will do better."

"Understand me," Donald Johnstone went on, "I am disgraced. Your wickedness is undiscovered as yet; but I am amazed with the shame of it, and I feel that I shall not be able to hold up my head as I have done."

"Oh, father!" Lancy interrupted again, "don't say it. Have pity on me."

"For better or for worse, I and mine are so far one that we must rise or sink together. I have a thing now to hide. When I meet my neighbors — especially my poor neighbors — I shall hope they will not find it out. I shall be ashamed — I am ashamed."

"Father, I cannot bear it."

"And nobody but us knows," murmured Maria Collingwood; but happily poor Lancy cared nothing for her opinion. The only severe punishment he had ever suffered in his life was now being inflicted on him, and he felt it most keenly.

"Will there never be a day when you can forgive me, father?" he sighed.

"Oh, yes, I can forgive you even now; but not the less I know that you are on the very brink of ruin, as I am liable at any moment to your being detected and my being disgraced."

After this, though Maria Collingwood perceived the salutary contrition it had wrought on Lancy, she hated Mrs. Johnstone and Mr. Johnstone too; for Lancy could not think about her — could not care that she had to part from him; could not even take thought for his birds, and his tortoise, and his skye puppy, which he had hitherto been making so much of.

Nothing that concerned her signified much. He knew he had been wicked, but he felt it most because the other mother had wept over her adopted son, and he felt the shame of what he had done because of the words of his adopted father.

"Oh, to save them for the future! Oh, to lead a better life!" That was what Lancy felt now; and when Mr. Johnstone drew him aside, and told him that he was to part from this poor mother of his, and he was to do it affectionately, he could hardly give his mind to it, though he was left alone with her. But her distress was like his distress, though it was from a different cause.

"It's hard, my son," she sobbed, "to come from the other side the earth to see you, and then find (I have plenty of friends there) that you neither care to go back with me, nor to stay with me here."

He was deep in his own painful thoughts, and made her no reply.

"But you'll call me '*mother*' once, won't you, Lancy?"

"Yes, I will, mother; you have been kind."

"I did the best I could."

"But I don't understand it at all, mother."

"And I may n't explain it to you. No; I know it would do no good to explain it to you." He was not listening, and she forbore to go on; but as she sat beside him on a sofa, she drew his head for a few moments on to her bosom, and he allowed her to hold it there.

"Lancy," she whispered, "if you get into a scrape again —"

"I never will," he answered, and groaned.

"But if you did, my own only one, you'd come to me, would n't you, to get you out of it?"

"Yes," was the answer. She waited some moments for it. Then releasing him, he lifted his face. "Good-bye, *mother*," he said. She kissed him, and in another moment he was gone.

Poor woman! She looked out of the window, and saw Mrs. Johnstone step forth from the hotel and enter a carriage which was waiting; and then, Lancy having got in, she gazed at him, till the reins were given to Mr.

12

Johnstone, and they drove off, and the carriage and her treasure disappeared.

He had left all his pets behind, and as they had consoled him while he sat disconsolate in his lodgings, so they consoled her a little. She took to the starling most, because she had seen her boy at work on his cage. She let the puppy set his little white teeth in the trains of her gowns, and worry her slippers, and drag her knitting over the floor; and she thought about Lancy, and felt how lonely she was, and considered, as many another has done, not only how she could have been such a sinner, but such a fool.

And now, having made voluntary confession so far, the boy's involuntary confession of other delinquencies was soon made to follow. Don John had told his father of the suspicions which had fallen on Lancy, owing to certain petty peculations, and then of the more serious theft, followed by his own adventure and his broken arm.

After this, as Don John believed, all had gone well. He had hoped that Lancy was cured; and yet when it was found that he had run away, just after the ten pounds had been stolen, he could not help dwelling on the recollection that "the lodger's" room had been entered by Lancy for a moment in order to bring away a book.

But why — Mr. Johnstone pondered — why had he done this? He was not a child now, that he could thoughtlessly yield to temptation not knowing the consequences. He had felt the fear of detection, and the bitterness of danger already. So far as was known he did not care to hoard; could he have risked so much misery that he might have ten pounds to squander away?

Thinking thus, and pursuing his advantage now that Lancy was penitent and crestfallen, Mr. Johnstone pressed him with questions. One admission soon led to another. Lancy did not dare to prevaricate, and very soon the miserable story of his last fall found out by the boy who was now his tyrant was told. He had con-

cealed this from Don John as he now declared because
he could not bear to be despised by him. Don John
had no idea of the misery he had gone through, constant threats of exposure hanging over his head.

" And it can never be put an end to," sighed poor
Lancy ; " he will soon write to me again."

" Oh yes. it can be put an end to. Where is his last
letter?" asked Mr. Johnstone. " Did you leave it
behind in your desk?"

" No, father, I was afraid it would be found. He is
at the seaside now, and when I got the post-office order
for him, I put it in my pocket to be sure that I sent it
to the right address."

" Give it to me."

Lancy produced it, and Donald Johnstone having
read it sealed it up. " Now you can write to this fellow," he said. " Tell him you have made full confession of everything to your father, who has taken his
last letter from you. ' He remarked,' you can say
' that at first he thought of sending that letter to your
father, but that on second thoughts if you at once wrote to
me promising that under no circumstances should I ever
hear from you again, he should not do so — for if your
father was an honorable man, it would make him miserable,. while you were too old to be flogged, and no
other punishment was likely to reach you.' "

Lancy looked amazed, but he wrote the letter, and of
course was delivered from that form of bondage ever
after, but he had a good deal to endure. It was soon
explained to him that he could not go to school again
with Don John, or indeed to any school. He was not
to be trusted, he might disgrace himself and the family
that had adopted him. " Father always used to say
that Don John and I should both be articled to him,"
he remarked to Mrs. Johnstone.

" So you shall," she answered, " if he has every reason to believe you are quite cured. I pray to God
every day, Lancy, that you may be cured."

Mrs. Johnstone in fact never admitted the least doubt
that he would be cured. She was ardently hopeful, and

always loving; taught him a prayer against his beset-
ting sin which he promised to say night and morning,
and did all she could to make him ashamed of his propensity and afraid of himself.

But Lancy was not taken home, he was sent to be
the private pupil of a clergyman, to whom his fault
was duly confided, and who watched him, prayed with
him, and also taught him. It was not so pleasant as
being at school with Don John and many other boys
for companions, but he was there shielded from temptation, and he also knew and felt that he was watched.
Besides the frequent letters both from father and from
mother had some effect upon him, while every now
and then his new mother as he called her wrote to
him by permission, and always sent him a very handsome " tip," which, by way of being candid and truthful, he mentioned in his letters home; he had thus
always plenty of money, as well as absence of temptation, and he appeared to himself to loathe the sin of
theft, because the constraint and distrust it had brought
upon him were always in his way.

He longed for his home, and even for his sisters
and Charlotte, whom he had not specially cared for;
but at the end of the year he did not go home.

The Johnstones came as they had done several times
already to see their adopted son, and brought Don John
with them; and they told him he should take a tour
with them and Don John on the continent, but that
they could not let him be with his sisters, and close to
the scene of his last delinquency at present.

So he was still during these holidays to be exclusively
with those who knew of his faults. Well, he thought,
he did not much care — anything to get away from this
dull place, and if he was still to be exhorted, to enjoy
at least a change of exhortation.

Lancy was grown, and was a fine, good-looking fellow.
There was something not unpleasing to him in the deep,
loving anxiety of them all for his welfare. It made him
so important; and as his moral sense was weak, he did
not despise or reproach himself so much as to diminish

his enjoyment of the holiday tour. He had done very wrong. It would have been strange if after so many tears, such fervent prayers, such tender letters, such loving care, so much as this had not been impressed on his mind. He said to himself that he should never do such a thing as that again *of course.* The consequences had been very unpleasant and the risk very great. Besides father had taken great pains to let him know that he would never be poor — never want, for that he should leave him a provision by no means to be despised; and the new mother had expressly told him that everything she had would be his.

Lancy was seventeen years old and perfectly cured in the opinion of everybody when at length his eyes lighted on his own home again, and he saw with delight and surprise the two grown-up sisters, and Charlotte, and the old garden, and the still prized and unaltered playroom.

He might have come home a year ago, but that the so-called " new mother " pleaded so sorely to have him during the midsummer vacation, that she was allowed to do so. She crammed as many pleasures as she could think of for him into the time, and sent him back loaded with presents, but to her sore discomfort he was just as urgent the following year to be allowed to go home as she had been to be allowed to see him. Home he went accordingly, and was every hour aware that it was a different home. There had been a tiresome, shy child in that former home called Charlotte — a child who teased him and whom he teased, that child's frock was always crumpled, her hair, like a mat or a bird's nest as he had loved to declare, used to hang over her forehead; she often pouted. He remembered that she had always possessed most beautiful blue Irish eyes with long black lashes, and that he had not cared about them the least in the world.

Charlotte — well, this was Charlotte now — Don John called her five feet nothing — in fact, she was a small creature and looked specially so among the tall young Johnstones.

Charlotte, the morning after Lancy came home, was
sitting at the schoolroom table writing, her rosebud
mouth pouting, and her lashes hiding the blueness beneath.   What a pretty little figure she had.

Charlotte was very youthful looking ; Don John, only
seventeen, looked much older.   Charlotte was his little
slave, and still his partner in the *minutes*.   Lancy rather
wondered to see him order her about.   He observed
what a charming air and manner she had — how the
small waist was graced with an ample chatelaine.   He
thought she had a pretty gown on, and admired the
little feet which in their trim slippers were perched on
the cross-bar under the table.

"Poetess!" the voice of Don John was heard to
shout from the garden below.   Charlotte was too deep
in thought to answer — her fingers were inked.   She
took up a bit of blotting-paper and dried them on it,
and looked at the tips of them, but as if her thoughts
were far away.   Her lips moved.   "She's muttering
her poetry," thought Lancy, very much amused, and in
another moment Don John burst in.   "Wasting the
morning in this way, Charlotte," he exclaimed ; "and
Lancy has never even seen the new pony carriage."
Charlotte turned her dreamy eyes upon him and gradually woke up.   "Here you sit all in a bunch with your
shoulders up to your ears — like a yellow-hammer singing on a rail — what are you doing? — some of your
rubbish of course."

"I was only putting a bit of Chaucer into modern
English, for the minutes."

"Modern fiddlesticks! — come on, Lancy, and you
too, Charlotte.   They've found three snakes in the
dairy, and one of them was drinking the milk."   Charlotte sighed, she was writing of thoughts and things
which had never come near her yet, excepting in a poetic vision.

"I must copy it out first," she said, "or I shall never
remember how it goes."

Don John sat down to wait with a tolerably good grace,
and he too came in for a share of Lancy's observation.

Don John would have been a difficult person to describe to one who had not seen him — he was neither short nor tall, he was neither handsome nor plain, he was not graceful, he was not awkward. He had extremely light hair, light eyebrows, a specially open, sweet-tempered expression, a good many freckles about his face and on his hands, extremely white teeth, and twinkling eyes full of fun. In manner, he was blunt, in behavior to his sisters he was affectionate, but peremptory — as yet it was firmly fixed in his mind that " the masculine gender is worthier than the feminine ; " he was lord and master at home, reigned over Charlotte more despotically than over any of the others — scarcely perceived at present that she was grown up, admired and loved his mother above all creatures, and looked on most young ladies not related to him, as mistakes of nature and bores.

Charlotte with her pretty head on one side and her eyebrows slightly elevated, copied out her version.

> " Still for your sake — by night I wake — and sigh,
> By day I am near — so sore my fear — to die,
> And to all this — no care I wis — ye deign,
> Though mine eyes two — never for you — be dry ;
>
> And on your ruth — and to your truth — I cry.
> But well away — too far be they — to attain,
> So plaining me — on destiny — amain,
> I mourn, nor find — how to unbind — my chain,
> Knowing my wit — so weak is it — all vain.
>
> Think on your name — why do (for shame) — ye so,
> For it shall be — thou shalt this dree — sweet foe,
> And me think on — in such wise gone — this day,
> That love you best — (God, Thou wottest) — alway."

A deep groan from Don John. " Oh, very well," exclaimed Charlotte, " if I am not to finish it now, I never shall."

" Of all the unreasonableness in this world," replied Don John, " there 's no unreasonableness like that of you people who pretend to be poets." He looked round the room. " And what 's the good of poetry ? " he burst forth.

Charlotte felt a certain fitness in Don John's honest indignation and sincere scorn ; she wiped her pen.

" I never said it was any good," she pleaded — " only I cannot help writing it."

" Even when there are snakes in the dairy ! and you are expressly told of it."

" Yes, I do want to see the snakes," said Charlotte. " Why do you try to make out that I don't care about interesting things ? "

CHAPTER XVI.

THE young people now ran down into the dairy, where three snakes were twisting themselves about under a wire meat-safe, while Marjorie and Naomi, standing well away from it with their backs against the wall, held their skirts with needless care, and regarded the silvery things with distrust and curiosity.

Little Mary, the only creature about the place who could still be considered a child, was perched upon the slate shelf.

Lancy and Don John poked slender skewers between the wires of the safe, and Charlotte no sooner heard the snakes hiss in acknowledgment of this attention than she sprang on the top of a covered bread-pan, and demanded to be saved, to be set on the shelf beside Mary, to be got out of their way.

" They 're perfectly harmless," said Mary, looking down from her elevation with complacency ; but she took special care to keep high above them.

Charlotte, by the help of Lancy's hand, perched herself beside Mary, and began to feel safe and brave till the cook, coming in, said to Don John, —

" I hope, sir, you are certain sure there are no more of the artful things lurking about on the top shelf ? "

" The top shelf ! " cried Charlotte, " how could there be any there ? "

"Oh, no," said Don John, "there are no more; and, besides, I told you they were perfectly harmless."

The cook put her hand on her side. "No peace have I had in this place at all," she remarked, "since you said, sir, it was a pop'ler error, — 'Cook,' you said, 'it's a pop'ler error to think of a snake as if it could n't glide up a steep slope.' I've been in here for milk and eggs times out of number as innocent as could be, and have heard a kind of rustling, and little thought the deceitful things were perhaps lolling their heads over and looking at me."

All the girls shivered in sympathy.

"But there it is, young ladies, when once you let yourself down — begging your pardon for saying it — let yourself down to go into the country (being London-born and one that ought to know better), why, you can never tell what may happen."

"Hiss—s—s" again.

"And me always taught that they lived in dung-hills, the only proper place for them, and then to hear that Mr. Don John with his own hands, pulled two out of Mrs. Clarboy's thatch, that they used to climb up to by the ivy — and found a long string of leathery eggs as well — such a respectable woman as Mrs. Clarboy is too!"

"They did n't require a reference as to character when they went to lodge there," said Don John.

"And had n't need, sir." cried the cook, smiling. "I should hope the wickedest family that ever lived was too good for such reptilly things as they."

"Mrs. Clarboy's roof comes down at the back of her house to within three feet of the ground, and the old ivy is almost as thick as tree trunks, they got up it both here and there; a snake must be a fool indeed if he cannot climb that."

"Instead of which he is rather cunning," observed Lancy.

"Yes," said Charlotte, knitting her pretty brow into a thoughtful frown, "cunning, but not so cunning as to lead one to any painful doubts or speculations. I have never supposed that snakes were reasonable creatures."

Lancy looked up surprised. "Reasonable creatures!" he exclaimed.

"Oh, it's only one of her theories she's alluding to," said Don John, "read our *minutes*, and you'll see."

The cook now retired, having certain matters to attend to, and Don John, having managed to push a flat piece of tin under the wires, carried away the snakes. Marjorie and Naomi followed, but Lancy had found some curds on a dish and set it between Charlotte and Mary, who were still perched on the shelf, and, helping himself also, sat down on a wooden stool, and thought how pretty Charlotte looked. Charlotte in one respect much resembled her mother, her mind was full of speculations, and in general she was ready to discuss any of them with any person at any time.

Lancy wanted to hear her talk, so he said, "How about the reasonable creatures?"

"Oh," answered Charlotte. "I think that though we are in this globe at the head of the reasonable creatures, there are at least two other races that have reason and are able to commit sin."

"Queer!" thought Lancy. Her speech had so much surprised him that he had attended to it, no less than to the well-favored face that looked down earnestly at him, and to the shapely curves of her lips.

"Do you think they are responsible, then?" he exclaimed.

"I said 'can commit sins,' so I suppose they are responsible — ants, for instance."

"They're so small," pleaded Lancy, amazed.

"They are not in any degree worth mentioning smaller than we are — I mean with relation to the size of the globe on which we live and they live. In my own mind the more I think it over the more I feel that I ought not to shrink from the notion that they are responsible creatures."

"But what are their sins, Charlotte?"

"They go to war, planning murderous raids beforehand, they take slaves in battle, both living ants which they make slaves, and eggs which they hatch, and bring up the young as thralls — as subject races. But what makes me mainly sure that they are responsible is that they are punished just as we are, but more severely, through these very crimes. The eagle is not punished for stealing the lamb and picking out its eyes. The pike, for anything we can find out to the contrary, swallows a whole family of young fishes, and does not know he's a cannibal. They are not punished, but the ants are, for having used themselves to be fed, cleaned, and waited on by their slaves, they absolutely lose the power to do these things for themselves, so that if the slaves get away or die, they die too."

" And why may not all that be instinct?" said Lancy, cogitating.

" If it were — which still I think it cannot be — what do you say to their having domestic animals just as we have? We have tame creatures, flocks that yield us milk; so have they."

" It's queer certainly," said Lancy.

" If they were as large as we are, it would seem queerer still; we were ignorant of it all for a very long time because they are so small. But only fancy, Lancy, if they were as large as bullocks, and we met them every now and then driving their unlucky prisoners home, taking them to their underground dens and keeping them there, what a queer sensation it would give us! And then when we walked forth and saw them milking their flocks, the question is, whether it would be more strange to us than to see us milking ours would be to them."

" But if they have reason." said Lancy, " why cannot they communicate with us?"

" I don't know: most likely because one of their senses is different from ours, on purpose to keep us apart — they are deaf. I suppose if we had not only no hearing, but no consciousness of such a sense as hearing, we should have no real knowledge of one another, and none of other races."

" Does one sense less, then, make all the difference?"

" Oh, I did not say one sense *less*. If we had the greater and more perfect faculty that they possess, we should be very superior to our present selves, and be able to communicate also with them. It is our disability that keeps us back, not theirs ; and one strange difference must strike every one. Language, which we address to the sense of hearing, often deceives — it is inadequate and often false as well — but that direct touch by means of which they communicate seems to cause the actual flow of one mind into the other. We have no reason to think it can deceive, we do not suppose that they can lie to one another. In a minor sense they may be said on touching to ' know even as they are known.' "

" Yes, but all insects communicate by the touch — are all responsible?"

" Why should they be, any more than all beasts and birds are responsible because they can all hear?"

" But I think if they are reasonable creatures," said Lancy, " it 's an odd thing that they *never try* to communicate with us."

" Do we ever make any systematic efforts to communicate with them?"

Lancy laughed, the question seemed hardly worth answering.

" And how do we know," continued Charlotte, " that they never have made efforts to communicate with us? They too may have come to the conclusion that we have reason. How do we know what little longing crafty signs they may, after long consultation, have put out, hoping to attract our notice?"

" They may wish to let us know." said Mary, " that they do n't like to be trodden on. I never tread on them since Charlotte wrote of their ways in the minutes. Don John says perhaps the negro ants have found out that we have emancipated our negroes, and hope we shall some day by moral force get their masters to emancipate them."

" Yes," said Charlotte, who was very truthful, " but

Don John only wrote that in the minutes for a joke. He has no sympathy at all with the movement — at least with my cogitations as to how, if they have reason, we can possibly find out how to communicate with them. I ought not to call it a *movement* yet! But is it not a most extraordinary thing, Lancy, that considering what millions of worlds Almighty God has made, and considering the almost infinite vastness of space, that He should appear to act as if space was very precious, and He wished to make the most of it? How crowded this world is — every inch turned to account as it were! So many races under, over, and beside one another. Only think, if all the suns and worlds and moons should be as full as our world is, and all different!"

" It is strange," answered Lancy. " I suppose she will have a lover some day," he thought; " how it will *stump* that unlucky fellow, if she breaks forth to him in such discourse as this!"

" And which do you think is the third race of reasonable creatures?" he asked.

" Oh," said Charlotte, " I think the observant mind often gets hints of some such race, but I do not think it is visible to our eyes as at present constituted. I mean a race not angelic nor demoniacal — but that we (knowing so little of it) are inclined as a rule to be afraid of."

" Oh!" said Lancy.

" They're skinned!" exclaimed Don John, putting his head in, and he and Lancy darted off together.

" Oh, you cruel boy!" exclaimed Charlotte, for she knew it was the snakes that had been referred to.

Then she and Mary jumped down from the shelf, and Charlotte went and finished the minutes.

Lancy, in spite of the joy with which he had looked forward to coming home, found that thorns which had grown up in his absence encompassed the roses there.

Things were now and then said which made him feel hot; he was not always so much at ease as he could have wished. There were some places that he did not want to visit, some people whom he did not care to see.   And yet he would question with himself as to whether his brothers and sisters would not think it strange if he refrained from going to those very places, would not have their attention attracted towards him as acting oddly if he did not expressly seek those very people.

It was easy enough to go with Don John and see Lady Louisa, and hear her somewhat tedious talk about her children's delicate chests, and how she thought of spending the next winter at Nice, because Evelyn, the eldest son, had too long a neck.

Lancy bore a great deal of discussion as to sloping shoulders and the said long neck, almost with complacency.   It stirred no uneasy recollections.   He rose up to be measured by Mr. Viser as a proof that he was not taller than Evelyn.

Then he and Don John stood an examination as to their health.   Their experiences were mainly negative. They did not feel by any means disinclined for their breakfast.   They did not feel giddy when they read. They never heard any drumming in their ears, and they did not lie awake at night.

Lady Louisa sighed.

Then Don John burst forth with, —

"If Evelyn had no work to do in the holidays, he would not feel giddy."

Evelyn nudged Don John in a fitful, weak way, and Don John responded to the nudge by saying, —

" And German is one of the hardest things a fellow can have to get up."

" Oh," said Lady Louisa, " but Evelyn is devoted, perfectly devoted, to his German, and to the Herr Professor ; he quite enjoys his eight hours a day."

Evelyn, fixed by his mother's eye, gave the answer expected of him, but added, with a natural sigh, and in a piping voice, —

" But I wanted to dig out those water-voles with *them*."

When Lady Louisa remonstrated, " But you would get your feet wet, my boy," the long-necked student

succumbed, and Don John and Lancy made no observation.

The wild ass tossing his mane in the desert is so different from the flounder flopping on his mud-bank, that
he cannot hope to understand him and his fashions.

" Wet his feet. Ugh ! " thought Don John.

" I think Evelyn a very nice boy, poor fellow," said
Charlotte, as they were walking home, " and extremely
clever. I like him."

" Oh, yes, of course," answered Don John. " ' Like
loves like,' as the old maid said, when she bought the
primrose. You 'll be an old maid, Charlotte, I know
you will."

" Yes, I know I shall," said Charlotte, a little ruefully. " There 's no abstract reason but — "

" Nonsense !" Lancy exclaimed ; " why, Charlotte is
as pretty as — as anything."

Don John looked at Charlotte critically.

" She 's just as pretty — you 're just as pretty as
some girls who are sure to be married, Charlotte," he
remarked encouragingly. " It 's not that."

" But you 've often said I was improved since *Fetch*
wrote me those letters," said Charlotte.

Don John rejoined, —

" Fetch is a sensible fellow. *I always thought there
was a good deal in him.*"

" He did not show his sense in wanting to alter Charlotte," said Lancy, hotly, and easily perceiving that Don
John had written the letters himself.

" You don't know much about Charlotte yet. You 've
not heard her dash into abstract questions, and develop
her theories to fellows when they come to call."

Here Charlotte blushed consciously, and Lancy
laughed.

Then Don John said, " ' What 's the joke ?' as the
ghost asked of the laughing hyena. ' Dear sir,' he answered, ' you can't see a joke in the dark.' But is this
fellow in the dark? Charlotte, your blushes testify
against you ! Mary, I now feel that I 've done my duty
by you — this is meant for a Sam Weller."

"Oh," said Mary, "it's very nice, Lancy, to hear him sometimes remember *poor* Fetch and Sam. Don John, you're so grand now you know you're to be articled to father directly — you hardly ever come into the playroom at all. When I sprained my arm, you did Fetch for me every day, and Sam too —"

They were now close to the back of the house, and a piano was heard, together with two fresh young voices singing a duet. They were not both ladies' voices.

"There *he* is spooning again," said Don John, "and Naomi playing for them. No, Mary, I am always telling you that I cannot do Sam Wellers for you whenever I please. But I'll dance three times with you round this geranium bed, if you like, to Naomi's tune. Now, then, 'Do you polk?' as the Ornithorhyncus Paradoxus said at an evening party when they introduced him to the blue-faced baboon."

"And what did the blue-faced baboon say?"

"She replied that she would dance because she wished to conform to the usages of society, but that she preferred swinging from a bough by her tail, because that amusement was so much more intellectual."

"How jolly he is!" thought Lancy, "nothing to conceal, nothing on his mind." "When are we going to see the people in the houses?" he asked aloud, for he was impelled by dislike to an inevitable visit, to have it over as soon as possible.

"Oh, whenever you like. Shall it be after lunch?"

So some time after lunch, Don John and Lancy, with Mary and Charlotte, set forth. Lancy would have felt more easy if they had been a larger party, but it appeared that there was important practising to be done. Two *tenors* and a *barytone* had arrived: each evidently thought his voice suited best with Marjorie's. Naomi stayed behind to play for them.

"And how does the new boiler do, Mrs. Clarboy?" asked Don John, when the first greetings were over, and Lancy had been assured that he was almost grown out of knowledge.

"Oh, sir, it goes lovely — lovely it does — but it's

rather slow of heating — shall I light it now, sir, and show you?"

" Yes, do, and Lancy, you sit on the top and let us know when the water boils. You won't? Well, I never knew such a disobliging fellow! and when you 've been away so long too."

" Master Don John, he 's always full of his jokes," said Mrs. Clarboy.

" And how is Miss Jenny to-day?" asked Charlotte.

" Thank you kindly for asking, miss; and pore Jenny feels herself better this afternoon. It 's a great comfort to her our niece being with us." Here she made a show of introduction between Charlotte and a pretty young woman in a close cap. " My niece Letty Fane, miss; she is a trained nurse, and understands Jenny's nerves. Yes, Letty was in a regular hospital, Miss Charlotte, but she has taken a situation in a workhouse now."

" You must find that a pleasant change," said Charlotte.

" Ma'am," answered the young woman, with an ag-grieved air, " nothing of the sort, I find it very dull, there are no operations."

" But she thought it her duty to take the situation, having a widowed mother to help, and there being bet-ter pay," observed Mrs. Clarboy.

After this Letty Fane went upstairs, taking with her some food for the sick aunt, but her account of herself and her tastes had cast a chill over the guests, and Charlotte presently rose to take leave, Lancy alone re-maining behind to slip a little present of money into Mrs. Clarboy's hand for the benefit of the sick sister.

Mrs. Clarboy accepted it graciously.

" And I am sure, sir," she remarked, " I 'm right glad to see you at last. I 've often said to pore Jenny, ' Depend on it, this is only for a time.' They 'll forgive Master Lancy in the end, and have him back."

" It was very wrong of me to run away from home," said Lancy, with apparent candor. " I have long been very sorry I did it."

A look of indescribable intelligence darted into Mrs.

13

Clarboy's eyes. She had the air of one who feels that she knows more than she wishes to know, and would fain hide it. She colored deeply. "Yes, sir," she answered, without looking at him, and then added hastily, "And how might that lady be — her that we used to call the lodger?" Then she looked at him. He had drawn back a little, and seemed abashed. So she hurriedly went on: "You find all a good deal growed up about us, sir, you and Mr. Don John; while you're away at school, or at college, or where not, the trees grow on; we shall be almost smothered in them soon."

"Yes," said Lancy, looking about him rather forlornly. "Well, good afternoon, Mrs. Clarboy," and he withdrew.

There were the others standing at Salisbury's door a little farther on.

Oh, what should he do? Surely Mrs. Clarboy knew something, or at least suspected something; but it was manifest that no hint had ever reached the girls. He went on to join the party — he must, or they would wonder why.

"Good afternoon, sir," said Salisbury, with a certain gravity as Lancy thought. Presently Mrs. Salisbury came out, and she too said, "Good afternoon, sir;" and Lancy, who had intended to be patronizing and pleasant, found that he had not a word to say. That visit was made very short, and Lancy took special care not to be left one moment behind the others.

The manner and the words together amounted to so little — a look in one case, in the other a certain grave restraint. Is a boy who runs away to sea met in that fashion by cottagers several years after, when his withdrawal has been no concern of theirs?

Lancy considered this matter, and could not feel at his ease. He took the first opportunity to ask Don John, —

"I suppose none of the people about here know anything about *that* — about the unlucky time of my running away?"

"Of course not," said Don John, with conviction.

"But they might suspect something."

"How nervous you are! They know that Mrs. Collingwood is your mother. Father told them. They know nothing more."

"Were you present when he told them?"

"Yes, and they all behaved like country bumpkins as they are. They held up their hands, and some of them said, 'Lawk, you don't say so, sir.'"

"And none of them said anything about her having lost anything?"

"I particularly remember that not one said a word about it."

"Well, then, I think *that* was rather odd!"

"No, there was nothing odd in the manner of any of them. If they had known, they must have betrayed the knowledge."

"I consider that the poor are far better actors than we are. They knew father must hope they had found out nothing (I always hate myself when I think of the shame he felt about it). They like both father and mother; they may have known, and yet have spared them."

"Nobody knows anything," repeated Don John, yet more decidedly; "you're saved, dear old fellow, this once. Only hold your head up, or you'll excite surprise, and make people think there is something wrong."

CHAPTER XVII.

LANCY was still glad to be at home. He admired his two sisters; he thought his mother more beautiful than ever, and yet the pleasure of those holidays was made dim by his growing certainty that "the Lodger's" loss and his disappearance were in some way connected together in the minds of his humble friends.

Don John was of an open, joyous nature. He was

devoted and most dutiful to his father and mother; his abilities were not by any means above the average, but he was blessed with a strong desire to do his best. He was to leave school and be articled to his father; there was no talk of his going to the University. He was delighted at this, but he well knew that it arose from a change in his father's circumstances, not from any desire to please him that he was to escape from the hated Latin and Greek, and take to more congenial studies. Don John accepted all his father's decisions as if they had been the decrees of fate; he was no whit more thoughtful than most youths of his age, but he had somewhat unusual observation of character—he could make his influence felt at home, and much of his talk was seasoned with a peculiar humor. The friends of the family considered him to be a youth of great promise; so he was in a certain sense, and a thorough good fellow; but though he worked fairly well at school, and may almost be said to have done his best, he never brought home one prize during his whole career excepting for good conduct, while Lancy scarcely ever came home without one or two.

And Mr. Johnstone, having looked over their papers, always expressed himself to the full as much pleased with Don John as with Lancy, sometimes more so. Neither boy was surprised. This was only justice, and they forthwith subsided into the places that nature had intended for them. In the schoolroom Don John ruled just as naturally as he took the head of the table; he headed the expeditions; if there was any blame, it all fell on him. If any treat was to be obtained he went and asked for it. If any one of the party in childhood had committed an accidental piece of mischief of a flagrant nature, such as letting a pony down and breaking its knees, or making a great smash of greenhouse glass, Don John, whoever had been the delinquent, was always deputed to go and make confession, and he generally began thus: "Father, I'm sorry to say *we've* done so and so."

Lancy was almost as much loved as Don John, but

he was neither feared nor looked up to; he did as he liked, and was great in criticism, but not in command.

Lancy spent many an hour in thought during those holidays. He perceived that circumstances gave him a certain power. There was a great deal of cunning in his nature, he felt a little ashamed of Mrs. Collingwood because, as he perceived, "she was not a lady." He had always been told that in the course of time he should be articled to the father who had adopted him; but he had hoped for several years at Cambridge, where he should do much as he liked. Still he wished to be under Mr. Johnstone's charge rather than under Mrs. Collingwood's. Such love as he had in his nature he bestowed on the Johnstones, specially on Mrs. Johnstone and Don John.

But his first visit to "the houses" changed everything. He could not bear to think of being so near to those people, feeling sure as he did that they were aware of his delinquency.

Another inevitable visit soon took place, and set the matter at rest in his opinion. He was sure they knew, just as sure as that his sisters did not.

And the servants? Had they, too, been made partakers of Mrs. Clarboy's and Mrs. Salisbury's suspicions? He longed to live "at home" again, but his fault had risen up and faced him when he hoped it was dead and buried. Why, rather than walk home through that field three or four times every week, he thought he could almost find it in his heart to run away again!

But there would be no need for that; he would write to Mrs. Collingwood, and make use of her to get his own way.

So he did, he never called her mother, and he was not base enough to use more expressions of affection than just enough as he thought to serve his end.

This was his letter: —

"MY DEAR MAMMA,

" When you wrote to me about going on the continent to travel with you for a whole year, I did not con-

sent to ask father's leave, for in the first place I knew
from Don John that he would not give it, for he meant
to article me to himself; and in the next, of course I
like better to be with my own family — the Johnstones
I mean, of course, — than with you.

"But you are very kind, and I am not so happy here
as I expected — because I am quite sure those people
in the houses know about IT. You understand what I
mean. And so, mamma, if you like, I 'll go the tour
with you. I know I shall be disagreeable and cross
to you sometimes when I think that I 'm away from
them, but that I can 't help, and I can hardly bear to
. write this letter, but I must.

"I think the best thing will be for you to write to
father (not telling that I wrote this), and ask him if
I may travel with you — you have said several times
that if he wished one thing and I wished the same, you
had no chance ; but I think if you wish one thing and I
wish the same, he will have no chance ; but mind, mamma, if he is very angry and will not consent, I am off
the bargain.

"I am, yours affectionately,

"L. AIRD."

In a few days a letter was written to Mr. Johnstone
by Mrs. Collingwood, just such a letter as Lancy had
suggested, and when the adopted son was told that the
plan was out of the question he seemed much disappointed.

"You must either be articled to me or you must go
to Cambridge, you cannot afford to waste a whole year
on idle pleasure. It is my duty to see that you are put
in the way to earn a comfortable living —"

"But I shall have four hundred a year," pleaded
Lancy rather dejectedly.

"How do you know that? what makes you think so?"

"Oh, father, Mrs. Collingwood always says that of
course what she has will all come to me."

"She is young, she may marry again."

"She says she never will."

" Well, grant that. Do you think I married, and that I bring up my family, on four hundred a year? "

" No, father."

" Or on treble that sum? "

" Perhaps I shall have something more."

" Of course you will. We need not go into that question. There! forget this letter, it will not do — I wish to have you under my own eyes, and living here, at home."

" But the people in the houses *know it.*"

" Know what?" exclaimed Donald Johnstone, forgetting for the moment what Lancy meant.

" Father, must I tell you what? "

No reply was made to this, the suggestion that his poor neighbors knew what Lancy had done was as gall and wormwood to Donald Johnstone.

" May n't I wait a year, and then perhaps you 'll go back to Harley Street, and I could be articled to you, and not be in their neighborhood? "

" No; I shall never go back to Harley Street. I am not nearly so well off, my boy, as I was in your childhood."

" And yet you say that I shall have more than four hundred a year."

There was a long pause. Then Lancy said, —

" Father, will you tell me one thing? " And before any answer could be made, he went on : " My father, Lancelot Aird, did he — did he save your life? "

" No." said Mr. Johnstone. He felt as if he had been taken at a disadvantage by this sudden question, but he little supposed that Lancy had long meditated asking it.

" Then he must have done you some great — some very great kindness, surely, father."

" No," said Mr. Johnstone, " he did not."

" When you last saw him, did you promise him that you would bring me up? "

Had the secret been kept so long to be drawn forth by such a simple question as that ; such a natural question, one that it seemed a son might surely have a right

to ask? Donald Johnstone scarcely knew, but he looked
at Lancy; he was impelled to answer, and could not
help it.

"I never made Lancelot Aird any promise of any
sort."

"He was not brought up with you?" said Lancy in
a faintly questioning tone.

"No."

"When did you first meet with him, then, father?"

"I never met with him at all."

Lancy, on hearing this, hung his head. It was not
for his father's sake, then, that he had been brought
up.

"You have made a mistake, you see," said Donald
Johnstone, in a low voice. "You have got an answer
to a question which sooner or later you almost must
have asked, and it is a shock to you. There is another
that you now desire to ask, but it pleases me to observe
that you cannot do it. I will ask it and answer it for
you. It is, I think, 'When did you first meet with
Lancelot Aird's wife.'"

Lancy, who had colored deeply, did not move or lift
up his face.

"I first met with her at a time of deep distress, when
my son was about ten days old, and there was every
reason to fear that I should lose his mother. I went
once into her darkened room to look at her, and as my
eyes grew accustomed to the gloom, I saw seated at
the foot of her bed a young woman in a widow's dress,
who had my poor little infant son in her arms. She
rose and curtseyed when she saw me, and I perceived
at once that she was the wet-nurse of whom I had been
told, and who had been engaged. She was nursing
Donald. The first time, then, that I saw her, was when
her child was about two months old."

Lancy, for the moment, was overcome with bashful-
ness, but when Mr. Johnstone said with a sigh, "I am
not displeased with you, my boy," he put his two hands
on the adopted father's hand as it was lying near there
on the table, and leaned his face on it and kissed it.

Then he said with a better, sweeter expression than had dawned on his face for a long time, —

"I am glad you are such a good man, father, but — but that only makes it more wonderful that I should be here, and that you should be so fond of me. Why, when I was a little fellow I used always to think you were even more fond of me than of Donald."

"Did you, my dear boy? I am exceedingly attached to you, Lancy; and when you went wrong, and I was told of that former delinquency, I lost my spirits. I became ill."

"But I 'm cured," pleaded Lancy, with a sob.

"Yes, I thank God for that hope. And now you perceive that by this conversation you have learned certain things; you took me at a disadvantage, and I spoke. You had meditated for some time asking these questions?"

"Yes, father," said Lancy.

"I advise you, as loving you, which I have proved, and as deserving well of you — "

"Oh, yes, father."

"I advise you not to ask any more, but rather to court ignorance. Let things be, my boy. Even Donald is not more welcome to everything I can do for him than you are. Let that satisfy you, Lancy."

"I will let things be," said Lancy, in a low voice. "Father, if I never thanked you and mother *for all this* all these years, it must have been because till Mrs. Collingwood appeared it seemed so natural I should have it, that I never thought about it — any more than the others did."

"Nothing else that you could possibly have said — nothing! — would have pleased me as much as this does!" exclaimed Mr. Johnstone.

Lancy was surprised. He saw how true his father's words were, that he had given him *great pleasure.* He could not but look inquiringly at him, and thereupon, with an effort, Donald Johnstone recalled his usual expression; and when Lancy went on, "But I want to thank you now, and to say that I am grateful," he answered, "That is enough, my dearest boy. Now go. I am about to write to Mrs. Collingwood. I am sorry she ever proposed to you to take this tour without first consulting me, and I must tell her it would not suit my views respecting you."

So Lancy left Mr. Johnstone, and even in the going, though his heart was warmed towards him, and he respected him more than for some time past, yet a certain ease of mind with which he had of late accepted his benefits was now gone. He wondered, as he had not been adopted for Lancelot Aird's sake, for whose sake it could be? His opinion had been highly disrespectful also towards Mrs. Collingwood — perhaps hardly more so than she deserved ; but the least suspicion of anything like the truth, and that he had been adopted for his own sake, never entered his head.

So Donald Johnstone wrote to Mrs. Collingwood, and told her that he did not consider a lengthened period of idleness and pleasure at all suitable for Lancy at his early age ; that he did not approve of mere feminine supervision for a high-spirited youth ; and that he trusted to her known affection for him not to damage his prospects by making the restraints of professional life irksome to him. The first step was now to be taken towards fitting him for his profession. When Mrs. Collingwood got this letter she was excessively disappointed ; and then, on reading it a second time, she was exceedingly wrath. She felt the galling nature of this yoke under which she had put her neck. Lancy had made her so sure she should get her own way, that she was resolved to do battle for it ; and she wrote, urging her claim to his company, and begging that he might not be forced against his will to be frequently among people who knew of " the childish faults which he had been so long and so severely punished for." " And besides, sir," she continued, " you are quite wrong if you think my dear boy has no natural feelings towards me, his mother. He knows his duty to you, and he strives to do it ; but he takes it hard that he is never to be with me, and you may depend that I do." Then she went on : " And I think it is but right, sir, that you should ask Mrs. Johnstone whether she thinks I ought to be always kept out of seeing my dear boy. She knows what a mother's feelings are ; and, though she is always so high with me, she will tell you that no mother could put up with what I am putting up with much longer."

Of course Mrs. Johnstone saw this letter. She sighed as she folded it up. "Donald, I am afraid if she will have him, she must have him. When we met, you carried things with a high hand, and I hoped she did not see her own power. Now, on reflection, I believe she does."

"Yes," he answered, "she is sure, you are sure, and I am almost sure, Lancy is hers. Let her take him for awhile, and I think she will be appeased ; but withstand her, and she will tell him all."

"You might exact a promise from her as the price of your consent."

"Oh, a promise goes for very little, my Star, in such a case as this. There is nothing that we ought not to do for Lancy, even to the point of telling him ourselves, if he was in temptation, or seemed likely to fall again, and to know of such a possible part in us might help to keep him upright for our sake — only — "

"Only," she went on, when he paused. "Only that, for the chance of elevating him, we should be sacrificing Donald. We should break Donald's heart."

"A boy's heart is not so easily broken," he replied.

"But he is our good boy — a very loving son," she answered almost reproachfully. "Who has never made us ashamed of him. Shall we take everything away from him, and fill him with doubt and distress in order to give almost nothing to the other?"

"Not if we can help it, my dear," and at that moment Lancy came into the room. "I've got a letter from my mamma," he said, he would not call her mother. "She says you do not like me to take a long tour with her, dear father and mother, but will I ask if I may go for one month?" The letter was duly read; "one month or six weeks " was the phrase used, and the letter was both urgent and humble.

" You wish to go?"

" Yes, father, if you don't mind."

Then observing that the tender woman whom he called mother was moved, and that her eyes, more moist and bright than usual, seemed to dwell on his face attentively, Lancy blushed and said, " I think I ought to pity her, for, as she often says, I am her only child."

Mr. Johnstone looked at him deliberately, and without any tenderness of aspect, he seemed to take a moment's time to consider his words, then he said, " If you were my only child, I should hardly love you more ; certainly I could not be one whit more anxious for your welfare. Therefore, knowing her feelings, and considering that her present request is reasonable (her wish to take you away for a year was not), I think if your mother agrees with me — " Here he paused, and it pained them both a little, when, after waiting just one short instant for her rejoinder, he said rather urgently, —

" Oh, mother, you always wish me to have treats — mother, you 'll let me go?"

" Yes," she said, without looking at him.

He scarcely observed her emotion, certainly never divined that it was on his account, but he gave her the customary kiss they always bestowed when thanking her for any favor, and he took out of the room with him a vivid recollection of what Donald Johnstone had said. He felt a little daunted by it. He knew it would be a restraint upon him. But it was no restraint as regarded that only point at which just then he was in danger.

* * *

CHAPTER XVIII.

" WELL, now I have leave to go," thought Lancy, looking out of the window of his own bedroom ; " now I have leave to go ; and the question is, am I glad, or am I sorry? If it was not for the people in

the houses, of course I would never lend myself to aid
Mrs. Collingwood's plans. Is it really only because I
have not courage enough to meet those people's looks
that I mean to go? Of course things would be no better
at the end of six weeks." He reflected on a sentence
written on a distinct piece of paper and put inside her
letter by Mrs. Collingwood: "Show this letter, my
dear, to Mr. Johnstone, and I'll manage, when we have
once set out, to keep you as long as you and me think
fit."

"Yes, as long as she thinks fit, whether I like it or
not — for I shall have no money, I shall not even have
my allowance."

He sauntered rather disconsolately down the corridor.
After that short conference with "father and mother"
he had, as it were, dismissed himself that he might write
to Mrs. Collingwood. He looked out at another window, and there were father and mother in the pony carriage, and there was Mrs. Johnstone's maid behind with
some bottles and a basket.

"Father" for once had taken a holiday, and all the
party were to have lunch and afternoon tea in a wood
about four miles off. Don John and all the girls were
standing about the donkey — a babble of girls' voices
came up to him very pleasantly. The donkey turned
his head over his shoulder with an air of discontent and
disgust. Well he might, for little Mary was seated on
his back, and Charlotte and Naomi were filling his pan-
niers with crockery, a tin kettle, fruit, cakes, and all
sorts of miscellaneous prog. Lancy was to run after
them when he had written his letter. Really he hardly
knew now whether he would write it or not.

He sauntered on; the door of Mrs. Johnstone's
dressing-room was open, and he idly entered.

Lancy never had any evil intentions unless present
opportunity seemed to his weak mind to be ministering
to them.

He was thinking just then, "If I once go, then, however much I may long to get back, I shall have no money
to do it with."

There was a good large dressing-case of Indian workmanship standing on the table opposite to him.   Often
when a little fellow he had been allowed to open it.   He
remembered how mother used sometimes to let him and
Don John rub her little amber and agate ornaments with
wash-leather when she was by.   There was an upper
tray, with nothing of value in it, that he had often
helped to put to rights ; there were some ivory hearts
and some bangles in it — how well he remembered
them ! — and there were some Indian silver butterflies,
which trembled on flowers with spiral stems.   There
were two or three trays in that box; but when it appeared to be empty there was a little spring somewhere
on which they used to ask mother to put her finger, and
then they used to see a shallow drawer suddenly start
forth and display its contents.

" I have n't seen it for years," thought Lancy ; " some
old rings were there."   The color flushed over his
face ; he began to know that he was in danger, for he
did remember again that he had no money.   He made
no movement to go out of the room, but he half turned
his head, and so it fell out that his eyes lit on a book
which was lying face downwards on the table.   He took
it up open as it was.   " Mother," had evidently been
reading it before she went out.

For one instant it seemed as if, prescient of this visit,
she had put the book there as a warning ; for what was
it that he read?

" There are two kinds of sin — wilful sin and willing
sin.

" Wilful sin is that into which, because of the frailty
of our nature, because of the strength of passion and
temptation ; not loving but loathing it, not seeking but
resisting it, not acquiescing in but fighting and struggling against it, we all sometimes fall.   This is the
struggle in which God's spirit striveth with our spirit,
and out of which we humbly believe and hope that God
will at the last grant unto us victory and forgiveness.

" But there is another kind of sin far deadlier, far
more heinous, far more incurable, it is *willing* sin.   It

is when we are content with sin; when we have sold ourselves to sin; when we no longer fight against sin; when we mean to continue in sin. That is the darkest, lowest, deadliest, most irredeemable abysm of sin; and it is well that the foolish or guilty soul should know that on it, if it have sunk to this, has been already executed — self-executed — the dread mandate, ' In the day that thou eatest thereof thou shalt surely die.' "

" Who wants to commit sin?" exclaimed Lancy aloud. "Always preach, preach, preaching,— I 'm sick of it. And just as if I did n't know the difference you talk of as well as you do — or better. *Wilful* sin is what we are dragged in to do for its own sake, but *willing* sin is what we plan to do for *our* own sakes, because it will be to our interest at some future time. Well I had better go and write my letter."

But he did not stir; he gave the pages of the book a flick and they turned; he could not stand there with no ostensible occupation, he actually began to read again.

" For first, my brethren, let us all learn that the consequences of sin are *inevitable;* in other words, that ' punishment is but the stream of consequence flowing on unchecked.' There is in human nature an element of the gambler, willing to take the chances of things; willing to run the risk if the issue be uncertain. There is no such element here. The punishment of sin is certain. All Scripture tells us so. ' Though hand join in hand the wicked shall not be unpunished.' ' The way of transgressors is hard.' All the world's proverbs tell us so. ' Reckless youth, rueful age.' ' As he has made his bed, so he must lie in it.' ' He that will not be ruled by the rudder must be ruled by the rock.'

" Even Satan himself would not deny it. In the old legend of *Dr. Faustus*, when he bids the devil lay aside his devilish propensity to lying, and tell the truth, the devil answers, ' The world does me injustice to tax me with lies. Let me ask their consciences if I have ever deceived them into thinking that a bad action was a good one.' " [1]

[1] Sermon by the Rev. Canon Farrar.

Something quaint or strange or striking impelled him to read thus far, or it may have been that he was or-dained to have every possible warning this time; he could not smother his better convictions without a long struggle, and he trembled. Something seemed to whis-per within him that this time he could not say if he sinned that it was on the impulse of the moment and almost unawares.

But he stood stock still. He would not go out of the room. He sighed, and the color faded out of his cheeks. "But if I was not to do it again," he whis-pered, "I ought never to have done it at all."

He put down the book — and went up and opened the box, and lifted the tray and touched the little spring.

The small box started forth at once and displayed its contents before his eyes.

He chose out a little faded ring-case of yellow leather he found in it. It contained an old-fashioned, clumsy ring, a ring for a man's finger. Perhaps about once in two years " mother" wore it on her middle finger. It had belonged to her grandfather. A handsome dia-mond ring. He took it out, closed the leather case, and put that back in its place. He pushed back the drawer and closed the spring over it, put down the trays, then shut the dressing-case and walked slowly out of the room — with the ring on his finger. "Mother does not often leave her box unlocked," he said to himself, " she must have been in a hurry."

He thought with something like dismay of the good clergyman whose exhortations had been such a weari-ness to him. Then there flashed on his mind the only thing that had ever been said to him that had made an impression.

"Father" had talked to him but a few days before, and Lancy had without hesitation claimed as an excuse for his sin *a propensity* that he unfortunately had for laying his hands on what he saw before him. He was cured now — but there were unfortunate people who could not help stealing — and if great care had not been

taken with him — for which he was very thankful (!)
he might have become one of them.

His mentor answered, "No, my boy, a thousand
times no — what you have suffered from has been by no
means an instinct of covetousness, but an absence of
principle."

"I wished for the things," said Lancy faintly.

"But not for the mere sake of possession — not to
hide them and go in secret to gaze at them. No, you
took fruit that you might eat it — you took money that
you might spend it. There is no powerful instinct of
acquisitiveness against you: be afraid of the right
thing, a feeble sense of justice, a slack hold on good
principle."

He remembered this now because, of all that had
ever been said to him, it had most impressed him. He
was no Kleptomaniac, nothing of the sort. Reason
showed him that possession was good, conscience did
not govern him enough as to how he came into possession.

He spoke within himself from time to time as he
stood in his own room, looking out at the window.

"It's worth about fifty pounds, that ring."

"Mother does not want it; will not know perhaps
for years that it's gone."

"But suppose it should be missed — is it possible
that they would suspect *me?*"

"Oh, they never would, they never could!" — Lancy
was actually almost indignant at the thought of such a
thing. He appeared to see — as if he was one of them,
how unlikely such a thing was, what a shame it would
be in their opinion. No, they ought not to suspect
him. In fact, the thing was not done yet in such a way
that it could not be undone.

It was almost time to set out to follow the family
party.

"I can easily put it back if I like," he murmured,
"To rob one who has adopted me as a son!"

"It sounds bad —"

"In this house particularly —"

" But this will only be an ideal loss after all — "

" If it 's not found out, it can hardly be said to have been done — "

" Very likely at the end of six weeks, having had no need to sell it, I shall bring it back."

" He that will not be ruled by the rudder must be ruled by the rod."

" I 'll put it back."

" To-morrow I 'll put it back."

" Before I go on my tour I 'll put it back."

" Well, if I mean to overtake them in time for lunch, I must start."

He meant to put it back, but yet to keep it in his own power till the last minute, *for he might not have an opportunity to take it again.* Having said even this to himself, and provided for a possible future wish to be a thief, he went into a spare room which was carpeted all over, lifted the carpet in one corner, and hid the ring under it.

" I 've done it now ! " he whispered, with a sigh. " Well, then, they should not try to make me live down here where that other thing I did is known."

" Perhaps I 've done for myself too — "

" Perhaps. It 's Mrs. Collingwood's fault if I have. Does she suppose I care for her, that she suggests to me to cheat them as if I wished to do it? To cheat them in order to be in her company ? "

Lancy walked and ran through the fair woodlands and pastures till he came to the place where he was to join his people.

The father and mother, as more to one another than ever the children could be to them, sat a little apart, and looked on together. Two dark, eager young men hovered about Marjorie, ambitious to help her, desirous to absorb her notice.

Naomi and Charlotte cut up salad. Mary held the dressing, Don John laid the cloth on the grass and set out the viands.

" I care for neither of those fellows, my **star**," observed Donald Johnstone.

"Nor does Marjorie," she answered; "don't disturb thyself with any fear of an unwelcome son-in-law."

"I suppose this sort of thing will go on till she makes her selection among the youth of the neighborhood. It's rather hard on Naomi. When first I saw you, Estelle, you were seated just so — just two such aspirants heaved windy sighs in your near vicinity. In twenty minutes I hated them with unchristian fervor. In twenty minutes more I loved! I was blighted! I had attained to the very fanaticism of jealousy! And I remember even now, how a girl as graceful as Naomi and as pretty as Charlotte stood by, and none of us took the least notice of her. It was Leslie that I hated most."

"Poor Leslie!" she said, with a quiet smile; "you were always very jealous of him."

He laughed.

"I could find it in my heart to be jealous of Leslie even now," he answered.

"I know you could, love," was her thought, but she only said, "What! when our grown-up children are about us? Donald, how odd that you should have taken it into your head to say that just now!"

"Why just now?"

"Because I had a letter from him this morning."

"No!"

"He is coming home invalided. His health seems to be quite broken up."

"Poor fellow! What an ass he made of himself! but he is a very respectable ass."

"And so conscientious!" she added, with a little, irrepressible laugh.

He looked at her inquiringly.

"After expressing his unalterable affection, his deep respect for me, he desired that I would show his letter to you — 'it was only right that you should see it — and then if you permitted it, would I write him a few lines of sympathy?' There, now read his effusion; and Donald, you really should not talk about being jealous of such a foolish fellow as Leslie, even in joke."

"I am quite aware of it, my star; but look at our children."

She looked, and the scene before them often rose in the memory of both parents afterwards. Don John was dipping water out of a tiny clear stream with a cup, and pouring it into a large china basin which Naomi held, leaning towards him with supple grace, and keeping her feet away from the moist brink. Don John might now almost be called a fine youth. He only just reached the middle height, but he looked very strong, was well made, and had a charming air of contentment and intelligence. The two younger children, with Lancy, were hovering about the table-cloth, and Marjorie, with a somewhat pensive air, sat quietly on her throne; it was the trunk of a fallen tree. The two lovers, one of whom was a mere youth, a nephew of Mr. Viser, and the other a young officer, Campbell by name, gazed at her resplendent robe, her exquisite gloves, underneath which were yet more exquisite hands. They admired the incomparable grace of that hat with matchless feathers in it. A small locket rose and fell on her delicate throat, no jeweller's shop contained an ornament so deeply to be admired.

Marjorie and her sister were dressed and adorned precisely alike, even to the locket. Neither of the lovers knew it, the two looked so different in their eyes. Her hair was the reddest brown or the brownest red; wherever the light struck, it looked the precise color of rust.

Marjorie admired a trail of honeysuckle which depended from the bough of a tree. Both the lovers started up to gather it; then Campbell fell back, thinking that the occasion promised him a moment alone with her. Then Viser also held back; how could he leave her alone for that same moment with his rival?

Mary and Master Frederick Johnstone, now thirteen years old, perfectly understood this little scene. They burst into a laugh of keen delight; Lancy joined, and Marjorie felt very foolish. Freddy's surprised eyes somewhat daunted her. They meant that it was ridiculous to have a lover, and it was ridiculous to be a lover. They seemed to ask what the young fools could be thinking of, and Don John exclaimed, —

"It's all very well for a time, but 'Blow these sparks!' as the fire said to the bellows, if they don't soon burst into flame I shall certainly go out."

"You are a very vulgar boy!" exclaimed Naomi. "Mother hates slang, you know she does."

"Well, they should n't be so long about it, then. Let them propose, and she can accept one."

"Then that one would always be here!"

"And I shall go out. Grandmother has asked me many times; I shall go to Edinburgh."

In the meantime Charlotte had been walking up and down a short level space under the trees. There was a tree-trunk to bound her path at each end, and when she reached it she turned; but getting quite lost in thought, she at last walked up to one of the trunks, and, being brought to a stand, forgot to turn, but stood with her face close to it cogitating, and quite unaware that certain peals of laughter which she heard had anything to do with her.

Don John pelted her with little rose-colored fungi, and little buds of foxgloves, flicking them with such dexterity that several lighted on her shoulders. At last he threw a good-sized hedge rose at her hat. Then she half roused herself, and, calmly turning, gazed at them all. Even the lovers were laughing. Charlotte blushed; she knew not how to move, whether to join them or walk away from them. She was covered with confusion; but here was Lancy coming. Lancy held out his hand ostensibly to help her over the tiny brook, and when she put hers into it, he squeezed it. It was the very first time any one had squeezed her hand. With startled eyes she looked up. It was the same old Lancy, the familiar companion of her childhood, but somehow he looked different. Selfish fellow, he was only pleasing himself for the moment; she did look so pretty. His fine eyes looked into hers and told her that she was lovely, and that he thought so. The admiration of the other sex, and what effect it might have on her, she knew at present nothing of. Sweet little Charlotte never had pretty speeches made to her; nobody wanted to appropriate the flowers she had worn, the gloves she had laid down; nobody stole her photographs out of the album; nobody " on his bended knees " begged for one.

Charlotte was surprised to the point of feeling confused, and yet there was a little elation too; and when she joined the party she had forgotten that they had laughed at her. She hardly knew what passed.

But Don John knew all about it, or at least he thought he did. He had seen the look between the boy and the maiden.

" I did not think Lancy could be a muff," thought this sensible youth with scorn. " And Charlotte to be so pleased! Ugh! they 're all alike, I declare."

CHAPTER XIX.

MANY a long day passed before those who met at that picnic came together again.

The next morning Lancy took leave of his parents, not without guilty beatings at the heart, for he took with him the ring. The affection they showed him — the almost confidence in him — he could not accept without some very keen stirrings of shame. He was only to be away a month, as was supposed, but he received a great deal of wise, grave, and truly fatherlike admonition and counsel. " What would he think if he knew all!" thought Lancy, and he held his tongue, and yet he was shaken, he was compelled to think the world into which he was wilfully flinging himself was more full of danger, not than he had known, but than he had felt.

" I 'm a valuable article, and it 's manifest that Mrs.

Collingwood is not thought competent to have the charge of me. Well, father's right there; I should be a fool indeed, supposing that I wished to go wrong, if I could not do it in spite of her."

"And now it is fully understood that this tour is only to be for a month?" observed Donald Johnstone.

Lancy answered, "Yes, father," and to take a tour of one month he went away.

And yet when he had taken leave of his sisters and of Don John, and went to kiss his mother, she was aware of something in his manner, something which he could not conceal, which struck her as if it portended a leave-taking for a long time.

He looked at her; he was agitated as if in spite of himself. The diamond ring was in his waistcoat pocket pressed so tightly by his arm against his heart that he felt it plainly. It almost seemed to burn him. But that was not all. He knew that he was not to be trusted; he was sure that he should not come back. It flashed into his heart that this was hard on them, for they had treated him in all respects as a son. It flashed back to him in an instant that if he had been their own son he should have done it just the same, and then he gave Mrs. Johnstone his fresh young cheek, and having his free choice and time to think, elected to shake off the salutary yoke with the peaceful security of home, and if the tour proved to be delightful or exciting, leave it to fate to find him excuses for prolonging it, and to the same "agreeable party" to get him out of the scrape if the home authorities should be wroth.

In time circumstances would drift him home again, he would eventually render himself so disagreeable to "his mamma," that she would be glad to get rid of him, and then, throwing all the blame upon her, he could humbly beg pardon. And — would they forgive him? Of course they would.

At the end of the month, two or three letters having already been received from him, he wrote a very humble letter full of anxious excuses, and, as it seemed, of perplexity. He declared that Mrs. Collingwood, who, in other respects, was most kind, had suddenly informed him that she meant to cross from Brindisi to Alexandria, and spend some time in Egypt; that he had no money to come home with; that she was very willing to take him with her and pay all his expenses, "as was only right," she said, "but she declined to give him money in order that he might leave her." Certain phrases in this letter let Mr. Johnstone see plainly that Lancy had not concocted it without aid, perhaps prompting, from Mrs. Collingwood. He was not deceived, but he felt himself to be powerless. He had long, indeed always, acted as if both the boys were his own sons, now he was made to feel that he could do it no longer without their consent.

As for Lancy, he was generally amused, often excited, but not always happy. He could not respect, he did not love the woman who was helping him to outwit his best friends. He soon got into idle habits, and the longer he stayed away the less willing he felt to go home and work and submit himself to the restraint of a well-ordered English family.

Feminine supervision was of little use to him, and he soon began to take advantage of Mrs. Collingwood's want of education, and more than once or twice helped himself to money of hers in the changing for her of one sort of currency into another. But even that was not enough; before they left Europe the ring was gone, and Lancy was the worse for a quantity of loose money always under his hand, yet not wanted for any good or needful expenditure. And he was the worse also for a fear that he could never dare to come home now lest the ring should be eventually missed and he should be suspected of the crime. Lancy pitied himself and he pitied "his folks," as he called them. "It's not so bad for them, though, my running away as it would have been if I had been their own son. It might have been Don John. Yes, and if I had been Don John — no, I mean if I had been the son and he the adopted fellow, I should certainly have done it just the same. Why, what a fool I am! I should have done it without half as much worry and conscience-pricking as I feel now, because I should have been so much more sure they would forgive me. Numbers of fellows run away — hundreds of fellows, in fact — but — well, they don't take any family jewels with them. How do I know that? Why, I don't know it. I dare say I 'm no worse than other people."

All the winter in Egypt — wonderful things to see, strange fashions, a floating home, sunny temples in the sand, and blank-faced gods to find fascinations in ; perfect impunity yet from any questioning as regarded the ring, and any calling to order, or even inquiry as to when he meant to return. And then having written several somewhat moderately penitent letters home, he got answers before they went up the Nile. " Father " at first was manifestly displeased, and yet Lancy thought he was restraining his anger, he wished almost, as it were, to propitiate the scapegrace. And " mother " did not so much blame as reason with him. He could have remained at the hotel if he had pleased, she said, and there telegraphed to his father to send him money — he could easily do so now. Not so very easily. He did hesitate for half a day, but to spend almost a whole winter on the Nile, and see so many marvels, and have nothing to do but to please himself — how could he give this up? He did not give it up. And to see so much, increased his thirst for seeing more. So the winter wore away, and before the cherry blossom was out in the orchard behind his old home, just as the buds began to turn white, and the girls were saying, " Lancy must be on his way to us by this time," there came a letter from him dated Jerusalem.

It really was a very nice letter, and it seemed to make out, though it did not exactly assert, that he had not heard from home for a long time, and he felt sure they would be pleased to know that Mrs. Collingwood, though she would not allow him to leave her, was yet very kind, and gave him every opportunity to improve himself. He said nothing of how " father " had proposed to send him money, but left it to be supposed that he had never received that letter.

Mr. Johnstone felt that he was foiled. Mrs. Johnstone was very jealous of the other woman, and, with yearning love, began to admit for the first time that much as she had been wronged, Maria Collingwood had wronged herself more. She knew perfectly well that Lancy did not love her ; he never spoke of her as " my mother," only as " my mamma."

As for Don John, he got accustomed in the end to the loss of this life-long companion. He ruled and reigned over the other young people and allowed Marjorie's lovers to perceive the good-natured pity with which he regarded them, not so much for " spooning," as he called it, for that, as he graciously observed, was natural, but for being so long about it.

" I shall take the matter in hand myself," he observed to Naomi. " Marjorie likes Campbell best, and, besides, Viser will not be able to marry for ten years, by what I hear."

" Why, what can you do ? " exclaimed Naomi, laughing at him.

" And after that," proceeded Don John, " I shall look up some lovers, one each for you and Charlotte. If I don't, I shall have you both on my hands all my life, so far as I can see."

Naomi still laughed ; " You can do nothing," she repeated, " a boy like you ! "

" We shall see. Campbell is horridly cast down because he's ordered to Edinburgh. And I feel sure that ass Viser is putting off making his offer till the powerful rival is out of the way. I shall write to grandmother, and — well, I shall tell her my views."

" No, Don John."

" I shall ! She will invite Marjorie to visit her ; and I shall take her down."

" Well ? "

" Well, father admitted the other day that though he had not cared for Campbell at first, he now thought he should like him very well as a son-in-law."

" Well ? "

" He never has the least chance here, always some of

you present, generally one at least of you laughing at him."

" Well?"

" I am not going to stand any more of this questioning. If Marjorie's frocks and feathers and things are not in good order, you will have to lend her some of yours, and Charlotte may lend her pearls — for she is going to Edinburgh in about a week, and I do not intend that father should be teased for any money for her just now."

He turned as Naomi, still laughing, but believing that he was in earnest, walked on to the house.

He was in the middle of the cherry orchard, and, behold, there was Charlotte advancing! The sky was blue above ; a cup of azure light without a cloud ; the trees were one mass of pure white blossom, and under foot the ground was covered with the glossy flat leaves and yellow astral flowers of the celandine. A blue and yellow world — all pure white and pale glory. Was there no red at all in it?—nothing to give a hint of coming damask roses and the intense pure blush of the carnation?

Yes, Charlotte drew near ; she was reading as she walked. Don John's time to rave about beauty was not yet come ; but he did look at Charlotte's damask lips and carnation cheeks ; and somehow he perceived that she supplied a deficiency, that she carried about with her all that nature and April possessed of a very precious color just then.

A smile of joy broke out over his face ; something occurred that was a revelation to himself, and that in an instant he communicated to her. A crisp sound, as of a foot treading on last year's leaves and fallen twigs, was heard behind them ; and there emerged from the side path, and evidently was making for Charlotte, a somewhat jaunty-looking young man, whose buoyant tread made him almost seem to dance up to her. Yes, he knew what he was about ; he had a deprecating and yet a somewhat elated air.

It was the youthfullest of the curates. It was he of whom a very ancient dame in one of the cottages had said, " He been a father to me, he have."

" At last ! " whispered Don John. " Now, Charlotte, remember Fetch's admonitions. The best of cousins withdraws."

He turned, and deliberately marched off, but so slowly that he heard the young man's greeting to the maiden. He heard him assure her that the weather was all that could be wished.

Don John joined Naomi.

Naomi was very much his friend. She thought it was not fair that Marjorie should have all the lovers and Charlotte none. For herself, a happy carelessness made her more than willing to bide her time. Meanwhile she and Don John shared confidences, passed family circumstances under review, and in their youthful fashion tried to throw good chances in the way of their sister and cousin.

And what was happening now?

Charlotte ought to have seated herself on the wooden bench in the orchard, and there the youthfullest curate, sitting cosily beside her, should have been allowed to say pretty things — that is, if he had any in his mind to say : but no, it appeared, after Don John had told the news to Naomi — the remarkable news that somebody had actually come to call whose manifest object was Charlotte — and while these two, standing behind a white thicket of bloom, were deciding that mother should be informed of this call, and asked to invite the youthful one to lunch — it appeared that Charlotte, so far from sitting on the bench, was walking towards the house with a brisk, elastic step, he after her ; and he was not talking at all ; it was she whose words were heard.

The brother and sister drew themselves closer together behind the bushes ; they did not care to be eavesdroppers ; but when they inevitably heard a few words of what Charlotte was saying, they looked at one another with just indignation. Charlotte had naturally been put out of countenance when Don John, with a good-humored but somewhat threatening air, withdrew, having let her know both what he thought and what he expected of her.

She glanced at the young curate, and he immediately became shy, ridiculously out of countenance and awkward. He opened his mouth, and, finding nothing to say, left it open for an instant, then actually fell back on the weather again, repeating his encomium on it, and declaring with earnestness that it was all he could wish.

Now shyness is almost as independent of rules as it is of reasons; but if any one thing may be said of it with certainty, it is this, that to encounter shyness greater than itself kills it on the spot. This is why shy people never think others shy. The one who has the quickest perception is instantly cured, and the other has to bear it all.

Charlotte pitied him, and became quite at her ease. She began to converse; he, more and more out of countenance, found nothing to say. So in a short time she came to the conclusion that he had nothing to say " of that sort." Young men never had anything of that sort to say to her; there was no abstract reason for it, but so it was.

Now, if it had been Marjorie! She had often heard young men talk to Marjorie, and knew the style quite well of that sort of thing. In her modest mind, she could not see anything in herself to give rise to that sort of thing; she felt no leaning towards the curate. He asked after her aunt. Charlotte promptly replied that her aunt was well, and would be glad to see him.

So she proceeded slowly towards the house, and, as silence was awkward, began to talk about the book she had in her hand.

It was one of Max Müller's. He, glad of anything which, while detaining him in her presence, granted him some delay, while he recovered from this shyness, which was an astonishment to himself, responded gratefully. Everything she did, said, and looked, was right in his eyes. He thought she perceived the state of his affections, and with sweet maiden modesty — for Charlotte had a peculiarly modest manner — was occupying the time (thus, in fact, giving him the best kind of encouragement, and all with perfect tact) — the time till he could recover his manly courage and pour forth his heart, at the same time laying himself metaphorically and his prospects actually, at her feet.

But Charlotte, who at first had talked coolly enough about the book, presently began to warm with her subject. He responded as well as he was able; but, as she became earnest and eloquent, he found himself completely drawn away. from what he had intended. He could not think what she meant. Surely she was overdoing her part! He was quite ready to begin now, and she actually would n't let him!

No; nothing was farther from her thoughts. With hazy half-perception the youthfullest curate heard her explain that in some respects she dissented from the view of Max Müller, as she did from the school of those who had mainly founded themselves on him.

But before he knew what he was about he was assenting, while with keen regret she spoke on the instability of language. What was the instability of language to him, particularly just then, when they were drawing close to the edge of the orchard? He was so lost in astonishment that he opened his mouth again, and it was at that instant that, passing the thicket of young trees, Don John and Naomi heard Charlotte say, —

"Yes, of course, mere pronunciation is a matter of secondary importance; and yet even in that respect any civilized nation must desire to escape change."

The curate assented with a forlornness which imparted an air of doubt to his words.

"It is always loss and never gain that an old, settled language has to fear," proceeded Charlotte. "I think I see one if not two losses not very far ahead of us. The Italians have utterly lost their aspirate; and it certainly appears to me that, even during the last twelve years, for I have noticed peculiarities of language about that length of time, it certainly appears to me that we are losing it too. This is sad, but I fear it is inevitable."

A murmur repeated at her side that it was sad.

"Even the pains we take (that is the more cultivated.

among us) to give the letter ' h ' due force, the increasing notice it attracts, the manner in which we measure
culture by its absence or presence, all these symptoms
show that we keep it and use it with difficulty and
against the grain.   Yet that we are in process of losing
it I cannot doubt, and that we have been doing so for
nearly 200 years ; before which date, as you have no
doubt noticed, there is nothing in literature to show that
our common people used it amiss any more than they
now do the letters T, M, or D."

The curate could not assert that he had noticed anything of the sort in literature ; but in a feeble sort of
way he foundered through an answer, which amounted
on the whole to dissent from Charlotte's opinion.

" If you think so," answered Charlotte, " only take
notice of the first conversation you are present at.   The
aspirate is at present always given with due distinctness
at the commencement of a long or an important word,
specially if it begins the sentence ; but I must say I
often hear good readers and speakers soften the sound
far too much in the little words when they conclude it.
' And what did you say to him ?'   An Irishman will
say, ' What did you say *toom* ?'   ' She handed me her
own bouquet ; ' when you next hear such a sentence as
that, remark whether the first aspirate is not sounded
much more strongly than the second.   I might give ex-
amples by dozens, but the fact is the danger is immi-
nent, and I greatly fear the worst symptom is our
unconsciousness.   It almost makes me weep ; but I
plainly foresee what the end will be."

The curate was lost in astonishment ; he would have
liked to comfort her ; but here they were at the hall-
door, and if any one had told him beforehand that he
should have found Charlotte alone, and been quite unable to make his offer, and that in his ensuing state of
discomfiture to be with a dozen other people would seem
to him more desirable than to be obliged to talk about
the instability of language, he would not perhaps have
easily believed this ; but he knew Charlotte better now,
and himself too.

CHAPTER XX.

WHEN Naomi and Don John appeared to take their places at the luncheon-table, Charlotte and the young curate were seated one on either side of Mrs. Johnstone. Charlotte was full of enthusiasm, and the youthful one was staring at her with an expression of countenance which Don John understood perfectly.

He had entered the orchard fully intending to do a great deed, a difficult deed, and one that he dreaded inexpressibly. He had greatly feared a dismissal, and had many times pictured himself to himself as returning crestfallen and dejected to his lodgings, with some such words as these ringing in his ears : — "I have the highest esteem, Mr. Brown, for your character, and I always find your sermons most interesting ; but the fact is my cousin, Don John, has had my heart from my childhood, and we are only waiting, &c., &c. ;" — and not having a high opinion of his own courage, he sometimes thought he might return without having been able to make his offer at all ; or, having bungled through it, might find himself confronted with a face full of wonder at his audacity ; for, of course, Charlotte must have a just idea of her own merits.

Thus he had tormented himself for some time, but nothing like this had occurred. A strange revulsion had taken place in his soul. He was not dismissed : he was quite at his ease with Charlotte opposite to him, and her aunt making him welcome. He had not committed himself in any way. Committed himself! What an expression, he marvelled, as he turned over in his thoughts the undoubted fact that it had occurred to him. And now, was he glad of this state of things? He could not tell ; but he had a kind of involuntary sense of having escaped. He ate his luncheon with a·

certain urgency; laughed, and was more hilarious than usual; trembled, and felt rather cold. Oh, certainly she was handsome, handsomer than he had ever thought. He had never seen on any cheek such a pure perfect carnation. Her eyes did not sparkle in the least — they shone. She had the deepest, the most bewitching dimple in one of her cheeks — only in one — that he had ever set his eyes upon. It almost prevailed to plunge him again into his dream, and thereupon he looked at Charlotte; his shyness and embarrassment returned, and with them a necessity to talk — he must needs say something. He took up what had so much astonished him — the instability of language — Charlotte's favorite despair.

For a few minutes it did well enough. He found himself half listening while she and Don John argued together. Then he lost himself in cogitations over the situation, till his wide-open eyes encountering Naomi's, he saw that her attention was attracted — she was observing him. He wrenched himself away from his inner self and listened.

"Yes," Charlotte was saying, "hopeless to stem the flood when once it has begun to rise."

"Well," Don John rejoined, "what then? The language has no abstract rights, the nation has. The nation must, it will, use and even change the language as it pleases."

"And, my dears," observed Mrs. Johnstone placably, "I think it was only yesterday that you two were rejoicing in some changes that you felt to be improvements."

"In pronunciation," Don John put in.

"Oh, yes, aunt; it was a very curious circumstance, we were saying, — that while some provincial defects of pronunciation are handed down for generations, others even in our own day and since Dickens wrote (Dickens, who only died ten years ago) are completely gone out, at least in the South and in London. 'Spell it with a *We*,' Sam Weller says to his father — and he always calls himself Veller. All that has van-

ished. I never hear any one say winegar or weal; I
never hear William called Villam. And that shows that
this peculiarity was less dialect than slang. Slang is
always to be deplored."

"Deplored!" echoed Don John solemnly.

"But dialect to be cherished — one dialect is just as
good really as another."

"Just as good as another!"

Charlotte appeared to find a protest rather than assent in this behavior of Don John's. She went on:
"It is only because our literature is written in one particular dialect of English that we give that the preference; this is intolerant, to say the least of it."

"Very; and after all a great deal of literature, and
even poetry, is written in what we unkindly call provincial English. We have but to step into our own fields,
for instance, to hear language very like ' the lay of the
hunted pig:' —

> 'So sure as pegs is pegs,
> Eight chaps ketch'd I by the legs.'

I have often wept over the affecting beauty of that
poem; I could now, only I would rather not.   And
how beautiful, how tender is the speech of the Wilt-
shire maid to her lover, when, feeling a little jealous of
a rival, she persuades him —

> 'From her seat she ris'n,
> Says she, Let thee and I go our own way,
> And we 'll let she go shis'n.' "

"Quite impossible to reason with you when you are
in this mocking humor, and yet what I said was quite
true, the London interchange of V and W has suddenly
gone out, but one hears people leave out or soften the
aspirate more and more every day, particularly in
church and by clergymen," she added, after a moment
of reflection; "and really and truly I have sometimes
felt as if the service and the lessons were arranged on
purpose to make this defect conspicuous."

Mr. Brown here felt a tingling sensation down to his

finger-tips, he colored deeply, and knew not where to look. His own aspirates were not conspicuously absent, of course, but he felt a miserable doubt whether they were always adequately present.

Mrs. Johnstone for the moment could find nothing to say, but Don John suddenly burst out with, —

"Ah, those are 'school of cookery' tarts, Marjorie! I am sure you and Naomi must have made them after your lesson."

"Of course we did, but how did you know it?"

"Because they bulge out in all directions, they are as slovenly as a bullfinch's nest. Let me give you one, Mr. Brown."

The curate accepted one. Charlotte meeting Don John's eyes as he looked straight at her, began to perceive that she had made a blunder, and forbore from any further remark. The conversation meanwhile became general, and any contributions made to it by the guest were received with flattering attention by Mrs. Johnstone and Marjorie, who managed to put him at his ease.

"Aunt, have I made a very terrible blunder?" said poor little Charlotte, while Don John and his two sisters accompanied Mr. Brown as far as the schools, which he had asked them to visit on his way home. "I mean an unkind blunder," she added.

Mrs. Johnstone was always specially tolerant of Charlotte's *gauche* speeches, and gentle with her shyness.

"It was a pity, my dear, that you made that unlucky remark. I am certain you did not mean to be unkind; but he felt it so keenly as to confirm me in an idea I had that he admires you, Charlotte."

"I thought so too," said Charlotte, "just at first, but after we had talked a little while I was sure he did n't, and then—"

"Well, and then?"

"Why, we got interested in our conversation, and I quite forgot it."

"So you thought he admired you?"

"Yes, but that was because Don John put it into my

head.   And it made me feel so shy and so ridiculous at
first that when I found it was not the case, of course
I was more at my ease than usual.   And so I talked to
him."

"You should have let him talk to you."

"He had nothing to say.   At least he had nothing
to converse about of any real or solid interest."

"Well," said her aunt, taking care not to let the
shadow of a smile appear on her face, "if he comes
again, let him have time to lead the conversation to
any subject he chooses."

"I could never take any particular interest in him."

"How do you know? you are almost a stranger to
him."

"I am so sorry I said that," repeated Charlotte with
a sigh.

Her aunt kissed her.   What was the use of arguing
with Charlotte or laughing at her? she would only be
made more shy and more *gauche* by such a course.

She went to the playroom feeling very angry with
herself, and began to turn over the leaves of the book
of "Minutes," to look for the letters Don John had
written to her on her behavior to the "conflicting sex."
This was the first : —

"CHARLOTTE,

"The mind of man (in which I include the mind
of woman, even of young woman), the mind of man, as
I have read in books, ever feels impatient of doubt.

"Thus when a fine young fellow, such as I am, one
at the acme, point and prime of his life, at which time
he is most interesting, and justly so, to the youthful
female, viz. forty-five last birthday — one of good estate
and old family — when, to come to the point, Fetch
Fetch, Esq., begins to pay frequent and somewhat long
calls at a house where there are three marriageable
young ladies, it is very certain that his motive in so
doing cannot fail to suggest hopes to each of the three
which she would fain translate into certainty, and doubt
which she longs to solve.

" Yes, doubt. ' Why,' she will sigh to herself, ' does this, the — shall I confess it? yes I will — the cherished hero of my dreams come day after day with a buoyant, an almost tripping foot, when the school-room duties are over, and having just put our prettiest frocks on, and our best lockets, we repair to the drawing-room to afternoon tea?'

" I think I see you now, Charlotte, as standing before your mirror you clasp your hands, while blushing at your own thoughts, you exclaim, ' Naughty one ' (it is your own heart that you thus apostrophize), ' art thinking of thy Fetch again? Oh' (I hear you go on) ' can it be for my sake he stuck that bunch of daisies in his button-hole? Is it because I kissed a daisy one day when I thought he was not looking (at least, I think I thought so), and murmured over it, "Innocent poetic flower, come to your Charlotte's heart" (at least, I think that's what I said, or something quite as foolish). Who,' you go on, ' shall resolve me this harrowing doubt?'

" Charlotte, I have an imaginative, and so far as such a thing is desirable in a fine young man, I have a poetic mind myself — and in the silence which would be complete, but that our dog is barking, and that my sister, Fanny Fetch, is chattering, and a dozen at least of sparrows are chelping at the top of the rick — in the silence I hear your spirit calling to me as plainly as possible, and I consider that it is only generous in me to resolve the doubt you have with so much maidenly reserve and modesty felt impelled to mention, at the same time telling you for your future guidance why you are not my object when I sit spooning over your aunt's Bohea.

" Among the many reasons, Charlotte, why this is the case, one of the foremost is that you have such a vehement desire to be instructed. A fine young fellow seldom knows much. (I do not say that this is my case.) It frightens him to feel that he is liable to be put at a disadvantage by being asked questions that he cannot answer. And then, again, you have a no less ardent desire to instruct. If you have picked up any piece of information, you think it must needs be as interesting to a fine young fellow as to yourself. Now I may say for my own part that there is nothing I hate like being instructed and having to give my mind to learning out of school; when I am unbending among a lot of pretty girls, I like to spoon. It is my wish to feel that I belong to the superior sex. It is their business to make me sure that I am an agreeable specimen of that sex. I must be set at my ease.

"But I do not wish, as is too much your own habit, to talk at large and utter aphorisms. I wish rather to persuade you for your own good to alter your manner. I have heard that remarkably sensible young man, Don John, say of his schoolboy brother, that if he declined to obey any of his behests, he should persuade him with a stick. But the custom of thus persuading the fair sex has, to some extent, gone out in this country. Also it is almost decided now that woman is a reasonable creature; in fact, if we did not think so, we could not blame her for being the most utterly unreasonable creature that ever lived, because this would not be her own fault, which it is. Observation and experience are counted among the gifts of reason. I appeal to these. You observe that fine young fellows fly from you, and you experience mortification; therefore, Charlotte, I leave these to guide you, and will no more use (metaphorically) the stick; but remind you of the conduct of the charming Marjorie your cousin: when a stumpy young man with high heels to his boots stands talking near her and showing himself careful, by holding himself scrupulously upright, not to lose the tenth of an inch of his stature, Marjorie always keeps her seat if she possibly can; you never see her rise and from her graceful height look down upon him; when a stupid fellow blunders in an attempt to pay her some compliment, the best he knows how to fish up out of his foolish heart, she respects his dulness, she never smiles, she feels for him a gracious pity, and while encouraging no ridiculous hope, she saves his self-esteem by helping him to show himself to her at his best.

"With that last sentence, which I feel to be worthy of me, and very neatly put, I remain, Charlotte, your sincere friend, and your cousin Marjorie's lover,

"FETCH FETCH."

Charlotte laughed a little over this letter. "But after all," she said almost aloud, "I do not want a lover! It is not because I cannot have one that I need distress myself so much about my *gauche* behavior, my shyness, my unattractive manner and stiff conversation. It is because I bore them at home so much with what they call my 'poetic faculty' and my 'intellectual fads' that I wish to be different. I lay down one subject after another, and urge it on them no more, but the fresh one, as I take it up, they laugh at just the same. I know there is something in what my aunt says, that there is no malice whatever in their teasing, and that if I became just like everybody else, it would make them all very dull, myself included, for I should miss that attention now bestowed on me, and they would miss what helps to stimulate them and draw their interest to various abstract subjects, which otherwise (particularly the girls) they would never take any notice of at all.

"How kind and sweet my aunt is! Is she right, does it really amuse me as much as it does them?

"Yes, of course I do not want a lover — I should not know what to do with one — and yet, perhaps, even I might have a lover some day.

"Ah! here's Don John's ode that he wrote to make game of me for thinking that they could take any interest, any of them, in my essay on the nature and province of poetry. How they all laughed! Lancy more than any of them. It was two days before he went away — before he helped me over the brook. Don John declaimed it in the playroom in a voice of thunder, putting intense emphasis on every short line."

She glanced at the composition in question, it had been copied into the "Minutes" in a round text hand and ran as follows: —

" To Charlotte on her demonstrating to me that poetry was altogether independent of rhyme.

"Unto thee, O Charlotte,
Unto thee,
Do
I indite this
Ode,
For thou hast removed, O joyful
Day, an insurmountable obstacle
To
My being a poet.   I may compare it
Unto a considerable obstacle,
Which,
This time last year, I being in the steamer
Crossing from Holyhead,
Rear'd itself right in front of me,
Looming to North and South ever nearer
And nearer.
I said, ' Now if I were minded
To
Cross the Atlantic to America I could n't, in
Consequence of this insurmountable
Obstacle,'
Which at that moment we ran
Into,
Being prevented by a buffer from
Doing
Ourselves any harm.
The obstacle was in point of fact
Ireland.
And as to this day,
Whoso would cross the Atlantic,
Must needs sail round that
Con-
siderable obstacle,
For,
He cannot sail through it
So hast
Thou taught me, O Charlotte,
Sailing clear of the obstacle of rhyme,
To
Be a poet."

Steps on the stairs.   Charlotte pricked up her head; Naomi and Don John entered.

" Here she is ! " exclaimed Naomi, " and not tearing her hair."

" Let her alone, Nay," said Don John. " We have business on hand, and she is only a poetess."

" I am very sorry, I am sure ; I never could have believed I should have made such a blunder," said Charlotte.

" Well, we forgive you. We feel that it is of no use to reason with you ; and if that speech is not severe enough to cure you, nothing is."

" And besides," proceeded Don John, following up his sister's remark, " if that young ass had anything better to do, it can hardly be doubted that he would do it instead of — "

" Instead of wasting his morning," interrupted Charlotte, " in paying such a long call. He only came here to while away the time."

" Well, he has not much to do ; he told me himself that he walked to the railway station, which is three miles off, every day to buy a penny paper — for there being only 200 poorish people in the parish, and they being almost always quite well, he felt a delicacy about paying many visits. ' You are quite right,' I said, ' not to harry your parishioners.' Well, now, Charlotte, you are actually forgiven, and going to help us — going to be of use to the best of cousins."

" What am I going to do ? "

" Help us to write a letter to grandmother ; you are not the only person in this house who has poetic visions — I have had a vision too. Methought (that is how your last vision began ; I read it, for you left it in the playroom blotting-book) — methought, Charlotte, I saw Dizzy and Gladstone playing at pitch-and-toss with the British lion, as if it had been a halfpenny. ' Heads I win ! ' shouted Dizzy."

" And which did win ? "

" You should not interrupt the vision. Why, the lion methought came down upon his head of his own accord, and, winking on them both, spake in pretty good English. He said fair play was a jewel ; and it was now time that the public should see how he looked when he was wrong end upward. Then the Lord

Mayor, for methought he was looking on, the Lord Mayor said, ' That was a beautiful and affecting speech, " heads I win ; "' and when he saw what the lion had done he put up his hand to feel whether his own head was in its place. Then the vision brake and faded (that's a quotation); and pondering on it, methought I too will play at pitch-and-toss with circumstances, as this gracious vision (that's another quotation) suggests to me. I will see what will turn up, eke I will write to my dear grandmother; and Charlotte and Naomi shall help. Well?"

CHAPTER XXI.

"WELL?" repeated Don John: "are you quite lost in amazement? I like to see a poetess gazing at me with her mouth open."

Charlotte hastily shut her mouth.

" And we want you to give us some of your large copying paper," observed Naomi, " because, as we told you before, we are going to write a letter to grandmother — a very particular letter."

" Why? " asked Charlotte.

Don John told her in much the same fashion as he had told Naomi in the orchard — having first arranged their chairs in a triangle that the party might have a " three-cornered crack."

" I know Marjorie likes Campbell," said Charlotte. " I know she feels his going away."

" You do?"

Don John glanced at Naomi, who nodded.

" Why did n't you take that for granted," she observed, " when I consented to help with the scheme?"

" But as you did not know it," observed Charlotte, " why this sudden zeal for match-making?"

" Well. if you must know, it is partly because I have within the last few days heard a piece of news which I know makes father uneasy."

"From whom?"

"From Lancy."

Charlotte blushed, and wished to ask, but did not, whether Lancy was coming home.

"Mrs. Collingwood has four hundred a year of her own, that is, as she told father, it is absolutely at her own disposal, and she could leave it to whom she would. She added that she should of course leave it to Lancy. She made a will before she went abroad, and deposited it with father of her own accord. Father has sometimes alluded to this will to me, and said it pleased him."

"Well?"

"Of course we know that Lancy being adopted by both father and mother, they have always said they should look after his interests in the future."

"Lancy is a dear boy," said Naomi, with the least little contraction of her forehead as if for thought. "And if father and mother had any real *reason* for loving him so much, of course they would long ago have told us; therefore I have for some time been sure they have no reason: they let him come to stay with them for a while, they got fond of him quite unawares, and kept him on and on, till at last they loved him almost as they love us; and it seems to them quite natural that they should, and also quite natural that we should think so. I never grudged Lancy anything in my life, but though it does seem natural that we should all love him, yet surely his place in the family is remarkable."

Don John looked keenly at his sister and listened attentively while she spoke. This was a subject on which, from his boyhood, he had thought a good deal, and nothing that he had arrived at as a reason for Lancy's place in the family had satisfied and pleased him so well. "After all," he thought, "why should there be any great and important reason? Why will not this reason do, which is hardly a reason at all?" His thoughts went on while both the girls were silent. "Perhaps if I had not instinctively been so careful to hide from father and mother that I felt the least surprise, I might have been told."

"But the news," asked Charlotte at last, "what is it?"

"Mrs. Collingwood is going to marry again."

"Lancy says so?"

"Yes; it seems that she was very desirous to keep him with her, and she proposed to go back to Australia, and over-persuaded him, he says, to go too. She took passage in the P. and O. steamer as far as Colombo, where she promised him they should stay a month. And there was a man on board whom Lancy calls 'a gentleman of position and fortune,' but father says the account he gives of him sounds as if he were an adventurer. He declared that he fell in love with that short, fat, little woman at first sight; he landed with them at Galle, and when Lancy wrote, his mother was to be married to him in a day or two."

"And that will make a great difference to Lancy?"

"Of course, because, if there were no settlements made before the marriage, every shilling she has is now her husband's; and she cannot make a will. As to the will she made before, it is no better than waste paper."

"Then Lancy will have to work?" said Charlotte.

"Oh, yes, of course; so have I — still —" he paused suddenly, and did not add, "but my father's children are worse off than they were by that four hundred pounds a year, for Lancy and I cannot both be wrong, and we think that in our early childhood we were told we should be left equal in father's will, and Lancy thought afterwards that he was to have less from father by four hundred pounds a year."

"And that's very odd," he said aloud; "it's very extraordinary," and while the girls bothered him as to his obliging desire to get lovers for them, and declared that there was no chance of his succeeding, he sat lost in thought.

"This news is only part of my reason," he said at last, "and I did think Marjorie liked Campbell, though I was not sure as I am now."

Don John was still almost a boy in years, and he was young for his years, otherwise he would hardly have concocted such a scheme, and deliberately detailed it to his grandmother, which, with the help of the two girls, he now actually did; saying, however, nothing about his father's circumstances.

His grandmother was excessively amused, and wrote forthwith, telling him that she would decide what to do in a day or two, and desiring that he would on no account mention the matter to any one. By the same post she sent his letter to her daughter-in-law, requesting to know her opinion, and asking her to name her wishes, but not to betray the confidence reposed in her. Marjorie's father and mother had a long, loving consultation over it, the father not without shouts of laughter, the mother with somewhat admiring amusement.

The family was at breakfast three days after, when the letters came in, and Mrs. Johnstone, turning one of hers over with the quietest of smiles, said, "Edinburgh, I see." The three conspirators blushed furiously, Don John was pink up to the roots of his very light hair. Mrs. Johnstone began to read the letter aloud. It set forth that the grandmother had, for some time past, not seen any of the girls, and had quite suddenly determined to ask her dear Stella to spare one of them. Here, with the gentlest audacity, she paused, and beginning again at "quite suddenly" repeated the sentence. "One of them to spend a couple of months with her; she should prefer to have Marjorie," here Marjorie blushed as rosy red as the others had done, not one of the young people could look up, the father and mother exchanged glances, Mrs. Johnstone went on. "And, my dear Stella, will you let Don John bring her down, for I have not set my eyes on the young rascal for some time."

When she had finished reading, she folded the letter quietly, the conspirators neither spoke nor looked up, so she looked at Marjorie, and said, with a gentleness which was almost indifference, "Do you think you should like to go, dear one?"

And Marjorie replied, with unwonted hesitation, that she did n't know.

That settled the matter in the mother's mind, she immediately said, much more decidedly, " Oh, I think you should accept your grandmother's invitation, and besides, as she asks Don John too, you should not deprive him of the visit."

" Oh, yes," Marjorie interrupted, sparkling all over, and blushing with pleasure, " and he has actually never been to Edinburgh yet; you would like to go, Don John, would n't you?"

And so the matter was settled. And all that Don John had proposed was done to the letter: Charlotte did lend her pearls, and Naomi her prettiest feathers, and scarcely any money was asked for, Mrs. Johnstone, from the contents of the Indian box, fitting out Marjorie with various beautiful ornaments, and having some most becoming dresses made for her from her own wardrobe. Nobody knew what was becoming to Marjorie so well as her mother, and she sent her forth to conquer. The daughter had no more than her mother's beauty, but she had inherited the same reposeful serenity and convincing charm.

Don John, with pride and confidence, took charge of her; brother-like, he declined to let her have anything to do with the taking of the tickets or the looking after her luggage. It was therefore all left behind, as was that of a young man in the same carriage. When this was found out, which was in consequence of Marjorie's looking out of the window, and seeing it with her own eyes as it stood on the platform, she made at first some lamentation, but Don John and the young passenger became friends over the telegraphing for it at the first stoppage, after which Marjorie was almost persuaded by her brother that it was safer on the platform than in the van, and would reach Edinburgh almost as soon — if not sooner!

. But there is no need to enlarge upon this experience of Marjorie's. There is probably no woman living who has not gone through it; a more uncommon part of the matter was that the three young people thus left together discovered that they had many friends in common, that they knew all about each other's families, and were going to visit at houses situated not a hundred yards apart.

The young man's name was Foden. "Campbell is too common a name to please me," thought Don John, "but I like it better than Foden." Why this thought came into his head will appear very shortly. "Marjorie Foden sounds foolish, so does Duncan Dilke Foden," he cogitated thus as they reached Edinburgh.

"Why, she's as tall as her brother!" thought the grandmother, when the two young people presented themselves. "An awkward height, and her hair as red as rust."

"Campbell's laid up with the chicken-pox," she whispered to her grandson, as soon as Marjorie had been escorted to her room.

"The chicken-pox?" repeated Don John, with scorn.

"Yes, all the children of the regiment have got it, and he caught it."

"Oh, well," answered Don John, rather dreamily. "I don't know that it particularly signifies."

His grandmother looked sharply at him.

"I suppose you know that he's a great flirt?" she went on.

Don John woke up suddenly.

"No, grandmother, I did not."

"Yes, after I had decided to invite you both down, his old aunt — Miss Florimel Campbell, coming in, amused me, as she supposed, with tales of his flirtations."

Don John repeated, with rather more decision, "I don't know that it particularly signifies."

And it did not signify at all, for Duncan Dilke Foden, presenting himself almost immediately after breakfast the next morning, to pay an outrageously early and outrageously long morning call, passed through a succession of changes in manner, mind, and face, which the grandmother read as easily as from a printed book. He

was elated at the sight of Marjorie, and expressed as
much delight and surprise as if she might have been expected to evaporate in the night, or to melt like a lump
of sugar; and then he became suddenly humble, as one
who had no right to be glad; and then he was afflicted
with a great desire to talk sensibly and seriously, as one
desiring thereby to excuse too long a presence; but at
this stage of affairs Marjorie broke in quietly with some
commonplace question. Duncan Dilke Foden was taken
in hand, first set at his ease, and calmed, then made to
show himself at his best, and finally let alone to remember that he had paid a long visit, and with a tolerable
grace to tear himself away.

Pondering on this visit soon after, the grandmother
said quietly to Marjorie, " What sort of a fellow is young
Campbell?"

" He 's not very wise, grandmamma," answered Marjorie.

" Did not I hear something about his paying ye a
good deal of attention?"

" Oh, yes, he did."

" And not the only one to pay it — at least, I have had
hints to that effect."

Marjorie lifted up her fair face, " But that is not my
fault, grandmother, I do assure you."

" Meaning that ye have no wish to be a flirt. No, it
is not your fault, I dare say; but, Marjorie, it *is* your
misfortune."

" Yes, I used to be a great deal happier before I had
all these ridiculous compliments," answered the young
girl, mistaking her meaning. " And yet, grandmother,
though I have never had any attentions from any one I
cared for — no, I mean I never have cared for any one
yet — "

" Well?" asked the grandmother.

Marjorie laughed, but answered, not without a little
ingenuous blush of embarrassment, —

" I used to be so happy at home with the others, and
now though I could not, on any account, marry any one
of my lovers — "

" No?" exclaimed the grandmother, interrupting her.

" Oh, no, certainly not — yet you cannot think how utterly flat and dull everything seems when I have n't got one. I did not care in the least for Campbell, for instance, yet I had got so accustomed to his compliments that when he went away I hardly knew how to do without him. You think me a very foolish girl ! "

" Just like her mother," thought the grandmother. " And so ye did not care for Campbell, my dear ; well, so much the better for Foden."

" And yet I do wish to be different," proceeded Marjorie.

" If the men will let ye ! " interrupted Mrs. Johnstone.

" And I was so glad when your letter came. I am sure I shall enjoy this visit so much."

" And Foden — what are ye going to do with him ? "

" I sent him away as soon as I could this morning, without hurting his feelings."

" There has been a great deal of harm done by that false proverb, ' Marriages are made in heaven.' "

" Grandmother? "

" In one sense everything is decreed above ; but in the other sense it may fairly be said that marriage is the one thing heaven leaves to be made on earth. Her birth, her station, her fortune, her beauty the maid had not the making of ; but if she does not exercise her wits, and her best discretion as regards her marriage, nothing her people can do can much avail her."

" Of course we ought not to marry for money," observed Marjorie, demurely ; " nor," she went on after a pause, " without being in love."

" How many lovers might ye have had already," asked the grandmother ; " six? "

Marjorie laughed.

" Well if ye cannot deny it, six it is ; and, as I said, not your fault, perhaps, but certainly your misfortune, for if ye cannot love one of the first six, why should ye love one of the second six? The girl that is really well off is she who waits some time, has one chance, and, it being a reasonably good one, takes it thankfully."

"Oh, I shall like some one well enough to marry him in the course of time," said Marjorie, who was very much amused at her grandmother's way of putting things.

"That is how your mother used to talk. She felt no enthusiasm, she once told me, for any of her lovers, and I answered, ' Consider which is the best worth loving and on the whole the most agreeable to ye, then dismiss the others, and let that one have a chance.' If it had not been for me," she went on, with perfect gravity and sincerity, "your father never would have won the wife he wished for. She had many lovers, and did not care to decide between them; but I talked to her. I said, ' Yes, many lovers, but one is old, and one beneath ye, and one above ye, and one is not a good man; and here are two left that are thoroughly suitable, but one of those even has an advantage not possessed by the other, or indeed by any one of the others.'"

Marjorie was interested, she had not expected to find that her father had needed any assistance in his wooing.

"Well, grandmother?" she said.

"Well," repeated the grandmother, "I said to her, ' There are women, Estelle, that long to keep their sons single, and there are those who look to patch up fallen fortunes with rich daughters-in-law, and there are women of such a termagant nature that all their sons have quarrelled with them, and there are women illiterate enough to make their daughters-in-law ashamed of them, and I know of one who dreads a beauty more than anything, and thinks such a one must needs be a spendthrift;' and now said I, ' I have named the mother of every lover you have but one, and that one longs to see her son married, looks for none but a small fortune, and would willingly help him from her own, desires an equal match and a beautiful young wife for him, has loved him more than anything mortal since her widowhood, and would thankfully resign him to — you.'"

" And what did mother say?" asked Marjorie.

" She said she would think of it, and she did."

" Mother always talks of you with so much affection. She always says you are so good to her." Marjorie did not add, " and I often hear her remind father that it is his day for writing to you;" that would have given pain, but it was true.

There was something rather sweet, as Marjorie felt, in being thus shown a glimpse of the past. Something so fixed, so inevitable, so without alternative as the marriage of her father with her mother had hung in the balance then!—had been a matter for discussion and for persuasion.

" Your mother was greatly admired," proceeded Mrs. Johnstone, senior, " and as was but natural, she soon found out that all the good and worthy young men were more alike than she could have supposed. As the proverb runs, ' *She wanted better bread than can be made with wheat*,' she went on seeking for it. She did not want merely a good and worthy young man; she told me so. But said I, ' Ye do not propose to live and die single?' — 'Oh, no, she proposed no such thing.' — ' My dear,' said I, ' men are not made of better stuff than yourself, far from it! But ye have had choice of some of the best of them, and I think your real difficulty comes from this, that you put your fancy before your duty.'"

" Duty!" exclaimed Marjorie, drawing herself up, and speaking for her mother as well as for herself.

" Yes, it is a woman's duty, if she has many lovers, to set them free from vain hopes, by choosing as soon among them as she can, even if she make some sacrifice to do it, with only a sincere preference for one, and as your mother said, ' no great enthusiasm.' Such a self-sacrifice is almost always rewarded. There is nothing so sweet as duty, and all the best pleasures of life come in the wake of duties done."

CHAPTER XXII.

DON JOHN thus announced his sister's and his own safe arrival at Edinburgh : —

" DEAREST NAOMI,

" We reached our destination last night just as it was getting dusk.　Grandmother is not at all grown.

" I am much impressed with the magnificence of this city.　The streets are fine, the populace polite, and the various methods of locomotion, omnibuses, cabs, tram-cars, &c., are admirably arranged, and convey the traveller cheaply and expeditiously in every direction.　The view from Arthur's Seat is remarkably fine, as is also that from Salisbury Crags.　I will not expatiate on the prospect from the ancient castle, its reputation is European.

" I am writing before breakfast, and have not yet quitted the house since my arrival.　Immediately after breakfast, I propose to do so, in order to view the various objects which I have so graphically described. I trust, my dear girl, that they may be found to justify the terms in which I have spoken of them.　With this ramble I shall combine a visit to the railway terminus in search of Marjorie's luggage, which I left behind at King's Cross.　Grandmother appeared to think this strange, but I reminded her that we are all subject to the law of averages, and as, on an average, half a box per thousand of all that this railway carries is left behind, lost, or delayed, and somebody must be owner of that half-box, she ought not to be surprised if that somebody proved to be her granddaughter.　She said that as Marjorie had three boxes, and had lost them all, her average was rather high.　A truly feminine answer, which shows that she did not understand the question.

Ah! I see a railway van coming up with those three boxes in it. Yes, the luggage is come.

" Best love to father and mother and all of you.

" Your affectionate brother,

" DONALD JOHNSTONE."

When Naomi read this letter aloud at the breakfast-table, one more person listened to it than Don John had counted on. Captain Leslie was present, a sunburned, stooping man, very hoarse, very grave, and very thin. He had called on Mr. Johnstone the day before in London, and when he found that he was not recognized, it appeared to hurt his feelings very much. But he was so much changed by climate and illness, that when he had been invited " to come down and see Estelle," Mr. Johnstone carefully telegraphed to his wife of the expected arrival, lest she also should meet him as a stranger. He was a distant cousin of Mrs. Johnstone's, hence the use of the Christian name.

When he had seen his first and only love with her children about her, in a happy English home, and looking, to his mind, more beautiful than ever, when he had heard the cordial sweetness of her greeting, such a glow of tender admiration comforted him for long absence, such a sense of being for at least the fortnight they had named to him delightfully at home, that his old self woke up in him ; isolation on staff duties, irritating heat, uncongenial companions, exile, illness, all appeared to recede. He had thought of his life — excepting his religious life — as an irretrievable failure ; but for that first evening he felt strangely young. He was very stiff, and when he reared himself up, his own iron-gray head, seen in the glass, confronted him, and appeared for the moment to be the only evidence about him of the time that had passed. Estelle was a little different, but it was an advantageous difference, motherhood was so infinitely becoming to her ; and as for Donald, he took the honors of his place so quietly that the old bachelor and unsuccessful lover did not grudge them to him as he had done at first. He spoke but little to his wife, being even then aware that the old love in Leslie's heart was as intense as ever.

With a keen perception of everything said and done in the presence of Estelle, Leslie felt that her husband scarcely looked at her; but he could not know the deep pity with which his successful rival regarded him, — what a short lease of life he appeared to him to have; how little, as he supposed, there was yet left for him to enjoy in his native country.

That night Leslie thought a good deal of Estelle's eldest son; he was much disappointed to find him away; his letter the next morning presented him in a rather unexpected light.

"Is that your boy's usual style of writing, Johnstone?" he inquired.

"Yes, I think it is; he is a dear, good fellow, but quite a character, and he always had naturally a whimsical way of looking at things."

"I am glad the luggage has arrived," observed Mrs. Johnstone; "but is it quite fair, Donald, to speak of our boy as an oddity?"

"My dear," exclaimed her husband, "I wish him to be what pleases you; but I have thought of him as an oddity ever since he was six years old, when he said of the cook on his birthday, 'She put my cake in the oven, and it rose ambrosial as Venus rose from the sea.'"

"It was clever of him," said little Mary, "for he had not been to a cooking-class as I have."

Leslie smiled.

"And Don John invented Fetch, you know, mother," observed Naomi, "and Fanny Fetch and the 'Minutes.'"

Mrs. Johnstone made no reply, but Leslie had a real motive for wanting to investigate Don John's nature and the character he bore at home; so after breakfast, when left alone with the girls, he easily got them to talk of him, and at the end of less than a week he was quite intimate with them, made welcome to a place at the playroom tea, treated to Charlotte's opinions on things in general, consulted by her as to her poetry, and even allowed to read selected portions of the "Minutes."

These abundantly bore out his father's opinion that he was a character; but Leslie made one mistake about Don John at once, for finding how many of the papers consisted of criticisms on Charlotte's opinions, remarks on her behavior, or counsels to her on her literary productions, he jumped to the conclusion that Don John must needs be half in love already with the beautiful little cousin; he wondered whether Estelle knew it, and he forthwith began to take a keener interest in Charlotte also for his sake.

The girls liked him; little Mary loved him, "though he almost always talked," she said, "as if it was Sunday."

He had not been in the house ten days before he was in the confidence of all the young people, and at liberty to turn over the leaves of the "Minutes" for himself.

He thought he knew Don John thoroughly, and Charlotte too. His religious counsels, his unconscious betrayal of a life-long interest in them and their parents and their home; his unexpected knowledge of various incidents before their birth, which had hitherto been unknown to themselves, all combined to make them think of him as one who might be trusted absolutely, and who had a right almost to the position of a near relative. He gave them presents, too, and discussed with them beforehand what these should be. As the days went on he found himself more at home with the children than with the parents. Estelle was the love of his whole life; but she was in a sense remote. Her children and Charlotte became intimate with him, as much by their own wish as by his, and they in the same sense were near.

He felt towards them as an uncle might have done; he perceived that the parents consciously allowed them thus to ally themselves with him, and he did not know the reason.

On the mother's part it was done because it made more easy her personal withdrawal. He must needs love her; but it was better for him to widen his interest and love her children too, and amuse himself with them

than have opportunity to sit apart with her, and waken
up again the old want which for so many years had
slumbered in absence.

On the father's part it was from pure pity. Why
should not Leslie enjoy the flattering consciousness that
these young creatures liked him? His time was so
short; the sods of his native valley would be laid over
his head so soon.

Leslie did not think so. He supposed that he had
come home to recruit his health. Estelle and her husband had no reason whatever to suspect the scheme
which was taking form in his mind; he delighted himself with the certainty of this fact.

Various little hints let him perceive that Mr. Johnstone, if not actually somewhat embarrassed in his circumstances, was assuredly not well off. "As to my
making their son my heir," he would cogitate, "they
have no reason to think I have anything worth mentioning to leave; but it is sweet to know that when I am
taken to my rest, Estelle will reap a benefit from me,
dead, which living I could not give; she will dwell
more at ease if her eldest son is provided for. Johnstone cannot feel jealous of my memory as he might
have done if I had left it to her; and Estelle will
know well that all I did for her boy was for her sake."

"But he is a character," continued Leslie; "his
father was quite right!"

Leslie had strolled into the playroom, the girls had
gone to their cooking-class, and he had wandered
through the downstairs room without finding their
mother. It might have been supposed that he would
go out, but no, the girls had strictly charged him to
wait for their return, when there was to be an early
lunch, and he was to go with them to a farm-house to
choose some lop-eared rabbits which he had promised
them.

"He's a character," repeated Leslie, and he turned
over the leaves of the "Minutes," as he had full leave
to do. "Here's some of his handwriting — all about
Charlotte — always Charlotte. Let me see.

THE POETRY OF MISTER BARNES, DONE IN THE DORSET DIALECT.

"What is it you do find in thik theer book?"
   Says I.
"They poems," says the maid, "they be so high;
   When on un I do look,
They fill my heart wi' swellin' thoughts, Idyllic,
   The most ecloguey thoughts they do!
     And I attain to view
The worrold as though 'twas made anew.
   And I do feel," she says, says she,
"So frisky as a lamb under a grete woak tree,
   So light 's a little bird,
A hopping and a chirruping
      Over the fuzzen."
    (Thinks I, "My word!")
    Says she, "You muzzen
Laff," for she read my thoughts in a trice.
   Says she, "This here 's the poet's vice
A speaking to 'ee." "Oh," says I, "shut up."
I couldn't stand no mwoor 'ee see.
They all cried, "What a vulgar bwoy he be!"
And I did call out passen drough the door,
   For I was forced to flee,
     "Do 'ee shut up."

"Innocent enough all these writings," he observed to himself, "and they show activity of mind in an unusual degree. Oh, that these dear children had the root of the matter in them! I must not shrink from talking to them on their best interests."

To do Leslie justice, he never did shrink from uttering anything that was on his conscience, and all his religious discourse was considerate and evidently devoid of affectation.

The fortnight came to an end. Leslie by that time was so desirous to see Don John, that if any opening had been given him, he would have proposed to prolong his stay.

He went away one morning, accompanied by all the girls to the station. The next afternoon Don John returned, and was in like fashion accompanied from it.

After he had seen his mother he was borne off to the playroom, where, at afternoon tea, he ate as much cake as would have spoiled the dinner of most young men ; but Don John's appetite at that stage of his career was spoiling-proof.

Mary being present, a certain caution was observed in the discourse. "You hardly ever wrote to us," said Naomi.

" But I wrote to mother — "

" Yes, — well, there could have been nothing particular to tell us. How is Campbell?"

Don John looked a little confused during the first part of Naomi's speech ; he answered the second part.

" Campbell? why, we never saw him once."

Charlotte and Naomi looked as if they thought this very bad news.

" Not well yet?"

" Grandmother thought that for another day or two he was just as well away. But, I say, what about Captain Leslie?"

"Oh, we liked him so much!" exclaimed little Mary, " but he's a very good man."

" But!! — Yes, I know he's very religious."

" And very evangelical, of course," observed Charlotte. " Officers in the army always are when they are exceptionally religious."

" Why should they be?"

" Well, my theory is that they have so many rules to enforce and obey — so much to do with discipline and drill, that it is natural they should take to that sort of religion which is the most gentle and free from hard rules, which insists least on the letter and most on the spirit — "

" How many officers of that sort do we know, three, is n't it? Quite enough for you to found a theory on. I think Captain Leslie must be an odd fish."

" No, he is not," said Naomi, " but he talks often just as father does when on some rare or serious occasion he has one of us into his own room and — "

" What! did he pray with you?"

" He asked mamma if he should pray with us before he went away ; she said ' yes,' and so we all knelt down in this room," and here little Mary in all simplicity attempted to give an account of this prayer.

Don John opened wide eyes of surprise at his sister, but they had sufficient reverence for her childhood not to offer any comment.

" And he says that God loves us," she continued, " and so we ought to love people — and poor people too."

" But, my dear little woman," exclaimed Don John, not at all irreverently, " I think we knew that before Captain Leslie came here."

" Yes," said Mary, " but I did not think about it; and now I am going to love the poor people, you know."

" And Mary took one of her birthday half-crowns to give to Miss Jenny; she asked him if he thought that would be a good thing to do; and I went with them to give it," said Naomi, still quite gravely. " And Mrs. Clarboy, who generally knows how to adapt her talk to her company, made rather a mistake, and got herself reproved, for she told us her nephew had taken her to an entertainment in London, which she had very much enjoyed. Captain Leslie asked what it was about, and she said, ' Well, I can't hardly tell you, sir, what it was about, but there was a good deal of music, and Cupid came down and sang something sacred, his wings were beyond anything, sir, they were as natural as life.' Then Captain Leslie said he hoped she was not in the habit of frequenting the theatres; and she assured him she had never been to one before, poor old soul! and she was vexed with herself for having told, and Miss Jenny groaned and was very much edified."

" And then we went on to Mrs. Black's to give her my other half-crown," said Mary shrewdly, " and he asked her if she went to church, and she said ' she 'd been so massacred with the rheumatism that nobody could n't expect it of her,' and then Captain Leslie laughed, and he said afterwards he was sorry he had done it, and it showed a great want of self-control."

" Poor old Clarboy!" exclaimed Don John, "the idea of her frequenting the theatres! I don't think she has been in London more than three times in her life."

Then Naomi went on: "She said afterwards, ' I know your pa's rather in the same line as that gentleman, miss, and never takes you to the theatres, but yet I should n't have minded letting him know, for he 's not so straitlaced. However,' she went on, 'Captain Leslie 's a powerful pious gentleman, no doubt, and one like him it was that sent a tract to poor old Mrs. Smart on her death-bed. It was called ' The dying Malefactor.' If ever there was a peaceable, humble, blameless creature, it was that woman, and a joined member too of the Methodist connection, but this world had got that hold on her still, that when I 'd opened the envelope for her, and she saw it began in large letters " To you," she burst out laughing, and she and I talked a good bit over it. It seemed such a queer thing to have done. I don't deny that we did let a few sec'lar words pass over our tongues, till her daughter that is a Methodist too got vexed, and she says, ' Now, mother, you have no call to think of these worldly matters any more, you lie still and mind your dying.' Miss Jenny had groaned a good deal during this talk, but she never dares to interrupt her sister. As soon as there was a pause she said, ' True it is that Sarah Smart laughed on her death-bed, but I have good hope as it was never laid to her charge.'

" ' No,' exclaimed Mrs. Clarboy, who never can understand Jenny's point of view, ' she was a good-living woman, and the Almighty (I say it reverently) would never take notice of such a small sound such a long way off.'

" ' It 's not that,' cried Jenny, ' it was that she was not one to put the least trust in her own works, she trusted in the Rock of our salvation, and three days after she died triumphant.' "

" If I was a guardian angel," exclaimed Charlotte, " and might choose, I would never wait on people like

us, but always on the poor — such people as these.
When do we ever say things so beautiful in their simple-
ness?"

"Yes," observed little Mary, "the angels must be
very much amused with them."

Charlotte and Don John exchanged glances; "I ·
think, if I were you, I would include children in my
choice," he said.

"But I forgot to add," observed Naomi, "that Miss
Jenny ended her account of Mrs. Smart by saying,
'She's gone where there's no more sorrow — nor laughing neither;' and Charlotte said, 'Oh, Miss Jenny, I
hope not, I think we shall often laugh in heaven.'"

"But don't we think that at least angels can laugh?"
asked Mary.

"There can be no laughing in heaven or among
heavenly creatures that has malice in it — but many
things witty and droll are without that."

"But, Charlotte, if I met Don John in heaven, I
should like him to call me 'button-nose;' do you really
think he never will?"

"I am almost sure of it, — he invented that name
to make game of you, only for fun, you know, but still
it was malice."

"Well, then, I shall say to him, 'Though you are
not to say it here, you must not forget that you used to
say it.'"

"But why do you want it to be remembered?"

"He never said it when he was cross, but when I
sprained my ankle and he used to carry me about the
garden he did, and when you used all to be doing
'Fetch,' and Freddy and I knocked at the door, if we
were not to come in he always shouted out, 'No, you
two kids must go;' but when Fred was gone back to
school and I knocked sometimes, he said, 'Oh, it's only
button-nose,' and then I knew I might come in. So, as
it's kind malice, I should like him to remember; for you
know I couldn't help being the youngest."

"Well, no, I do not see that you could, but, Mary,
I shouldn't wonder if when you get to heaven you find

you're the eldest; don't you know that it says in the Bible, the last shall be first and the first last?"

" Do you think I shall be older than you, then, Don John?"

" It might be so — "

" I shall take great care of you, then, and if you are a baby when you come, I shall carry you about and show you all the beautiful things."

CHAPTER XXIII.

DON JOHN, now that his short holiday in Scotland was over, fell at once into his regular work, going up to London daily with his father. Meanwhile Captain Leslie spent a few weeks at different English watering-places in search of health which almost to his surprise he did not find. He meant eventually to live in Scotland, where he had some distant cousins, his only relatives excepting Mrs. Johnstone, but first he had wanted to see Don John and Estelle's eldest daughter Marjorie.

Don John had said in joke of his grandmother that she was not grown. Marjorie, under the auspices of this same grandmother, grew very fast during the months she spent at Edinburgh and its neighborhood.

She was of a grave and gentle nature, moderate in her demands of life as to pleasure, and she was high-principled and tender.

This same girl, who had not cared for an early marriage for her own sake, found a certain charm in it now that her grandmother had linked it in her thoughts with duty and even with self-sacrifice. She would not make more men unhappy, nor unsettle any for her sake, but she would essay to be an elevating hope and then a helpmate and a comfort to one; she would do her part to make one man and one home what God meant that they should be.

There are such people in the world, they need sometimes to have it discovered to them that such they are,
and then they need a little guiding. Marjorie had only
a very little of this last, but she had also the advantage
of being away from a sister and a cousin who were
much inclined to criticise and make game of her lovers ;
and, further, she had the advantage of a lover who had
many manly qualities, and among them a capacity for
all the improvement that comes to manhood from loving
a beautiful and pure-minded young woman.

Marjorie, instead of amusing herself with this lover,
looked out for his good qualities. He was of average
height, of average good looks, his position in life was
such as her own, he had excellent principles, he could
afford to marry, and he loved her. This was his case,
as she said to herself at the end of a week ; and hers
was that she was inclined to be pleased with him, and
to think a good deal of the self-sacrifice which life as a
general rule demands of woman.

At the end of another week, she thought about this
again, but as to average good looks, anybody might
see that his was a face which grew upon one. It was
while she was dressing for dinner that she passed him
in review on this second occasion, but there was not as
much time as before to think of the self-sacrifice, because she had not quite finished considering his agreeable countenance when it was time to go down to dinner. He was coming to dinner. Don John was to go
away the next morning. The brother and sister were
alone together for a few minutes at night before they
retired. Marjorie, seated by a little table, was untying
some tawny roses and putting them in water.

Don John had never said a word yet to his sister
about young Foden. He now remarked that her flowers
appeared to require a great deal of attention.

"Yes," answered Marjorie, "I shall take care of
them because I have told Duncan that he is only to
bring them every other day."

"Oh," said Don John, and presently Marjorie said, —
"What do you think of him?"

" I think he is one of the jolliest fellows I ever knew," answered Don John ; " he's so jolly straightforward and manly."

Marjorie was pleased with this tribute to Duncan Dilke Foden, boyish though it might be.

" He beats Campbell to fits," continued Don John.

" Oh, you don't care about Campbell, then?"

" No."

" Nor do I."

Then after a pause, —

" Don John?"

" Marjorie."

" Though Campbell paid me so much attention, he — he went away without making me an offer."

" Just like his impudence."

" Oh, but I was going to tell you that he wrote to me at home, where he thought I was, and yesterday mother sent me on the letter. He said he felt that on reflection he could not bear to be parted from me, and he had made up his mind to offer me his hand."

" Just like his impudence again! Made up his mind, I like that. I call it quite a providence his having the chicken-pox, quite a providence and nothing less."

" I should like you to take his letter back to mother, and tell her —"

" Well, *tell her?*"

" Of course till he made me an offer I had no right to consider him a lover —"

" No, any more than you could any other fellow who had not yet offered his hand —"

The last two remarks probably came in by way of parenthesis, but Marjorie went on as if she found the second very much to the point.

" Of course not, so I want you to tell mother that even if I was sure no one else would ever ask me to marry him, I must have answered Campbell as I did this morning. I said it could not be."

" I will tell her that."

" And nothing else."

" Well, so far as your having offers, there is, as I suppose, nothing to tell."

" Of course not."

" All right," answered Don John, and then they were silent for a few minutes, when Marjorie suddenly asked, —

" What is the middle height for a man, Don John?"

" Oh, from five feet seven to five feet nine. I measure five feet eight."

Marjorie reflected awhile, then she said, —

" They always say the strongest men are those of middle height. It 's just as well not to be too tall."

" Just as well," echoed Don John. He was in the habit of thus fervently endorsing his sisters' remarks when he wished to call their attention to them as absurd.

Marjorie laughed, but she blushed too, and then the brother and sister kissed and took leave of one another, for Don John was to start early the next morning, almost before dawn. He left his grandmother in rather an uneasy state of mind. She saw no reason to think that Marjorie cared for young Foden, but she perceived that she was giving him every kind of modest encouragement, and from time to time Marjorie sent a stab to her heart by making remarks which evidently showed that she had taken her grandmother's advice in good earnest, and would be actually glad to follow it if she could.

This good lady had all her life loved to give advice; she had been liberal as to the quantity of it, and fervent as to the manner; but she had become fearless, because, weighty though she felt it to be, it hardly ever took effect. She remembered but two instances in which it had. These were important ones, it is true. She could not regret the first; she might have cause deeply to regret the second.

" And it was hardly advice at all," she would sigh, when thinking this over. " It amounted to no more than suggestion. I have put something into her head; who would have expected her to be so docile?"

So the grandmother thought; but she could do no

more in this matter than her son had done, when, Donald being a little boy, he had once come in from the garden with a large basket of very fine pears just gathered, and had set them on the hall table.

The little fellow ran up and regarded them with open admiration, and his father said, in a bantering tone, "Do you think, Donald, if you were to try, you could eat all those pears before dinner?"

"I'm not sure whether I could," answered the child, scanning the half-bushel basket seriously.

"What, not to please papa!" exclaimed the father, bantering him; and being just then called away, the boy and the pears were left alone for about twenty minutes, at the end of which time Donald the elder coming back, Donald the younger greeted him in all good faith with, —

"Well, father, what do you think? — I'm getting on — I've eaten nine."

Nine very large pears, — their stalks and their cores were laid in a row for his inspection. Donald the younger, strange to say, was none the worse, but Donald the elder was much the better: in talking to his children he took more pains ever after to make his meaning plain.

And now Don John had come home again, and was holding his head rather higher than usual. Like many another very young man, he had a sufficiently high notion of his own importance both in the world and in his family.

None but the unthinking or the cold-hearted are seriously displeased with this quality in the very young. It is in fact rather pathetic, rather touching; a proof of ignorance as to what life, time, and trouble really are. And it often goes so soon! Perhaps it is just as well that they should begin by thinking they are to do a good deal, and have a good deal, for nothing can be worse than to despond beforehand.

Despond indeed! Who talks of desponding when things are so jolly? Don John exulted every day of his life. It is true that he had been perfectly wrong

as to Campbell, but then if it had not been for him
Marjorie never could have met with Foden. When he
thought of this he whistled and sang every morning
while he stropped his razor preparatory to the morning
shave. He only shaved his very light moustache as yet,
to encourage it to come on. His whiskers were but a
hope at present, they had not sprouted.

His father's dressing-room was next to Don John's
little bedroom, and when he heard the outbreaks of
whistling, singing, and other signs of good health and
good spirits that the young gentleman indulged in while
dressing, Donald Johnstone sometimes thought of the
pleasure expressed by the poet Emerson on hearing
a young cock crow. It is somewhat to this effect:
"When I wake in the morning, and hear a young cock
lustily crowing I think to myself, Here, at least, is a
fellow-creature who is in the best of health and spirits.
One of us, he would have us know, is well, and has no
doubt as to his right to a place in creation. And this,"
he goes on to remark, "is a pleasant thing to be assured of in this doubting, low-spirited, dyspeptic age."

Somebody rapped at Don John's door, when he had
been at home two days. He opened it with a little
lather on his upper lip. It is possible that he was not
sorry to exhibit this to Naomi, who was standing there.

"Come into the playroom as fast as you can," she
exclaimed; "something has happened!" and she darted
off without telling him what it was.

The celerity with which he obeyed the summons may
be held to prove that shaving was not actually necessary,
it must have been performed daily more as a pleasure
than as a duty.

Charlotte was in the playroom, she had a letter in
her hand, and looked at him as if so much flustered, so
much overwhelmed by the weighty event which had taken
place, that she knew not how to utter it.

Don John sat down on the deal table — a favorite
place of his. He surveyed Charlotte and his sister.
"It's an offer!" he exclaimed. "Charlotte, you've
had an offer; it can be nothing less."

" Oh, dear no," exclaimed Naomi; " it's nothing so commonplace! Your conspiracy that we helped you with came to nothing; but we contrived a better one while you were away, and it has succeeded, and nobody knows what it may end in!"

" Yes," said Charlotte, " I can now see a vista opening before me!"

She handed him a piece of paper: as it was a post-office order for 2*l*. 10*s*., he may have been forgiven for exclaiming, " I don't think much of the vista if this is it."

" But we hope it's only the first of a great many. Now listen; Charlotte and I, when you were gone, looked over all her verses and essays and things, and chose out four, which I copied beautifully at her dictation, and we sent them to four magazines; three were rejected, and we were getting rather despondent, but one is accepted, and this money is come, and here's the magazine with her thing in it — and among the notices to correspondents, ' We shall be glad to hear from a Daughter of Erin again.' "

" Poetess! I'm stumped!" exclaimed Don John. " Even if you'd had an offer, I could not have been more surprised. Shake hands; to think that anything should have been written on this inky, rickety deal table, that I have cut my name in with a buck-handled knife, and burnt my name in with a red-hot poker! To think, I say! No, I am not equal to thinking or saying anything — the most burning words would not blaze high enough — they surge disconnected in my brain. Type — Fame — Wealth — Pica — Epics — Colons, and last, not least — Cousins. I am your cousin, Charlotte; when you become famous I should wish to have that remembered." He fell into thought. " No," he went on. " I never could have believed it."

" Of course not," said Charlotte, " you always made game of my things, and now you see!"

" Some of those poems, whoever pays for them, were the very mildest lot I ever set my eyes on. Everything you have ever done is the better for my criticism."

"Yes, I know, I always said you had good taste and great critical faculty — and now I consider that really — in order that I may not lose all this money, &c., it will be your duty to help me as much as you can."

"The young person, though she laughs, is quite in earnest. Yes, that is what things are rapidly coming to. Some years ago this might have been thought affecting. Here is a young man, shall I say it? in his early prime, I think, girls, a fellow of my age —"

"Just beginning to shave," interrupted Naomi.

"May so characterize himself —"

"As he swings his legs, sitting on the playroom table."

"Without undue self-laudation (the voice of a poetess should never be strained to such a shriek as that!) —a fellow, I say —"

"He says," echoed Naomi.

"A fellow, I repeat," shouted Don John, "just launched into the responsibilities of life, and it is suggested to him as the most useful thing he can do, to criticise the poetry of a girl; I say it's enough to make a Stoic grin; yes, she belongs to the dominant sex."

"My dears," exclaimed Mrs. Johnstone, looking in, "are you aware that your father has been calling you for some time? What is all this laughing and shouting about?"

"And what is Don John roaring out for *about the responsibilities of life?*" said Donald Senior, looking over her shoulder.

"Oh, father and mother!" exclaimed Don John, "I hope you'll take my part, I am so crowed over by the superior sex!"

"Is that all?" said Donald Johnstone. "Do you good. Come down to breakfast, my Star, and teach your son to imitate his father; put yourself in your right place, my boy, and you will never be crowed over; you should submit the moment you find out what they wish, and then they will have no occasion to crow."

A henpecked man never talks thus; but the wife in this case was well aware that either her husband's love

for her, or his deference to her wishes, or his depend-
ence on her judgment, made her very much what he
often called her, his guiding star. As a rule he found
out what she wished, and did it. But he was so absolutely blind to this fact that he rather liked to boast of
it, and talk about the yoke of matrimony, which he
never would have done if he had felt it.

But there were occasions when he would announce an
intention, and then she never interfered.

"It never rains," says the proverb, "but it pours."

This remarkable news concerning Charlotte had not
been half enough wondered at and discussed when the
letters came in: one was from Edinburgh, as Don John
saw at a glance before his father opened it, and one in
Lancy's handwriting, which was handed to his mother.

"Duncan Dilke Foden" was the signature of the
Edinburgh letter, and before breakfast was over Charlotte and Naomi heard, to their great astonishment, that
the said Duncan Dilke Foden, having made Marjorie
an offer, she had desired him to write to her father.

With one consent his two fellow-conspirators looked
fixedly at Don John, he must have known that this
event was probable, and he had kept them out of his
counsels. But the event was very interesting. Mrs.
Johnstone read the letter, and handed it back again,
when it was read aloud.

"Just like Foden," thought Don John, who could not
help noticing that neither father nor mother showed the
least surprise.

As no one spoke, Don John said, while Mr. Johnstone folded up the letter, "I call it jolly respectful to
you, father. Foden is such a fine, straightforward
fellow."

"Yes, the missive really reminds one, in spirit, at
any rate, of some of the old Paston letters, ' *Right wor-
shipful, and mine especial good master, I commend me to
your mastership as lowly as I may, and do you to weet that
an it please you I am fain to seek your favor with the fair
maid, my Mistress Marjorie, your daughter.*' This must
be a great surprise to you, my boy?"

Don John looked a little foolish when his father said this; he wondered how much his parents knew, or suspected; was it possible that his grandmother had betrayed him?

A look darted at him by Naomi showed that she was thinking of the same thing.

He could not help glancing at his mother, but she gave him one of her benignant smiles that told nothing excepting that she was " weell pleased to see her child respected like the lave."

And the other letter? Well, there was to be no end to the surprises of that morning. Lancy was coming home.

CHAPTER XXIV.

IN another fortnight letters were received again from Lancy. They appeared to show an altered frame of mind, and opened a question which hitherto he had managed to evade and put by. " He knew he had acted very badly, he had felt this for a long time. It was wrong to have thus gone away and kept away. He humbly begged pardon — would his dear father and mother forgive him?"

This in the first letter. In the second, by the same mail, but dated a week later, Lancy said that he and his mamma were miserable; that she was very much afraid of her new husband; she had no settlements, and could not draw her own dividends. He had been very kind to her, till he had got her property into his own hands, and he now said that her son was an undutiful fellow, and ought to go back at once to the good friends whom he had left in England. That he would advance him enough money to pay the passage, which was all he should do for him. He ought long ago to have been earning his own living.

This second letter was addressed to Don John, who

for a week or two after its arrival was almost as miserable as Lancy said he was himself.

But another mail-day went by, and there was no letter at all; then again the day passed, and Don John made up his mind that Lancy must be coming. He still retained an affection for Lancy, though in the minds of his sisters such a feeling had begun to fade. Don John knew all Lancy's faults and delinquencies, yet he clung to him without effort. The girls knew none of his delinquencies, but sometimes one would say to another, " We ought not to forget him, poor fellow, considering how fond father and mother have always been of him."

As for Charlotte, she thought of him a good deal, but his behavior, which at first had given her very keen pain, because she would not understand it, began in time to show itself in its true light. At first she would not see that he had meanly taken advantage of the Johnstones, had got away and kept away against their will; that he was shifty about the letters; that he pretended not to understand; that he was amusing himself as long as he dared, hoping to come back when he must, and throw himself on their bounty and goodness again. When Charlotte did begin to see this, she was ashamed for him, and all the more because her own ideas of right and duty and gratitude were high. She also had a home in the same house which had sheltered him.

She scorned herself when she found that she had for many months been tacitly excusing his conduct to her own mind, as if it was not his duty to do the same things which in such a case would have been her duty; as if wrong could possibly be right for his sake. " Could I misunderstand as he professes to do? What should I deserve if I treated my uncle and aunt thus?"

Charlotte for several months thought a good deal more about this than was consistent with her own peace. She could not help arguing the matter over, she was often weary of the subject and of Lancy too. Yes, at last she began to feel this, and then — well, then, happily for her, she ceased almost suddenly to think about it. The tired mind, which was vigilant in its desire to forget, fell asleep over the subject unawares, and when it woke up again, the importunate presence was withdrawn. Charlotte soon began to forget how importunate it had been. Of course she had not loved him, but he had touched her imagination, and she soon must have loved him if he had not made her ashamed for his sake.

"It has been a rude shock to me," Charlotte sometimes thought. "I am obliged to see that he is mean, and not straightforward. I never can care for him as I might have done."

In the meantime Marjorie stayed three months at Edinburgh, was now engaged to young Foden, and about to return home.

The summer was passing, Charlotte had been invited to contribute to a well-known magazine, and when Lancy and his return, and Marjorie and her engagement had been discussed in all their bearings, this affair of hers continued to afford constant talk, in which no one was more interested than Don John.

Even Mrs. Johnstone appeared to find the subject interesting, at least she frequently came and sat in the old playroom after Don John had come home in the afternoon. There she would quietly work and look on, and weigh in her mind something that Captain Leslie had said. She saw no good ground for his supposition, but she made many reflections as to whether any change in existing arrangements would tend to bring such a thing on or not.

But, no, there was no ground for such a thought, none at all. Don John was almost uncivil to Charlotte; but though he gave his opinion about her writings with a lordly air of superiority, he wished her to get on, because as he graciously remarked "she is one of us."

"Now, look here," he was saying once, when, the conversation getting animated, she was drawn from her considerations about Marjorie and about Lancy to look at and to listen to him; "you always talk about the poets as if they were such sacred creatures that it is

quite taking a liberty to see that there was any humbug
in them even after they are dead. There is Wordsworth, for instance —"

"Any humbug in Wordsworth? how dare you!"

"I grant you that he was *crammed full* of human
nature. He was full of us and the place we live in.
We take a beautiful pathetic pleasure in reading him,
because we like that a man who knew us so well should
love us so much. But it was humbug in him to say that
everything the poet writes is valuable and interesting
because he writes it — for — for it is n't.".

"Splendid reasoning," exclaimed Charlotte, "and
quite unanswerable!"

Don John, seated on the table, was making a cherry
net. Charlotte and Naomi, standing at two easels,
were painting decorations for a cottage hospital. Don
John brandished the mesh and went on, delighted to see
Charlotte fire up.

"I've never thought so much of that old boy since I
found out that he did not know how to pronounce his
own language."

"My dear," exclaimed his mother, beguiled into remonstrance, "what can you mean?"

"Well, mother, listen to this —

> 'I've heard of hearts unkind, kind hearts
>   With coldness still returning,
> Alas the gratitude of men,
>   Hath oftener left me mourning.'

You see he pronounced 'mourning' as if it rhymed
with 'returning,' which is the north country provincial
way."

"Accidental," exclaimed Charlotte; "it would have
been out of the question to spoil such an exquisitely
beautiful verse for the sake of a more perfect rhyme."

"I quite agree that the verse is beautiful; but, Charlotte, he always rhymes 'mourning' with such a word
as 'burning' or 'returning.' I defy you to find a case
where he did not."

"Then," said Charlotte, after a moment of cogitation,
"perhaps that is the right way."

" That answer was just like you. As to Pope, I am almost sure he spoke with several provincial peculiarities. Look at his inscription on his grotto : —

> ' Let such, such only tread this sacred floor
> As dare to love their country and be poor.'

You see he pronounced ' poor' as Miss Jenny does ' pore.' "

" Nothing of the sort. It is a modern invention to be so particular about rhymes. Pope felt a noble carelessness about them. So did Wordsworth. At the same time I must admit that one has sometimes very deeply to regret his carelessness in other respects. That most beautiful poem, for instance, on ' The lesser Celandine,' how he took away from its perfectness by not being at the trouble to arrange the last verse properly ! I dare say he dictated it first to his wife or his sister, and never looked at it afterwards. The states mentioned in the first two lines are meant to be contrasted, not the one *worse* than the other, but he says, —

> ' To be a prodigal's favorite — then worse truth,
>   A miser's pensioner — behold our lot !
> O man, that from thy fair and shining youth,
>   Age might but take the things youth needed not!' "

" Well, I see nothing the matter with it excepting that it is a pity he put in the word ' youth ' twice. But he was obliged to do so in order to have a rhyme for ' truth.' To be sure this rather spoils the climax."

" Of course it does. I have so often wished he had written just a little differently, it would have been so easy. Thus : ' To be a prodigal's favorite — then forlorn, — (forlorn of that delightful favoritism, you know, and made) ' a miser's pensioner.'

> ' To be a prodigal's favorite — then forlorn,
>   A miser's pensioner, — behold our lot !
> O man, that from thy fair and shining morn,
>   Age might but take the things youth needed not!' "

" Well, that is what I call audacity ! That's the

real thing.   If the critics could only hear you improving Wordsworth, would n't you catch it!"
    "Of course I should; but they never will!   And
now be quite fair, for once.   If you had first seen the
lines according to my version, and had thought it was
the original, should you not have been very angry with
me if I had proposed to alter it and put it as it now
stands?"
    "I shall not argue with you, arguing as a rule sets
me so fast in my own opinion.   And, Charlotte, you
are not asked to write reviews, you know; if you were,
there is no evil and contemptuous thing that reviewers
may not say of authors and their works; but I never
met with one yet who after saying that a poet was a
fool wrote an improved version of his lines to show the
reader what they should have been."
    "Why should you be surprised at my criticising
things?" said Charlotte.   "All intelligent reading is
critical.   Even our admiration of a masterpiece is our
criticism of it; we judge it to be fine and true."
    "She said the other day," observed Naomi, "that
Keats wrote of Greek scenery as if he was describing an
English market-garden."
    Charlotte excused herself.   "I said he wrote not
differently of 'The sides of Latmos' and of an English
wood and brook.   He is here in spring, —

> 'While the willow trails
> Its delicate amber, and the dairy pails
> Bring home increase of milk,'

and he hopes to write a good deal before the daisies

> 'Hide in deep herbage, and ere yet the bees
> Hum about globes of clover and sweet-peas.'

Then forthwith he is in a mighty forest on the sides of
Latmos,

> 'Paths there were many,
> Winding through palmy fern and rushes fenny
> And ivy banks.'

Then he comes to a wide lawn —

> 'Who could tell
> The freshness of the space of heaven above
> Edged round with dark tree-tops through which a dove
> Would often beat its wings, and often too
> A little cloud would move across the blue.'

Is not that England?"

"Certain sure. But you must not forget that in classic times there were forests in Greece, though it is as bare as a down now."

"But was there 'rain-scented eglantine'? did the cold springs run

> 'To warm their chilliest bubbles in the grass'?"

Don John reflected — then shirked the question and disposed of the poets.

"I don't know; Keats is a muff. I could n't read him half through. Wordsworth I respect, he knows all about me. But I think, as you delight in him so much, it is odd you are so fond of choosing out pretty and beautiful things to write about, instead of choosing to make homely things beautiful as he did."

"I write of what I see," said Charlotte. "We do not all live in the same world. In the swallow's world, though it be our world, there is no snow."

"Yes, but though the swallows never heard of snow that is not the less their own doing. They live always in the light and the sunshine because they go to seek them. You mean that you too may go in search of sunshine if you please."

"I suppose I do."

"But the swallows are inferior to the robins for ever, because these last have experience of summer and winter too. However," continued Don John, "I am rather sick of the fine things written lately about birds. I suppose we shall hear next that they admire the sunsets."

"But it is nice," said Naomi, "to know that they delight in gay colors just as we do."

"Yes, and to be told almost in the same breath that

man has himself only developed the color faculty very lately indeed. Well, all I know is that I have frequently with a pewter spoon taken a pink egg streaked with brown, and put it into a nest full of blue ones. If the bird I gave it to could see the difference between blue and pink, why did she sit upon and hatch the alien egg?"

"Perhaps *some* birds are color-blind, as some of us are," said little Mary, speaking for the first time.

"I have sometimes thought," said Charlotte, "that whole generations and ages saw things differently as to color. The ancients all agree that a comet is a lurid, a portentous and a red-colored light in the heavens. Up to about two hundred years ago we never hear them spoken of as anything but red; but the comet I have seen could never have suggested anything but a pathetic calm, infinite isolation, and it had a pure pallor which made the stars look yellow."

"I saw one once when I was a little girl," said Mary, "it had a long tail, but the next time they showed it to me the tail was all gone."

"That tail," said Don John, "was the comet's ' horrent hair,' it got in between the sun and the planets, so it is probable that they sent for a number of old *Daily Telegraphs*, the largest paper in the world, you know, and twisted it all up in curl-papers to be out of the way."

"They did n't."

"Well, then, perhaps the sun pulled all the comet's hair off to fill up his spots with."

"No, Don John," said Mary, with sage gravity, "I would rather believe about the curl-papers than believe that."

"Thereby you show your discretion, Mary, always believe the most likely thing."

Whether he would have gone on to explain this celestial matter to her, will never now be known, for at that moment a servant, one new to the house, flung open the door, and not at all aware what a commotion the name would excite, announced, —

" Mr. Lancelot Aird."

Lancy was among them; he had kissed his mother and sisters, Charlotte had greeted and shaken hands with him, and Don John was still clapping him on the back, laughing, shaking hands with him over and over again, then stepping back to exclaim on his growth and altered appearance, then coming close and shaking hands again, when he suddenly caught sight of his mother's face, and both the young men paused surprised.

There was for a moment an awkward pause. Mrs. Johnstone, who had risen, was winding the loose worsted round a ball with which she had been knitting; when she looked at Lancy, her eyes, more moist than usual, had a pathetic regret in them.

She said calmly, " Have you seen your father yet? "

" No, mother," answered Lancy, looking very foolish.

" Father 's in the orchard, I 'll go and tell him! " exclaimed little Mary, dancing out of the room, and almost at the same instant Naomi and Charlotte, each feeling that the manner of Lancy's reception at home was unexpected, stole quietly after her.

Don John felt his mother's manner with a keenness that was almost revolt against it. If he had been away so long and had been so met, he thought it would have gone near to breaking his heart, but he also saw instantly, because it was quite evident, that Lancy was not hurt in his affections, he was only a good deal ashamed. He had planned to take them unawares.

" You should have asked his leave before you appeared among your brothers and sisters," she went on — oh, so gently. And then she sighed, and the two tears that had dazzled her eyes fell on her cheeks, which were colored with an unusual agitation.

If Lancy had fallen on her neck, and kissed them away and implored forgiveness, it might even at that pass have been different.

But no, it was Don John who did that, while Lancy, looking red and irate, turned to the window, and appeared to look out.

"Oh, my mother!" exclaimed Don John, in a voice full of remonstrance and astonishment.

She answered calmly, looking into his eyes, —

"Yes, my son."

"You will beg father to forgive him, if — if indeed there can be any doubt about it. Mother! what can this mean — mother?"

His arm was still on her shoulder, she took her handkerchief, and wiping away her tears, said, "Lancy;" and when he turned from the window she kissed him a second time.

"Father has come in and gone into your dressing-room, mother, and he says Lancy is to go to him there," said little Mary, returning.

"No, mother, not there!" said Lancy, turning white to the lips. He had hoped to the last moment; now, before he knew what he was about, he had betrayed himself.

When Lancy appeared at the dressing-room door with his mother, Don John was there, pale, shocked, faltering, choking, he had been entreating, questioning, what could Lancy have done? what did it mean?

"You will forgive him!" he exclaimed. "I don't know — I cannot believe that there is no more than I know — but I cannot bear my life unless you forgive him."

Lancy listened with eager hope. It was but an instant. Then before any greeting was given to himself, Donald Johnstone put his two hands on the young Donald's shoulders, and looked aside to his wife.

She said, "Your poor son Lancy comes to submit himself to you, and to confess."

"You will forgive him, then, whatever it may be, father?" cried Don John.

"My much-loved son," was the reply. "If I had no better and stronger reason, I would forgive him for your sake."

CHAPTER XXV.

SOMETIMES one who has very good cause for suspicion against another, repudiates it heartily for a long time, and obstinately holds on to a hope that it is groundless.

On the memorable day of the picnic, the day when Lancy stole the ring, his mother, as she entered her dressing-room after coming home, noticed a small piece of folded writing-paper on the floor, under her table. She picked it up carelessly; it was one leaf of a ridiculous letter from Don John to Lancy. It had been shown to her already, was full of jokes, in fact it was droll enough to make her wish to read it a second time, and she put it in her pocket.

She had a good deal to think of just then besides parting with Lancy, and as soon as he was gone she went into her dressing-room, to revolve a little plan for producing, as she hoped, about two hundred pounds. Before she went to the picnic she had put in order all her jewelry; there was much more than she ever used. Her husband had told her of a loss he had lately had on some shares; if he would let her part with some of it, this loss would be made up without the least inconvenience of any kind.

Lancy had only been gone a few hours; her mind was still full of him, of his eagerness to get away, of the little love with which he repaid theirs — when she went up to her jewel-box again, and found to her surprise, but not to her dismay, that it was unlocked; she must have left it so, but it was most unlikely that any one should have noticed this fact. She began gently to take out the jewelry she meant to part with, and was not in the least disturbed till she missed the ring. It had been in her hand so recently, she would not believe that it was gone; but it was not till the box had been searched a second time that the finding of that little piece of folded paper flashed into her mind, and made her feel sick at heart. She told her husband, and at first, as Lancy had foreseen, they both felt very angry with themselves for having harbored such a suspicion. It seemed a shame that they could, for an instant, believe him base enough to steal from THEM. And yet the letter had been found there — and yet the ring was gone!

He had perfectly believed that no suspicion attached to him, because, though the letters had expressed displeasure and surprise, no mention had ever been made of this ring. But his guilty conscience accused him to such a degree when he saw Mrs. Johnstone's face, that he no sooner heard where his so-called father meant to receive him, than he gave up all for lost.

And yet, in one sense, all was not lost. Whatever he did, they would not, they could not, altogether give him up.

"I shall receive him in this room," Donald Johnstone had said of his adopted son, "and if he bears the ordeal badly —"

"Yes," she answered, "if he bears it badly, we may get him once more to confess and repent; but what if he bears it well? We cannot accuse him."

There was no need to accuse him. The deed which had been done was not named — it was taken for granted.

"Our taking this thing for granted," said Mr. Johnstone, "ought to show you how deep is your disgrace."

The adopted son hung his head; he was alone now with his parents.

"If you had been my own son — do you hear?"

"Yes, sir," said Lancy; he did not dare to say "father."

"If you were my own son now standing before me, and accusing his conscience of having robbed me, even me — if it had been Don John that had done this, I never would have spoken to him more; but you — you have no father — and you are unfortunate in your mother."

He paused, appearing to hesitate; and Lancy, though very much frightened, was astonished too — he lifted his daunted face. The adopted father had turned away from him, and gone to the window. Yes, it actually was so — he perceived that he was to be forgiven.

He was intensely relieved, but he felt, almost with terror, that he could not call up that amount of emotion, and above all of deep affection, which could alone meet suitably the love and grief that he saw before him.

He bungled through this scene as well as he could.

He meant to live at home again if they would let him, and submit himself to the yoke — at any rate till he could get some more money, for he was penniless. But work and restraint were now more distasteful to him than ever; money and idleness had afforded him ample opportunity to cultivate the knowledge of things evil, and he had done this with diligence.

He still retained a certain degree of affection for Don John, but he was so surprised by a few things incidentally said by him, that he paused to make further observations before talking confidentially to him on life, as he now unfortunately thought of it, on its fashions and experiences. He hardly knew, after a day or two, whether he looked upon Don John with most astonishment or most contempt, for he was not only very straightforward and honorable, very desirous to learn his profession, very high principled, but he was in some respects a good and blameless youth; he had everything to learn, as Lancy thought. This was a contemptible state of things; but on the whole Lancy elected not to teach him.

Don John had something on his mind just then, he was penitent and disgusted with himself, he had begun to perceive that in plotting Marjorie's flight to Edinburgh he had very much forgotten himself, as well as what was due to her. He was much displeased also with his grandmother for having played into his hands.

He thought this over till there seemed to be no peace but in confession, and he told his mother all.

She took his confidence very calmly, and paused before answering. "Your father will be glad of this," she said at last, "for, as time went on, your want of perception in the matter has disappointed him."

"Mother! then grandmother told you?"

"Of course!—I knew perfectly that Marjorie did not in the least care for Campbell, and we agreed with your grandmother that while she stayed in Edinburgh he should never be invited to the house."

"I'm stumped," was all Don John replied, and he retired, feeling much relieved, and a little humiliated. "The human mind," he reflected, "is deeper than I had supposed!"

And now Lancy was fitted out with proper clothes and personal possessions, for he had come back shabby and almost destitute; and then he was told that something had been found for him to do in London, and he was to board in the family of a clergyman, for it would not be just towards the other children that he should live at home.

He understood that he was under probation—was well aware that his host and hostess, probably his employer too, knew perfectly of his propensity. It pleased him to receive frequent letters from "mother," with as frequent presents of fruit, books, or the various trifles that she thought he might want or like. And sometimes "father" would send round on a Saturday to the office where he was employed, and propose to take him down with him to spend Sunday. Lancy liked this very well just at first, but he soon made many friends for himself, not by any means all of an undesirable sort; some were old school-fellows and their families, some were people whom he had met with on his travels. He had shortly a circle of his own, and seemed to take a certain pleasure in letting the Johnstones see, that as they would not any longer have him to live with them, he should make himself independent of them as soon as possible.

At present his salary was extremely small, and Mr. Johnstone paid for his board and his clothes; his pocket-money was all that he provided for himself.

There was only one thing in this world that he deeply dreaded. This man who still watched over him, and had been a true father to him, would on some rare occasions take him into his study, and after certain fatherly admonitions and counsels would kneel down and pray with him. Lancy regarded this as a very awful ceremony, so did all the children of the house. It came so seldom that it never lost its power. It was far worse, as Lancy felt, than any punishment; in fact the recollection of it actually kept him, and that not seldom, from doing wrong; but it was an additional reason for wanting to get free, to throw off the paternal yoke altogether.

So things continued for nearly a year, and all, including himself, appeared to be going on satisfactorily.

Captain Leslie had not been able yet to see Estelle's eldest son.

Early in the autumn he took a tour on the continent, and was detained there by illness. He was almost always ill, and could not think how it was. He was prudent, he never fatigued himself; he would like to have spent his strength, and money, and time for the good of others; and all he could do was to care for himself.

He consulted several physicians: "Perhaps he had better remain in the south of Europe for the winter," said one, and he submitted, finding the charge of his own health, of himself in fact, very dull work. It was not till the hottest days of the English summer, the middle of July, that he found himself in England again, and on his way to the Johnstones'.

He longed to see Estelle, and her son. He felt that he had almost asked for an invitation, but not the less that his welcome was spontaneous and sweet. The girls had corresponded with him, they were all charmed to see him. The mother gave him a shaded comfortable corner in the drawing-room, and sent for some tea. She perceived at once that he was quite an invalid, and for the first time he fully admitted it — to himself. And Don John?

Could anything be so unfortunate? Don John was away again. He would be disappointed, for he had wished to see Captain Leslie. They did not think he had been away for nearly a year.

But Lancy — "Did he remember that they had told him about Lancy?" asked little Mary.

" O, yes."

" He is our adopted son," said Estelle ; " we brought him up with our own children."

" But he lives with his own mother now," proceeded Mary ; " her name is Mrs. Ward, and she is come home from Australia. And Lancy has been ill, very ill; so Don John and Mrs. Ward took him to Ramsgate for a change. Did you ever see Mrs. Ward?"

" No; I have not the pleasure of her acquaintance."

" She used to be rather rich, and had the grandest rings, and the thickest chains and bracelets you ever saw ; but this is very fortunate, for she has married a very bad man, who treats her so unkindly that she ran away from him, and now she has all that jewelry to sell. She told Lancy it was worth four hundred pounds, and she keeps selling it when she wants money ; and she and Lancy live together. Lancy says he shall go to law with that man soon, but it will not be any use. Don John knows all about law, and he says so."

" But Don John will be back in about a week," said Mrs. Johnstone, " so you will see him."

Captain Leslie was very well amused, falling as before into the possession of the girls, to whom Marjorie was now added. As before, he made them talk a good deal about their brother. Freddy, a fine boy of fifteen, was at home, but he excited no interest. Don John, his doings, his writings, and the photographs of his honest face, were what pleased Leslie. He was a very joyous young fellow, as was evident — the leader of the young brood, Marjorie's confidant in her peaceful happy love affair, Naomi's comrade, Charlotte's critic, Mary's patron — looked up to by Freddy as one much exalted, but whose various doings were not beyond hope of imitation, and whose privileges might one day be shared.

He was of age now, and gave himself occasionally

the airs of a man of thirty, taking it much amiss that his two grown-up sisters were older than himself, and almost as tall.

However, as he frequently said, their being so tall was their own lookout; he was himself quite up to the average height, in fact, half an inch taller than his father.

Charlotte and Don John, about this time were frequently seen sitting with their heads together, in doors or out of doors, and manifestly concocting somewhat that amused them; but though Mrs. Johnstone took notice of this fact, she was not careful to influence either party in any way. The brother and sister-like intimacy, the old habit of writing "the minutes" together, kept them always familiar, but neither ever surprised the other; they were never absent, and then, uniting, saw each other in that new light which is apt to produce a new feeling.

The fact was that about this time Mr. Brown began to cultivate Don John's friendship with a certain assiduity. The young gentleman was not taken in. "It won't do," he would think; "Charlotte does not care about your prospects a bit; why must you need confide them to me?" But in their next conversation Mr. Brown with much diffidence let Don John know that he thought he might have mistaken his own feelings as regarded Miss Charlotte, and he felt sure she did not look on him with any favor. Don John assented with needless decision, and added, of his own proper wisdom, that he was sure Charlotte was not a girl who was ever likely to marry anybody.

But there was always something curiously deferential in Mr. Brown's manner when he called upon the ladies of the family. Don John was sagacious; he felt that his society was not sought for his own sake. He had been told that it was not for Charlotte's. He consulted Charlotte. Charlotte said it must be Naomi. Manifestly she did not care about his turning away from her so soon. But Naomi would care.

And yet Mr. Brown was decidedly a good fellow.

He was rather a fine young man. Would it be a good thing to let him have a chance?

Of course, if Naomi knew anything of this beforehand he would not have a chance. They were some time reflecting on the matter, and Naomi often thought they had more conferences than usual; a dawning suspicion occasionally induced her to surprise them. They may have been adroit, or she mistaken, it was almost always "the minutes" they were discussing, for by this name all Charlotte's contributions to literature were still called.

Evidently it must have been the minutes, for if there was any conspiracy nothing came of it.

Mr. Brown frequently called; Charlotte often went out of the room on these occasions, and Naomi had to entertain him; but when Charlotte came back again it never appeared that Naomi had been well entertained.

And in the mean time Lancy was frequently in the house. He delighted to make Charlotte feel shy, and yet he saw that she resented his half-careless compliments. He would often try to squeeze her hand, for he liked to see the pale carnation tint rise on her clear cheek; and when she was distant to him, or when displeased, he would laugh and enjoy it. He did not truly care for her, but he would have been very well pleased to make her care for him, and he flattered himself that she did.

Leslie, true to his interest in Estelle's eldest son, was pleased to learn all he could of Charlotte and her writings.

It was the afternoon of the day when Don John was expected home; seated where he could see the path by which he would arrive, Leslie easily beguiled her into conversation. She and Naomi were doing "art needlework," and Leslie was so fixed in his opinion that Charlotte and Don John were all in all to one another, that it surprised him when she sat down with her back to this path. All had hitherto favored his idea, and the talk as usual came round to Don John. That afternoon, for the first time, Naomi noticed it, — started a subject which had nothing do with her brother, and then fell silent to observe what would happen; but her attention wandered. She knew not how this was, but when it returned there was Don John's name again.

" Then why does he think that story was rejected?" Leslie was asking.

" Oh, because I had tried to bring in some of the old-fashioned courtesies. It is such a pity that we are obliged to do without ' madam ' and ' sir.' Don't you think so?"

" I *think* I have not *thought*. So it is; we must make the best of it."

" Such expressions as ' my lady ' and ' your lordship' must always have been a hideous incubus on a polite tongue; but English has not been so pretty since we left off ' madam,' nor so terse since we parted with ' sir.' I do allow myself in conversation to use those words now and then, for the mere pleasure of hearing them, but it does no good."

" How do you mean, no good?"

" Oh, it does not help to bring them in again."

" No," said Naomi; " when you do it in society it only makes people think you know no better."

" I fancy, madam, that their day is gone by," said Leslie, smiling.

Charlotte sighed, as if she really cared about the matter. " We are growing so rude."

" And so Don John counsels you to do without ' madam ' and ' sir'?"

" Yes, and without my theories."

" What theory, for instance?"

" Oh, in that paper I brought in my notion that birds have an articulate language."

" Articulate?"

" Yes, some birds; he has shown me that no creatures differ so much from one another, in point of intelligence, as birds; but I am sure some have a real language, bank-swallows, for instance. When you hear them chattering together at the opening of their holes, does it never occur to you that if you heard any language you do not understand, such as Malay-Chinese or Hottentot, it would not sound more articulate than swallow-talk does, particularly if it was uttered as hastily and in as low a tone?"

Leslie smiled, as if he would put the question by.

She went on, " Of course their verbs must be very, very simple."

" What! you believe that they have verbs?"

" Certainly, for they possess the idea of time; they must be able to say, ' *We were there,* and ' *We are here.*' And as they are perfectly aware that they shall go back again, and as they do it in concert, I think they must be able to say, '*Let us depart.*' "

" They may have signs which stand for such ideas," said Leslie doubtfully, " as we have."

" Yes."

" And we call them verbs."

" Irresistible reasoning! and yet I resist it altogether."

" But how will you resist it? What theory will you set up instead?"

Leslie considered : " The verbs I cannot admit," he said doubtfully ; " I could rather think your sand-martins have a monosyllabic language, like Chinese."

" Yes ; but I don't think that idea will help you, because the latest books about Chinese show, and I think prove, that originally that language had parts of speech, verbs, and inflections ; but it has gone to decay, partly from isolation, partly from the idleness of those who spoke it — from their letting their phonetic organs pass out of use. Chinese is not simple and young. It is as it were in its second childhood, going to pieces from old age."

" Indeed."

" And you must have noticed that it is the tendency of language to have, as time goes on, a richer vocabulary and a simpler grammar."

" You are going to found some theory on that, as regards your swallows?"

" No ; but I think it likely that theirs being only a rudimentary language, what fails them most is their store of nouns — not of verbs."

"Charlotte," said Naomi, "Captain Leslie cannot help laughing at you."

"Perhaps you picked up these theories from constant companionship with Don John?" said Leslie with an air of apology.

"Oh no; Don John is always criticising my theories; but for him I should indulge in many more."

"I must admit that in this one I think you claim far too much for the martins."

"Do you think then that all their chatter conveys no knowledge from one to the other — no intention, no wish?"

"Why should it more than the lark's song? He pleases his mate, but he tells her nothing."

"No, any more than we do when we sing without words; but sand-martins cannot sing — they talk. Some birds, for aught we know, can only sing. But our sense of hearing is very dull. It may be that besides singing the thrushes can say many things, and yet their speech may be too low and too small to be audible to us. Sand-martins are the only birds I know who talk manifestly and audibly."

"Ah, here is Don John," said Naomi, and she laid down her work, and went out at the open window to meet him.

Leslie lifted his eyes, and looking out into the garden saw a young man slowly advancing along the grass. Could this be Don John? Mary came running up to him; he stooped slightly, and she kissed his cheek. He looked languid, and tired; and while Mary chattered and danced about him, seeming to tell him some interesting piece of news, he gazed fixedly on a bed of petunias, and with his hands in his pockets stood motionless, as if lost in thought. Naomi came near, and the two girls advanced towards the house, one on either side of him.

"Captain Leslie is here," Naomi said, as they came up. Leslie heard this, and the answer —

"Oh!" That was all.

Rather a gentlemanly looking young fellow, Captain

Leslie thought. The extreme gravity and seriousness of his manner made his smile appear sweet; but it was soon gone again, and after the first greeting, he sank into thought.

And so this was Estelle's son! Of how much consequence he had been to Leslie! Leslie was of no consequence at all to him.

CHAPTER XXVI.

AMONG the minor surprises of his life, none had ever struck Leslie so much as the behavior and air of young Donald Johnstone.

He had gathered a good deal of information as to his voice, his manners, his laugh: he appeared, and scattered it all; the picture was not like, in any respect. There was something almost pathetic in the gentleness, the serious and silent abstraction in which he sat, and, remote in thought from everything about him, cogitated with folded arms.

His light eyelashes concealed in part rather expressive blue eyes; he was pale with that almost chalky hue of a fair skin not naturally pale. He only spoke when spoken to — and Leslie did not speak. The girls, evidently surprised, asked if Lancy was worse.

No, it appeared that Lancy was almost well again.

" Nothing is the matter then?"

" The matter! with whom?"

" Why, with you. Did you come up by the boat, Don John?"

" Yes."

" Ah, then you were sea-sick! You always are! It is such a mistake to think that, to be often on the sea at intervals, just for a few hours will cure you."

Oh, what a sigh for answer!

" I wish you would n't do it, dear," said Naomi, leaning over the end of the sofa on which he sat, and touching his light hair lovingly; " it has made you look so pale."

"I've got a headache," was his reply; and then, all in a moment, there was a step heard, and the tall graceful mother came in the door. Don John roused himself, he almost seemed to shake himself, and rose up and met her, and kissed her, and seemed quite cheerful.

"My dear!" she exclaimed, "how pale you are!"

"Yes, mother!" cried Naomi; "and he's been on that steamer again."

"A fellow looks such a muff," said Don John, "if he is sea-sick. I wish to cure myself."

Leslie looked up, and met Don John's eyes; he knew as well as possible that there was something more than sea-sickness the matter.

"When he got up from the sofa," exclaimed Mary, "he staggered; he is quite giddy."

"There!" said Don John, impatiently; "no more! It's more muffish to talk of it than to have it."

"Yes," said the placid mother, soothingly; "I'll ring for some strong tea, and when you have had it you will be quite well."

"Shall I?" he answered; and then he seemed to make a supreme effort again, and this time with better result.

It appeared to be almost by his own will and resolution that he cast over the matter that had held him down, and that the natural hues of life came back to his face. The tea came in, perhaps it helped him; he ate and drank, and seemed to feel a certain comfort in his mother's observance, so that when in the course of time Donald Johnstone himself entered, all that was remarkable in the young Donald's appearance and manner had passed away. He was still pale, that was all. Could it be, Leslie thought, that all this pathetic air and abstracted expression had come from a mere fit of sea-sickness? He almost despised young Donald when the thought suggested itself. But the night undeceived him.

There is something so pathetic in the anguish of the young.

Leslie had a feeling heart, and when, lying awake in

the dead of the night, when the healthy and the strong should have been asleep, he heard a sound of sobbing in the next room to his, he could have wept too.

This was his heir — bemoaning himself in the night on his pillow, when he did not know that any one could hear. But the heads of the two beds were close together, one on either side of the wall.

What could it be? He was not yet twenty-two years old; could he be breaking his heart already for some woman's love? Or had he committed some grave faults, and was he craving forgiveness of his Maker? or was he sick — was he in pain?

The sobbing went on so long that Leslie almost thought he must rise and enter the young fellow's room. But no, he controlled himself; he feared to do more harm than good; and at last, but not till day had dawned, there was a welcome silence. Don John was asleep; and Leslie, who had offered up many a prayer for him, fell asleep too.

Leslie did not hear that midnight mourning only once; but for several nights there were no articulate sounds with it. Don John, though in the morning he appeared grave and dull, and though he looked pale, went every morning to London with his father, and had the air of striving to behave as usual, so that Leslie felt that to speak to him or to his parents would be to make matters worse — it would be a breach of confidence. But once before dawn, waking at a now well-known sound, he heard words as well as sighs: " Oh, father! Oh, mother! " He started up; these were about the last words he should have expected to hear; he could not risk being obliged to hear more.

The heir, for whom he had already begun to feel some affection, must surely be mourning over some fault which he knew would distress his parents when they found it out. Was it not possible that he could help him? He rose, and lighting a candle, began to move about in the room without making any attempt at special quietness.

There was absolute silence. In a minute or two a

tall figure in a quilted dressing-gown appeared at Don John's door, shut it behind him, and came in.

He set down his candle, drew a chair, and seated himself.

" I must have disturbed you," said Don John, deeply vexed and disgusted with himself, and perhaps with Captain Leslie too.

Leslie answered " Yes ;" and when Don John made no answer, he presently went on : " And if I feel a very deep and keen sympathy with your sorrow, whatever it may be, there are reasons for that, dear fellow, which probably you never knew."

Surprise had for the moment mastered emotion. Don John raised himself on his elbow, heaved up another great sobbing sigh, and stared at him.

" Are you aware that I have loved your mother all my life," he went on, while Don John was considering that it was no use to say anything, he must let him alone — " all my youth — and I never had the least chance with her? A hopeless attachment, and to such a woman, is very hard discipline for a man. I say it that you may feel sure of my sympathy ; but I have had faults to deplore as well. Sin has full often been standing at the door. If that is your case, feel sure of my deep sympathy there also. And now tell me — you, the much-loved son of my first and only love — if there is anything in the world that I can do for you, do you think I should be thankful to do it ?"

" Yes," said Don John, quite simply, " I think you would ; " and he laid himself down again, and made no attempt to say more.

" You have got into some scrape : you have, perhaps, done something that you deeply regret, and — "

" No," interrupted Don John, " I have n't."

A little thrown back by this, Leslie paused, and after a short silence the youth went on — " But I feel that what you have said is extremely kind : and perhaps now I may be able to sleep. I have not slept well the last few nights." A hint surely to Leslie to go — but he stayed.

" Are you so sure then that there is nothing at all I can do — with my advice, my assistance, my property?"

" I am sure."

" There remain only my prayers."

" And they cannot help me to anything but patience."

" My dear fellow — "

" But I am as glad you came in as I am sorry for having disturbed you, because I am sure you will promise me not to mention this to any one — any one at all."

" Not even to your parents."

" That was what I meant."

" But if I promise you this, you will owe a certain duty to me in return."

" What duty?"

" If a time should ever come when I can help you, I shall have a right to expect that you will claim my help, to any extent and in any way."

" Thank you."

" And I must not ask what this sorrow is?"

" I cannot tell you."

Leslie thought of Charlotte. She had treated him with composed indifference, but he had appeared to the full as indifferent to her. He could but speak carefully.

" I hardly like to give this matter up," he said. " When I first loved your mother I was scarcely older than you are now. If there had been no other bar to my hopes, it would have been enough that I was poor. Now, if you feel any likeness in my case to yours, and if the young lady's father — I mean, if two or three thousand pounds — "

" In love with a girl!" exclaimed Don John with a short laugh, whose bitterness and scorn it would be impossible to describe. for he was contrasting an imaginary sorrow with a real one. " Fall in love with a girl, and cry about her in the night! I am not such a muff."

" What!" exclaimed Leslie, rather shocked.

" I am not come to that yet," continued Don John with unutterable self-contempt; " but perhaps I shall " —

and the suddenly arrested storm asserted itself with another great heaving of the chest. Then he begged Leslie's pardon, for he saw that he was hurt. "That's not my line," he said. "But what you say, or seem to say, perfectly astonishes me. You are very good; I have no claim on you in the world — and — I am sorry I disturbed you."

"I think you mean that you are sorry I have become aware of this."

Don John made no answer; Leslie turned towards his candle; the gray light was beginning to wax, and it was burning dim.

"I must go, then," and he held out his hand. But the next day, when his heir came down, he deeply regretted that he had promised silence. Don John was not able to go to town; he had low fever hanging about him, and his already wasted hands looked whiter than before.

The day after that a medical man was sent for. Don John could get up, but he complained of his head; and in another day it became manifest that both his father and mother were alarmed about him.

Leslie's visit had nearly come to an end — he felt that he must go; but it was bitter to him. He longed to talk to his heir, and offer him the best consolation that he could; and Don John was aware of this.

In his shrewd but somewhat youthful fashion, he perceived the real affection that Leslie felt for him. He thought it would be very unfair if he did not have his innings before he went. Expressing himself in these words to Leslie, on an occasion when he was feeling slightly better, and not being understood, he explained — "I meant that I thought you would like to pray with me; father does sometimes. I should not mind it at all — in fact, I think, I should like it."

"Out of kindness to me, dear fellow?" asked Leslie; but of course he took the opportunity offered. There could hardly have been anything appropriate to the peculiar circumstances of the patient in that prayer, and yet he derived from it his first conscious desire to sub-

mit — his first perception that if he could submit he
could get well.   He knew that he had rebelled hitherto,
and thus when the thinking-fit over this misfortune came
on, rebellion was at the root of its keenest sting.

He had merely meant to be kind, and he had his reward.

He was very ill, and both father and mother lavished
observant tenderness on him.   Sometimes he could get
up, come down stairs, and talk almost as usual.   Then
all on a sudden something which had been held at bay
appeared to get hold on him, and low fever devoured his
strength.

One day he could hardly lift his head from his pillow,
but he was yet not quite in such evil case as before, for
there was that in the manner of both parents which
made Leslie sure that they knew now what had pros-
trated him.

It was very hot weather, his door was set wide open,
and the family came in and out, not aware, and not informed, that there was any anxiety felt about him.

And there was little in the placid mother's manner to
show that she felt any.   She was generally with him.
It was not so much tendance as consolation that she
seemed to be giving him ; not in words.   And his father,
too, he spoke bravely and cheerfully ; yet the patient
lost strength and flesh daily.

" As one whom his mother comforteth," thought Leslie, when he saw his life-long love watching by his heir.

Who could fail to be consoled?   Yet Don John did
not appear to derive direct comfort from their manner,
only from their presence ; he could not ·bear to be left
without either one or the other of his parents.

And yet it was he himself who had first consoled ; and
he went away, and endured a very anxious fortnight,
till the girls, who had promised to write frequently,
could at last say that Don John was better.

With what gratitude he heard this.   He was going
up shortly to Scotland, and could not help proposing
to stop on his way, and pay a call of one hour on the
Johnstones.

There was the beautiful Estelle, and there were her tall daughters, and her invalid; he was lying on the sofa, undergoing a course of indulgence and waiting on, from all parties. His hands were thin, and as white as a girl's, his cheeks were thin, and his eyes were sunken ; but the struggle was over between youth and death, and youth had won.

And yet it was not the same Don John. Leslie was just as sure of this as the others were.

His mother put down the book she had been reading to him, and looked at him with anxious love. "He must go out soon for a change," she said, "and then I hope he will be well."

"I don't want to go away, mother," said the young invalid ; "but if I must go anywhere, perhaps Captain Leslie would have me."

The beautiful mother actually blushed ; the way in which all her children took to Captain Leslie was almost embarrassing to her. She could not see any charm in him herself ; but that was an old story.

Leslie was highly flattered.

She was about to say, "I really must apologize for my boy;" but when she saw Leslie's pleasure she had not the heart to do it. He looked as if he would have liked to hug Don John.

"Captain Leslie ought to have me too," said Mary ; "I've done fourteen errands for him this very day, finding books for him, and fetching his eau-de-Cologne, and handing him his beef-tea, and all sorts of things."

Mrs. Johnstone did not speak, but she looked quietly at Leslie. The look was not an apology to him for not having given him her love, but it expressed an affection she had never shown him before, and she said, "If you can have Don John" ("And me too," interrupted Mary), "my husband and I could trust you with him with more comfort than I can say."

"And me too," insisted Mary.

"Don John, and you too," answered Leslie. His mahogany-colored face could not change its hue, but short of that it expressed all the pleasure possible.

"Invited themselves, did they?" exclaimed Donald Johnstone, when he was told of this by his wife. "My children invited themselves into this man's house, who has of all men least reason to like their father! How did he stand it? and how did you get him out of the scrape, my Star?"

"He was delighted; so I let them alone."

"Let them alone! But it will be a great inconvenience to him; very likely he will have to get in more furniture and other servants. I believe he has a mere shooting-box."

"Yes, I felt all that, and was very much out of countenance."

"And doubtless he perceived it. I don't see how you could have done less than blush, my dear. You are actually repeating the performance, and very becoming it is."

"Perhaps he wishes that old attachment to be forgotten — perhaps he feels only friendship, now that he has seen me again."

"Perhaps!"

"Well, we must make the best of this now. They proposed the visit with the greatest composure, and he accepted with acclamation."

So in a couple of weeks Don John and Mary were in Scotland, in a moderately convenient house, wedged into one corner of a triangular valley. Its one carriage road led down beside a prattling stream to the sea. Mary was intensely happy, and Don John was convalescent. The sensation of returning health and strength is in itself delightful, and the refreshment of clear skies, long sunsets, scented air, and mountain solitude, all helped to console and calm.

Don John gained strength daily, but Leslie did not observe any return of the joyous spirits for which he had hitherto been conspicuous in his little world. He never ventured to ask what the sorrow was, but he perceived that its cause was not removed; and sometimes there would come over the pleasant but somewhat commonplace countenance an expression which removed it into another world of feeling and experience. An ardent yearning would come over it, the outcome it seemed of some impassioned regret, which made it look more noble, if less young.

CHAPTER XXVII.

"FATHER is ill," cried Mary, running down one afternoon to the shore of the long loch beside which Don John was sitting, watching the little wild ducks as they crept into the shelter of the reeds; " not very ill, but rather ill. Captain Leslie has got a letter from mamma. He is better, and we are not to be at all disturbed, and not to think of coming home."

Father ill! Such a thing had never taken place for one day in the memory of the oldest of his children.

Leslie followed closely on Mary's message. Don John read the letter, and neither he nor his sister were so uneasy as might have been expected.

He looked at them. " They have this composure from their parents," he thought. " It was one of Estelle's great charms that she never was in the least nervous, never apprehensive."

The nearest telegraph station was fifteen miles off, and did not open till eight o'clock in the morning. Leslie had waited behind to make arrangements for having a servant there, to send a message off at the earliest moment for the latest news.

The sick man's children slept in peace. As soon as possible the next morning, an answer came from Naomi to Don John. " Father is not worse. You need not be uneasy; but mother wishes you both to come home."

Don John had been prepared for this, for his packing was found to be ready. All little Mary's effects by his decree were to be left behind, excepting what could be put into a hand-bag. Thus they were all ready as soon as the horses could be put to.

"But why are you in such a hurry?" asked Mary.
"Mother says we are not to be uneasy."

Leslie listened for the answer.

"And therefore I am not uneasy about father's illness; but he is sure to want me, and I want to go and
help."   .

"I am glad to see that you have your mother's delightful temperament. Why indeed should you be uneasy? why anticipate disaster?" said Leslie.

Don John's eyes dilated with a startled and gratified
expression. "My mother's temperament," he began,
almost vehemently, and then checked himself.

"Yes, you often remind me of her, both of you."

Though Leslie was driving, and the horses were
rather fresh, he could not help noticing that he had produced a great effect by this speech, and that it was a
pleasurable one. That his own feelings should be of
the most romantic cast towards Estelle, seemed to him
the most natural thing in the world; but that her son
should share any such feeling was, he well knew, a very
uncommon circumstance. But then she was not an
ordinary mother; so he presently told himself. Why
then should hers be an ordinary son?

Don John lost himself in cogitation. This remark
of Leslie's appeared to be such a spontaneous testimony
to his sonship. Very slight, but the more sweet.

Undoubtedly his handwriting was extremely like his
father's, but he had tormented himself with the thought
that this might be because he liked it, had admired and
copied it, as remarkably firm, clear, and round. It expressed the qualities he wished to have.

And then his manner, and the carriage of his head:
he walked just as his father did. The remembrance of
this consoled him just at first, but his sick fancy turned
that into poison also: "I constantly walk with father,"
he thought; "and when I was a little fellow I liked to
go as if I was marching, because he did."

Leslie parted from Don John and his sister with much
affection. Neither the son nor the daughter anticipated
evil; but Don John sent a telegram on to mention

at what time he hoped to reach King's Cross, and requesting that one might meet him there with the latest news.

He found all as he had expected.

His father had been ill, but was better — still in bed, and not allowed to get up.

" And you are not to ask him how his illness began," said the mother.

" But how did it begin, then?"

" That is what we do not know, my dear. We thought he had had a fall. Dumplay came home quietly, and your father not riding him."

" But that fat, old, peaceable creature could not have thrown him. Impossible, mother."

" So I think. Mr. Viser found him sitting up leaning against the gate of the long field, and brought him home just after Dumplay came into the stable-yard. He was a little cut about the face, seemed ill, and that first day gave no account of the matter. We were told he was not to be questioned at all, or teased about it. The next day he roused himself, and said, when he saw Dr. Fielding, 'Now am I better?' 'Better than I could possibly have hoped,' Dr. Fielding answered, ' wonderfully better;' and then, to my distress, your dear father went on: 'I cannot think how this came to pass.' But we are assured that there is no danger. That evening he said he remembered dismounting and opening the gate; he remembered seeing Dumplay walk through it, but nothing more. If he fainted and fell, he must have hurt his head and cut his face in the fall." Then she put her two hands on Don John's shoulders as he stood gravely listening, and said, " My much loved son, what a comfort it will be that you will be with him, able to help him, and knowing all about his affairs. It consoles me to see you looking well again."

The new expression came into Don John's face then; and after that again, when sitting by his father he found that he could calm and satisfy him, and that his mere presence was doing good.

He went up to London the next day about such of
his father's affairs as he could attend to, and walked
home from the station through the long field.   Several
people out of "the houses" waylaid him to ask after
his father; perhaps that was the reason why he did not
notice, till he almost reached the shrubbery gate, that
Charlotte was standing there waiting for him.

Charlotte.   He perfectly knew Charlotte's face, and
yet it was true that he had never looked at her with any
particular attention before.   It was a light green gate
that she was leaning on, just of the proper height to
support her elbows.   She was dressed in white, and
had no color about her dress at all; on her head was
rather a wide white hat, limp, and only suited for a
garden.   Her whole dress, in short, was dazzlingly white
and clean.   Her small face seen under the hat was in
shade; a pure pale carnation suffused her cheeks, and
the lips were of the hue of dark damask roses. · The
same Charlotte! and yet the beautiful Irish eyes seemed
almost new to him.

Don John stopped.

" I thought I would come to meet you," said Charlotte, not moving from her place on the other side of
the gate.   " My uncle is so much better; he is up, and
sitting in the playroom."

This was certainly Charlotte, and yet he looked at
her with wonder.

" Well?" she asked with a little smile, and added,
" I knew you were uneasy, you always look so .grave;
so I thought I would come and tell you that Dr. Fielding says he is more than satisfied."

" It was kind of you, it was good of you," said
Don John.   " What a beautiful gown you have on,
Charlotte!"

" This old thing," said Charlotte, lifting her arms,
and letting him open the gate; " why, I have had it for
a year!"

" Oh," answered Don John; and how long he would
have stood gazing at her it is impossible to say, if she
had not turned and moved on, saying, as she preceded

him in the narrow path, " No doubt you will want to see my uncle first ; but after that 1 want to consult you about something."

Charlotte and Don John generally were consulting together about something or other ; he was always expected to criticise her essays and tales, and did not regard this as by any means a privilege, but as he often thought, " she is not likely to marry, and therefore she ought to have something else to give a meaning to her life." On this occasion he did think of the coming consultation as a privilege, and ardently hoped that Naomi would not be present. His past thoughts were full of images of Charlotte, and for a moment he was not aware that he was looking at them with different eyes.

His father was so much better, that but for the cuts about his face it would have been difficult to be uneasy about him. These, however, reminded them how sudden the seizure had been, and made them long to know whether it was ever likely to recur. Don John had tried to discuss this in the morning ; but when he found that he was put off with remarks about symptoms that he knew could be of no consequence, he said no more, but he looked so much alarmed that the friendly doctor said, " I have told you that there is no danger — for the present. But if I allowed you to get anything out of me, your father would very soon get it out of you, and that would be bad for him. When he asks questions, you know nothing."

" Excepting that there is something to know," thought Don John.

Marjorie was away, staying with her grandmother, as was often the case now. Dr. Fielding went on : " I would not let your sister be sent for, but I wanted you ; your presence will be of the greatest use, and may be of the utmost consequence."

Don John took easily to responsibility, guessed that his father was not to be left alone, and found a great solace in the consideration that he had so arranged his life as to have his son almost always at his side.

The dinner that evening was a very pleasant meal. The head of the family was so manifestly better that no one could be uneasy about him. A nurse was in the house, and she sat with him.

Little Mary was allowed to dine late, and was full of talk about Scotland. Don John was in better spirits than he had been since before his illness, and sitting in his father's place surveyed the family.

His mother looked tired, but peaceful and thankful. Mary and Naomi had on white muslin and blue ribbons — pink does not look well with reddish hair; but Charlotte had on pink ribbons. How much prettier pink is than blue! Her almost black hair, not glossy — how soft and thick it looked! A twisted rope of pearls was embedded in it. Her mother had just sent it to her, and at the same time some silver ornaments to Naomi. Don John did not know that, but he could not help looking at Charlotte, and she and Naomi kept glancing at one another.

"Don't they look sweet, both of them?" exclaimed the admiring little sister; and then Don John was told that the girls had put on their best to do honor to these ornaments, which had just arrived; and before he had reflected that he should have included Naomi in his remark, he had burst forth with "Well, I thought I had never seen Charlotte look like that before — look so well, I mean."

It was the end of September, remarkably hot for the time of year, and though they were dining by candle light, all the windows were open.

"Girls always look better when they have their best things on," said Mary. Don John glanced at both the girls; Naomi looked just as usual, Charlotte's appearance was really indescribable.

"You never say anything civil, excepting to mother," said Naomi to her brother. "Now there was an opening for you to have said that we look well in everything."

"Only he does n't think so," observed Charlotte.

"No; he often says, What a guy you look when you

have a crumpled frock on! and, How horrid it is of you to ink your fingers!" observed Mary.

" Yes," said Charlotte, with sweet indifference; " but I 'm not half so untidy as I used to be."

Don John would like to have made fervent apologies for his past rudeness; he would like to have put Naomi's hint into impassioned language, but he had just sense enough to hold his tongue; and he thought his mother's encomium very inadequate when she said, " Yes, I am pleased to see a great improvement in you, my dear; you almost always look nice and neat now."

Charlotte's cheeks blushed and bloomed; a deep dimple came. Her smile was naturally slight, but it always lifted the upper lip in a strangely beautiful way, and then the teeth showed. One never saw them but then.

Nice and neat! Go out at dawn and apply those words to a dewy half-opened damask rose. Charlotte for her part found this praise very much to her mind, and both the girls continued to remark on one another's ornaments in a way that enabled Don John, with wholly new shyness, to glance at them. He tried to make his glances impartial, but the silver chain was only an ornament round his sister's neck. The pearls twisted in Charlotte's hair appeared to be almost a part of herself, he felt that if he might touch them they were close enough to her to be warm.

When he opened the door for them all to go out, that vision of beauty was last, and she whispered to him. " In the orchard, Don John; you won't forget?"

No, he was sure he should not forget.

He argued with himself for some minutes as to the length of time he was accustomed to sit at table.

He reminded himself that when the evenings were light he generally rose when his mother did, and strode straight into the garden. It was rather dark now, but hot, and the air was still. He could hear the girls' voices, they were all out of doors. He could not wait any longer; he ran upstairs to wish his father good night, and then came down to give a cheerful message to his mother, who was alone in the drawing-room.

After that he too stepped forth into the dark. Naomi and Mary were together; Charlotte was walking on just before them, and held a lighted candle, which she was protecting with her hand. There was no stir in the air to make it flicker. Naomi was very fond of Charlotte; when Don John teased her, she always took her part.

"Another 'thing' of Charlotte's has been declined," said Naomi—and added in a persuasive tone, "you've never written one word about the minutes since you went away; and I think Charlotte would like to discuss some letters she has got; you'll ask her to read them to you?"

"Yes," answered Don John; "what letters are they?"

"Oh, from some of her editors, no doubt; no one else writes to her. I have advised and criticised as well as I could while you were away, and now you must; but we need n't all be there, need we?"

"No," said Don John with an air of impartial fairness. It was a piece of hypocrisy, which for the moment he really could not help. So Naomi, as he stood still, gave him the gentlest little push towards Charlotte, who had now got on a good way before them, and with her arm over her little sister's shoulder, turned her down another path, saying, "Well now, Mary, tell me some more about the gillies."

Don John, like a moth, went after the candle.

He got into a long walk, sheltered on one side by the shrubbery, and at the end of it, in a small arbor where was a little rustic table, sat Charlotte, her candle burning before her. She seemed to be poring over some letters, but as Don John drew near she folded and put them into her pocket, and sat perfectly lost in thought, till, standing in the door of the arbor, he spoke to her.

Then, to his great astonishment, she put her hand in her pocket again, drew out, not the letters, but her handkerchief, and leaning her elbows on the table, covered her face and began to cry.

"Why, Charlotte," exclaimed Don John, "what can be the matter, dear?"

When Charlotte got into a worse scrape than usual, he generally said "dear" to her, so did she to him on grave occasions — she had often done so when he was ill; what a valuable habit this seemed now.

"I told you I wanted to consult you," said Charlotte trying to recover herself — her lovely color had fled, her hands trembled a little, and her long eyelashes were wet — "but I don't know how to begin," she sighed, almost piteously.

"I'll begin then," said Don John. "If that editor has declined your last thing, he is a humbug; it is the best you ever wrote."

"But he hasn't," said Charlotte.

"Oh, it's not that!"

"No, but it's everything else — it's all, excepting that."

"It's not the curate," exclaimed Don John with sudden alarm. "Surely he has not turned round again to you?"

"Oh, no — of course not;" then the color came back to Charlotte's face. Don John sat down on the other chair, and Charlotte said, "If you were in my place — I mean if, instead of being the son of the house, you were (as I am) only here because my uncle and aunt are the kindest people in the world, you would understand —"

She fell silent here — he had become rather pale. "I should understand?" he repeated.

"That I cannot bear, having never had the least chance of even showing that I am aware of their goodness — I cannot bear to put away from me a possible means of returning it, even at the risk of perhaps making myself unhappy." Then she leaned her elbow on the table again, and said with pathetic simplicity, —

"I could easily make myself love him, if I chose."

Don John made a movement of surprise and alarm, but she was thinking of far more important matters than his feelings, and went on, "But he is not good — I

know he is not good — and I don't believe he really
cares for me."

"Then, for heaven's sake, Charlotte — for all our
sakes — don't 'make yourself love him.' Why, what
does the fellow mean, that he should dare to ask it?
Whom can you be talking of ? who has presumed — "

She was thinking too intently to notice his agitation.
" You always said, you know," she presently went on,
" that I should not have lovers — and it 's quite true ;
but there might be some one whose interest it is to
marry me, particularly now. When Christmas comes
this year I shall have a hundred pounds from those two
editors. I am ashamed to think meanly of him, but I
know — I am almost sure, he does not love me."

"Then he is even more a fool than a knave !" Don
John burst out ; " and you will not be so cruel to us all ;
you will not so make us sure that your welcome has not
been warm enough here — "

"Gently, gently !" interrupted Charlotte ; " but I do
like to hear you burst forth in this way beforehand.
When I tell you his name do not forget what you have
said, for you are the only person whose opinion I have
truly feared in this matter — you love him so."

Don John almost groaned ; he thought he knew then
what she meant. " Who is it ? " he inquired.

And she whispered, " Lancy ! "

CHAPTER XXVIII.

DON JOHN looked forth to right and to left, as if
casting about in the dark garden and shaded sky
for somewhat to comfort or to counsel him.

Some of the stars were out. It never comforts any
human soul to contemplate them ; they are so change-
less. And there was a crescent-moon, sharp as a sickle,
and too young to give any light. The old moon had

waned while he was in Scotland; sometimes he had found in this familiar show a new significance. So, his happiness had waned away — his careless joy! He was a man now, and must abide what manhood and sorrow might bring him.

And the new moon! almost as young as this fast-waxing love. Oh, what should he do! They would both grow.

His eyes had only just been opened to see what Charlotte was, and what she might be to him, and now she was to tell him of a lover who, of all young men in the world, he would fain not try to supplant.

" For it is not *impossible*," he thought, with a sharp pang, " that I may already, without my own will or knowledge, have ousted him out of everything in the world that is worth having. Not *impossible*, though, as my father and mother both declare, the chances are a thousand to one against it. All that is *to me* worth having," he continued, in mental correction of his first thought. " But though I should never call her mine, it is not fit that poor Lancy should get her."

" That would indeed be sacrificing yourself," he said, in a low voice.

" You think so," answered Charlotte, in a tone of relief.

" Because, as you have said, he is not good."

" I know he is not good," she answered, " but he said if I would take him it would make him good. He said he was no worse than other young men, excepting in that one matter, which he declares he most sincerely repents."

" What one matter, Charlotte?"

" Oh, the affair of — the ring."

" He did not, of course, lead you to think that he had never erred in that way but once?"

Charlotte looked up at Don John, as he stood leaning in the doorway, with an air of such amazement that he could not meet her eyes. He turned away. Charlotte should not be sacrificed in ignorance of this, he was determined; but he knew his heart would accuse him of

baseness forever if he tried to set her against Lancy for
any other cause.   And then he struggled hard with himself.   He knew Lancy was on the road to ruin ; that he
was not in the least worthy of a lovely, pure, and high-
minded girl.   He could have told Charlotte things of
more than one nature, which would have been quite
enough to set her against Lancy for ever.

But she herself — was she not setting him an exam-
ple? Why was she inclined to yield?   Only because
she longed to return the goodness she had experienced
from those who so manifestly loved him, and for some,
to her, inscrutable reason had linked his lot to theirs.

Might not Lancy, in this one matter, prove himself
good and true, if he could be made so by anything or
any circumstance?   But why must the experiment needs
be tried with what was so precious?

The gulf when one leaps into it does not *always* close.

Don John knew well that this fancy for Charlotte, or
rather that this plan to obtain her, must be a very sudden one on Lancy's part, and with a flash of thought he
felt that if he had heard of it a week ago he should certainly have blamed him in no measured terms for daring
to think of her.   He would have left no stone unturned
to make Charlotte give up the thought of such a sacrifice — why was he not to speak now?

All this took but a minute or two to think out.   Then
he turned again and looked Charlotte in the face.

" I thought he did not love me," she faltered, " because there was something so fitful and so sudden in the
way that he poured forth his devoted speeches — yes,
they seemed devoted for the moment — and then ap- .
peared almost to forget me and them.   I believe it
was nothing but an unlucky blush of mine that put it
into his head that I liked him — and — I was rather near
it once."

Don John had suspected this, but he did not hear it
without a jealous pang, and Charlotte went on.

" But I think however fond you may be of Lancy —
and you always used to say that you loved him better
than some of your own brothers and sisters — and

though, to do him justice, I believe he returns your affection, yet if you know — not that he has actually stolen anything more than once — that I do not of course suppose — but I mean if you know him to be unprincipled — "

" But I do mean that ; I do mean that he has erred in that one way more than once or twice."

The color flushed into Charlotte's face. " Do THEY know it ? " she whispered with an awestruck air.

" Father and mother ? Yes."

" They never could wish me to take him then ; and yet, if he should go from bad to worse, and they should hear that I had refused him ; — they might feel what his mother wrote to me, that I was cruel, for he wanted only such an attachment to make him all that could be wished, and I, it seemed, did not believe in his deep and abiding repentance."

" She is a base woman," exclaimed Don John. " It always makes me shudder to think of her."

" Oh, you dislike her ? "

" I cannot bear her ; but I am not so wicked or so unkind as to say that he does not repent ; or so false as to say that I do not see in a marriage with you his very best chance of a thorough reformation."

Charlotte looked pleased — she hardly knew herself what she wished. It was sweet to think herself beloved, but yet she was inexorable in pointing out things which had made her doubt it.

" Do you know I could not help thinking when I saw his mother's letter, that it was she who had put it into his head — of course, if I was sure of his love I could not talk of him in this cold-hearted fashion."

The tone of inquiry, and almost of entreaty, was evident. " You have made it difficult, you know, for me to believe anything of that sort ! "

Don John forced himself to say, " It was an unparalleled piece of imprudence on my part to put such nonsense into your head ! "

Charlotte looked up at him, her smile increasing till the dimple came. She was pleased. " The event justi-

fied you!" she said, "and your finding it out so early
did you great credit. But do give your mind to this,
and your opinion about it, for you are thinking of something else. I want you to understand how queer his
declaration was; and it was mixed up with remarks
about my uncle, who was severe to him, he said, and
about how splendidly he was getting on — he should
soon be quite independent of him."

"Lancy getting on!" exclaimed Don John; "Lancy
independent! How can he be getting on? I never
heard a word about it. It is all since I saw him."

"I am sure he said so, and also sure that he came
to ask for his quarter's allowance. My aunt and I were
both sitting with uncle, and when he saw Lancy, who
came in gently, he seemed a good deal distressed."

"My dear father! What did he say?"

"He said, 'That's my prodigal son: it embitters
my bread to know that he will some day bring himself
to want bread.' He was a little confused after the blow
on his head. Aunt Estelle took Lancy away, and then
my uncle said to me, 'I hope you will never forsake
him.' I said, 'No.' Well, afterwards Aunt Estelle
came back, and sent me away, and Naomi and I cried
together a little in the playroom. In the garden, after
that, Lancy talked to me. Oh, I cannot be ungrateful! He came again the next day, and I laughed at
him; and I cannot help laughing now. It seemed no
more real to me than *Fetch* does! I do not know how
it was, but I did not think he talked like a lover. I
thought of you."

She laughed a little nervously.

"Thought of me," repeated Don John. Her words
were rather ambiguous: they made his heart beat.
Charlotte turned the pearl bracelet on her arm and
blushed excessively.

"I am sure it was not the right thing," she said.
"He asked me to marry him — to be engaged at once;
but if my uncle has been very much displeased with
him, as his mother's letter seems to hint, and if Lancy
is almost afraid that he should give him up, how natural

that he should wish to marry into the family, and so make such a thing almost impossible. Laney cannot get it out of his head that I love him. He never had any tact any more than I have. First he urged me to accept him on account of his love, then he as it were threatened me that if I declined it would be the worse for him. I don't think he was considering me much; and I formed this theory as to why he wanted me almost while he spoke."

Don John did not know what dangerous ground he was venturing on. Who could have supposed that he was not to agree with her? He said, —

"I think that shows you do not really care much about him. You have given the verdict yourself, why ask for one from me?"

"I do care," said Charlotte, looking dreamily at him, "and I must read you the letters." The candle was low in the socket. She began to sort them, but had hardly opened the first, when the leaping light covered her with its yellow flickering radiance, and then sank and was out. "Some other time you shall hear them," she went on. "No, I have not decided; I could make myself marry him if I chose."

"And you might be miserable."

"Not if I saw that I was improving him, saving him, and so relieving Aunt Estelle and my uncle; only what you have just told me is such a sad surprise as almost to render that impossible which I had been trying to make up my mind to. But you speak with a kind of restraint — I am sure you do."

"I speak like a fellow who feels that he must and will repeat and justify all he has said to the person whom it most concerns. I must and shall tell Laney what I have said against him. And I speak, remembering how Laney and I were bound to one another all our childhood by a great affection, which I know he depends upon to this moment."

"And that makes you wish to be as moderate and fair as you possibly can."

"That, and other things."

" You will talk to him then ? "

" Certainly."

" What shall you say ? "

" Would it be fair to him that I should tell you ? "

" I think it would be fair to *me*. You seem to forget *me*."

Silence here for a moment; then Charlotte put her little warm hand on Don John's sleeve, and added, " But perhaps you have no fixed thought in your mind as to what you shall say ? "

" I knew before you spoke what I should first say."

He did not lay his hand upon hers; but when she withdrew it, and said, " Tell it me," he answered, —

" I shall first say that I am aware — at least, I know — that he does not love you."

" You will ? " exclaimed Charlotte rather bitterly. " Oh yes, of course *you* would be sure to think that; and secondly, I suppose you will say that you know he is not reformed."

" I certainly shall."

" But you need hardly add, for it does not matter, that you should not care to see your cousin dragged down through any foolish hope of serving yours or you; or that you see any presumption in his offer; for that, in fact, the son of an English carpenter is quite equal to the descendants of Irish kings." Thereupon Charlotte broke down again, and began to cry with vexation, and perhaps with mortified self-love.

" I beg your pardon," blundered Don John. " You said yourself that you felt he did not love you, or I should not have presumed — "

She had started up by this time.

" It is quite time to go in," she remarked, interrupting him; and she stepped forth into the dusky garden, when, having dried her eyes, she presently answered some further apologetic speech by asking him some question about his visit to Scotland.

Charlotte had never had a lover in her life. She was quite capable of expressing doubt as to the truth of this one; but when it was taken for granted, by the person who should have dissipated her doubts, that he could not be true, it was rather too much for her philosophy. She would have sacrificed herself without mercy, if she had heartily believed that she was beloved ; and now — well, Lancy, poor fellow, was certainly not worth having. It would have been a great convenience to this family if she could have reformed him ; but since her great ally KNEW that he only wanted to make a convenience of her, all the sweetness of a sacrifice would be taken away if she made, it, and only degradation and misery would be left.

Charlotte was very disconsolate the next.day. So was Don John. She did not meet his efforts at reconciliation, but simply passed them over.

A woman, young, beautiful, warm-hearted, it was a peculiar mortification to her not to be beloved.

She must have lost her heart at once if she had known that any eyes found the light in hers sweet.

That there was a foolish young fellow close at hand, who found every nook in house or garden complete and perfect if she was in it, treasured up all her sayings with approval, thought the changes on her cheek more fair than the flush of sunset — she could not have believed without due assurance ; but she was not to have that assurance. She never mentioned Lancy now, and she could not get over the mortification which she had, however, brought upon herself; and Don John soon knew from Lancy himself that she had refused him, and yet had so far yielded to his mother's deprecating letters as to promise that she would not utterly decide against him, she would let him speak again in the spring.

That was a long, cold, dark winter. It appeared as if the spring would never come. Don John had anxieties common to himself with all the family, and he had some which oppressed him alone. Among the first was the putting off of Marjorie's marriage. The two thousand pounds promised to his eldest daughter could not be produced without expedients which Donald Johnstone considered unjust to his other children. So he put it off till "the spring," hoping to produce it then; but only Don John knew how this told on his health and spirits, surprised and annoyed the family of his intended son-in-law, and disappointed his daughter.

As to Don John, he groaned in secret over the assurance which had suffered him so fearlessly to interfere. If he had but left Marjorie alone!

In the meantime Donald Johnstone soon recovered from his accident, and began to resume his usual habits. He thought himself well, and it did not come under his observation that he was never long alone.

He might have a sudden fainting fit again. He must not go to town or walk or drive alone, but quite naturally it came to pass that he hardly ever was alone. His wife saw to that when he was at home — his son always went to town with him, lunched with him, sat in the same room, and came back with him.

Such consolation as was to be got out of the increasing love of both parents Don John received that winter, but his life was dull, and time and events seemed hard upon him. A good deal more money was lost that winter; and Lancy caused Don John a world of worry, for Lancy was getting on — so his mother said; but how could this be? He was only a clerk — he had never been articled. Sometimes Don John went to see his mother, Mrs. Ward. She had possessed a good deal of handsome jewelry, and was parting with it by degrees. She had easily persuaded Lancy that it was to his advantage to share her lodgings, and the Johnstones had not been able to prevent this. Little enough, if any, of her four hundred a year ever came to her; yet a certain air of triumph appeared sometimes in her manner, and surprised Don John, no less than did the sullenness and reserve of Lancy when he would come from time to time to see his adoptive father, and receive his quarter's allowance.

So the winter dragged slowly on. Don John had much more to do than before his father's illness. Charlotte was a good deal away with her own people, and she had soon appeared to forgive him after their unlucky conversation ; but there was seldom anything to discuss as of old.

Don John knew that several letters had been written by Lancy's mother to Charlotte, and he often longed to tell her that she ought to confide the matter to his parents, who were her natural guardians. He was sure of this, but how should he say it? why did he wish it, excepting because he knew they would not approve? No, Lancy must and should have his chance, however bitter this might be to his foster-brother.

It was not till the end of March that Charlotte, who had just returned from a long visit, said to him as they were walking home from church, and a little behind the others, —

" Mrs. Ward has been teasing me again about Lancy, asking whether I consider that this is the spring. You have said that you know he does not care for me now, but I suppose you can hardly say that you know he never will? "

" No, I am not so base as to say that. But then, Charlotte, you are not so poor in affection that you do well to hang on the hope of his, if it is yet to come. There is not one person in our house that does not love you heartily."

" More than Lancy is ever likely to do? "

" ' *Comparisons are odious.*' I only say that we all love you heartily. My father and mother do."

" Yes."

" And the girls do."

" Yes."

" And I do."

" Well, now you say it in so many words I remember that I have had no cause all these years to think other- wise. And yet why should you, there seems no reason? "

" There is every reason."

A short silence here, then Charlotte looked up at him and said, " Sometimes we have quarrelled, and often we have argued together, and I have not been nice to you at all."

Don John felt a singing in his ears, it appeared to repeat to him "Lancy — Lancy — Lancy;" he set his teeth together, and was silent.

She went on in a tone of sweet elation, "But that was because I did not know. So many people in the world who love me heartily — almost as heartily, he appeared to say, as I loved them. And it sounded quite true. Now the world seems much more beautiful and happy, and I am enriched, and that other talk of Lancy's is all the more sham. I forgive you, Don John; I am consoled, and I shall never quarrel with you any more."

Was not this the right time to speak? If so Charlotte did not know it. She found the former speech complete.

CHAPTER XXIX.

AND now, the very day before Lancy was expected — Lancy, who was to spend a fortnight, and do no one could tell what mischief — have all opportunity to plead his cause, and perhaps to win Charlotte, under the open eyes of her true lover — now, when Don John, quite out of heart, almost wished himself old, that he might have lived through and forgotten the bitterness of his youth — now, while he was tossed about in twenty minds what to say and what to do — his course was suddenly decided for him. At breakfast-time there came in a telegram, setting forth that Captain Leslie was dangerously ill and desired exceedingly to see him.

Such a scramble to get him ready, that his travelling up to London in his father's company might come to pass naturally! Such fervent thankfulness expressed by his mother that Lancy, as would be equally natural, was to be his companion for some time to come!

Nobody had much time to consider that to request Don John's presence was strange; and as for him, he never thought about it.

So far as any comfort that he might have been to Leslie, or any counsel he might have received, he was too late. Captain Leslie was insensible, he was fast passing away; but Don John sat in his presence for many hours of several days and several nights, and the solemnities of death came on and showed themselves, surprising both his sorrow and his love.

This would certainly be the end, whatever might come in before it. He had time to contemplate its absolute isolation as well as its majestic calm. At last one day at dawn, while he half dozed, the doctor touched him on the shoulder. That impassive form had taken on an air of rapturous peace; he saw at once that all was over, and he shortly went downstairs, and prepared to depart.

A paper had been left giving directions about the funeral, and mentioning where the will would be found. It was at a banker's in London — Don John remembered afterwards that he had heard this said by Leslie's lawyer — and he then set forth home, thinking how little there had been in the letters from his family.

He had telegraphed, so that they knew when to expect him; and after his long journey, he approached the garden gate, through the field, about eight o'clock on an April morning.

A white figure, glorified with morning sunshine, stood and waited.

So far off as he could see her at all, he knew that it was Charlotte. Lancy was not with her, and she did not look up. No, a sort of tender shame touched the rose-hued lips, and made the long black lashes droop. "Charlotte! Are you well? are they all well?"

" Yes."

" Where's Lancy ? "

He wanted to know the worst — suspense was torture.

She only answered, —

" I thought I would rather see you at once, and — and you would have a minute to think before you met them all."

"I can easily think what it is, dear," he answered, trembling.

"No, you cannot," the color faded from her face. "You were quite right about Lancy."

Don John drew a long breath. What did she mean? was she not come to tell him that she was engaged? She seemed to be overcome with a shy, sharp pain. "Lancy is not here," she almost whispered. "*He never came!*"

"Never came!"

"No, he wrote to uncle that he had an indispensable engagement to fulfil. Uncle was so much displeased and so much hurt: he went and saw Mrs. Ward, and she told him that Lancy had been sent into the country by his employers. But it's false, Don John. Uncle believed the story; she said she was not at liberty to say where they'd sent him. She wrote to me the very same day, imploring me, if I knew anything of Lancy's whereabouts, to let her know, for she feared the worst — he had run away. He had taken all his best clothes and possessions, and he had been gone twenty-four hours."

Don John, pale to the lips, looked at her, and for the moment found nothing to say, of course she knew nothing of what was passing in his mind.

"There," she said with a little movement of her hand, as if she would put Lancy from her, "it is agreed between us that you would say something kind to me if under circumstances of such ignominy there was anything to be said." She looked almost more distressed than ashamed.

"Don't cry, Charlotte," was all Don John found to say; he was so dumfoundered that his thoughts were all scattered abroad. "But this letter," he presently exclaimed, "what was the post-mark on it?"

"His mother says he left it behind, with the envelope not fastened. She read it, and not knowing what better to do, sent it on without comment or explanation."

"Of course he has not written to you?"

"No, and uncle has not been told what Aunt Estelle and I dread, for I went at once and related all to her;

and we have had a miserable week, for there was no one to go up and down with uncle. Happily he is well, and you are come home, so that trouble settles itself. I do not forget that you too have had a solemn and anxious week. But I have not told you half about Lancy yet. He has changed his name, as his mother tells me, and that bodes no good, I am sure. But, Don John, this is not the only scrape we are in." She had dashed away her tears now, and an air almost of amusement came into her face. They were emerging from the cherry orchard by this time. The starry celandine was glittering all over the grass, and the cherry blossom was dropping on Charlotte, when she turned, and standing still for the moment, "Yes, we two," she went on, "and nobody else."

"Not Mr. Brown's affair?" exclaimed Don John.

"Here they all are coming forth to meet you! Yes, Don John, Mr. Brown's affair. This time, I suppose he thought he had better not conduct the matter personally; he got his father to write to my uncle. The old Canon seemed therefore to think his consent very doubtful, but he wrote politely; gave some hint, I believe, that his fortune was small, but spoke of his high respect for uncle; and said that in about ten days he should be in the neighborhood staying with the vicar, and if by that time the young lady had made up her mind to accept his son, he hoped to be asked here, to make her acquaintance and assure her of a welcome."

"And Naomi?"

"O, Naomi! when my uncle showed her the letter she did not attempt to disguise her delight."

"What on earth is to be done?"

"When I consider how we encouraged his modest hopes, how we set him before Naomi in the best light! Oh—"

"Why it is not without the greatest difficulty that father will be able to produce the two thousand pounds he promised to Foden with Marjorie. It will be years, if ever, before he can give the same to another daughter. Oh! what a fool I have been."

" You must not meet them with such an air of consternation. You must make the best of it."

" But there is no *best*. It's all my own doing. I have already brought father into pecuniary straits, and now I am going to make Naomi miserable."

And thereupon they all met.

It was not an occasion when smiles could have been expected, but even the parents who shared all their anxieties with Don John were surprised at what Charlotte had called his consternation.

Marjorie was present; she looked serene now, the day for her wedding was fixed, her fortune was to be ready, and she little knew at what a sacrifice.

And Naomi was present.

Don John was very fond of Naomi; when he saw her face he felt a lump rise in his throat. It was all his own doing! What had they said to her? Perhaps they had told her the whole truth, that she was dowerless; perhaps they had only hinted at a long engagement. What was it that she knew? Well, he could never forgive himself; he had meddled, and he had his reward.

" I'll sit down," exclaimed Don John suddenly; " I don't feel as if I could breathe."

His mother was at his side instantly. He was close to a bench, and she took him by the arm.

He sat down and battled with the lump in his throat.

" I dare say he has been up for two or three nights," observed his mother, " and perhaps has had nothing to eat for hours."

" I'm all right," said Don John, almost directly, and the whirling trees seemed to settle down into their places, so did the people.

A strange sense of disaster and defeat was upon him. And Charlotte was gone. He felt with a pang that though Lancy was off, Charlotte had never spoken of him in a tone of such pity, nor to himself with such unconscious indifference.

But presently here was Charlotte again, in one hand a roll, in the other a glass of red wine. He had time

to notice her solicitous haste ; two or three drops of
. the wine had flowed over the brim. There never was
such a precious cordial before ; he clasped the little
hand that held it, without taking the glass from her,
and she held it to his lips ; a delightful thought darted
into his mind.

He was quite well again. He looked up at her as
she leaned towards him, and she whispered, " Never
mind, perhaps it will all come right in the end."

A prophetess of hope, how lovely she looked as she
stepped aside ! He often thought of her words afterwards ; just then they only meant kindness, the consolation was only in her good intentions. And so she
stepped aside, and Mary came running up with a
telegram, addressed to Donald Johnstone, Esq., the
younger.

Donald Johnstone, Esq., the younger, took it in his
hand and turned it over. His mother was beside him,
and the others were grouped before him as he sat.

He really for the moment could not take his eyes
from Charlotte's face.

At last he read the telegram ; and then he looked at
her again. His air of helpless astonishment was almost
ridiculous — Charlotte thought so — that dimple of hers
showed it. It was very sweet.

" Well ? " exclaimed Marjorie.

Then he read the telegram aloud. It was such an
important one that they forthwith forgot to notice how
he was behaving. It ran thus : —

" Sir, — The will has arrived, and we look to you for
orders. You are respectfully requested to return for
the funeral, the deceased Captain Leslie having left you
his sole heir."

Nobody had a word to say. Each one looked at some
one of the others.

Don John presently rose, and in absolute silence
they all walked in to breakfast.

Don John was relieved to find all the blinds of the
breakfast-room down, he was in a state of elation which
he felt to be almost indecent ; he was trying hard to

conceal it, and hoped that the green gloom made by
these blinds would help him.

It was not about his inheritance ; no, that was astonishing, but hardly yet understood. It was not that
Lancy seemed to have given up Charlotte ; no, for Charlotte was distressed at it — how much distressed he
could not yet be sure. It was because he had felt that
morning a momentary faintness. Such a thing had
never occurred in his life before ; but just as he felt
as if about to faint, a flash of ecstatic pleasure at the
thought completely restored him.

"I should not wonder," he said to himself, with
boyish delight and pride, "if I've got a heart com-
plaint ; and if so, I'm all right. I *must* have inherited
it from father. I'll never give myself an uneasy moment
about that cruel woman's story any more."

He had been up four nights, and had travelled many
hours without food — he wished to give these facts their
due attention ; and while he ate his breakfast he got
deeper and deeper into cogitation over them, all his
people letting him alone. At last, but not till breakfast
was nearly over, he began to look at Charlotte and
Naomi. Naomi was so pale, and Charlotte was so
nervous, and so perturbed.

He longed for time to talk to them, but if he meant to
go back to Scotland there was absolutely none to be lost.

"Time's up, my boy," said Donald Johnstone. Perhaps he was a little disappointed, considering the pecuniary straits, which had all been confided to his son,
that not one word was said to him in private before the
young man started off.

As to the mother, she was more than distressed, she
was almost displeased. He had scarcely mentioned
Leslie. He meant to go, and not first tell her anything
of the solemn days he had spent. He would give her
no chance of telling him anything of Lancy. She had
wished so sorely to consult him about Naomi.

Even when he kissed her, he was so lost in thought
that he gave no answering glance to hers that seemed
to wonder and to question him.

No, before the morning meal was quite over, he was
off; and she went up to her own room to look at him
as he went down the long field, running rather than
walking.

It was an unsatisfactory parting. In the two or three
letters that followed it hardly anything was said. The
meeting at the end of a week was quite as strange. He
came in unexpectedly, just before dinner, and the whole
evening he seemed to be fencing off any discussion.
Then, before his sisters had withdrawn he fell asleep
in the corner of the sofa, and soon took himself off to
bed, tired out, as it seemed, with travel and with business.

But the next morning Don John was up as early as
usual, and his father heard him bustling about. It was
a brilliant morning, and Don John was taking out basket
chairs, and placing them under a certain tree at the edge
of the orchard. After breakfast he said, " Won't you
spare this one day for talk, father? Don't go to town ;
you have never said one word to me yet. Why, you
don't even know what was in the will, though I did let
you know how absolutely, and without conditions, all
comes to me."

" So be it; I will stay," answered Donald Johnstone.

" I have made a place in the orchard," said Don
John. " I could tell you and mother best out of doors."

His mother finding herself included, took up her work
and a parasol, and followed.

" It will be less awkward for me to do it there," he
went on.

" Less awkward, my boy," repeated the father.
" Why should it be awkward at all? "

There was silence after this till they reached the three
basket chairs, which he had set into the shadow of a
young lime-tree. The parents seated themselves. The
son threw himself on the grass at their feet.

" It's more than you expected," he said, looking up
at them. " There's seven thousand pounds in different
investments, and then the land is worth at the very
least ten thousand more."

" That is more than I expected."

" And I suppose, father, though it is left to me as Donald Johnstone, the eldest son of Donald Johnstone and his wife Estelle, I suppose no one can dispute it with me."

" No, my son ; no one can dispute it, since I acknowledge you. I do not care to hear you bring forward that subject. It can only give us pain."

" But I consider that if this inheritance had come to me before I was of age, it would have been your business, and your right, to say what should be done with it."

" I don't catch your meaning."

" There are two, if not three courses, that you might have pursued, or at least wished to pursue, and I should have had nothing to say against any of them."

" Well ? "

" You might have wished that it should all be equally divided between me and Lancy — money and land."

The father made no answer.

" Or you might have wished that I should give, or leave the land, to Fred (for that is in my power), and that I should divide the money with Lancy."

Still no answer.

" Or you might have wished that I should keep it all."

" Yes, I might have wished that you should keep it all."

" And yet it was left me for my mother's sake."

The father and mother fell silent here. What more indeed could be added to all that they had felt, or even to the little that they had said ?

" I owe a great deal to Captain Leslie," said Don John, after a long pause. " When I was so ill, he came and prayed for me. I did not like it, but afterwards I could not help thinking about it. How anxious he was to console me. I thought I should die of misery. He could not make out what the misery was, but he suffered it too for mother's sake."

" I know he felt for us."

" And he said he knew I was under the shadow of a

great grief, but that if I could trust God, He could turn
it into a ground of consolation. He said, take this
grief and lay it in the Saviour's hands. He will show
its other side to you, and you shall not feel its bitterness any more."

"Good people," said his mother, "have said like
things to me;" and she remembered how she had felt
when the doubt about her child first fell on her: "this,
at least," she had said "could never be made a blessing
in disguise."

"Well," continued Don John, "I used to lie and
think that no fellow had ever been so basely used; but
after that prayer of his, I felt suddenly consoled by the
very last thought that you would have said could have
in it any consolation."

"Why should you think of that time at all? You
are our dear son."

"I like to think of it now. He was a very curious
man. He spoke to our Saviour that night just as if he
was sending up a message by Him to the Almighty
Father which was sure to be duly delivered. They were
very reverent, but yet they appeared so intimate — those
things that he said; and he spoke of his love for mother,
as if it was perfectly well known up there, and as if
they pitied him."

"His love for mother." She had not been able till
his last days to give Captain Leslie even a moderate
degree of kindly liking in exchange for his love; but
now she sat back in her chair, and covered her face with
her hand. An almost unbearable pang smote her, and
made the tears course down her cheeks. She could not
get beyond the thought that he was hidden away in the
dark, and she was out in the bountiful sunshine of early
summer, there was such a peaceful spreading forth of
young green leaves about her. It was so well with the
world; but he was gone, and she had not been kind
enough to him. She longed to get away from any sense
of death and darkness for him, and said to her son,
"I cannot bear more of this; tell me about Leslie's
prayer."

CHAPTER XXX

DON JOHN looked at his mother. "Why are you distressed?" he said. "What Captain Leslie wanted was to comfort me. I soon let him know that he had done it. He took the sting out of that cruel story that he knew nothing of."

"Then he had his reward," remarked Donald John-stone.

He and his son hardly ever so much as mentioned "that cruel story," against which Don John had at first raged, and then fallen sick. Both parents had done all they could to comfort him, and inspire him with their own intense belief that he was theirs.

"It was a base lie," continued Don John. "You told me to think so; and you said the chances against my not being your own son were a thousand to one."

"Yes, my boy, a thousand to one against it in fact, and far, far more than that in our opinion and feeling. I feel always, that nothing could ever disturb the fatherly affection which belongs to you, quite as much as to any of my other children."

"But I thought it was so hard that such a tale should have been told to me," said Don John. "I hated it, and that woman, and could not get well because I raged against her so. But it stole into my mind all at once as he prayed for me, that I was not unfortunate after all, for by those nine hundred and ninety-nine chances I certainly had all I wanted — all the right in you and mother, in this brother, these sisters, and this home, that I could have; but there was yet that one other chance to be thought of. It should not be left out altogether, faint, and slender, and slight as it was. If that one of the thousand chances was mine, how then? Had I any quarrel against my life, and grudge against my destiny then? It was not so; then I had all. It was so; and then the most singular piece of good fortune had fallen to me that was ever in the lot of man!

"But father, how good you have always been to me — more than most fathers you have let me know all your affairs; you have even consulted me; and I should not like — I mean, I do not like to surprise you."

He had surprised both parents now, but though he looked confused and shame-faced, he laughed. Then taking off his "chimney-pot" hat, he remarked on its being such a queer thing to wear in the country, but it was the only black one he had; and he smoothed it with his sleeve, and appeared to examine the band of crape upon it with interest. It was a transparent device for gaining a little time.

"As *he* chose to leave this property to me," he began, and then came to a dead pause.

"Well?" said his father.

"Of course it's mine," continued Don John, after a very long pause.

"That's rather a flat conclusion to your speech," said Donald Johnstone, and laughed himself.

"Of course it would seem only natural that I should consult you about it."

"It would indeed!"

"Yes, father, I am glad you could laugh. I believe you will trust me. I am sorry — I am dressed in a little brief authority you see, and mean to use it — I am sorry, but I cannot consult you at all."

"I always told your mother you were a very odd young fellow."

Don John looked up at him, "Like father like son," he murmured, but not at all disrespectfully.

"What, sir! do you insinuate that I am an odd fellow too? But take a little time to consider, my boy, before you do anything, or promise anything. I hope you are not proposing in your own mind anything Utopian."

"Have I not always lived in Utopia? What could

have been more Utopian, father, than your conduct and mother's, unless indeed it is Captain Leslie's?"

"Take a little time," repeated the mother.

"Not till I have told you, which I want to do at once, that poor Lancy must not have any of it."

Rather a surprised silence here. He presently went on, "Because that would not be just to mother, and the younger children.

"But I wanted to tell you at once, father, that two thousand pounds of the money is absolutely at my own disposal at this moment. We shall want it for Marjorie."

"We!" exclaimed his father.

"Yes, thank God," said the mother. "Let him alone, Donald. What better with it could he do?"

"You know very well with what difficulty, and at what a disadvantage you were, to borrow it. Marjorie's dower is to be paid down by me to-morrow."

"Yes," repeated the mother, "quite right. Let him alone, Donald; let him show himself your true son."

"Only," continued Don John, "nobody knows that you have done anything Utopian, father, and we cannot afford to have people talk as if I had; so you will have to accept the money from me by deed of gift, and forthwith settle it on her; and neither she nor anyone else must know."

The father drew a long breath, and found not a word to say, the relief was so opportune, the advantage so great.

"And then there is Naomi," continued Don John. "I do not believe the old boy (well, I mean him no disrespect; he has a right to expect what his son has no doubt told him you were to give to your other daughter), I do not believe he would welcome her without it. I make over another two thousand pounds at once to you. I hereby declare the fact; and to-morrow, when the Canon calls, I hope that matter will be settled."

"Stop, my boy, it is too much for you to despoil yourself of."

"Me — for me to despoil myself of! — What does that mean?"

"I did say to you that I did not wish Lancy to have any of this —"

"Yes."

"Then I cannot either."

"Wait a minute," exclaimed the mother. "I foresaw this; but, my dear boy, decide nothing more at present; do wait."

"I will delay to tell you, mother, if you please."

"Do advise with us," she repeated tenderly.

"I have made a vow that I would not, but I will delay."

"A vow, not that you would do this or that, but only that you would not consult us?"

"Yes, mother, that I would not consult you."

"I do not care to wait, then; so far as your decision is made, I wish to know it."

"Mother, you must not be vexed. I decide, that when Fred is of age, he is to have the house, and the farm, and the land."

"And you think *that* would not cause talk, and appear strange?"

"Not if my father takes me into partnership at the same time."

"And are you really proposing all this only that Lancy may not feel himself aggrieved?"

"No, mother, and yet it is mainly on Lancy's account; but we have no time to talk any more."

A gleam of amusement lighted up Don John's eyes. A tall girl was ushering into the orchard a fat old divine. Blushing, and very becomingly shy, she came slowly forward, he waddling beside her. Don John had met her that morning on the stairs. She looked pale, drooping, dull. Don John in brotherly fashion, which means with intimate and somewhat bluff kindness, devoid of chivalry, and devoid of deference, had kissed her, and whispered in her ear, "Don't mope, Nay. I'm sure it's all right."

A light leaped into Naomi's eyes.

"How do you know?" she replied. "I thought it was all wrong; father —"

"Well, father?" replied Don John, following her into the playroom.

"Father said almost as much as that he hoped I should not be disappointed if — if it could not be arranged."

"And why should n't it be arranged?" said Don John, with a stolid air.

Naomi's face took on a soft blush of pleasure.

"I wish you had been at home," she said naively; "I have been so miserable. I thought father meant that he could not give me the same fortune he is giving Marjorie, and I was afraid — Oh, I knew Canon Brown depended on my having it."

"There's no occasion to think of such a thing," exclaimed Don John; this in a whisper, "Mark my words, father will lay down the two thousand pounds like a brick."

"He will be able then? dear father!"

"You 'll see."

So now Naomi was seen between the trees, sweet in her maidenly dignity, and trying hard not to show in her manner that she supposed this to be more than an ordinary morning call. She came on, and as her father and mother rose and advanced to meet their guest, Don John accompanied them far enough to bow to him; then, bestowing on his sister something uncommonly like a wink, he gravely withdrew, or, as he would himself have expressed it, "sloped."

He had a great deal to think of, and many things to do which were not likely to be as easily arranged as Naomi's dower. Naturally he was drawn to the house, for there Charlotte was. The playroom was generally given up to her in the morning, and as he came round he looked up at the window, and saw her as she sat writing.

He entered the room, and when he shut the door behind him, she said, "I knew you would come as soon as possible." Don John had hardly time to feel agitated and pleased before she went on — "I hope you will not be disappointed; there is nothing more to tell you about Lancy; neither his mother nor I have heard anything of him." Her mind was too full of Laney just then to admit anything else, so it seemed; but presently she looked up, and as if surprised at something that she saw, contemplated Don John for a few moments with a musing expression in her deep blue eyes. He was at once very much out of countenance, but she did not notice this. She said, with the downright straightforwardness of a sister, "I 'm sure Marjorie is right; you look different. We never used to think you were at all — I mean particularly — good-looking when you were a boy."

An implied change of opinion gave Don John unfeigned delight. He tried to hide it. "No; but, as Mrs. Nickleby said of Ralph, you two used always to declare, ' but it 's an honest face.' "

" Yes," said Charlotte, and went on, oh, so dispassionately, " but I always liked it; I mean, I liked the look of you." Here she folded her arms on the table, and leaned forward, as if about to dismiss that subject for something of real interest. " But have you heard anything?" she went on; " do you think that anything can be done?"

Don John succumbed at once. There was only one way to interest her — it was to talk of his rival! To do him justice, he was almost as much distressed for her as for himself; and Laney — he had the best reason to know that Laney cared for her nothing at all.

" Yes, I have heard a good deal," he began; and went on, making a pause between each sentence, as if not to overwhelm her with the waves of a too sudden disaster, " I did not mean to tell you just yet. If anything can be done, I am on the look-out to do it. Laney is gone away to America, and does not intend to return. I have seen his mother."

" Seen her! Oh, where?"

" As I stood by the grave during Captain Leslie's funeral I felt as if something obliged me to look up; I did, and there she stood among the bystanders. Laney was gone! He had written taking leave of her, and saying that he should never see her again. He has

changed his name also, and desired her to tell his old
friends that it was useless to try and communicate with
him.   And yet she wished to follow; she had heard of
my inheritance, and came and asked me to give her
thirty pounds.   I did, but I begged her at least not to
sail till she had given him time to write, in case he
changed his mind."

"And she did not tell you why he is so urgent to
leave his own country for ever?"

"She could not; she knows of no reason at all."

"She does," said Charlotte, indignantly; "she does
know!"

"What! have you seen her too? has she told you
anything?"

"No; but before you came home from Scotland the
first time, I told you that she had written to me.   In
that letter she said she had too much reason *to fear that
it was the old story*.   Almost by the next post she wrote
again, and begged me to return that letter, telling me
that she felt she had made some groundless charges;
she desired to have both her letters, and I sent them
back to her, hoping against hope.   But if Lancy is
really off, and really in hiding, as I consider he is if he
has changed his name, I cannot hope the best — I fear
the worst."

"I never thought of this," said Don John, quite
aghast; "but I have known for some time that he
plays high.   I thought he had got himself so crushed
under the weight of these shameful debts of honor that
his only chance was to fly."

"How distressed Aunt Estelle and my uncle will be
if it is anything worse."

Two large tears had gathered in Charlotte's eyes, and
now they trembled on the long, dark lashes.

"And the mother said nothing more, but only asked
you to give her this thirty pounds?" she continued.

"Oh, yes," exclaimed Don John, "she said a great
deal more!"

In fact, this is what had occurred; Mrs. Ward had
reminded Don John that his father had always said the

two boys should be equally well off. She did not see " but what his wish ought to be binding on Mr. Don John — to divide all honestly. She might not see her way to keep silence any longer," she observed, " unless she had his promise that this should be done."

To her great surprise Don John laughed scornfully at her, and defied her, bidding her do her worst. " Look at me," he exclaimed, almost in a passion, " look straight into my face and tell me whether if you were my mother it would be possible for me to dislike you as I do. Look at me, I say, and if there's any truth in you speak it out and tell me how you hate the sight of me. Is that possible to a mother — that?"

" I did n't mean to put you out," she faltered. " It was only when you made as if you'd shake hands with me that I —"

" That you shrank! you trembled from head to foot. You can't bear me. And now hear this, I would rather all the world knew your base story — I would rather all this property was sunk into the sea than that it should go to pay the debts of an inveterate selfish gambler."

" Mr. Johnstone always made out that he had a claim ; " she was very much frightened by this time, and perfectly pale, but she still dared him.

" A claim!" repeated Don John. " Oh, yes, a fine claim! You know best what it amounts to. But granted that he had the utmost claim — granted that he was the son, the eldest son — is this prodigal son, who has run away twice from his family, disobeyed his father, and disgraced himself, is he to be allowed *more than any other prodigal would be* to share this property with the younger children, and lay it out in paying for his vices."

" You need n't be in such a passion, sir. I'm a poor weak woman, but it's my duty to speak up for my Lancy. He's the only creature I've got in the world to love." She spoke in a faltering tone, but no tears came. She was too much frightened for that. " Ain't it his right to have any of it then?" she went on. " Mr. Johnstone would say very different, I know."

"Lancy shall never touch a shilling of it," exclaimed Don John, "unless I utterly change my mind."

"Well then," she cried, flaming up, "I will say it's hard. It was a shame to bring him up like a gentleman and then leave him in the lurch, and you used to pretend you were so fond of him."

"Yes, I did, and do. There is nothing that is not unjust which I would not do to save him even now."

"I don't care to hear talk like that," she answered, rising, but trembling so that she could not get away, as she had meant to do. "I shall go to Mr. Johnstone; he was always Lancy's friend—"

"And so am I. I hope to help him. There is hardly anything I long for so much."

"I hate to hear such hypocritical talk," she cried out, almost more angry than he had been. "Don't tell me what you long for—and do nothing. I don't like it."

"Then," he answered, with a bitterness that surprised to the point of calming her, "I will tell you something that you WILL like." Here, however, he fell into a musing fit, and paused.

"Yes, sir," she faltered, "something that I shall like?" All this time she had kept the purse in her hand which contained the thirty pounds; she now slipped it quietly into her pocket. She wished to defy him to the utmost, but not to give him his money back.

He lifted up his face, and went on: "This property—I have decided that as I cannot share it with Lancy, I cannot keep any of it for myself."

Though she had been so angry with him she was shocked when he said this, and experienced a keen sensation of shame. This was not Don John's fault, nor Lancy's either. It was all hers. Did she dislike him heartily enough then to be glad that he must forfeit his inheritance? And did he know it? *Something that* YOU WILL LIKE. It was of no use denying it, he read her better than till this moment she had read herself.

"I shall keep nothing in my own power," he added, "but the disposing of it."

Now, indeed, she had nothing to say, and she shed a few contrite tears.

Don John went to the window and stood cogitating when Charlotte asked him whether Lancy's mother had said anything more. He revolved the conversation just detailed in his mind, but did not see what he could do, or what others could do, supposing that Lancy really was off. A man cannot be followed to America and made to pay falsely called "debts of honor." And Charlotte seemed to be taking his utter withdrawal with very consoling calmness.

In fact she had taken up her pen, and was beginning to write.

He turned suddenly: yes, she was writing, and she took no notice when he came and sat down opposite to her at the table.

He went and fetched a little box of pens. He had a sort of notion that he should like to break a certain matter to Charlotte; how was he to begin? He came again, and began to pull out the pens from the great playroom inkstand. Such a sorry lot they were. The girls were all by nature untidy; sometimes they put them down without wiping them. Interesting pens! crusted with dried, rust-like ink. Charlotte so often had one or another of them in her little tanned and dimpled fist.

Don John had already put a fresh steel point into every one of the holders excepting the one Charlotte held. He was naturally rather neat with his possessions. He glanced at her as often as he dared — she often pouted slightly and knitted her brow when she wrote. Of course, as he remarked her she became conscious of it — people always do. She noticed his occupation, and that all the holders were clean excepting the one she held — Don John had rubbed them with a piece of blotting-paper. The inkstand had been put to rights, and looked quite creditable.

It was rather a narrow table; Charlotte put her pretty hand across — with the one old pen in it, and Don John seized it and looked at it. Now? No, not now — some other time. He could not kiss her hand — he did not dare.

Charlotte was a little ashamed of the pointed way in which, as she thought, he had called her attention to her inky fingers. She snatched away her hand, and rushed out of the room to wash it.

" What a calf I am ! " said Don John to himself in unutterable self-abasement. " Why did n't I do it then ? "

There was company to luncheon that day — very important company. Canon Brown and his son were present, and were made much of.

The next time Charlotte went into the playroom she saw two large new pen-wipers on the inkstand, each with a gold tassel.

CHAPTER XXXI.

DON JOHN was not present at luncheon on the occasion of Canon Brown's visit; he had gone up to London, to see if he could find Mrs. Ward or any traces of her. But he could not; she had gone from her late lodgings, and left no address.

She had said nothing to him when she had hunted him up in Scotland, as to why Lancy was off. Whether he had lost largely at play, and was gone to hide his head abroad; or had won largely, and was gone to spend his ill-gotten gains, was what Don John could not decide. But now this third reason for his absence forced itself on his foster-brother's attention. That he had been getting on — that is, that he generally had plenty of money — might be owing to play ; there were several families of the better class in whose houses he often visited, and was known to play high; he was much sought after, for his manners were charming. But his mother's hint about " the old story " could only mean, if it was true, that he had been a thief again. If so, he might be followed to America and brought back, and, spite of all the love and care, and all the

prayers that had been expended on him, he might yet
be a disgrace to his bringing up. The miserable story
might yet come out, and in the most public and painful
way.

Don John was marching off to the station after his
unsuccessful inquiries. He wanted to catch the train
which would take him home in time for dinner, when he
heard some one calling after him, and a lad caught him
by the arm.

"What is it?" cried Don John, not best pleased.
The lad pointed to a man with a monkey under his arm;
he looked like an acrobat — perhaps a Christy Minstrel.
"He called to me ' *That gen'leman has lost somethin',*'"
said the lad, and he passed on.

The man had come up, was almost close to him.
Don John had instinctively slapped his pockets — his
watch was safe, and his purse. He darted a look at
the supposed acrobat; he was a fellow of about the
middle height; he had on a shirt made of pink flannel,
a pair of white duck trousers; he wore an old barris-
ter's wig; his face was chalked, and he had a triangular patch of black on each cheek, and one of brick red
on his nose.

He tapped his wig with his forefinger and whispered,
"You notice it." It was tied under his chin with blue
ribbon.

Don John heard the bell ring and the train start, but
he stood as if spellbound. "I've been hanging about
between this and father's chambers looking out for you
for nearly a week," muttered the acrobat, "and I'm
half starved."

If Don John had stared at the patched and painted
face for hours he would not have recognized poor Laney.
But the wig, and a long scarf that he had dressed
himself up in, had been used time out of mind in the
playroom at home for acting charades. These he recognized at once. "What does it mean?" sighed Don
John, drawing in his breath with a gasp, and his legs
shaking under him. "What on earth is to be done?"

"There's a policeman," muttered Laney; "he'll tell

me to move on.　*Good gen'l'man, give us a copper to buy the monkey his nuts."*

"Now you move on," said the policeman, just as had been foretold; "you're not wanted here."

Lancy, who seemed very footsore, accordingly moved on, with a limping gait; and Don John noticed the direction, and followed him as soon as he could do it without exciting attention.

"What on earth does it mean?" he repeated when he ventured to pass him and speak, for they had got into a quiet back street.

"You go into that shop and buy a tract," said Lancy, "and I'll tell you."

"A tract I said," he repeated impatiently, "and give me a shilling, do."

Don John produced the shilling; Lancy darted into a cook's shop, and presently came out with cold meat and bread in his hand. Don John was looking into the shop he had pointed out (it was a depôt of the Tract Society), and trying to marshal his scattered wits. "Buy tracts," whispered Lancy as he limped past him.

There was nothing for it but just to do as he was bidden, and he presently came out with some tracts in his hand.

"Now we can talk as long as need be," said Lancy, who was eating ravenously. "Since I have been rigged up in this way, city missionaries and Gospel fellows often offer me tracts. Look out and keep your wits about you, do! There, offer me one. If there is no obvious reason for such as you are talking to such as I seem, it will excite attention, and I shall be spotted, and perhaps nabbed."

As he hurried through this speech, Don John offered a tract to him: but the monkey sitting on his shoulder was quicker than Lancy. He put out his weazened hand to the very great delight of some passing children, and snatched it, then turning it over smelt it suspiciously, after which he rolled it up into a tight ball, and persistently tried to get it into Lancy's mouth. There was soon a little crowd; poor Lancy groaned.

"Go on," whispered Don John; "I'll not lose sight of you." The crowd gathered and followed with delight, halfpence were forthcoming, and the children took it amiss if he did not stop while the monkey received them in his little hot hand. It was almost sunset, and Lancy's strength was nearly spent, when, getting a little beyond Hornsey, they reached some green fields and got over a stile, finding themselves alone at last.

Lancy threw himself upon the long grass among the buttercups. Don John had bought some food and a bottle of beer as they walked; he made him eat and drink, after which poor Lancy lifted himself up, and they walked together through the deep meadow grass, and sat down on the small bank on which grew a tall hawthorn hedge.

Their disaster seemed to be too deep for any words of comfort on one side or of explanation on the other.

"Oh, don't," groaned poor Lancy piteously; "I haven't cried since this happened, wretched as I have been — and if you do! Oh, how shocking it all is, how hateful!" Then they both broke down utterly; the one wept with a passionate storm of sobs, the other weakly and piteously, like a tired child. These two still had such an amount of affection for one another that the misfortune had to be borne in common.

Lancy hoped now that something might yet be done for him, and while the stars came out, and the summer dusk gathered, he told his miserable story.

But not without many pauses of sullen silence, not without much questioning. "That old fellow was such a fool," he began, while his chest was heaving still with sobs; "what business had he to put temptation in my way?"

"What old fellow do you say?"

"Why, old Cottenham — old Cottenham. I was his clerk. I've no patience with him. He took such a liking to me from — from the first, and he knew nothing about me — nothing at all."

"I can't help you unless you'll tell me what you have done."

" Done! I 've done what you can never set right. I
nearly got away — I got to Liverpool — I was all but
off, and had paid for my passage."

" You robbed him, then? Lancy, I can help you if
you 'll only tell me all."

" Yes, I robbed him then. I had paid for my passage, when I saw a face that I knew, a porter old Cottenham employed, looking at the passengers as they
went on board. There were detectives with him. I
edged myself back. In short I got ashore and hid myself."

" But tell me what you had stolen."

" I used to play high; sometimes I won — very often
I won — and had such sums of money as you never
fingered in your life. But there came a run of ill-luck,
and I lost all — and got nearly three thousand pounds
into debt. And that old ass — that old fool — when
I was in despair about my debts he sent me to his
bankers with a large sum of money. He had often
sent me with securities of different kinds, but not such
as I could use; but in this parcel were two cheques for
large amounts, the rest all in notes and gold; and I
cashed the cheques, for it had flashed into my mind, as
I went, that play was a misery and a bondage, and if I
could get away *I could lead a more innocent life,* and yet
not have to pay these debts at all."

Don John groaned.

" Before I had time to think, I had got home and
packed up my clothes. I told mother, Cottenham had
sent me on a journey for him, and I was off."

" But where 's the money, then? You did not go.
There 's yet time, there 's yet hope; give it to me and let
me pay it back. He might forgive you."

" There 's no time, and there 's no hope. I 've lost it."

" How? "

" I gave away — I had to give away — a large part of
it, to some fellows who found me out. Hush-money.
Don't you understand? "

" And the rest? "

" I 'm sorry; it cuts me to the heart to know that the

police are after me, and to dread that I shall be a disgrace to you. It's gone; I thought I would risk what was left, to get perhaps all back, and repay it; and I did. I risked, and lost. It's all gone; I gambled it away. Oh, I wish I could die, but I can't. I found out next that I was followed, and I put on this disguise."

" There's one thing more that I want to know," said Don John, " and you must tell it me as carefully and as plainly as you can, for on it mainly depends my yet being able to help — "

" You can't help, dear boy, as to setting me right with old Cottenham, so that I can show my face and not be taken up."

" I want to know about your changing your name. Your mother said you had changed your name."

" Yes, I called myself John Ward. Cottenham only knew me as John Ward."

" Why did you do that?"

" I suppose because I foresaw — "

" Foresaw what? Are you going to sink yourself lower yet in this abyss of crime and disgrace by admitting that you did it with a view to making a future crime easier?"

" Your father is so sensitive," said Lancy, " he would feel any disgrace that came upon me, as if it was a reflection upon him, on my education that he gave me, on my home and my bringing up; and so — so I did it *in case.*"

Don John noticed the unusual expression, "*your* father." Lancy had the grace to feel his position. For the first time in his life he spoke as if not claiming this father for himself.

" You'll act like a brother to me," he said, with a heavy, despairing sigh.

" Yes," answered Don John, " if it can be done consistently with acting like a son towards him."

Lancy was surprised; he turned towards Don John, who was aware that in the dusk he was scanning him attentively.

" So far," he repeated a little faintly ; and when Don John made no answer he went on, "What I want you to do of course is to help me cross the water. I dare not leave off my disguise, but even as I am I can get to Liverpool begging and walking ; and if I had money enough from you, I think I could get over."

" That would do you no real good. You are not reformed, not repentant, not aware of your disgrace, and sin, and misery."

" I am ! "

" You wish you had got over to America with that money in your pocket."

" I tell you I do repent. I am miserable, I am lost, and I know it."

" I am going to help you, dear boy, as well as I can, but I shall never call you Lancy again. The only chance of your not disgracing father and mother and me, is in what you did for a wicked purpose. You can be helped as John Ward — unless the police are too quick for us, and you are taken up on a charge of felony before I can see the man whom you wronged."

" Only help me over, that is the thing to do. What can you be thinking of ? Going to see Cottenham would be bearding the lion in his den ; it would be almost like betraying me. Surely you don't hope to make him say that he 'll not prosecute, that he will forgive me. He liked me, I tell you ; he trusted me though I was almost a stranger. He cannot forgive me, for he 'll have found out by this time."

" Well ? "

" There were things of his in my desk," whispered Lancy.

" You 're sunk so low — so low, that I — "

" I 'm not sunk so low that I would do *you* any harm," exclaimed Lancy. " You know very well that when mother told us two that base story at Ramsgate, and you were so dumfoundered that you could n't say a word, I told her to her face that it was all a lie, and, by Jove, I almost made her own as much."

" You have never *taken* any advantage, though you

have had every possible advantage given you with regard to that story."

" I know."

Thereupon followed the account of Captain Leslie's bequests; and Lancy listening, found once more that there was hope for him, in spite of everything that he had done to throw himself away.

In a hurry and in a whisper, for Don John and he did not dare to risk being found together, the poor young criminal was told to keep himself in hiding only for a few days longer; and as he did not dare to go to post-offices, and could not tell in what part of the country he might be, he was to buy every day a certain penny paper agreed on between them, and there he should, in as short a time as possible, find an advertisement telling him what his foster-brother had been able to do. In any case he was always to be John Ward; and even if he had the misfortune to be taken up by the police, in that name he was to abide his prosecution. And so his disgrace and punishment would cause no pang to those who had so loved him; they would never know. And on this condition his foster-brother promised never to forsake him.

It was nine o'clock when Don John stole back along the hedge, leaving Lancy sitting under it alone. Don John perceived, as he turned the matter over in his mind, that it was the misery and disgrace of the situation, not the crime he had committed, that weighed on Lancy's heart.

Even if Don John's conscience could have suffered him to procure the money, and help Lancy over to America to escape from justice, this would do no real good — he might be followed there, and the Johnstones might have to suffer. The crime of this still dear adopted son would be such a life-long distress and misfortune as almost to swallow up the sense of his disgrace.

All Don John's determination that Lancy should have none of Captain Leslie's money melted away. He must be set right, and the sum he had taken must be restored, as the only chance of saving him; and with this money it must be done, and no other.

Little more than twelve hours after this, in a small dusty office in the heart of the city, a young man sat writing, and opening his eyes from minute to minute so widely that he could not see the page. His pen spluttered — he sighed with excitement; it was no use trying to write, he put it down.

In a minute or two a remarkably sweet man's voice was heard outside, and the speaker came in and took up a row of letters, all addressed " Locksley Cottenham, Esq."

" Now for it," thought the clerk.

" There 's — there 's somebody upstairs who wants to speak to you, sir."

" What did you show him into my room for? " said Locksley Cottenham, Esq., frowning.

It was not much of a frown ; the face was as pleasant as the voice — a round chubby face, open and smiling ; it did not look wrinkled, but it was surrounded by perfectly white hair, as soft as wool.

" Did he tell you his business? "

" It 's not a man at all," answered the clerk, " it 's a young lady."

The clerk felt a certain joy in communicating this astonishing piece of news. That it might lose none of its effect, he did it as abruptly as he could.

Locksley Cottenham, Esq., went slowly upstairs, his little den door was open, a worn oilcloth was on the floor, a writing-table heaped with papers was in the middle, and there were two chairs, in one of which, sure enough, sat the young lady.

Oh! what a pretty young lady! His old heart warmed to her at once. What an air of shyness, and sweet blushing confusion! What color might the eyes be that were veiled by those downcast lashes? She gave him time enough to think all this before ever she lifted them. It was Charlotte.

She looked at him, and half rose as if to acknowledge his presence ; then she cast her eyelids down again. It was a very little room. He stood in the doorway and said, —

" I have n't the pleasure of knowing your name?"

Then she spoke, with an air perfectly sweet and confiding; it was not he, it was the circumstances that made her shy.

" The friend who brought me said I was not to tell you any name."

As she spoke she looked at him, and thought what a nice old gentleman he was. He was so very chubby; his face might almost have been called a sweet face, it had so much of the child in it.

" This parcel," she continued, trying to untie a piece of pink tape, and not succeeding, for her hand trembled a little.

He had seated himself in the other chair, with the table between them.

" Shall I undo it for you?"

" Yes," said Charlotte, " and look at what it contains." She perceived a certain gravity now in his manner. He did not seem altogether pleased with her; but in a minute or two, while she watched him, so much depending on what he might think, she saw the chubby face take on an air of utter puzzlement and surprise.

" A friend gave you these to show to me?" he inquired, lifting up some parchments.

" Yes."

" Do you know what they are?"

" Of course; they are the title-deeds of a Scotch estate."

" The title-deeds of a Scotch estate, which seems to have been sold by the executors of the late Fraser Macdonald to Patrick Leslie. I never heard any of these names before. What has this to do with me?"

" The friend who sent them wants to pay you a sum of money which — no, I am not saying this aright — he is going to pay it as soon as possible. He prays you to keep these title-deeds as security till he can produce it, and in the meantime, if you could be merciful and kind."

She looked at him and paused: she observed that he was startled, and that he hastily put down the deeds.

"It appears that certain things are understood here which are not expressed," he remarked.

"Yes."

"Your friend — I need not mention him by name —"

"You do not know his name."

"Indeed! I thought it might be John Ward."

"No, it is not."

"That makes the matter no better — quite the reverse."

"But I want to explain this to you, so far as I may."

"If I understand you aright, you offer me money to stop certain proceedings."

"That is not at all how my friend expressed it to me."

"Perhaps not." He began to tie up the parcel with its pink tape. "I am very sorry. I must return these deeds."

"You will not consider this again? you will not be merciful?"

"You must take the deeds."

He put them into her hand.

"Then you will see my friend. I am sure he can make you understand better than I have done. We never counted on your refusing."

"I am very sorry for you, my dear young lady."

"But you will at least see my friend?"

"It is much better that I should not. I will send a message to him instead."

"Yes. You will advise him how to act, as this way does not please you. It will be a kind message, for you look so kind."

She looked at him appealingly, and when he made no answer, she went on in a faltering tone, —

"Then what am I to say to him?"

"You can ask him if he ever heard of such a thing as compounding a felony?"

CHAPTER XXXII.

THE dusty, smoky sunbeams were shooting down into Mr. Cottenham's room about three o'clock on a warm afternoon, when his clerk knocked at the door. He may have been dozing, for he seemed desirous to show himself more alert, and to speak a little more sharply, than usual; while some one was shown in, and the door shut behind him.

"Decidedly I must have been asleep — bad habit. Don't remember saying this young fellow was to be shown up — don't remember what he is come about," thought Mr. Cottenham. "Can't recall it at all." He looked at his guest — at Don John, in fact, remarked his very light hair and fair complexion, the frank, good-tempered air, and was sure he had never seen him before. He said to himself, —

"A gentlemanly-looking young fellow, and in no hurry to speak. I see that he knows I have been napping."

The young man spoke at last, not without a slight air of deference, which was very agreeable.

"You sent a message to me."

"A message?"

"By a young lady."

The smiling, chubby face took on an air of concern and wonder.

"She was to ask me whether I had ever heard of such a thing as compounding of felony."

"Yes."

"I am an articled clerk to a lawyer. Criminal cases are not in his line, but I have access to the best law-books."

"I consider that the young lady, innocently of course, and in ignorance — " interrupted Mr. Cottenham.

"Pardon me, I come only in reply to your message,

to inform you according to the best authorities what is meant by compounding of felony."

" Well, well, this is remarkable."

Don John unfolded a sheet of foolscap paper, on which was some writing in the round hand of a copying clerk, and began, —

" ' Compounding of felony is the taking of a reward for forbearing to prosecute a felony ; and one species of this offence (known in the books by the more ancient appellation of theft-base) is where a party robbed takes his goods again, or other amend, upon agreement not to prosecute.' "

" I thought as much ! "

" It could not be more clear. Shall I go on ? ' This was formerly held to make a man an accessory to the theft, but is now punished only with fine and imprisonment.' "

" Only ! " ejaculated the listener, " *only with fine and imprisonment.* Now what could possess you, to read all this to me ? "

" It defines the compounding of felony."

" It defines it very clearly ! I am much afraid of the law. I have got into the clutches of the law three times."

" That could only have been innocently, as you said of the young lady, and through ignorance."

"You are sure of this ? You don't require much time for making up your mind."

" I have had time enough already to feel grieved to think that when a certain thing is explained and arranged I shall probably never have the pleasure of seeing you again in this world. I shall be obliged to wish indeed that you may never know even my name."

The round, childlike face took on its sweetest expression.

" Explained and arranged ! Well, well, the confidence of youth is amazing ! "

" There 's a good deal more of it," said Don John. " This perversion of justice in the old Gothic constitutions was liable to the most severe and infamous punishment.   Indeed the Salic law ' *la troui eum similem habuit,* *qui furtum* '—"

" Stop !   That I will not stand.   What is such jargon to me?"

" I had better go on then to the English, ' And by statute 24 and 25 Vict. c. 96, s. 102 (amended by 33 and 34 Vict. c. 65), even publicly to advertise a reward for the return of property stolen or lost, and in such advertisement to use words purporting that no questions will be asked ; or purporting that a reward will be paid without seizing or making inquiry after the persons producing the same ; or promising to return to a pawnbroker or other person any money he may have advanced upon, or paid for such property ; or offering any other sum of money or reward for the return of the same : subjects the advertiser, the printer, and the publisher to a forfeiture of fifty pounds each.' "

" Is that all?"   There was the least little touch of sarcasm in the tone of this question.

" I could have multiplied authorities, I could have copied a great deal more, but I thought that was enough."

" I think so too.   Compounding of felony is now very clearly explained ; what I still fail to understand is the meaning of your conduct !   I am not expected to consider it disinterested, I suppose."

" I had something to hope for, of course."

" And I should like to know whether, when you searched through the law-books for these definitions, you instructed yourself as to what compounding of felony was, at the same time that you prepared to instruct me?"

Don John for a moment endeavored to preserve a stolid expression, but as he could not, — as he felt himself detected, he glanced furtively at the round, chubby face, and then looked again, and seemed to gather confidence and comfort.

" I want to dismiss that subject, now if you will let me, and mention to you a poor young man who has behaved very wickedly to you, and who is very miserable."

" In short, John Ward. I trusted John Ward; I was very kind to him."

" He told me so ; it aggravates his crime. He robbed you of the sum of three thousand and fifteen pounds and fifteen shillings."

" He told you that! you have seen him then."

" Yes ; he is very miserable. He says that he deeply repents —"

" I am sorry for him,— and for myself,— and for you."

" By a quite unexpected circumstance, some property was left, on which both he and his mother thought that he had a claim ; at first his claim was disallowed, but now it is admitted."

" Indeed, indeed. Well, I don't know what to make of this."

" I have seen him a second time, and I am thankful to say that when I was explaining to him about this claim, he asked whether the money would amount to as much as three thousand and fifteen pounds and fifteen shillings. I was less miserable about him after I had heard him say that. It shows that he really does repent."

" You are his good friend."

" He humbly begs your forgiveness for what he has done, and he humbly desires to restore to you by me the whole of the money that he stole. Here it is." He handed over the table a parcel neatly sealed.

" Here it is," repeated Mr. Cottenham, as if this unexpected turn of affairs confused him to the point of leaving him devoid of any original words. He took up his eye-glass and leaned over the parcel without touching it. Then he drew towards him the paper Don John had read, and carefully considered that. In the shrewdness with which he scrutinized it there was something childlike and simple ; but in the silent pity with which he turned over the yet unopened parcel, there was something that childhood cannot attain.

At last he broke the seal, and slowly spread out the notes, and opened the little packet of gold.

Don John's heart danced.

"It was a large sum to lose," muttered Mr. Cottenham. "And his behavior cut me to the heart too. I suppose," he went on, but not addressing Don John; "I suppose I cannot be bound to prosecute now?"

He appeared to fix his eyes on a map which was hanging on the opposite wall, and to address his remark to that. "I have been bitten by the law three times already."

Don John chose out an opposite map, and in his turn made some cautious remarks. "A fellow must be prosecuted on some particular charge, either he is accused of a crime against the prosecutor, or against 'Our Sovereign Lady the Queen.' Now if a man tried for murder could produce in court the supposed murdered man, and prove that he was alive and well—"

"The two might walk out of court, arm in arm, for aught the judge could say! There was no crime!"

"Or again, a man accused of a robbery, if he can produce a receipt in full, for the money in question, cannot be brought to trial, the intending prosecutor has no charge to bring against him. Only," continued Don John, "if writs are out against such a man, and when he has paid he is arrested before he has the receipts to show, his people are liable to be disgraced; his story might get wind."

Mr. Cottenham lost himself in cogitation here, then he said,—

"I shall give John Ward a receipt in full, and write him a short letter by you. What can I say better than, 'Sin no more, lest a worse thing happen to thee'? You may trust me to do all I can for you."

He began to write, and having put a certain stamp at the end of the letter, handed it to Don John, who received it with eager joy and fervent thanks.

"This has been a great trouble to you, since you first heard of it."

"Yes."

"So it has to me. I felt that he had ruined himself, and I had trusted him."

" But I felt not only that he was ruined, but that his trial would disgrace my people. They know nothing of this, not one word."

" Well, if it depends on me, they never shall; for I think they never need. You have conducted this case very well for your first client. I suppose I am your first?"

" Oh, yes."

" Father and mother both living?"

" Yes, both, I thank God."

" As doubtless they do for you. It is a fine thing to have a son. I lost my son — he was my only one. I have still a daughter, about the age, as I think, of that beautiful young girl whom you sent to me. She is not your sister, of course."

At this mention of Charlotte, a sudden change came over Don John's face in spite of himself. The denial had leaped out of his eyes before he answered, " That young lady is not my sister — no."

" If she is in any sense under your charge, or influence, I cannot but express a hope that you may never have to send her on an errand again which has to begin by her informing the one person present that she must conceal her name — "

Don John looked up.

" I fervently hope that young lady may never be sent on such an errand again. Being what she is, and looking what she is, you could not have thought any evil of her, for a moment — any evil at all."

" I did not."

" And you being what you are, and looking what you are, she could think nothing but good of you. On what better errand (if you had understood it) could I have sent her to you, unless I had sent her to ask for your blessing?"

" Sir! no man was ever so acceptably reproved."

" We are not strangers to you, we both know you by reputation."

" Indeed! there is nothing else that I can do for you?"

" Unless you will shake hands with me."

Thereupon they parted, and Don John with the precious receipt buttoned up in his coat, ran clattering downstairs, and sped towards the Great Northern Railway, getting out at a station agreed upon between the two, and walking about in search of the poor acrobat. He wandered through the suburban streets, and stared into the eating-houses, till he was getting tired out; but he did not feel alarmed, for he knew Lancy might have taken fright, thinking himself watched.

At last he came home.

The next morning before breakfast, his mother with an ivory paper-knife was cutting open the newspapers, and laying them before his father's plate, when glancing one over, she remarked, " I often wonder what some of these queer advertisements mean. Here is one odder than usual: ' The acrobat may wash his face.' "

" I 've been told they concern some smuggling operations; they are signals it is thought," said Marjorie, " signals to vessels that have smuggled goods on board."

" Perhaps the ' Acrobat' is the name of one of those vessels," observed Mary.

" Perhaps," answered the father carelessly, and with a smile.

Don John and Charlotte exchanged glances: that was all which passed. The talk concerned Marjorie's wedding, which was to be in three days. The bridegroom was already in the house, the grandmother was expected in an hour. The wedding presents were frequently arriving, and all was pleasant bustle and cherished confusion. It was so nice to have so much to do. Nobody wanted to think about the parting, especially the bride's father.

But the acrobat made no sign, and one day, two days, and then the wedding-day passed over, and still he was not to be found. Don John wearied himself with researches under hedges all about Hornsey, and out beyond Barnet; he had large bills posted up over

walls in waste places, on hoardings, and outside the
railway stations. "It's all right. The acrobat may
wash his face." A great many eyes became familiar
with that strange announcement, but apparently not
Lancy's, and yet Don John was moderately easy in his
mind. He felt sure Lancy had not been arrested. Mr.
Cottenham would have taken care of that.

At the wedding everybody behaved very badly; almost all wept, some because they were sorry, some because they were glad, and some because the others did.

The bridegroom stuck fast in returning thanks, when
his bride's health was drunk. Her grandmother openly
prompted him. The bride's father stuck fast in remarking how much he was blessed in his dear sons and
daughters. People will say such things. This happy
remark caused a good deal of piteous sniffing. The
grandmother prompted him also, but not so audibly;
he was glad to avail himself of her words, and then she
counselled him to sit down.

The day was hot, and there was an intermittent
downfall of pouring rain. The bridesmaids' gowns, in
spite of awnings, got wet at the bottom. The rain
poured through openings in a tent which had been
pitched in the field, and splashed into the bountiful
bowls of custard, and weakened the claret-cup, and
cooled the gravy. In that tent, the inhabitants of
"the houses" were being feasted. The rain was not
held on the whole to be a disadvantage, because, as
some of the guests remarked, it cooled the air, and
made the victuals seem to go down more sweetly.

At last, in a heavier downfall than ever, and with
more tears, both from gentle and simple, the bride
drove away. The father shut himself up in his study;
the mother and her little Mary went upstairs to console
themselves together. All the guests took their leave;
and Naomi and Mr. Brown, settling themselves comfortably in a corner of the drawing-room, sat hand in
hand.

There was nobody left in the great dining-room but
the grandmother, Don John, and Charlotte.

" I shall not come up to Naomi's wedding," re-marked the former, " if ye all mean to go on in this way. I 'm quite ashamed of you! Charlotte too; what had you got to cry for, I should like to know?"

" It was so affecting," said Charlotte demurely, and trifling with the flowers of her bouquet.

" Affecting! Yes; your little nose is quite swelled with crying!" (Charlotte went and peeped at herself in a glass) " and your eyelashes are wet yet. I hope ye 'll behave better when your own wedding-day comes."

" I shall never have one," said Charlotte, in the same demure fashion, and with a little smile, which seemed to betoken superior knowledge.

" What, do ye really mean to tell me that ye never intend to marry?"

" Oh, no!" said Charlotte, " I think I should like to be married. I always have a theory that I should." She laughed. " If anybody that was nice would have me."

The grandmother sat bolt upright.

" What!" she exclaimed rather sharply.

" I shall not be married, because nobody wants to marry me," persisted Charlotte, not the least put out of countenance. " I never had a lover " (excepting once for a day or two, and then he changed his mind), " and they think I never shall have."

" ' THEY,' " repeated the grandmother, with infinite emphasis; " and who are *they*, I beg to know?"

" Oh," said Charlotte carelessly, " Don John and the girls."

The grandmother looked steadily at Don John, and he appeared confused.

" Don John said it, did he? said ye had no lover! I thought he knew better!"

Charlotte had not eaten much breakfast, and was dip-ping some ripe strawberries into the sugar, and eating them with bread. " But I forgot," she continued, " that we mean to call him *laird* now. Marjorie made us promise not to forget. Laird, shut the door."

" He may hold it open a moment for me first," said

the grandmother, rising, and slightly tossing her head
— there were a good many feathers in the wedding-
bonnet, and they wagged as she walked.   She laughed
when she reached the door, but before it was shut behind her she was heard to murmur, —

"No lover has she.   Well, I thought ye knew better, I did indeed."

———◆———

CHAPTER XXXIII.

"SHE means Lancy," exclaimed Charlotte, "and I
do think"— Don John had come up to her by this
time — "I do think, considering what friends we have
always been, and considering how I have helped you
about him, you ought not to let her suppose it."   She
put her hand to her throat.   "No, I am not going to
cry again ; but two or three times grandmamma has
hinted at this kind of thing to me, and remembering all
the piteous truth, I feel as if her thinking of him as my
lover was almost a disgrace to me, and that was why I
was so anxious to tell her that I had no lover."

"She did not mean Lancy," said Don John.

Charlotte had finished her strawberries.

"She must have meant Lancy," she answered, "for
there's nobody else."

The grandmother had much exaggerated the traces
of tears.   Charlotte had never looked so lovely in her
life.   That may have been partly because she had never
been so beautifully adorned before.   The shimmering
white silk set off her dark hair, and there was lace
round her throat, from which it rose like a small ala-
baster column, and then the rosebuds in her bouquet,
how they matched the hues of her mouth ! and it soft-
ened, and the dimple came in her cheek.

"Look," she exclaimed, pointing into the garden,
and there was the grandmother marching about among
the dripping flowers, with a certain air of determination, "she is quite cross still."

"Yes; but not with you. Do not be vexed. She did not mean Lancy."

"Then whom could she mean?"

"A mere nobody; for as you have said (and I deserve it), '*there is nobody else.*'"

"Don John!"

"She meant ME."

All the sweetest changes that Charlotte's face was capable of came into it then. She pouted as one cogitating, and her long lashes drooped, then she blushed — it was that real old-fashioned maiden blush, which is rather rare now, and so exquisitely beautiful that when seen under such interesting circumstances it can never be forgotten.

She sat down on a sofa in the corner of the room, where she could not be seen from the garden, and quickly recovering herself, began, "Then go to her at once, of course, and say — "

"Yes; what may I say?"

"I ought not to have been told this at all," said Charlotte, in a tone not quite free from reproof. "It is your affair to find out how to say — that she is mistaken."

"But she is not mistaken."

"No!"

Charlotte had got the corner of the sofa, and looked forth from it. Under such circumstances people cannot sit side by side; but Don John sat as near to her as he could.

"No?" she murmured again, almost in a whisper, and she lifted up her eyes, and looked into his, which denied and denied that there was any mistake, in a fashion more convincing than words.

Just for a moment she felt as if a kiss was impending. Don John did not kiss her. He thought that was owing to his own new-born modesty, deference, and devotion, and did not know that she had already made him remote from her lips. He wanted to take her hand, but she scarcely let him hold it for an instant. Even at that pass it flashed into his recollection how often in their childhood he had lent her his own pocket-handkerchief to dry her fingers on, when they were inked. All was different now, and he must make the best of the change. It would seem so natural to go down on his knees — but would she laugh at him? On one knee — but would she laugh at him? He started up on his feet, and burst forth with his love, and his entreaty, that she would not remember his boyish impertinence, and before he knew what he was about, he was on one knee, and the door being suddenly flung open, his grandmother entered. She was heard to utter a short laugh, and she hastily withdrew.

Don John sprang to his feet. He and Charlotte looked at one another, and they both laughed also. Charlotte as overcome by a surprising and absurd incident, Don John as one who accused his fate.

He had been pleading with her for a rosebud — only one, out of her bouquet — and Charlotte had been so taken by surprise, that she knew not what to do. But she was mistress of the situation now, new as it was to her.

"Come and sit down here," she entreated. "Let us be our old selves again, and tell me what this means."

But he still wanted the rosebud, that he might get her hand to kiss, and when she withdrew it, she looked at it as if it might be changed.

"All this is very amazing," she began; and repeated, "Let us be our old selves again."

"I cannot be my old self; I love you." He looked down: her little feet in their white satin shoes peeped forth, and seemed to nestle on the carpet, he thought, like two young doves; but of course he had the sense not to say this, he knew she would laugh at him if he did.

"But I meant that I want you to explain what all this means. You always had a theory, you know, which — which I thought a very sensible one," said Charlotte, suddenly giving her sentence a fresh form.

Don John heaved up a great sigh. "Yes, I know I have chiefly my own insolence and folly to thank, if you cannot understand or believe me."

"At any rate there's no occasion to be so melan-

choly about it," said Charlotte; and then, overcome by
the absurdity of this sudden change in her old comrade,
she burst into a delightful little laugh, which was quite
irresistible.

Don John could not possibly help seeing how ridiculous the thing was as regarded in the light of his whole
former conduct, and the two young creatures laughed
together, both at themselves, and at the irony of fate.

"I never would have believed it of you," exclaimed
Charlotte, recovering herself.

"It's poetical justice done upon me."

"I suppose it is."

"I deserve it."

"I had not reached to the point of thinking so!"

"But what are you going to do with me?"

"Do with you!" exclaimed Charlotte, laughing
again.

"Yes. You make me laugh, but it's no laughing
matter. If you only knew. Don't you think you can
say — something?"

"Something appreciative?" suggested Charlotte,
when he paused. "Yes, laird; I can say that your
property becomes you vastly in the giving of it away.
I can say that this must certainly have been a pleasant
day to you, for you have got uncle out of a pecuniary
scrape, made Marjorie happy, and are going to do as
much for Naomi. I did say the other morning that I
thought you had grown better-looking. I now see the
reason of it; your bosom was glowing with virtue and
generosity; you pose before my mind's eye as on your
first return I saw you — classically bundled up in your
new plaid, and smoking your cigar like a sort of Scotch
Apollo."

"It was only right you should know I had parted
with that two thousand pounds. You, and only you!"

Charlotte blushed; the hint was rather a strong one.

"I shall have something much more difficult to tell
you soon."

"Don John!"

"Well?"

" It's not at all becoming to you to be tragical. You cannot have forgotten that in our charades you never would do the tragic parts ; because, as you said, a fellow to act tragedy well ought to have a Roman nose."

" But I am not acting now."

" No ; I never meant to insinuate anything of the sort. But look how the sun shines and glitters on the wet roses, don't you think if you were to take a cigar and go out, and think this over, you would come back in a different humor? "

" I am always thinking it over."

" Since how long? "

" Since I came home from Scotland the first time, and you met me — waiting for me at the green gate — don't you remember? "

" Remember ! No. Why, that's months ago."

" You leaned on the green gate — and I saw you."

" I always lean on the green gate. It couldn't be that."

" I saw how beautiful you were, and how sweet — and — I loved you."

" All on a sudden? "

" Yes."

" But what for? "

" What for ! ! "

" It was not for anything in particular, then? "

" It was for everything in general. I am always finding out more reasons for loving you. If you send me out to walk among the rose-trees I shall find them in the shadows at their roots, and in the rain-drops that they shake from their buds. All the reading in the book of my life is about you, and the world outside tells me of you. Things fair and young and good I must needs love, because they are like you ; there is pity in me, and I find a pathos in what is unlovely and old, because it is unlike."

" Extraordinary ! "

" Don't be unkind, Charlotte."

" Oh, no."

So many charms in one small face — such dimples

and blushes, and shy dropping of black lashes, and such a whimsical pathos, and almost tenderness — when she was not laughing at him — were hardly ever seen before.

" Don't you think you could afford me one kiss, Charlotte ? "

" Certainly not."

" But you will think of all this — you are not displeased ? "

" Displeased ! I always used to think nothing was so interesting as — "

" As love — such love as this — as mine ? "

" Yes ; and so I think still. Nothing can be so interesting, *in the abstract !* "

" Well, you might at least let a fellow kiss your hand ; I never heard of a lover yet who was not allowed to do that."

" If it were any other ' fellow ' — but you ! Don't be so ridiculous."

" It 's cruel of you to make game of me."

" And yet I love you better than any excepting Aunt Estelle, and my uncle and mother. I liked you, I believe, better than any one at all till now."

" Liked me best. Oh, do tell me what is the difference between that and loving ? "

" People whom we like are those who (we suppose) will never astonish us ; people whom we are not obliged to explain things to, because they know ; people whom we perfectly trust — they are partners, comrades, friends."

" You *like* me less now ? "

" Perhaps so, laird."

" It is my belief that your poetic mind eschews with distaste the notion of prosperity ; if a fellow has, as you . think, all he wants in this world, he is less interesting to you."

" That is not impossible."

" And it is nothing to me. Not that I allude to Captain Leslie's bequest. Between Lancy and the girls, I have despoiled myself already of most of the money, and I shall not have the land much longer."

" What can you mean, Don John ? "

" Why you knew that I had parted with enough money to set poor Lancy straight. You helped me to do it, my lady and queen."

" But the land?"

" Ah! yes, the land; there's the rub. You have always thought of me as rather a jolly fellow, haven't you? Not a fellow that had ever known misfortune, or had anything weighing on his mind."

The rose hue faded out of Charlotte's face now, and by absence helped its new expression to a deeper emphasis.

" When you were ill," she began, " I thought you had something on your mind. My heart ached for you. I felt that you must have some sorrow clouding your nights and days. Even when you were getting better, I often saw it come over like a dark cloud to veil out all the sunshine."

" And you *liked* me then, better than any one, and understood — "

" No, I did not understand; for I could not help thinking, that in some way it had to do with Lancy, and your distress at his going wrong."

" It had something to do with Lancy."

" Lancy, and his place here, and their love for him, and yours, have been wonderful to me all my life; but at least he can have nothing to do with this strange thing, that I thought you said about Captain Leslie's land. You cannot possibly want to give that to him?"

" Certainly not, and yet it has to do with him, that I cannot keep it for myself."

" You make him more important than ever," said Charlotte faltering, and obviously shrinking from she knew not what.

" But he became ten times more important after I got better, after I had seen you leaning on the green gate, and you had told me about his trying to make you like him, and of his mother's entreaties. I thought indeed for a long time that you did care for him. Till in fact you went with me to offer old Cottenham the title-

deeds as a pledge. Then I knew for the first time that
you did it for all our sakes rather than for his."

" Laney is at least not going to have that estate."

" No ; nor I either."

" Amazing ! Oh, my uncle is no doubt in debt more
than we had thought."

" No ; nothing of the sort. Mother is going to tell
you why."

" Your mother ! Aunt Estelle. Why should she tell
ME ? "

" Because it might concern you."

Charlotte blushed and flushed, and the dimple went
away into hiding. " Aunt Estelle," she repeated ; " but
how should she know ? "

" How should my mother not know? Could she see
me day by day, and never divine that I loved you? She
always knows without being told what concerns the happiness of her children."

" And she *consented to* — "

" She *proposed to* tell you several things. She said
I ought not to ask you to be my wife till you knew
them."

" Aunt Estelle ? "

" Yes ; whether you can ever love me, or whether you
cannot, you will always love mother ten times more when
she has told you."

" Wait a minute, let me think."

Don John had no objection. He leaned over the end
of the sofa. He knew all the expressions of Charlotte's
face — the beautiful pouting mouth, and shining tender
eyes. How she pondered and wondered !

" There really is something? " she sighed at last.

" Yes, really."

" And I cannot catch the remotest glimpse of it." But
the mother's knowledge, and the mother's apparent
sanction, gave a strange, sweet surprise and reality to
the thing.

True love it was evident had come near her. She foresaw that there would soon be a response to it ; but she
thought most of the mother, her aunt who had brought

her up, and been so loving to her. It was manifest that
nothing could be denied to her; but how amazing that
she should be brought into the story. " I cannot make
it out," she exclaimed.

" No."

Then remembering how she had laughed at this
mother's son, and teased him, and denied him the
small comfort of a drooping rose-bud, she went on, —

" But Don John, if you will let me tell you beforehand exactly what it means, I think after all I had
better give you that kiss."

" Oh, yes! do tell me then what it is to mean."

" First, it is to be for the past, for a parting with all
the old yesterdays. We used to be such friends, and I
am glad we were."

" Tell me the rest, and give it me."

" I knew so little of my mother. I always loved
yours best of all. There was something more, but I
forget it."

" But give me the kiss."

" Yes."

CHAPTER XXXIV.

AFTER all, when we read the parable of the Prodigal Son, we find him for all his faults more interesting than that blameless brother who was at work in
his father's field.

It was now twelve days after the wedding. In a
small bare room, on a truckle bed, a poor disfigured
patient was lying. A medical man without touching,
leaned towards him, and regarded him with attention.
He gave directions to two women, one of whom was
seated on either side of the bed, then said, before retiring, " He'll do now. You'll do very well now, my
poor fellow. Do you hear me?"

The patient assented, but scarcely in articulate words, and presently dozed again.

After he had taken some food, and had his pillows altered to his mind, he began to look about him with interest and attention, specially to look at the face of his elder nurse, a simple and rather foolish face, but full of goodwill.

"I should like to see myself in a glass," he presently said.

"There ain't a glass in the house, my pore young man," she answered. "It's an empty house that you was brought into."

"What is it that has been the matter with me?" he next asked.

"Well, it's what they call an eruptive fever," said the younger woman.

"Is it infectious?"

"Yes, it is; but it's my business to nurse such cases."

"I thank you for your goodness to me."

"You should thank God, my pore boy," said the other, "that He has made some of us with a liking for such a business."

"That's my aunt, Miss Jenny Clarboy," said the younger; "I had to have somebody here to cook, and wait, and help; so she came."

"For the love of God," explained Miss Jenny.

The patient sighed distressfully. "Then I am not to have a glass; but if I tell you that I hope my face *is* very much changed, you'll let me know whether it is, or not, won't you?"

"My poor young man, we don't ask you why you should want it to be changed; but I may say, that though you'll be like yourself again some day, your own mother would n't know you now, though she should look at you hard."

"I'm thankful," said the patient faintly; but whether for his present disfigurement, or for the promise of recovery, did not appear.

The younger nurse now retired to take some rest.

The patient for awhile was very still. He looked about, but there was little in the room for his eyes to rest on. The clean ceiling and the sloping walls were white-washed and bare. A small green blind was hung before the curtainless window. There was nothing to look at but his nurse, and he contemplated her till the circumstance attracted her attention, and the simple creature was a little put out of countenance : for she had a clean, but exceedingly shabby, old print gown on, which was patched in various places. She actually began to explain.

" It's a one as I've kept for cleaning, and washing days. I've respectable things for going to my chapel in."

" Anything is good enough for me, Miss Jenny," said the patient gently. " Won't you draw the other chair nearer, and put your feet on the spoke to rest them ? "

" I will, my pore young man. Now you can talk so as to be understood, I warrant there's not much of the tramp on your tongue."

" I was only a tramp, because I've thrown myself away."

" That's a sad hearing."

" I heard you pray by my bed, when you thought I should die."

" There was little else to be done for you."

" And you said I was a poor lost creature."

" We're all lost till Christ finds us — Jesus Christ, the Saviour of the world."

" Till Christ finds us — yes — but I have tried hard to prevent Him from finding me. I have tried to hide myself from Him under the darkness of a great many evil deeds."

" You talk very faint and very hollow. I may not let you go on, and I'll only say this, my pore lad, that if nobody else will have anything to say to you, and you are so lost that you have nothing but misery to call your own, why then lie still and wish (for you're too weak to pray), wish that He may find you, and He will, for you are the right sort for Him."

There were many days of pain and sickness after this; there were many drawbacks, and sometimes it almost seemed as if the poor young patient would sink. "Who's going to pay for all this?" he one day asked.

"You've no call to think of that," answered the younger nurse, "for there's nothing asked for from you, John Ward."

John Ward sighed; how could he tell that he ever should be able to repay this money. During the first stages of his illness, which had come on suddenly, he had been delirious; he was lying under a hedge wet with dew, and ghastly with smeared paint and white-wash, when a policeman found him. He had some recollection of this, and that he had been able repeatedly to make known his wish that a penny paper might be bought for him. Of course no notice was taken of this request; but his intervals of sense for several days were spent in repeating it; and even after he became so weak and confused that he by no means knew himself what he had wanted it for, he could often be soothed by having some old piece of newspaper put into his hand, when he would fumble over it, and guard it jealously. Thus his desire for a newspaper was always regarded by these women as a proof of delirium, and one of his worst symptoms.

Of course, though they did what was right by him and never left him, his sick-bed was not surrounded by those delicate, attentive cares that he would have had if he had been in the midst of a loving, cultured family. Nobody tried to find out a meaning in his fancies, or made experiments to discover whether this one or that would please him. So when he was a little better and again approached the subject of the papers, he was cut short by the remark that the doctor would by no means let them go to the book-stalls fresh from the sick-room; for the doctor was a very conscientious gentleman, and particular to prevent the spread of infection.

"As you may *jedge*," Miss Jenny would say, "when you see saucers here and saucers there full of *Condy's Fluid* that costs a pretty penny; and that he does n't grudge you, my pore young man, more than if it was water."

Miss Jenny finding herself for the very first time in her life in a position of authority, took advantage of it, and seemed to rise to it strangely. She gave John Ward a good deal of advice, and he listened to it, wide as it was of the mark, with wonder and interest. It was advice suited to an acrobat and a tramp. Such she thought him. That this should be possible was a thing so piteous as to give it often a keener edge than any satire; but then she would go on in her simplest fashion to teach some of the most comforting doctrines of our faith. John Ward had heard these all his life, and yet they seemed new now. It is only those who have known what it is to be lost who can truly long to be found. He listened, and was comforted. The Saviour does not often walk in high places. John Ward, who knew himself to be a disgrace, and felt that he was wretched, had been cast out as the unclean thing, and lying in the dust had met with Him.

He was sitting up in bed for the first time when his nurse thus let him know that he had been dependent on charity. His head had been shaved again during his illness.

"And those wretched calicoes and that sash and wig of yours were burnt because of infection," she continued; "but see what good friends have been raised up for you, they are going to make a gathering for you at our chapel to get you some decent second-hand clothes and a pair of shoes so soon as you are strong enough to wear them."

"Her brother," said Miss Jenny, indicating her niece, "is a waiter, and waits in the best of families, so you'll *jedge* that he has to wear good clothes in his calling. That white shirt you have on is an old one of his."

"Yes," said the niece; "he gave it to me for you, being fine and fitter for a sick patient than the coarse things they sell in the slop-shops. And he says he'll give you a waistcoat when you go out, one that he has done with."

John Ward cast his eyes on the frayed wristband of
his shirt. If ever in his life he had felt shame for himself it was then. "I am very much obliged to your
brother that is a waiter," he said, with the peculiar gentleness of intonation that he always used towards his
nurses.

Miss Jenny was about to depart home. The patient
could now be very well attended to by one person. She
talked of her sister, who was a respectable dress-maker,
and always paid her way, and then of the Johnstones.
Not, of course, as the poor speak of the rich to the
rich — but as they speak to one another — "My sister,
'Mrs. Clarboy,' and 'Johnstone's people,' that live at
the great house."

What a pang it gave poor John Ward to hear these
familiar names, and feel himself remote!

"Well, good-bye, aunt," said the niece, "you're
not to shake hands with the patient now you're dressed,
nor go nigh him."

"I'm truly obliged to her," said John Ward.

"How respectable and how well you look in that
Sunday gown," continued the niece. "And nobody
knows what a deal of use you've been to me."

"Kept up your spirits, did I, dear?" answered Miss
Jenny complacently.

"No, I don't say that," replied the niece; "I never
feel my spirits half so good as when I've got a right
down bad case, that anybody else might be afraid to
come near; nor so well in my health neither."

"It's a providence," replied Miss Jenny; "and as
for my pore nerves, I don't know where they're gone
to, since here I came."

So then she nodded to John Ward, and was gone.
He might not send any message by her: shame and
probable danger to himself prevented that. He laid
himself down again and cried feebly. Then his nurse
gave him food.

"Don't you take on," she said, "it's bad for you."

"But I don't seem to get well," said the poor fellow.

"Get well," she repeated with the merciless directness always used by the poor to those of their own class,
"there's a deal to be done before you get well."

"What's to be done?"

"Why, for one thing, there's your skin to come off
— when you see it coming off your hands and face in
bits as big as sixpences you'll know you're getting
well."

John Ward inquired whether the process would hurt
him much.

"Not a bit," she replied; "but I may tell you for
your own comfort that the parish authorities are very
particular in this union; they'll keep you here, and let
you have the best of food till that's over. In short,
they won't let you go — or every lodging-house you
went and slept in you'd spread the infection, and that
would soon raise the rates."

John Ward perceived that he was a pauper, and felt
it. Also he felt that charity, at least national charity,
was largely indebted to enlightened self-interest.

"As cold as charity" has become a proverb; he was
guarded here, and lodged and fed, as he was informed,
because by coming out he might raise the rates.

"And how thankful that ought to make you," she
continued; "all your meals coming up as regular as
can be, and there's a gathering to be made, to buy you
clothes, and you've time to think upon your ways."

John Ward was not at all thankful to the parish authorities; but he did much relish his meals, simple as
they were, and for many an hour he did lie still and
think upon his ways.

With a certain humbleness and simplicity he tried to
pray. The chapters in the Bible that his nurse read
to him appeared fresh and interesting; the words were
familiar, but they meant something new, and her homely
comments, which seemed to take for granted that he
had broken almost all the commandments of the Deca-
logue, did not rouse in him any resentment. It was all
true, truer than she thought; the wonder was that even
now, even yet, there might be found a remedy.

And so the hours and days went on, till at last, a poor, hollow-eyed young man, he went forth from the cottage where he had been nursed, with a benefaction of two shillings in his pocket, and an ample meal of meat and bread tied up in a pocket-handkerchief, for the gathering at Little Bethel had provided even this last article.

He had a loud, hollow cough, and with faded eyes he surveyed his grotesque habiliments — one of the waiter's old coats, very white at the seams, a shirt and hat contributed by the preacher, and trousers a world too wide for him; also a pair of new boots, of strong workmanship, and heavy with hob-nails. He must spend the half of his money in sending a telegram, and before he reached the station he saw, torn and faded, and not perfect in any case, the token he longed for. On hoardings and walls, and on empty houses, glaring and disreputable portions of it greeted him everywhere. His heart leaped with joy once more, and echoed the words, —

"It's all right; the acrobat may wash his face."

He doubted awhile in sheer delight, and spelt over the disjointed sentence; but at last he found a perfect copy, and creeping into the railway-station, sent his telegram, and rested on a bench to await the event.

His troubles now were soon over. In less than an hour Don John appeared. Lancy was very quiet, very humble; he could say little more than that he had been extremely ill, and he was thankful to be taken in hand, decent lodging found for him, and proper clothes bought for him; then, weak as he was, shaken by his cough, and ashamed of the pauper position that he had just emerged from, he asked to know nothing but that he was safe from prosecution, and laid himself on his bed, leaving Don John to do and say what he pleased.

So he was left to rest and food, and his own salutary and bitter reflections. He did not betray much emotion the next day, when his foster-brother gave him old Cottenham's letter; but he wept when he was told how anxious the Johnstones had been at his disappearance.

They often said it was certain he had gone to America, but no suspicion of his crime had ever crossed their minds. They hoped he would write soon to them. So far so good; his crime had been condoned, and had caused them neither misery nor disgrace, and of his sufferings they had not known. But what next? Could it be right, or would it be possible to bring him under their roof again? Fortunately the deciding of this was not left to Don John.

Lancy had no sooner found himself alone, than he had written a letter to "his mamma," setting forth that he had been extremely ill, and giving her his address with directions to come to him. He directed the letter to her old lodgings in which he had left her. He knew nothing of her visit to Scotland, or her wish to follow him to America.

Fortunately for her, Don John's advice, that she should wait in England for tidings from Lancy, had taken some effect on her mind.

She felt that if he did not want her, he would take care she did not find him, whether she followed him or not; but if he did want her he would certainly write to her at the only address he knew. So, after waiting awhile in the north, she came back as cheaply as she could, took a garret in that same house, and waited and hoped.

At last a letter came; and he was close at hand.

She hastened to him, bringing with her the few clothes he had not taken with him when he went on his nefarious errand. She was much shocked at his appearance and his cough, but there was little for them to talk about. He merely told her that he had had a dreadful illness, which he had entirely brought upon himself. She saw that he was humbled, and that all the spirit seemed to have gone out of him; but he said little more, and never complained.

"I wish you had another suit," she said, holding up a dress-coat, "for that one you have on seems rather heavy for you this weather."

" I have another," he answered, " a whole suit, I left in the box in our old playroom at ' the house.' "

" Then ask Mr. Don John to send it you."

" Perhaps I shall some day; he has enough trouble with me just now."

" And how did it come there?"

Lancy seemed confused, and did not tell her how, in the middle of a summer night, tramping down from Liverpool, he had reached that once-beloved home, and wandered about in the garden; then, knowing it, and where everything was kept so well, had got the longest fruit-ladder and put it against the playroom window, which was open, and there, the better to hide himself, had put on the wretched clothes and the wig, in which he had been found, and had folded up his own clothes and put them into the box. The rubbish in which they had been used to array themselves when they acted their charades! He put on the worst of it. There was bread in the room; Mary had been having her supper; he took the loaf, went cautiously down the ladder, and replaced it, then filled his pockets with fruit, and went his way.

CHAPTER XXXV.

WHEN Mrs. Ward heard that Lancy still had property at "the house," she was at once tempted to make that an excuse for going there, claiming it, and giving her own view of matters to Mrs. Johnstone.

Mr. Johnstone and Don John would be away; it seemed such a good opportunity for wringing the other woman's heart, by describing Lancy's cough — talking of his sufferings, how he had been picked up under a hedge, and how, if he had died, he would have had a pauper's funeral.

Lancy was generally kind to her, he was even glad of her company; but when she told him of this project, he was exceedingly angry, and desired that she would do nothing of the kind.

"You were always promised a share of everything," she grumbled, "and it is my belief that they are forgetting all that, and you too."

"If they can forget my past, the better for their own peace," sighed Lancy, "and as to my share, I have had it already. I was never promised a certain sum. I was only promised a certain proportion of the family possessions."

"And you have had nothing yet," she answered, "but just your bringing up."

"Yes, I have. I have had three thousand pounds from Don John."

"Mercy!" exclaimed Mrs. Ward. "I thought — yes, I'll allow that I thought — it was bluster and vaporing, when he said that on your account he should keep his hands from touching Captain Leslie's fortune. Three thousand pounds! Wherever is it, then? You told me we were living on money Mr. Don John sent to you — living as I thought from hand to mouth; but if it's on the interest of three thousand pounds, I call that handsome, and I don't feel that it's at all the same thing."

She laid down her work and pondered.

"Three thousand pounds!" Lancy having justified Don John, felt too weak to enter on his own terrible story, and he let her alone. Many bitter and salutary thoughts had possession of his breast; and when she added, "And yet it might be — I mean it may be — that you've a right to all —"

"You don't think so, you are sure of the contrary," Lancy burst out roughly.

"Yes, my blessed boy, that I am."

"And yet you're not at all thankful for this three thousand pounds, this great sum of money, which has saved me from a trial for felony — from becoming a wretched convict."

"Don't talk so wild," she answered soothingly. "You are as weak as can be still. It's too much for you."

" God forgive you, and me too," muttered Lancy, fretted almost beyond endurance by the knowledge that he had not strength to tell her all.

" It is you who talk wildly, mamma," he began. " It makes me sick to hear such nonsense. We cannot both have a claim to all."

" No, I allow that," she answered, as if it was a great concession.

" Well it's their own doing that has made me talk and think wild about it." She presently added, " They treated you both exactly alike."

" But they loved me the most," said poor Lancy, with something like a faltering in his voice. " I always felt and knew that though they were just, I was the favorite ; nothing could have been done more for me."

" And then you had me to be fond of you as well," said Mrs. Ward, " as soon as I 'd set my eyes upon you in the field, a pretty little fellow, jumping and shouting, I loved you so as nothing could be like it."

Lancy did not appear to notice the appealing tone in which this was said, he went on, —

" It is only of late years, since I have gone on so that they could not have me with them, that I have felt I was becoming less and less to them all, and Don John more and more."

" But you had me," she repeated.

" Yes," he answered, with unconscious indifference ; and when he saw presently that tears were dropping on her hand, so that she could not see her work, he said fretfully, —

" Oh, mamma, don't."

" I often think you don't care for me a bit," she replied, with the short, sobbing sigh of a sick heart.

" I feel so weak," said poor Lancy, trying to put off a discussion. " Is n't it time I had my stuff ?"

She got up and poured him out his tonic, and as she handed it him she went on, —

" You 've often made me feel, in particular of late, that you 're only willing I should live with you because it 's a conveniency to yourself."

" Don't cry, mamma," said Lancy, a little touched.

" I 'd rather by half that you 'd reproach me and tell me it 's all my own fault (if you 'd be like a son to me at other times) than treat me so cold as you do."

" You 'll not love me so well when you know all," Lancy began, but he stopped short, for his conscience, and even his heart, told him that this would make no difference.

She hardly heeded ; taking his self-accusation merely for an acknowledgment of gaming debts, and delinquencies yet more to be deplored but not punishable by any human law.

" Besides," he went on, much more gently, " what would be the good of reproaching you with its being your own fault?   Why that is what makes you feel it so keenly and be so bitter about it.   Mother was not bitter ; I am sure she did not feel it half so much.   You have had the worst of it every way.   But anyhow I am not the fellow that has any right to find fault.   I could not have had more if I had been their own son, and if I had not been yours you could hardly have had less."

" It 's true.   I have had the worst of it."

" And I am often sorry for you."

Still the remonstrance, though said gently, was not to her mind.   She went on, having checked her tears, —

" But as you never doubt I 'm your mother, no more than I do, I wonder you don't love me more."

" I like you.   Well, I love you as well as I can," said Lancy fretfully.

" I 'm often afraid that when you get better you 'll be off again, and leave your poor mother.   It will break my heart as sure as can be if you do."   •

" I promise you that I never will."

" They 'll invite you to stay at the house for change of air — I know they will — and then you 'll forget me again."

" I do not think Don John will ever let me go there again."

" What ! set himself up against you ! — and pretend to order you ? "

"And if he does allow it, I am not sure that I shall think I ought to go."

"You speak quite solemn, my Lancy!" she exclaimed, looking at him with alarm.

"But you'll stand by me, I have no doubt," continued Lancy: "and I begin to think, mamma, that I have behaved badly to you. I'm pleased (now I consider it), to know that it's natural you should be fond of me. I don't mind kissing you —"

Remarkable speech, but quite to her mind; he raised himself up, and turned his hollow cheek to her.

He had always greatly objected to her bestowing on him this form of caress. There he drew the line.

Mrs. Ward rose, and carefully drying her face with her handkerchief availed herself of the present gracious proposal. She kissed him; and he kissed her, almost for the first time, and then, exhausted, laid himself down to rest, and to consider.

He had hitherto so much despised her; she had proved herself to be a mean and sordid person, without principle, and indeed without common honesty; still she was a great deal better than himself, as he now discovered.

When he was a little better he asked her to read him a chapter in the Bible. It was characteristic of Lancy, now that he felt himself to be much changed, that he should think of this Bible-reading as likely to improve her; for his own part he was improved.

She took the book, but she turned white even to the lips. "You don't think you're going to die, my only dear."

"Oh, no!"

"This seems like it though."

"We were always brought up to think a great deal of the Bible," said Lancy, "they were always teaching us things in it."

"But you told me you hated those puritanic ways."

"I did then; but now those things comfort me, and seem to do me good."

" Oh, well, if it 's only that, my Lancy, and if you 're sure you 're not going to die." Thereupon she found the place he mentioned and read to him for some time.

" And what did you think of it?" asked Lancy, not without a certain gentleness, as she closed the book. He had chosen chapters that he thought might be useful to her.

" I was so taken up with thinking of your poor father, I could not attend to the reading much."

" Oh, what about my father?"

" When he was on his death-bed he asked me to read to him just as you did ; I was that terrified that I ran down to the lodger below us. ' Mercy, Mrs. Aird,' said she, ' what now? how white you look !' so I told her. She was a play-actress of the lower sort, and not a good-living woman ; in short, Lancy did n't like my having anything to say to her. ' I cannot do it,' said I, ' it frightens me so.' ' Nonsense,' said she, ' I 'll go and read to him as soon as look at him ; he will die none the sooner for it.' Well, if that woman did n't go up as bold as brass and read to him, as if she 'd been a saint. He died the day after."

" It was of decline, was it not? "

" Yes, my Lancy."

" Did his cough sound like mine?"

" Don't say such heart-breaking things to me ; you 'll be all right soon."

" But did it? "

" Well, it did."

" There now, you need not cry. As the ' play-actress ' said, *I shall die none the sooner* for knowing this."

" What with you making me read the Bible to you, and then talking about your poor father, you 've quite overcome me," she exclaimed, starting up, and she went into her little bed-room to recover herself, for Lancy hated a scene.

And almost as she went out, the other mother came in, and Don John behind her.

She came in calm, tender, observant, and sat down beside his couch, taking him in her arms, and holding his head with her hand for a minute upon her bosom.

"Mother," said Lancy, "I am not worthy that you should come to me."

She did not contradict him, but releasing one hand, wiped away her quiet tears.

"I have never been worthy of you — never," continued Lancy. "And all my faults and my sins against you and father seem much worse now that I feel how I have sinned against God." She arranged his pillows again and let him lie down on them.

Don John had been looking out of the window, he now came forward to say, "Father and mother know nothing about your last three months — excepting that you have been very ill."

"And that you wished to go to America without taking leave of us," put in the mother. Oh, what a small delinquency for her to know of!

"I am afraid, indeed I feel sure, that if we did know how you have been conducting yourself, we should be much hurt, perhaps displeased — but Don John (and we have trusted him in this) — Don John thinks it best we never should know."

Lancy and Don John looked at one another, the old bond was just as strong as ever that bound them, but it had never been one that seemed to admit of any deep sense of obligation. They were both lucky fellows if the one could get the other out of a scrape, and save the parents from disgrace and pain.

"I am afraid it will be a long time before you are well enough to go back to your situation," she said tenderly.

"Yes, mother," was all he answered.

"Will Mr. Cottenham wait all that time?" she next asked. So far as she knew, Mr. Cottenham was not aware of Lancy's intention of going to America, and this had been prevented by illness.

Lancy could not answer.

"Mother," said Don John, "I have seen Mr. Cottenham twice. Lancy has lost the situation."

"Oh, but I hope he was kind?"

"He was kind."

And then she began to talk to him. A deep sense
of the presence, nearness, and love of God had gradually grown up in her heart. Sorrow had been the
earthly cause of this. She had dwelt long in the presence of a great doubt. It had first become sweet to
her to feel that God knew which of these was her own
son, and then opening her heart so fully to both of
them, she had begun to think of them as both God's
sons, and to perceive that He was giving the one who
was not hers very unusual blessings, care, guardianship
from evil, love, prayer, teaching, warnings. It was
true that one of the two had persistently turned away
and done evil, but she believed firmly, that the same
God who had turned sorrow of hers into blessings for
him, would certainly go on with him. The last stroke of
bitterness had been dealt to her when the other mother,
angry at some lordly airs of Don John's, when he was
indignant at a base thing which Lancy had done, had
dared to tell both the young men their story ; and her
own, as she had long known him to be — had come
home, and fallen ill, and almost broken his heart.

But how much more truly he had been her own, and
his father's, ever since. How much more fully than
ever before she had now become able to sympathize in
her husband's religious life, and receive and partake of
those consolations that he offered to his son. She
deeply loved Lancy .still : we do love those whom we
have been so good to. She talked to him, and Lancy
answered her humbly, and with what seemed very true
penitence ; but that he had been so lately hunted by
the police, in hiding among the lowest of the low, and
within an hour of being taken up to be tried for felony,
she never dreamed.

When she rose to go away — " I suppose you send
your love to your father, and all of them," she said.
Lancy darted a look at Don John, which said as plainly
as possible, " May I ? "

She saw this, and saw the nod of assent given. Then
Lancy said, " Yes, mother." She had just been going
to add, " And of course as soon as you are fit to be

moved, you will come and stay with us till you are well again." But the sight of this permission, asked and given, arrested her. She put her gloves on, considering all the time, then took leave of him, and went her way.

Don John soon observed that his mother was displeased. He knew she had noticed that Lancy all through the interview had seemed to look to him for guidance, and had got it. Don John was not penitent of course, but he knew that he had got into a scrape.

His mother presently said, "I meant to ask poor Lancy whether he could come down to us to-morrow, but I did not care to hear you answer for him, and tell him whether he could or not."

Don John pondered. He and Lancy had already discussed this very question. Miss Jenny had never been inside "the house" in her life, and he could easily keep out of the fields. Besides, though looking wretchedly ill and thin, he was like his old self, not like the poor disfigured creature whom she had helped to nurse. When first they both talked of this, and Lancy pointed out that Miss Jenny would not recognize him, he was surprised to observe that, as to his going again to the house, Don John made still the same demur.

"I am not a felon!" Lancy exclaimed, rather bitterly; "that you should look as if you thought my presence would be a disgrace."

"No; because it takes two parties to make a felon —the criminal and the law. You have done your part, the whole of it, it is the law that has not, and therefore you are not a felon."

Lancy quailed a little. He had not been arrested, he had not been in the dock, his name and antecedents had not been published in the newspapers, his adoptive family had not been put to shame. He seemed to himself to be indeed a sinner, and in need of God's forgiveness, but to be, somehow, nothing like such a sinner as if the law had found him out, and had taken its course.

"I do not wish to excuse myself," he began, "and I owe it to you that I can hold up my head among my fellow-creatures ; but if I am not to hold up my head, how am I the better?"

And now Mrs. Johnstone was hurt, displeased in fact. She knew nothing of the facts of the crime, of the hiding, of the giving up on Don John's part of the three thousand pounds.

" His coming to us, poor fellow, is of course a matter for your father to decide, not for you," she remarked. " It was indeed very wrong of him to break away from us, as he has done. I cannot quite understand why he should have wished to go to America, having a good situation, and so kind a person to work under as Mr. Cottenham ; but it is not for you to judge him, my dear, and if your father is inclined to forgive and have him home for a time, you will of course acquiesce, and I hope I shall never see such evidence of his being subservient to your wishes as I have seen to-day. I know you are allowing him what he lives upon, but — "

" But that's a mere trifle," Don John put in here, for the attack was unexpected and he did not know how to meet it.

" That you should be in the least hard or unjust towards him I cannot bear to think."

No answer.

" Still less that such a feeling as jealousy should — no, I do not think it, and the more because you have no reason."

Still no answer.

" It is a long time now since that lamentable affair — "

Don John's face appeared to ask a question.

" Of the ring," she continued ; " and since that he has been I fear little better than the poor prodigal ; but, my very dear son, though your father has lost so much that it would sound unreal if he were to say what that father said, yet so far as love, approval, trust and pride go, we may truly say each of us, ' *All that I have is thine.*' "

Don John's face was almost a blank. She knew all its expressions. He did not intend her to find out what he thought.

"But I must not be hard upon you, my dear," she went on ; " youth is naturally severe."

To this general proposition Don John expressed neither assent nor dissent ; but he presently said, in a somewhat constrained fashion, —

" I have never been jealous of poor Lancy — never."

Just then the train ran into their station ; some of the home party were in it and they all walked through the fields together ; but in a few minutes Don John turned back, and sent a telegram to Lancy, —

" If you are invited to come here, pray make no objection ; accept at once."

Don John was already in the midst of trouble about money. It had been difficult to get the three thousand pounds for Lancy without his father's knowledge, he now wanted seven hundred more ; for to debts to that amount Lancy now confessed ; and he was daily liable to be arrested. These creditors had to be called upon and appeased, some were paid, some had advances made them on account. A farm, in order to meet these demands, had been already mortgaged. Don John did not feel even yet that he could trust to the truth of Lancy's repentance. He feared that if he came again to " the house," other creditors might appear, and claimants of no very creditable kind might dun him under Mrs. Johnstone's eyes. He had expressed this fear, Lancy had earnestly declared that he had no other debts than those he had named. Don John hoped this was true, but he must now take the risk of its being false, and if it was they would all have to abide the consequences.

CHAPTER XXXVI.

" I THINK after all," Charlotte had said, " I had better give you that kiss." So she gave it. It was a sister's kiss, and he knew it.

And.she was so kind, so true, so helpful to Don John. They were comrades, friends and conspirators again. They had a sad and damaging secret in their sole keeping, and held the family honor in their own hands. And Naomi's affair went on prosperously; and Mr. Johnstone in a great degree recovered his health, so that constant companionship was not needful for him; but Mrs. Johnstone had not yet talked to Charlotte, and Charlotte held Don John remote.

Charlotte was so beautiful! But a young man's love not uncommonly is beautiful. It is a way she has.

Lancy had his invitation, and accepted it. He was very weak still, had still a hollow cough, and used to lie on the sofa in the drawing-room, or in the old play-room, and he too perceived that Charlotte was beautiful, and he liked to be in the same room with her, and observe her sayings and doings.

The same Charlotte, talking about things that so many people cared for not one straw, and bestowing on them the most impassioned feeling and sincere interest.

And once when "mother" entered the room, he saw her come to a pause, and regard them all, and especially regard him, with a certain attention. Why? And then she quietly went out of the room, again looking as if lost in thought.

It must be something they had been saying, and yet how could it be?

The girls had been laughing at Don John because they said he was such a complete John Bull, and he had justified himself, had even confessed to a conscious wish to keep up the old style and form of patriotism. He would like, if he could, still to believe that one Englishman could beat three Frenchmen. "As to slavery," he went on, "I hate to hear the old English horror of it made game of. 'Down with it at once, sir,' as nurse said to Fred the other morning when she brought him the black dose, 'for the longer you look at it the worse it is.'"

Fred, a great fellow of eighteen, made a sulky rejoinder: "How came Don John to know anything about his physic?"

No, it could not be their talk which the mother had noticed. In about a quarter of an hour she came in again, and sat down in her own corner on the sofa, taking up her knitting.

She still appeared to notice them all, and Lancy felt that he must not look at Charlotte so much.

Charlotte and Don John were talking and arguing playfully, as of old, only that Don John treated her remarks with more deference. There was nothing to interest Lancy in the conversation, but he listened idly, because the mother did.

"Poetry! What! poetry, our finest English endowment! poetry destined to become a lost art! Surely, Charlotte, you cannot think that?"

"Not destined to decline at once, but in the course of years. The first move has been made already. We have begun to admire the wrong thing."

"Other arts have been lost certainly."

"And why? Partly, I think, because we try so many experiments; it is not enough to have perfection. What could be more beautiful than an old seventy-gun ship, or a wooden full-rigged merchant ship, or a sloop?"

"But we do not want our ships only for their beauty."

"No; and yet we came nearer to the Creator's work when we made our finest sailing ships than man ever came before."

"Nearer than when he built the Parthenon?"

"Oh, yes; there is almost the same difference as between a lily and a nautilus. The Parthenon is beautiful and stationary, but ships are beautiful, and they can move."

"It does seem as if the ship of the future was to be like a giant polony, or a vulgar imitation of a turbot, with horns fuming out blackness on its back. But, as I think I remarked before, we do not want ships only for their beauty."

"No."

"And so we change them to gather speed, or to get power, or to save expenditure."

" And we do want poetry for its beauty, you mean.
Yes, only for its beauty ; for its moral power over us —
its teaching, comforting, and elevating power all depend
on its beauty.　We know all this, and yet things come
to pass."

" Nothing particular is coming to pass that I can see,
excepting that just lately some poets and people who
think they are poets are getting excessively ingenious.
The French never had much poetry in them, but they
were exceedingly ingenious, as the old Italians were.
And this sort of thing is being naturalized here.　Is
there any danger in it ? "

" Yes ; because it makes the form of so much more
consequence than the spirit, that it will end in taking
the writing of verse out of the hands of the poets, and
we shall end by admiring ingenious, artful rhymes more
than a wonderful or splendid thought."

" I should have thought a poet, if there was anything
in him, would have been able to write even in that
style."

" But not better than an ingenious scholar.　The
future poets will be born in chains, and they used, especially in England, to be born free.　It will surely be
a great disadvantage to be born under the dominion
of a culture of the wrong sort."

" Well, I pity the poet of the future : he will have to
look out."

" The more art the less nature.　I think the poet of
the future will be like a wild bird in a handsome cage.
He will beat his wings against the wires instead of singing.　And as all these old formal and difficult descrip-
tions of verse come in, the themes must be carefully
chosen to suit them.　Lyrical poetry with us has always
been rather a wild thing : now we seem inclined to tame
it.　The French partridge you know has nearly extermi-
nated the English.　So I think the French and Italian
forms, in which we can only after all write a finer kind
of *vers de société*, will prevail to smother the English
lyric."

" Well," said Lancy, who did not care a straw for

poetry, "then let them, if they can ; we have got more poetry already written than we know what to do with."

" I should n't wonder," answered Don John, " and so we begin to want a change ; but I must say, Charlotte, that I think the indications you speak of are very few and faint."

" Like the straw which shows the way of the wind."

Mrs. Johnstone was at the door by this time. Lancy had felt sure that she would leave the room when this discussion began to flag, for he knew whom she would call to follow her.

" Charlotte."

He was right!

" Aunt Estelle."

" I want you, dear one."

Charlotte got up, and the door was shut after them. The glorious soft orange of the sunset was reflected only on the red carpet, and on the pale blue sofa. Charlotte's white gown was what it had rested on so beautifully, and her absence made everything look dull.

It came to Lancy almost as an inspiration that he himself was to be the theme of " mother's " discourse with Charlotte ; that he had looked a good deal at Charlotte, and that " mother " did not care that he should.

He was a little nettled. She was quite needlessly careful! It was true he frequently forgot what a bad fellow he had been, but then he only forgot what she had never known. Lancy thought a good deal about this during the evening and the next day ; but Charlotte did not seem to avoid him ; she played to him in the morning, and in the afternoon she took her share of reading aloud to him with Naomi.

Charlotte generally wore white ; either the sunshine was clearer or her gown was even whiter than usual that afternoon, for as she passed down the garden grass walk she looked like a pillar of snow. She gathered a red rose-bud, and went to the green gate, and leaning her elbows on it looked out.

Some thought, both sweet and strange to her, was lying at her heart, its evidence seemed to give a brooding beauty to her eyes, and she pouted slightly, as she often did when she was lost in cogitation.

So she was looking when Don John came up the field. His father went into the house by the usual entrance, but he, remarking her, came on and approached her as she leaned on the gate.

And she was so quiet, that though she looked at him, he wanted to partake of the joy of her presence as she was, rather than to accost her and make her move. He stood for the moment on one side of the gate and she on the other. It was such a slight affair, only three green rails and a latch.

Here he had first discovered her to be his love, and that on her answer to this hung his destiny.

The folds of her white robe were not stirred by any wind, all was as still as a dream. She had the rose-bud between her hands, and she touched it with her lips.

He had drawn off his glove when first he marked her, for sometimes when they met if he held out his hand she would put hers into it unaware. Now, he hardly knew by what impulse he took off his hat too, and laid it on the grass. What was she thinking of? what did this mean? The rose-bud was at her lips again, her shining eyes looked into his, and she said, "Dearest, shall I put this into your coat?"

It was such an astonishment. "Let me kiss it first," he stammered, for he could hardly think this real. How could any young man so much in love have been so unready!

Her hands were busy for a moment with the breast of his coat. "I might envy the rose if you did," she whispered; and when he had kissed her, she put her arms round his neck and returned the kiss.

How sudden and how vast a change!

But nothing, when one has it, appears so natural as delight.

They went through the garden together, hand in hand, and when Charlotte had said, "Aunt Estelle has told me all the story," there seemed to be nothing more to explain, and nothing so sweet as silence; for it was manifest to both that the world was their own — a new world not learned, and unexplored.

How can one utter the world?

No, " silence is golden," for at least it does this marvellous new world no wrong.

During dinner the musing, ecstatic silence was hardly broken at all.

In the course of the evening they began to consider how anything so remarkable as their love could be communicated to the family. They need not have troubled themselves, everybody knew. Even Master Fred, who generally stood upon his dignity, was not above stopping in the corridor that night to bestow upon his elder brother a neat and carefully modelled wink, and a very large smile — a smile in fact that spread over his face almost from ear to ear.

A chuckling, rolling sound burst from the young gentleman's chest. It was as if a small earthquake heaved when it was young.

He darted into his room and hastily bolted his door, his usual way when he had been " cheeky," for when that ceremony had been forgotten, Don John not unfrequently burst it open and threw at him anything that came to hand.

Once or twice he had elaborately screwed him in, so that, as Mary said, —

" If the fruit-ladder had not been long enough to let him out the next morning, he must have been fed through the key-hole."

But such are the ordinary ways of brothers when one is several years older than the other, and they are as these were, pretty good friends.

And Lancy knew. Somehow or other he thought it was rather unfair, — and yet he was very much improved. On the whole he was very penitent. When he came to review and consider matters, he did not see how if they had known all, they could have let him win Charlotte. And next he considered that there was reason enough against such a thing even in what they did know. This was a great advance to be made by such a young man as Lancy. Another advance was his not being afraid of his father's advice and prayers, he liked them.

But his visit to "the house" was a great anxiety to Don John, and even to himself. He felt that he was always liable to be hunted up by those who had known him as John Ward, and to whom he had owed small sums. Little bills might have been forgotten. His parents might yet know of his dreadful disgrace; and the fear of this, no less than his true penitence, left him on the whole humble and thankful.

So several weeks went on, and at last it was decided that Lancy should take a sea-voyage as the best chance of perfectly restoring his health, and that his "mamma" of course should accompany him. Mr. Johnstone found funds for this, and Don John arranged it. They were to go to Tasmania. And somehow Mrs. Johnstone felt, and yet could give no actual reason for it, that Lancy did not intend to return to his own country, and Don John did not intend that he should.

Lancy was an old traveller, he thought nothing of the voyage; and yet when he went away from "the house," taking leave of them all he betrayed, for the first time in his life, very deep emotion. It was impossible he could stay; not even Don John knew that as well as he did. And yet it was bitter to turn himself out of Paradise.

He felt how much dearer they all and every one of them were, than the poor woman whose all he was, and who was to go with him more because he needed her services than because he cared for her companionship.

She, too, was much improved. She had been told all by Don John. She knew the extreme difficulty with which he had found money to pay Lancy's bills, and yet how he had refused to let Mr. Johnstone know anything.

She blushed for Lancy over some of these bills, and felt that it was like mother, like son. He was untrustworthy, dishonest, and deceitful, as she had been.

Don John was the soul of honor and uprightness. She sank in her own esteem when he came near her — and yet he was rather kind too.

In the course of a few more weeks all was ready.

The two mothers went on board, and Don John was there and Mr. Johnstone. Then while these and Lancy went over the ship, the one mother wept and said to the other that she hoped she would forgive her.

" My husband, Collingwood, has said to me many a time that our having been suffered to plant such a doubt in you was enough to make you feel almost as if the ways of Providence were hard."

She sobbed.

" I did almost feel something like that at first," was the answer. " But I 've got my own, and the doubts and distress have long been over."

" Ay," was the answer, " and you 've had all the good and innocent years of the other too. I never had him back till I knew he would be a misery and a disgrace to me."

" You speak too strongly," said Mrs. Johnstone. " Poor Lancy is very much improved."

" But I 've brought it all on myself," sobbed Mrs. Ward. " I own it; I humbly ask your pardon. I 've had my punishment."

" I do forgive you."

" It is but reason you should, for we both know you 've got your own. But even if it was not so, why still you 've got the best of it. It is not so; but if it was, I should have given you my good child and got your bad one."

" Yes; I have felt that too; but you must not think that any distressing doubt remains. A mother's instinct, both in your heart and mine, soon grew too strong for any mistake to be possible."

So they parted friends, and even with a kiss.

It was Christmas when Lancy sailed. That was a pleasant winter, even Naomi did not think it long. She saw her lover frequently, and she was to be married in March.

She knew by this time, because her mother had told her, from whom was to come her dower, and Fred knew at whose instance and whose charges he was to go to

Oxford that his really brilliant talents might have scope. And Mr. Johnstone, feeling easy as to some matters which had weighed on his mind, improved again in health, so that it was a very cheerful winter for them all.

And Charlotte was brought to say after much persuasion, that the double-blossomed cherry was her favorite flower, and most appropriate for a bridal. Charlotte was very demure. Sometimes she held Don John remote ; their engagement, in short, by no means went on according to its beginning. But her mother was to come over that spring for six months, and he thought he knew what for.

There was not half so much crying at Naomi's wedding as at Marjorie's. They were said to behave extremely well, and the children from the houses strewed the aisles and the church path with yellow and white and purple crocuses.

As they all stood in the porch to see Naomi off, she said when she came down the steps and saw Charlotte standing by Don John, —

" Be good to him, Charlotte. There 's nobody like our Don John."

Charlotte's dimple came, but she blushed. In a minute or two the bride was gone, and the whole party excepting herself, Don John, and his mother had rushed back into the house to the dining-room windows to watch the carriage as it turned up the road.

These stood yet in the porch. The mother and Charlotte on the upper step and Don John on the lower.

" Yes," said Mrs. Johnstone, smiling, though tears were in her eyes, " there 's nobody like our Don John."

Her hand was on his shoulder.

" Oh, mother," he exclaimed, turning and looking at them, " if you did n't all make so much of a fellow — "

" Charlotte would not need telling to be good to him, is that it ? " she inquired.

" On the contrary," said Charlotte, " if his merits were not so frequently set before me I might never have found them out."

She laughed, and her blue eyes danced. How lovely she looked in all her fair adornments!

"That was a very unkind speech," said the mother, smiling. "You must say something to make up for it."

"Yes, to please you, Aunt Estelle!" said Charlotte demurely. Then she pursed up her rosy mouth, and first bestowing on him a kiss under his mother's eyes, she said, "There's nobody like our Don John, and I always think so."

Our Don John. He was always to be theirs; first their joy and then their comfort, next their aid, and in the course of years all they had of honor and distinction.

And yet, after all — though in this world they were never to know it, though he was bound to them by more than common dues of service done, and love bestowed — after all, this was the carpenter's son; and that Lancy, who but for him would more than once have been their sorrow and their disgrace, he was the true Don John. But he was to trouble them no more for ever. He was cast upon "the mercy of the Most Merciful." He was quiet in the keeping of the sea.